TESSER

A Dragon Among Us

A Reemergence Novel

Chris Philbrook

Edited by Linda Tooch of Insight Copy Editing

Designed and illustrated by Alan MacRaffen

Tesser: A Dragon Among Us; A Reemergence Novel

Published in the United States of America

First Publishing Date June, 2013

Edited by Linda Tooch of Insight Copy Editing

Cover design and interior layout by Alan MacRaffen

Mike! Amanda!

Dragons & swords & magic

OH MY!

Kris [signature]

Special Thanks to all of the members of the Inner Circle:

Carey Anderson
DeLaina Craft
Derek Carrier
Doug James
Ilox
J.C. Fiske
Jamie Rogers
Junior Black
Lindsey Carrier
Matt Chambers
Mike "Haus" Cartwright
Pistol Annie James
Rob "Ontos" Roche
Vincent Carrier

Also by Chris Philbrook:

Elmoryn - The Kinless Trilogy
Book One: Wrath of the Orphans
Book Two: The Motive for Massacre

Coming Soon:
Book Three

Adrian's Undead Diary
Book One: Dark Recollections
Book Two: Alone No More
Book Three: Midnight
Book Four: The Failed Coward
Book Five: Wrath
Book Six: In the Arms of Family
Book Seven: The Trinity
Book Eight: Cassie

The Reemergence Series
Tesser: A Dragon Among Us

Coming Soon:
Ambryn: & the Cheaters of Death

*Don't miss Chris Philbrook's **free** e-Book:*
At Least He's Not On Fire:
A Tour of the Things That Escape My Head

Table of Contents:

Prologue:
The Dream

I am flying.

I have done this before, many times, and it is joyous.

I feel the gusts buffet my body left and right, up and down. It isn't violent, though the wind is reckless. I feel the energy of the air lift me higher and higher through the cool mist of a thick cloud that clings to my face, and invigorates me. It is much like the first inhalation of the ocean's air after a long journey to the coast.

Far down below me I see green grass, lush treetops, and the grey pebbling of stones poking through the skin of the world. There is a single brown line of disturbed earth winding forward that I know to be a human road. I know this road. I have flown over it many times before, and I have walked it as well. It is familiar to me, but I cannot quite place where it has come from or where it is leading to.

It doesn't matter. I have eyes that see, ears that hear, and a nose that smells. In time, I will discover everything. When I flex my wings and dip below the clouds like a descending sparrow I can see that miles ahead the road ends at the tall wooden gate of a castle nestled atop a hillock. Centered in the fortified wooden walls is a castle made of stone, mud, and timber. It is majestic when compared against the hovels in the mud surrounding it.

I think it is my castle, but I don't live there. It is mine in the same way that a King owns a dog. Or how a Queen owns a King.

My dream is almost over. I feel it like a blue dawn rising on the edge of a long night. It has been a good dream for the most part, though in life no matter how much the sun shines storms always appear now and again. It is natural, unstoppable; it is the way of the world. It is the way of my kind.

I sense that I have been dreaming this dream a very long time. More than a night, a week, or even a year. Centuries have passed, maybe a millennia since I last laid open eyes on the waking world. The castle I am soaring towards in my dream is certainly gone, buried underneath centuries of revolution and crumbled empires.

These thoughts do not cause me alarm. Nor do I fear what the world will be like when I open my eyes soon.

I am beyond mortal fears.

Those that wear two skins are but a nuisance to me.

My skin breaks the teeth of those that drink blood and stalk the night.

Were it not for the teachings and lineage of my kind, the Magi would be ordinary, and not the wielders of primordial might that they are.

Goblins, monsters, and fae are my kind, and they pay me the respect that is my due.

I am the bringer of death from high above.

I am the giver and shaper of life in so many forms.

I am the bringer of light that illuminates all darkness.

I am the stone that cannot be broken and the blade that cannot dull.

I am the legend your grandfathers were told about by their grandfathers.

My footsteps shake the ground like the marching of a hundred legions marching to war.

My heart beats as the thunder shakes the sky, and if this body does not suit me, I will change it and become whatever will thrive in the soil of the times I awake in.

I am Tesser, and I am a Dragon.

And as I arc my wings once more to soar above the clouds, my mind elevates me away from my slumber; my fear finally makes itself known. A question, a single nagging lost memory that I suddenly fear occurs to me.

Why did I allow myself to be pacified in sleep for so long?

Long slumbers are not my way.

Acquiescing is not my way.

I think I'll find out why I have slept so long, now that this dream, this long, long dream is over. And those that have seen to my sleep had best have had good reason for my time lost.

Because I am Tesser, and I am Dragon.

Chapter One

Abraham "Abe" Fellows

BEEP! BEEP! BEEP!

Is that a car?

BEEP! BEEP! BEEP!

Nah, it sounds too electric.

BEEP! BEEP! BEEP!

God I hate technology.

BEEP! BEEP! BEEP!

Ha, God, that's a good one. I don't think Mr. Doyle would approve of me referring to God.

BEEP! BEEP! BEEP!

Why am I sitting in the coffee shop? Where is that infernal beeping coming from? Why does this latte taste like old chewed meat? Or is that a sock I taste?

BEEP! BEEP! BEEP!

Oh Hell, that's my alarm clock. Coffee shop is just a dream. Oh hell it's bright out. Dammit my hand is asleep again. Fingers are number than ever. I'll be fumbling with this shut off button for five minutes now. That Indian asshole in the apartment above me is going to start screaming again.

BEEP! BEEP! BEEP!

I'll cast a spell. I know that cantrip well enough, and my fingers can be as numb as they want.

BEEP! BEEP! BEEP!

The young man sat up on the edge of his worn mattress and addressed the phone sitting on the milk crate he used as a bed stand. The air stirred slightly as Abe gathered his thoughts to cast the spell. There was some magic in the air here in his apartment, in his sanctum. On the mantle of the nonfunctional fireplace he'd organized semi-precious stones that had mystical powers, and there was always the scent of incense on the nose. Scents had power.

I'm ready. Abe gestured with his tingly, stiff fingers at the touch screen of his cell phone still sitting a couple of feet from his hands on the plastic crate. He slid his finger in the air and spoke a word laced with arcane power, "Commoveo."

Abe watched as the image on the phone glitched. The LCD screen didn't feel the touch of his spell in the same way it would've felt a finger made of flesh and blood. He sighed at his newest failed attempt to mix technology and magic. The tingling in his fingers had abated, but he couldn't abandon the spell.

BEEP! BEEP! BEEP!

Fucking thing. "Commoveo," he said again, sliding his fingers through the air, this time with more emphasis and focus. Abe felt a surge of energy come from somewhere and fill his word and fingers with a different tingle altogether.

The red button reacted. Jumped. It slid across the screen smoothly to the other side, silencing the horrid alarm.

BEEP! BE—

"What the hell?" Abe said aloud, running his hand through his thinning black hair. He looked down at his fingers, his palms, turning his hands over several times, trying to find the source of the sudden energy he'd somehow tapped into. He stood on creaky morning legs and looked about his apartment for something new. Possibly some creature or artifact that Mr. Doyle had perhaps slipped in while he was asleep.

But there was nothing. Just empty pizza boxes, clothes in need of a washer, and Magic the Gathering cards.

His phone elicited another electronic bleat, and Abe had a sudden pang of failure. But he was wrong. This was just the ringer. He picked the phone up with living, breathing fingers and looked at the caller ID on the screen. It read simply: Mr. Doyle.

Abe thumbed the answer button over and lifted it to his ear. "Mr. Doyle?"

An older British man's voice came back, "Abraham."

"Yes, Mr. Doyle? What can I do for you this morning?" Abe asked quickly. Mr. Doyle didn't like it when he hesitated. Mr. Doyle said men who wanted to learn the art of magic should always act with confidence.

There was a pause on Mr. Doyle's end. *Is he at a loss for words? Has the apocalypse come?*

"Abraham, I think you need to call in sick to work. Someone else will need to tend to your company's accounting today. In fact, you should phone them that you can no longer work for them. Something rather large is afoot in the world, and your time needs to be redirected to more appropriate tasks." Doyle sounded somewhere between ecstatic and horrified. Abe had never heard him speak in such a way.

How the hell will I pay rent? "How the hell will I pay rent Mr. Doyle? I can't afford to quit my job at the firm." Doyle was an accountant at a large law firm. Emotionally it was a dead end position, but financially it was a homerun. You'd never be able to tell that from the décor of his apartment though. Abe looked down sadly at the milk crate again.

"Abraham, I can afford for you to be in my employ.

Many of my earlier years home in *The* United Kingdom were fiscally bountiful. I shall replace your salary in its entirety. Sack yourself via the telephone, and come to my brownstone immediately."

Abe smiled. This was what he wanted all along. He'd been an apprentice to the old British mage for nearly two years now, and all he'd learned were three minor spells and how to read ten ancient and long since dead languages. By this point, if the magic thing didn't work out all he had left was counting beans in a cubicle.

"Abraham, is this arrangement sufficient?"

Shit, I must've gone silent daydreaming again. "Yes, Mr. Doyle, my apologies. I was lost in thought. I wanted to tell you I was able to cast a cantrip a few minutes ago. It seemed far more powerful than anything I've ever done before. I think I'm getting the hang of it."

Doyle tsked several times, as a teacher might, "Dearest Abraham, something else is happening. Something large, and something that will certainly have rippling effects on the whole world, both mundane and magical. Some of my most precious possessions in my study have begun to… awaken, shall I say. Clocks ticking, candles burning again, things of that sort. All roused by something or someone."

Abe started to wonder what that meant, but caught himself. Daydreaming was unbecoming for someone who wanted to master magic.

"I guess I'll quit and head over then," Abe said softly. *I'll need to go in to get the stuff out of my cube.*

"You guess? I suggest you stop guessing Mister Fellows and start being confident and assertive. I haven't lived as long as I have to waste my time on someone who guesses at things. Come over when you are ready. And please don't forget to turn your alarm off." Doyle cut the call.

Abe let his hands settle in his lap. He looked around the room, wondering what had happened that made Mr.

Doyle call and ask him to make such a huge change to his life.

BEEP! BEEP! BEEP!

The beeping startled Abe, and he dropped the phone to the hardwood floor of his apartment. He reached down, picked up the smart phone, and laughed as he thumbed the snooze button permanently.

"How did he know my alarm wasn't off?"

Chapter Two
Tesser

I am buried in earth.

Tesser's body was immense. From the tip of his nose to the end of his tail he was nearly one hundred and fifty feet long, fully half the length of a modern football field. Right now he was coiled in tightly, wrapped up to be as small as was physically possible. Tesser had no idea what modern football was though. Not yet at least.

How did come to be here?

The earth holding Tesser's draconic body still was pressing down with enough force to crush coal into diamonds, but his ancient scaled skin held firm. Dragon flesh would not succumb to something so natural and primal. The mere presence of earth, no matter how crushing it may be, wasn't enough.

I need to reach the surface.

Tesser's eyes were already closed against the dirt and stones, but he furrowed his massive brows tighter and focused his mind. A swirl of sensations cascaded over his awareness as he opened up to all the information the world offered him. One by one each of the scales on his body registered what was against them and precisely how much pressure existed. His nostrils, still sealed with a flap of scales to keep out the invasive sand, opened a slit and took in the tiniest amount of matter. The scent of organic matter told him his depth. Within seconds Tesser realized which direction was up and how far he had to burrow to get there.

The muscles that corded the length of Tesser's body were unlike anything science had ever seen. Only the dinosaurs were comparable, but to compare a Tyrannosaurus Rex to Tesser was akin to comparing a garden trowel to a nuclear weapon. Both were capable of moving earth, albeit in a spectacularly different fashion.

Tesser's enormous hand opened, the fingers as large as tree trunks and tipped with curving black scythes of claws. The black tips ripped through the earth smoothly, loosening it in handfuls large enough to fit a small car.

Still too tight.

Tesser shrugged. The earth moved. Above in the city of Boston, the area in the Back Bay felt it. The media that night reported that there was a "small tremor" causing a 2.1 localized earthquake. The green line was paused for several hours as well at the beginning of the workday, which was unfortunate.

The immobile body of a dragon might register as stone to a geologist. The bones and muscles are far more dense and supernatural than simple flesh, and when several hundred tons of dragon chooses to move, anything preventing that from happening gives way.

Below Tesser, the earth gave way abruptly. Tesser's massive arms and legs shot out and arrested his fall, short as it may have been. Several yards of stone, some of it shaped in an unnatural way fell, into a passage that lay below. He immediately opened his nostrils and inhaled for the first time in thousands of years. He was assaulted by foreign smells that caused discomfort. Primarily he disliked the burning smells—sulfurous and unpleasant—that reminded him of the raw eruptions of volcanoes and the ancient pits of tar that swallowed so many creatures hundreds of thousands of years prior.

Tesser's eyes opened once again. Larger by far than many eyes to ever have gazed on the world, they were orbs of gold and slit as a cat's. He could see in any level of darkness, complete blackness if need be, and presently he looked down through the hole he'd made to the strange passage below. In the floor of the oddly lit passage he could see a uniformly wide channel with three metallic rails running along. One rail hummed with an invisible energy that was oddly reminiscent of magic. Tesser was intrigued. The opening was small, only a third of his length. He would have to shift to a smaller form to fall through.

Tesser was not limited to a single form. The body he found most natural, that of a massive winged dragon, was not his only choice. Tesser could take on the form of any living creature should he wish it, and right now, he wished to be smaller.

It was a form of magic, though not a spell. More ancient than the clumsy arts the tribal humans were just now grasping. Tesser employed magic the way a bird would fly or the way a fish swam. It was natural and happened without thought. Tesser shrank down into a form that would fit through the hole below him, starting with his hindquarters first. As his tail and hind legs compacted down, he dug his claws into one side of the space that he had been dormant in, clutching tightly so as not to fall. Once he had reduced to a little less than a third of his original size, Tesser unclenched his still massive claws, and he descended down until he fell, straddling the channel in the strange stone passage.

The sides of the fairly round tunnel were covered in small, straight shaped white stones that were uniformly smooth. Spaced every so often were images, clearly made by something that could write or draw. It took only a moment for him to realize there were strange images of humans as well.

The images were massive, far larger than the humans he remembered. The largest human he'd ever seen was a savage in a cold village in the far north. He was nearly as tall as Tesser's largest finger and claw. He was a specimen, and Tesser was glad to let him live after he threw a spear ignorantly at him. Needless death was not Tesser's way, and the man would be good breeding stock to improve the human lineage.

But these humans, many of them would be a head again taller than that one, so long ago. That human came from a village that had only just begun to make markings on hide to remember things. But these images with the large humans…

They have languages. And they are writing now. And some strange magic that allows them to capture perfect images of themselves. I must have slept a very long time indeed.

Tesser heard the small sound of tiny feet moving from the darkness nearby. He'd heard the same sound before, and when he turned he smiled. One of his most favorite of creatures ever had come out to greet him.

A dark furred rat scurried out, completely unafraid of the massive dragon crouched in the alien tunnel. The rat had come from a hole in the white stoned wall and sniffed emphatically, wriggling its tiny nose and whiskers, and taking in the powerful scent of the dragon.

Another sound came from far off down the tunnel, and even though he didn't know what the sound meant, he knew what creature it came from.

A human. I need to observe. I need to see this new world. Unseen.

Tesser shifted forms again.

By the time the MBTA security guard arrived, Tesser had taken the form of a second rat, though his tiny eyes were still golden. He stood fearless, his nose wriggling as emphatically as his new friend's had been a moment before.

The guard reached up to his shoulder and spoke.

Tesser didn't understand any of the strange words and thought his manner of dress strange. He wore dark colors, none of which was the skins of an animal like the humans had worn when he was last awake.

"Tunnel collapse, big time. We're gonna need to shut down the Green line heading west between Copley and Hynes. Holy shit."

Tesser cocked his head and realized there was much he had to learn. He had all the time in the world to do it with. As the other rat darted back into the hole in the wall, he decided to join him. The shrunken dragon would start with the lesson of the rat's tunnels.

Rats always knew how to get around.

Chapter Three

Matilde "Matty" Rindahl

Matty was on the phone.

"Relax, relax Matty. Your parents love you, and I know you're nervous they're here visiting from Norway, but there's no reason to be all amped up about it," Max said softly from the other side of Boston.

Easy for you to say, Matty thought. "I know Max, but this is the first time I've actually seen my mom and Dad since the miscarriage and since you and I stopped seeing each other. I guess I'm just freaking out for no reason. Maybe it's that silly little earthquake earlier. Stupid collapsed subway tunnel. Thanks for talking with me."

"It's my pleasure babe. You know I'll always be your friend," Max said.

His sincerity was sickening. He probably always would be her friend, despite their past year of awkwardness and pain. There had been physical pain as well as emotional pain. Matilde and Max had been engaged to marry, and her pregnant with their baby boy. Money was accumulating in their joint savings account for them to buy a condo in Boston near Boston College where Max was an assistant professor in the psychology department. Matty was a promising grad student with job offers lining up. Matty was a fair skinned, dark haired beauty with bright green eyes, and Max was tall, lean, and handsome. Their lives looked bright and full of inevitable happiness.

The fairy tale unraveled in the morning sun late last summer when Matty awoke to find a large slick of blood between her legs. Max had rushed her to the hospital, and after the emergency room did everything it could, she was told her baby boy would never draw breath. She had miscarried.

Try as they might, they could not conceive again, and a fertility specialist, paid for by Max's family's wealth, told her that she was no longer able to have babies. She was devastated. Max's dream had always been to be a father, and she knew that with her, his life would never be complete. There were more than a few tears, but in the end they agreed it was best to go their separate ways, wishing each other love and good luck.

Max returned to work and soon after met Amanda, a beautiful grad student not too unlike Matty (though blonde), and they were forming what looked to be a good life. Matty had returned to grad school, this time at Boston University instead of Boston College, and was about to graduate. The reason for her family's visit from Norway was for that graduation.

She realized Max had said something. "What Max, I'm sorry. I'm all discombobulated right now."

Max laughed, "You should've studied linguistics. You love all those big words. I just said that Amanda and I will try and stop by the graduation tomorrow. I'd like to say hello to your parents if there's time."

Matty winced, "Max I'm not sure my father is up for that. He's still a little bit resentful about the breakup after we lost Aiden." *Aiden. It would've been such a pretty name for a young boy.*

"I thought you'd talked to them about it? Explained the whole situation? That it was mutual?" Max sounded genuinely disappointed. More evidence of that sincerity that made her queasy.

"Yes, I'd explained everything Maxwell, but he's my father, and no matter what I say, you'll always be the man that left his daughter after her baby died. If you cured cancer he'd still never shake your hand again."

Max sighed. "I understand. That's sad. I guess maybe we'll just mail you a congratulations card instead. I'll pick you up a gift certificate to Legal. Can you tell your mother I said hello at least? Does Lindsey hate me too?"

"No, she understands far more than father does. I'll pass along your well wishes Max. I've got to go shortly. I need to drive to Logan to pick them up. Their flight was delayed a little, but I don't want to hit traffic on the way over."

"Yeah, the Storrow will be a bit of a bitch at this hour. Why don't you just take the T over?"

Matty had to swallow a laugh. "My father shouldn't have his slacks dirtied by the seats in Boston's public transportation system. Besides, I want to drive my new car over and show them how well I'm doing. He'll appreciate the new car."

"How is the new job? I was pleased to hear you got the job ahead of getting your master's."

Matty's inner joy surfaced. "It is outstanding Max. I love working in the lab, culturing all the cells, and running all the experiments and trials and all that nerdy stuff. Plus the money is ludicrous. If I can save like I think I can, then I'll be a very early retiree."

"Take that Italian vacation we talked about. That's terrific, Matty. Well go get your parents. Tell your mother I said hello, and your father too if he doesn't curse me out too much."

"I will Max, and tell Amanda I said hello," Matty was

as sincere as Max. She wanted him to be as happy as he could be, even if that meant it was without her.

"I will, good luck tomorrow, and toss that cap as high in the air as you can!"

They said their goodbyes, and Matty ended the call. The long legged young woman walked around the island in her new Beacon Hill apartment and spied all the boxes she'd not yet unpacked. The busy work of emptying the boxes would be golden busy work for her father. She'd also intentionally left some Ikea furniture unmade. He'd gobble up that busy work as soon as they walked in the apartment door together. That'd give her and her mother time together. She missed her mother fiercely since she and her father had moved to Norway. Her dad had missed his native country fiercely, and her mother was looking for a new experience anyway.

Matty sighed and scooped up her new car keys from the dish on the island. The traffic could be tough with everyone getting out of work, and she didn't want her father to wait any longer than was necessary.

Chapter Four
Tesser

The world was different. Wrong.

When last I wandered the world, the only things that man had made that reached towards the sky were squat towers made of logs and stones errantly piled up, held together by the hopes and dreams of immature minds. These creations, these new structures, are made of stone, glass, and iron and reach nearly to the clouds. They've sprung up like evil weeds, giant and infecting the earth.

These humans remind me more of lice than men.

I'm being bitter. So very bitter. I really do not know what these people have been through since I was sent to slumber.

I've remained in the form of the large rat. It has proven itself indispensable for moving about this settlement. Although, I feel the term settlement is inadequate. I sat in the shadows at high noon in a narrow stone alcove a few days ago and counted over ten thousand unique human faces as they walked by, oblivious. It is quite shocking to me to see all the different skin tones, facial features, and the range of size. When last I dealt with humans they were segregated geographically by design and had multiple distinct lines. Now they are clearly interbred, larger, and obviously smarter. It appears that their natural crossbreeding has been beneficial. This is a good thing.

And the languages! Some letters that are written on signs or on paper look familiar to me, but I've yet to piece anything together. I've learned none of the different spoken dialects, but I believe I've identified five different tongues. I'll learn the most common language soon. I've got a passion for communication.

Tesser's rat body paused in the orange light from the streetlamps high above. Towering buildings, ten, twenty stories tall loomed above like inorganic, steroidal sequoias. Several other rats froze solid as the alpha rat considered the world around him. Inside a nearby building, the bass from a club that had just opened for the night started to rumble. Tesser's rodent head started to bob slowly to the electronic beat.

I must admit, the music they have created is enthralling. All across this settlement I've listened to songs created by stringed instruments, as well as metal horns, and varying other tools to make sound, but this rumbling, thumping, grinding music that comes from this chaotically lit building is my favorite thus far. It has energy. Life.

Tesser resumed his trot down the alley and the other rats unfroze. Even in this relatively alien body, the creatures of the city were blatantly aware that he was in charge. A calico alley cat ten paces away that had been stalking a different, ordinary rat hissed at Tesser as he approached, though it dared not attack. Tesser paid the feline no mind and continued on his way. The fur on the back of the cat's neck stood on its end as Tesser marched past it, unworried. Only when he turned the corner towards a well-lit area of the city did the cat return to its hunt. It understood the food chain.

I must try more of the food. So many culinary delights have been made here. I've eaten out of nearly every refuse container in a wide radius the past two weeks, and no meal twice. Some of it is fetid, and clearly not made of natural ingredients, but some of it is quite delicious. Sometimes, no matter how much of it I've eaten, I'm still hungry.

The thought of the exotic human food made his rat

stomach growl eagerly. Tesser did the equivalent of a rat smile. Up ahead, at the end of the long alley that spilled out into the area of Boston known as Chinatown, three people stood talking, their voices rising in volume and anger. A woman had two men surrounding her, one on each side. She was shrinking lower and lower, trying to make herself smaller, trying to escape the building wrath of the men.

I wonder what makes humans angry now?

Tesser picked up the pace. He wanted to be close, to watch, smell, and learn. Examining people in all their heightened emotions was fascinating for him. He couldn't tell what they were saying, but he listened anyway.

The girl spoke, the presence of worry in her voice thick and strong: "Look, guys, I don't really know you all that well. I don't want to go back to your apartment. The night is early. Let's go into Pandemonium, get some drinks, and dance first. See what happens."

She is attractive. Her manner of dress reveals quite a bit of flesh.

"Look," the taller of the two men said. Tesser noted that as he spoke his mouth sounded... loose. Uncoordinated. "We've seen you like, three, four weekends here now, and we've bought you like, ten, twelf drinksh each. We put in our money and our time. Come back to our place, and we'll have some fun there, shugar tits."

She is frowning. Whatever he said did not appeal to her.

The shorter man behind her reached up and put two strong hands on her upper arms. She flinched as his stubby fingers pressed into her flesh. It would leave a mark.

"Look hoe, we're walking," he said brusquely as he moved her deeper into the alley, straight towards his little rat body. Tesser noted that both men had lumps in their clothing where their genitals were. He did not need to speak the language to understand what was going to happen. They were going to rape her.

A complex series of thoughts ran through Tesser's mind as he considered what to do. Almost all sex in the natural world is consensual. Every species that copulates is unconsciously bidden to do so to procreate their line. Saying no is not part of their equation. As Tesser watched the woman's struggle begin, he contemplated the dilemma at hand.

Humans are not the same as other animals. They think, speak, debate, care, and love. For them, with their heavily developed society and ability to use both the ancient magic as well as whatever new magics they have developed to build structures so high, they are set far apart from the rest of the animal kingdom. Yes, there were some animals that raped to intimidate, or to impregnate, but the whole idea of forced copulation for any reason made the dragon's skin itch.

Are this woman's feelings more important than her unconscious need to procreate? Are her emotions on the subject clouding her ability to judge that giving birth is important to further her line?

Tesser's mind raced as the three bodies in front of him moved in slow motion. He watched intently as the woman's face contorted from soft and pleading, to panicked and angry. She fought with all her might against the two men. The young adult males, however, had little panic in their faces. They had lust and anger.

Immediately, Tesser's mind discarded the strange debate as he felt his own emotions flare. This was not about sex. This was about domination. This was about ego. This was not about making a baby, and bringing new, wondrous life into the world. This was about causing pain and evoking a powerfully twisted form of justice. He'd seen it before in many places and he hated it.

And I will not allow it.

Tesser had no designs to shift into his dragon form to stop the rape from happening. His full form would never fit in the alley, and he knew far too little about this world. Revealing his greatest secret now, even for this, would be foolish. He would need to turn into something that would not be out of place.

Tesser became a man.

The shift from rat to human was painless, like all other shifts of which Tesser was capable. It took only the thought and desire to become something for him to change into that thing. As a human, Tesser preferred to shift into the same form over and over. It was automatic once he'd become comfortable. Akin to how one might button a familiar pair of jeans in the morning getting dressed, or how it is possible to tie a shoe without thinking about it, or even looking at it. Changing into an unfamiliar body took a few seconds longer as he decided how each and every aspect of his form would appear. What hair? What eyes? How tall?

Tesser's favorite people were the north men. He'd spent centuries amongst them, taking the form of a tall, muscular man. His hair was shorter than was the style then, as he made it now. He copied a hairstyle from a picture he'd seen in a window. His new body was lean and painfully perfect as he took his first steps forward. He was already very close to the men. The odd dark stone felt cool and rough under his bare feet.

The short man with the fat fingers turned and saw Tesser, naked and completely out of place in the alley. He challenged him after a moment of confusion, though Tesser didn't understand his words.

"Fuck off, hobo! Get some fucking clothes!" The man said, passing the frightening woman off to his taller, thinner friend.

Tesser watched as the fat-fingered man curled his hands into fists, preparing for the inevitable altercation to come. Tesser's bright, golden eyes nearly glowed with intensity. The thick person stood his ground, showing more courage than Tesser expected.

"One more step, faggot, and I break your jaw," the fighter said.

Tesser didn't understand him, and even if he had, he wouldn't have stopped. His mind was made. He was a dragon and this was a mere man.

The man angrily stepped into a punch that, had it connected, would've been powerful. Tesser's draconic brain and reflexes saw it coming long before he even threw it, so when the fist whistled out, Tesser was already stepping to the man's inside with enough time to watch the attempted strike pass by.

The other man and woman watched the entire fight end in the time it took to take a deep breath.

Tesser grabbed the man's right wrist with his left hand and squeezed hard enough to collapse the two bones at the base of the hand. It was the kind of injury that would have resulted in death when Tesser last walked amongst men. Before the man could let loose a scream, Tesser hammered his own fist up and under the man's ribcage, sparing him shattered ribs, but collapsing both his lungs violently. All of the fight had left him and it had only taken a second. Tesser guided the man down to the pavement carefully, though not gently. The man's nose broke against the hard surface they stood on, and he balled up into the fetal position, heaving air back into his empty chest and holding onto his ruined hand as his nose bled out a large pool of red blood. He groaned in pain.

The other man discarded the woman and bolted, abandoning his friend.

Cowardice. I see the humans still can suffer from it.

"Thank you, oh thank you. They were going to rape me," the pretty young woman said, her eyes boiling over with fresh tears of relief. Tesser couldn't understand her, but as she threw her arms around his bare shoulders he knew the essence of what she was conveying. Gratitude. She cried until the man on the ground got his breath back, and started to moan complete words, begging for help.

"Sweet Jesus, please! You fucked my arm up, man! I need help. Call 911! C'mon!" He cried out, rolling around on the ground in agony.

"Go fuck yourself, you North Shore guido! You and your fucking homo friend!" The woman yelled back, clearly out of control. She let go of Tesser and started to rear back a high-heeled shoe to kick the man in the groin.

Tesser again didn't know what she said, but could piece it together. He snatched up her wrists firmly, moving his body between hers and the man he'd just beaten senseless before her kick could reach the hurt man. He made eye contact with her, peering into her blue eyes with his golden orbs.

"Your eyes..." she said softly, entirely forgetting about the man who had planned on attacking her. The gold glittered like its namesake and she was entranced. Her rage melted away.

Tesser knew one word's meaning, and knew already it was nearly universal, and he spoke it softly, "No." He shook his head to match it, indicating that her behavior was too much. She simply nodded, all the will to be cruel gone.

Tesser smiled genuinely, happy that she was safe. He let her wrists go and turned, his long naked body causing the woman to catch her breath. His human form, the same as his rat form, was perfect. Tesser caught the tiniest whiff of her unconscious arousal and smiled. It pleased him enormously.

He crouched low and leaned down to the injured man.

"No, please, man. Take all my money! Take my ring; it's worth three G's! Just don't kill me!" The man scrambled on his back, getting his clothing dirty in the garbage. His shirt was covered in his own blood.

Tesser shook his head in disgust as he stood and walked down the alley, leaving the man and woman behind to sort out their futures. When he could, he stepped behind one of the large metal refuse containers and shifted down into rat form and disappeared. They had seen nothing.

The woman wiped her eyes, smearing her mascara terribly, and reached into her tiny purse for her smart phone.

Chapter Five
Abe Fellows

Mr. Doyle's home was expensive and everything inside it was expensive as well. The Beacon Street brownstone would list on the market for well over five million dollars, and that was a fraction of the value of the artifacts that the reclusive sorcerer had stored in it. Where Mr. Doyle had earned the money to own such a home was beyond the young man.

Abe let himself in and walked upstairs. He entered one of the upper floor study rooms and sat at the corner of a long table made of mahogany. Intricate scrollwork ran along all four edges of the table. Words and runes were delicately carved in a very precise and magically powerful fashion in languages that were spoken no more. The table had been enchanted over a century earlier to be used as a place for experimentation. The spells cast upon it would contain and nullify any accidents, protecting those sitting at the table and the room the table sat in. Abe called it 'The Error-Proof Table.' It alone would fetch half a million dollars at the annual arcane auction in Paris should Mr. Doyle want to sell it.

But the old man would never do that.

His employer sat at the head of the table. The British man looked no more than fifty years old, with a receding hairline that was turned well gray and a round face edged by soft wrinkles. Abe knew that was wrong. The wizard had been slowing the decline of his aging body for some time, and there was no way to tell just how old he was. Mr. Doyle had told tales of experiencing the First World War in person and that would put his age at no less than a hundred. He didn't look a day older than sixty.

Mr. Doyle sat at the head of the table, leaning over the invisible wall of runes at the table's edge and examining a large pocket watch. The watch was made of gold and like the table, had its own set of carvings and inset words and runes. Abe watched both the timepiece as well as Mr. Doyle intently, utterly and completely unsure of what was happening. He cleared his throat quietly.

"Shhhh," Mr. Doyle said softly, holding a finger to his lips.

He even shushes in a British accent.

"This watch, this marvel of magical engineering hasn't worked in nearly ten years Abraham. Ten years. It has remained in my pocket every day nevertheless. Yesterday, I heard it tick once at precisely noon. If you look at your wristwatch you will notice that we are just a few moments from noon. Your silence will be appreciated young man."

"Of course, sorry," Abe replied.

Why do I put up with his attitude? Seriously? I could totally apprentice under a different warlock or sorcerer now. Someone younger with a more modern take on magic. Maybe someone in a west coast coven? Yeah, it might take me a year or two to find someone new, but it might be worth it.

The pocket watch ticked. Abe's eyes had been pointed directly at the second hand, and when it ticked off a single second there was a brief flare of energy, almost like the watch had vibrated the very reality surrounding it, phasing into and out of our world. Abe felt the hair on the back of his neck stand up.

"Fantastic," Mr. Doyle sat up, pleased like a Cheshire cat. He adjusted his wire rimmed, circular glasses.

"Does this mean...?" Abe let the question hang in the air. In truth, he had no idea what it meant.

"It means that some of the magic that has faded from this world is coming back, Abraham. Some of my most trusted associates back in the old world have confirmed that some of the spells and enchanted items that haven't worked in a decade are starting to function again. Powerful magic, Abraham."

Abe looked at the watch then at his teacher. "What do you think is causing this? Alignments of the stars? A convocation of spellcasters? Some prophecy coming to fruition? Do we have any idea?"

Mr. Doyle sat back in his mahogany chair and wrung his fingers in thought. It was a habit of his. "I cannot say. Most of the prophecies of old are just the ramblings of mad men. Idiots and lunatics that thought they saw the future in tea leaves and the innards of a pig. Whatever has happened, or is happening, is unknown to me as of yet."

"What do we do?" Abe sat back in his own chair and looked through a doorway into a study that was lined wall to wall with ornate glass cases filled with all manner of strange objects. Velvet cases held jeweled rings and bracelets, while hooked mounts displayed swords, daggers, and more than one firearm. That room and all its arcane contents was Mr. Doyle's lifelong passion. All *things* magical were his obsession.

Mr. Doyle sat forward, eagerness in his voice, "We wait, and we watch. Something will happen soon. A sign. A magical portent of the supernatural will arise somewhere, and if we are vigilant we will see it; we will move to it, and investigate it as the scholars we are, Abraham. I am certain of this. Nothing this powerful happens without leaving a mark or making itself seen sooner or later."

"Are there divinatory spells we can cast? Can we get out your crystal ball or fill the scrying pool you've got in the other room?" Abraham's heart jumped. *Oh boy, this will be fun. Real, honest, clairvoyant magic.*

Mr. Doyle shook his head. "I'll see to that, Abraham, that is *my* forte. For now, I need you to do what you do best. I need you to search the internet. YouTube, Twitter, Facebook, and all those other foolish places you frequent so often. Use your modern savvy alongside my magical experience, and we will find our clue soon I suspect."

Are you shitting me? Abe frowned, and spoke before his brain could stop him from doing so, "Are you shitting me?"

Mr. Doyle frowned in a sad fashion. "No my dear, Abraham, I am not 'shitting you.' Swallow your disappointment, and get to work my son. You do your part, and I will do mine. Run to the Star Market and fetch yourself one of your energy drinks and perhaps one of those bags of ranch flavored corn chips you savor so. Bah. American snacks. We are in for a very long stretch, my apprentice." Mr. Doyle got to his feet, with a slight creak to his motion. Abe thought he looked a little older today than yesterday.

"Sorry Mr. Doyle. I just thought that with all this happening I'd play a larger role in the magical side of things. I am apprenticing under you to learn, and this seems like a learning opportunity to me. There isn't much else I can learn about the internet."

Mr. Doyle nodded like a grandfather might and adjusted the waistband on his slate gray slacks. "Abraham, this is a new day, filled with new questions, and answers even I can't guess at. What I can tell you is that your help with the computer and modern media will be far more effective than you helping me to operate a crystal ball that even at the height of magic and in the hands of an experienced wizard was imprecise at best. You wouldn't want me teaching you how to operate a trebuchet when an assault rifle was available would you?"

Abe had his own frown now. "No, I guess not."

"Then please go get your snacks, and load your assault rifle, young man. We're storming the trenches of knowledge tonight, and hopefully we'll rout the Krauts soon and find out what has sparked this resurgence in magical activity."

And with that, the old British sorcerer walked away.

"Fuck me," Abe murmured under his breath as he stood up and headed to the stairs.

I'm totally getting a six pack of Red Bull.

Chapter Six
Matty Rindahl

Gosh it's cold in here today. That's weird.

Matty sat down a microtiter plate that was about to be filled with a solution from a pipette. She was in the early steps of a culturing project and the chill in the lab air was causing her hands to tremble slightly. She looked over her shoulder at the white plastic thermostat on the wall. It read 62 degrees F. The room should've been at 65 degrees Fahrenheit.

So much for my cold resistant Norwegian heritage. I gotta go call maintenance and see what the deal is here. If the temperature is off, the lab won't function properly.

Matty stood up from her lab stool and sat her microtiter plate down, each tiny well in it still empty. She lifted her plastic facemask off, sat it down on the counter beside the plate, and walked away to the lab's airlock style exit door. They worked with nothing dangerous at this facility, but the lab's sanctity and cleanliness was important. Everything done at Fitzgerald Industries was done thoroughly and methodically, and it was a huge part of why they had seen so much growth in a down economy. It also helped that the company's sole owner, Alec Fitzgerald, was strikingly handsome and eloquent enough to be a liked politician. She'd only met him once and had been impressed by his sincerity, good looks, and wit.

Matty left the airlock after discarding her slip-on shoe protectors and leaving her white lab coat behind in a locker. Her black hair was tied back in a ponytail that was just tight enough to give her the onset of a faint headache. She tugged at the hair tie at the back of her head and freed the locks up a bit. Immediately she felt some of her tension dissipate. *Much better.* She walked down the sterile hall towards a large open space filled with cubicles. The room was surrounded by the open office doors of scientist managers, and she headed straight to her direct supervisor' office.

Matty winced at the bright sun glowing out the window. She was never a fan of the fiery orb that hung in the sky. Her skin burned in minutes and her life as a shut-in nerd didn't do her eyes any favors when the sun was out. Matty leaned on the doorframe and waited until she got off the phone.

"Hey, Alexis, the lab is running about three degrees too cold today. Can you get maintenance on the horn and get them to fix it? My fingers are about to fall off."

Alexis sat behind her desk, the city of Boston a few miles distant out the window. Alexis was a short lady with graying red hair. Matty thought she was pretty despite her mid-fifties age. She certainly was full of life. Alexis made a sour face and then nodded. "Yeah, sure Matty. I'll call 'em. You taking lunch soon?"

Whoa, I am hungry.

Matty looked at her watch and saw it was a few minutes shy of noon. "Yeah, I'll probably take off now."

"Did you bring a lunch? I was thinking of ordering delivery from that new Greek place on the corner." Alexis pulled out a large take-out menu from a drawer in her desk.

"I brought a lunch, sorry. But if you want to eat with

me in the break room, I'll be over in a bit. I think I'll check my email and maybe see if there's anything interesting in the news."

"That sounds great," Alexis said as she picked up her phone to call either maintenance or the Greek restaurant. Matty left before finding out which.

The young scientist wandered over to her cubicle which was just a few seconds walk away. She was still very new at Fitzgerald Industries and as such, her cube was only sparsely decorated. A few picture frames filled with snapshots of her mother and father were on the desk, and she had the obligatory kitten calendar hanging on the side of her cube. She was waiting for a few weeks to pass before she brought in the stuff that she really wanted to decorate with. Anime action figures, a few posters of her favorite B-grade movie classics, and an action figure of Bub the Zombie from the Romero flick Day of the Dead.

It's no wonder I'm single. Max was right to move on after the miscarriage.

Matty sat down and rolled her chair up to her computer. She logged on to the company network and opened a browser window. Her lunchtime ritual was ever the same, even here at her new job: first, she checked her Gmail account. From back in Norway her mother had sent her a recipe for a Mexican style baked dish that her father had loved. Matty deleted the email after replying, 'yum!' Second she skimmed Facebook (people were breeding, and then attempting to get that choice validated by sharing photos of baby bumps and kids acting like kids in public), and then went to a local news station to see what was happening in Boston. She'd had a strange need to check the news several times a day since the random Green Line tunnel collapse a few weeks ago. Terrorism scared the crap out of her.

A video on the station's homepage caught her eye. The article was titled, 'Naked vigilante hobo rescues woman from attempted rape.' The freeze frame on the header showed a naked man (genitals blurred, of course) standing in an alley, and he didn't look anything like a hobo. If anything, he looked like a model that had stood in an alley waiting for a picture to be taken for the cover of Men's Health or a snooty mail order catalogue. He was handsome.

Interesting...

Matty hit play on the video, and a pretty female newscaster explained the situation.

"A young woman who had gone out for a night of dancing and fun with her college friends had a nearly deadly turn of events. Parents, the following footage is not appropriate for all children. The lady, seen here on black and white ATM security camera footage was being accosted by two men when an unknown Samaritan appeared from deeper in the alley came to her aid. He was wearing *no clothing*." The news anchor placed heavy, heady emphasis on the last sentence before continuing. She smiled, and the video started to play.

"The naked, homeless man stepped into the attempted kidnapping and very quickly made short work of one of the men before the other assailant escaped unharmed. As the video plays on, you can see the naked man go so far as to stop the victim from taking revenge on her assailant in a showing of tremendous self-control and good will. The victim was unharmed by her two attackers, and the man who did not leave the scene was transported to Mass General with numerous broken bones in his arm and wrist. Boston police have arraigned the suspect on attempted kidnapping charges, and are looking for the other suspect. If you have any details, please call the number on the screen to talk to Detective Henry Spooner who is in charge of the case."

The video ended.

Wow.

Matty rewound the video and played the short

moments where the light haired man was visible. He moved faster than she'd ever seen anyone move. Maxwell, her ex-boyfriend, had earned his black belt in Tae Kwon Do, and she thought he was graceful and powerful, but Max had nothing on this mystery naked man. He was masculine, lean, strong, and embodied what Matty imagined to be nearly perfect violence. He used only the force needed to rescue the woman and no more.

Holy shit, I'm horny.

Matty took mental stock of her body and realized she was flush. There was a tiny amount of dampness in her lady parts and she leaned back in her chair and shook her head. *What the hell?*

"What's that you're watching? A movie trailer? Wow, that man is fiiiiiine," she heard Alexis say over her shoulder.

Matty sat back up, embarrassed for no visible reason. "It's uh, a video of some naked homeless guy rescuing some girl the other night nearby that new nightclub Pandemonium. He doesn't look homeless to me."

Alexis snorted. "If I met him, he wouldn't be homeless anymore. I've got a spot in my bed next to me he can have all night. My food's at the front desk. I'm gonna grab it and head to the break room."

Matty nodded, her eyes fixed on the grainy black and white paused video.

"Take all the time you need with that video," Alexis said, and the two women shared a laugh.

Matty sat at the desk, fantasizing about the vigilante for a good long stretch before chastising herself and getting up.

"I gotta get laid."

Matty grabbed her brown-bagged lunch and headed to the break room.

Chapter Seven
Tesser

To further my learning of the most commonly spoken language, I have opted to spend more time in a different area of the city. I've learned that word: city. It means a large settlement filled with constructions that reach towards the sky like this. I've also learned that this settlement, this city, is called Boston. I've managed to do all this by spending more time in my human form.

I was able to find some makeshift clothing out of a refuse container a few days after I helped that young woman. Near an area of the city where there were many crafters selling clothing I was able to see another young man throw away a large bag filled with what appeared to be clothing.

I shifted into my human form and as soon as the sun went down, I helped myself to several garments that fit. I kept the bag, and the clothing that did not fit as well. I don't know why the man threw the clothing away.

My first attempt at human interaction ended poorly. I went into a small building that served hot drinks and small baked goods under a green emblem of a woman. She reminded me of the legendary mermaids. A small woman with a green cloth smock became very irate at my entrance, and ushered me out. I didn't want to engage in hostility, so I left. I sat on the metal bench outside, in full view of the world when a young man, also wearing a green smock, brought out a small paper cup filled with a dark beverage. He spoke at me for a minute or two to no avail, and then offered me the cup. I sipped it, and it was dark, bitter, and flavorful. I pointed at the cup and tilted my head indicating I didn't know what it was. Even after all this time, body language has remained similar.

He said it was, "Coffee."

That was my first word of the language I now know to be called English.

He then pointed to his chest and said, "Alan. I'm Alan."

I nodded, pointed to my chest, and told him my name, "Tesser."

He spoke at me until the small woman came out and yelled at him. He told me her name was "Bitch" before he smiled and went back in to help other people who wanted some of the hot coffee.

Alan was my first human friend.

Bitch was not.

I stayed near the coffee shop for a week. Alan brought me a coffee on the days that he worked, and I was thankful for that. I have since developed a strong affection for the drink, but now I've decided I like mine with cream and sugar. Humans have certainly been ingenious with their foods.

Alan discovered my lack of English knowledge very quickly and provided me with the one item that Bitch required me to have to enter their establishment: shoes. Alan gave me an old pair of what appeared to be sandals, which fit perfectly after I readjusted the size of my foot to be a little larger. Sandals on foot, Bitch could no longer kick me out of the coffee shop.

Inside the shop I have sat attentively in front of a magical device called a 'television.' It apparently receives mass messages in both visual and auditory formats. While not truly magical in the ancient, primordial sense, the images that play across the device are remarkable. Alan adjusted the television to play images that are clearly designed for children for several hours a day and provided me with small books that have only a few pages.

I have seen far more complicated books at small crafter-shops in the city, so I know that these too are likely made for children to learn with. They will be perfect for my first few day of learning.

At night I relocate to another food establishment that is open very late into the night. Immersion into the human culture is key. This business serves round baked food covered in sauce made of tomatoes and then topped with cheese and various meats and vegetables. The painted sign on the front of the business calls this food "pizza."

With my bag of clothing in hand each night, I sit in the far back of the pizza shop and watch more television and listen to the younger people come and go, buying their pizza. I've noticed that at all of these places where things are served, they exchange small slips of green fabric-paper for the goods and services they want. A strange form of barter. I think I'll try and obtain some of the green slips of paper.

The owner of the pizza shop, or at least the man that everyone else seems to listen to, has a strange obsession with stories that center around two men. One man is tall, with long blonde hair he wears underneath a winter cap, and the other is shorter, fatter, and has long brown hair and a beard. He too wears a hat, but it has a brim facing to the rear. Because they have set their television to show the words that are being spoken, I've been able to learn many of the words.

Apparently the words shit, fuck, ass, bitch, and stoner are common in the English language. I've used them a few times in awkward, minimalist conversations to no good effect. Clearly, I don't know enough. I'm also trying to decipher how the woman's name at the coffee shop is also a word in regular use.

It confounds me, but I've already got a working vocabulary of perhaps a hundred words that I am able to use in very short sentences, some of the time.

"Hello?! Are you the dude in that video?" A rail thin blonde dressed in a tight mini skirt and halter top bleated not five feet from where Tesser sat in the back of the pizza parlor.

Shit. See, I'm learning already.

Tesser turned slowly, unsure of what she'd said. He understood that hello was a greeting.

"Hello," he returned in a friendly but deadpan fashion. He forced a smile that was only slightly awkward.

"Nissa, this is the guy, come look." The blonde grabbed her friend by the arm and dragged her from the line of people trying to buy a slice of pizza at the late night shop. The brunette friend stumbled over, angry at first, but when she laid eyes on the still disheveled Tesser, her eyes widened.

"Oh my god! I think that *is* him, get your phone, look up the video!" The brunette stared at Tesser in a way that Tesser had seen before, and it confused him. She thought she knew him. She thought she'd seen him before.

Shit. He continued to smile, still sitting in the bright orange booth in the corner near the television.

The blonde held up her phone and tapped on the screen rapidly, bringing up a YouTube video. Before long, both girls were squealing with delight. They had recognized Tesser from the ATM video.

"Is this you?" The blonde thrust her phone practically into Tesser's eyes. The dragon had to lean back to prevent one of her bright red nails from scratching his skin.

Tesser watched on the tiny screen as images of his alleyway altercation played out. His face stayed solemn as he watched his own violence. His nakedness caused a tiny, edge of mouth smile. It amused him and startled him that his image had been somehow captured, and without his realizing it.

"It's him," said the brunette seriously. Both women were oddly star-struck in Tesser's presence.

Tesser watched until the video finished playing, then smiled and nodded. He wasn't sure what the words were to agree with the girls.

They squealed again, and squished into the booth with him.

Tesser sighed.

Well, at least they are attractive.

Chapter Eight

Sergeant Henry "Spoon" Spooner

They aren't opening up.

Henry's adrenaline surged. His muscles were taut from head to toe as he stood in a breaching stack with the rest of the SWAT team. Everyone in the line with him was wearing full ballistic armor for the raid. Helmet, full ballistic plate, lap and groin protectors, kneepads, and shin guards were the order of the day. Some guys wore more. It was miserably hot in the armor. It was early in the morning, far too damn early to be up kicking in some drug dealer's door in Dorchester, but they needed the body, and Henry was available. SWAT wasn't his gig anymore, but he said he'd help.

"Go," said the Sergeant in charge of the breaching team. The warnings had ended.

Let's do this.

The man at the head of the stack held a battering ram, and in the dark hallway he looked the size of a medieval ram all on his own. He brought the steel crash bar back to hammer into the closed front door of the apartment they'd come to raid. Some of these SWAT guys dwarfed

Henry. He'd always been the runt of the litter.

Henry smiled.

The goliath carrying the battering ram brought the steel cylinder into the door right at the knob with a powerful underhanded swing. The sturdy wooden door burst inward, splintering the doorframe and cracking in half as it fell completely off the hinges. It was as if the door had been made of glued together toothpicks.

Shit Paul, that door sleep with your wife?

The man dropped the ram and stepped aside to let the rest of the men in the breaching stack pour through the doorway past him.

The first man into the apartment started yelling immediately, "Boston Police! Search warrant! Face down, hands on your heads!"

Henry's thumb twitched reflexively on the safety of his M4, moving the selector to fire. His index finger hovered over the trigger guard, ready to retract and send a high velocity round into anyone who threatened his life or the lives of the officers he was with. The tension was incredible. Delicious.

"Clear!"

"Clear!" The SWAT officers barked out as they moved into the apartment and fanned out, checking rooms for signs of life. These early morning raids were almost always successful at catching the suspects in their underwear asleep in bed, and in the first thirty seconds of this raid, it was looking good.

Henry's assigned job on this raid was the ass end of the stack. He was to push deepest into the apartment with one of the more experienced officers on the team and arrest the person in the last bedroom. Surveillance indicated that there was only one person in the apartment, and that's where they were supposed to be.

Henry and his teammate moved into the apartment quickly, past the other officers as they covered movement in every conceivable place. Like Henry, every man on the breaching team had military experience, and he felt comfortable with them.

Though anything could go wrong.

The officer in front of Henry raised his leg and snapped it out in a powerful kick at the closed bedroom door. The cheaper interior door was hollow and the kick well placed, causing it to blast inward on the hinges and bounce off the wall of the bedroom. The two men were moving into the room before the door had a chance to come back at them.

In the bed was their perpetrator.

There he is.

The leading officer yelled as he slung his M4 and grabbed at his cuffs, "Boston Police! Hands where we can see them!"

That's the point where something went wrong.

The suspect was curled on his side in the fetal position facing them, and as the other officer went to grab the man's arm, he launched a kick out and it struck the cop straight in the groin.

Fuck.

The lead officer let out a whimper and collapsed, bouncing off the edge of the mattress before hitting the floor.

The perp leapt up like a ninja in the darkened bedroom and launched his entire body at Henry. He screamed and spread his arms wide like some insane, drugged up bird of prey.

Henry might've been the runt of the litter his whole life, but one thing he had was speed.

Henry stabbed his M4's barrel out as a reflex, and caught the man square on the jaw as he came down on him. Henry felt and heard the man's jaw break, but could do nothing but fall as the now unconscious drug dealer's body fell on top of him, pinning him to the floor. Henry let out a grunt as all the dead weight squished him down against the dirty, smelly rug. Henry's finger never moved over the trigger.

Another officer stepped into the doorframe, saw the situation, and laughed. "Shit Henry, you're supposed to be on top of him."

"Kiss my ass, Ethan. Check on Lawrence, he got hit in the junk," Henry said as he pushed the drug dealer off of his chest.

Ethan stepped over Henry and checked on the downed officer, Lawrence. Henry cuffed the scumbag with the broken jaw and left him lying on his side. He moaned in pain as Henry started to walk away. He'd need to be checked by the EMTs before he was moved. Henry was sure the drug dealer's jaw was broken.

"What happened?" The team leader asked as Henry passed him on the way out of the apartment.

Henry put his weapon on safe and dropped the magazine as he replied to the sergeant in charge of the team, "He kicked Lawrence in the balls then tried to jump on me. I barrel-struck his face."

The sergeant laughed. "I'll need a report, Henry. Fucker's lucky you didn't just put a round in his face. Thanks for joining up last minute man, always glad I can call on another Rakkasan in a pinch."

Henry grinned. "You betcha." The two men shook hands and Henry left the ratty apartment and went down to the SWAT truck to have a seat and let the narcotics team enter to search the property. He grabbed a bottle of water off the bumper of the truck and watched as the neighborhood came out to see what all the commotion was about.

From his duffel bag in the back of the truck, Henry heard his cell phone ring. His department phone, not his personal phone.

"This is Sergeant Spooner," he answered after picking up.

"Hi, is this the detective investigating that naked vigilante thing? I saw this number on the news," asked a young woman's voice.

"Yes, this is he. Do you have some information you could share on the case? Anything said would be anonymous." Henry felt a rush. This was his first major case since being promoted to *Detective* Sergeant. A break this early in the case would be huge for his career in the BPD.

"Well, yeah sort of. My girlfriend and I met the naked guy a few nights ago at a pizza parlor near Fenway. That late night place?"

"Yeah, I know the place. Slice and a Coke for three bucks right? Best deal in town." Henry grabbed his small notebook and started to jot the woman's statement down.

"Well, I don't drink soda, but yeah, that place. Hey, that guy was like, foreign or something. He spoke like, next to no English. Super nice though, and was wearing like, used Abercrombie stuff. Like, dumpster used. He wasn't naked at all."

She's an idiot.

Henry smiled, "Well, that's good news. Does he frequent the place?"

"Dunno. But I saw the news thing online and thought like, you guys might be able to ask him some questions, maybe with like a translator or something."

Henry nodded and watched a young black boy of maybe ten years of age watch him from the steps of the building across the street.

That kid should be asleep. Where are his parents? It's a school night.

"May I ask why you're calling me at this hour? It's sort of an odd hour to phoning the police about a case."

The girl giggled.

She's drunk.

"My girlfriend and I just got out of a night dancing and we were talking about the guy. You know how HOT he is, right? Like, smoking manly hot. If you were gay, you'd be wicked in to him. Anyways, we were thinking it was like socially responsible to call. Plus maybe he could use some help here in America? Maybe he can lead you guys to the other dude who was trying to rape that girl. It takes a village, you know?"

Henry sighed. "It takes a village, yeah, for sure." *Complete with the idiot.*

"One last thing. You will totally be able to recognize him by his eyes."

"His eyes?" Henry asked.

"Yeah. They are like, golden, or like super brown or something. Never seen anyone with eyes like that before. Okay, well that's it. Thanks!" The girl hung up before Henry could thank her for the information.

Terrific. Now the naked hobo is a foreigner with weird eyes who likes cheap Back Bay pizza. That's better than nothing I suppose.

Henry shooed the young kid back inside the apartment building he lived in and proceeded to find a cruiser that could take him back to the station so he could change and fill out the paperwork for the raid. He would follow up on the phone tip as soon as he was done.

Chapter Nine
Abe Fellows

Abe sat alone at a desk in a study that had been assigned to him by Mr. Doyle. The room was sumptuous, the desk made of cherry. Everything felt old.

Daft Punk blared in Abe's ears through high quality headphones. The melodic, electronic music thumped and pulsated, and Abe's left index finger tapped on the desk to the beat. Abe's right index finger operated a computer mouse as his eyes scanned webpage after webpage for something… special.

Something weird. Something new. Something magical.

Abe's first stop on his internet adventure at the behest of Mr. Doyle was a series of websites dedicated to the mystical, and magical. These were the first sites that he'd stumbled on years ago that awoke his still budding magical talent.

He could thank the internet for bringing his magic to life.

The first site he visited was the one most likely to have chatter, but the least likely to produce anything meaningful. It was called Wizard's, Warlocks, and Sorcerers, though its domain name was something entirely innocuous. WWS as those in the know called it, was a forum dedicated for people to share their work in the magical arts. Hedge mages who could only work the barest of spells were the primary attendants there, but sometimes they saw something real and powerful.

The talk on WWS was heightened and excited, though not because they'd seen something specific like the reappearance of an incredibly powerful artifact, but because they ALL had seen something. Their magic was growing. Each of the meek spell casters had seen their own ability to wield the arcane art grow in the preceding weeks. One mage had only started to study reputable texts a week prior, and was already able to wield a fledgling form of telekinesis.

Man, what a lucky asshole.

The rest of WWS was crap. Nothing of note. No sightings, no truly substantial revelations worth telling Mr. Doyle about.

Daft Punk gave way to Death Cab for Cutie.

Abe's second internet destination was The Delphian Covenant.

The Major Leagues baby.

Abe would never dare to shorten The Delphian Covenant to The DC, not even in the secluded sanctum of his head. The circle of warlocks that operated The Delphian Covenant were the kind of people who would know if he did. He wouldn't dare risk their wrath however unlikely it was.

The Delphian Covenant was a news site dedicated to the arcane. Seven male warlocks worked for the site as the modern day magical equivalent of journalists. Abe's favorite writer was a man named Oliver Douglas. Oliver was a well-spoken man, an excellent writer, as well as a successful practitioner of water-based magic. Some of the other spell casters that had met Oliver claimed that he was able to do things like walk on water and form tendrils of it using highly refined spells, despite the overall waning of all magical power in the world. Abe was jealous once more.

Oliver lived in Europe somewhere and wrote about things that occurred there. His last article on The Delphian Covenant was about a circle of stones deep in the German forest that had begun to vibrate a few weeks ago. Abe had never heard of the stones. The date of the new vibration seemed to coincide with the morning that Abe was able to cast the telekinesis spell to turn his cell phone off. Oliver had taken some video of the circle of stones, as well as of the interviews he'd done.

Bingo, maybe this will good.

Oliver spoke at length about the composition of the stones, their placement in relation to constellations and moon phases, and commented on how the stones seemed to be vibrating in varying frequencies. There were seven gray stones, each the size of a modern refrigerator, and all but one was vibrating. Local mages filled in the backstory as they stood in front of the circled granite obelisks, with the voice over translation from German courtesy of Oliver.

"The Seven Stones of the Black Forest have always vibrated in some fashion. Six of the stones have vibrated for a very long time you see, centuries, millennia. One of the stones stopped vibrating about ten years ago, and that happened just before all the magic began to fade away," said a middle-aged German woman. She was clearly from the area, and looked halfway between elated and terrified.

"The sixth stone was the stone that stopped vibrating a decade ago. But just now, just this summer, the seventh stone began to vibrate once more." She turned and pointed at a stone that had a faint glimmer of gold to it. As Oliver zoomed in on the 'seventh stone,' Abe caught traces of actual gold filigree in the granite. Veins of actual gold were interlaced into the rock, and the stone itself was beyond beautiful up close. Oliver panned his handheld camera to each of the other stones and, in turn, each stone revealed its own strange quality. One had similar veins of a red substance that looked like iron, whereas one stone had scattered bits of an amber colored gem embedded into it. Each obelisk was unique. The sixth stone, the silent stone, had amethysts in it.

"The two most remarkable stones of the seven are the ones we call the water stone and fire stone." The woman gestured to two stones arranged conspicuously from one another in the circle. To the west was a stone that was unremarkable in any way, save for a small hole in the center of its peak that issued forth a gentle stream of water. The water cascaded down the stone, covering it in what looked to be a glossy film of water.

The Water Stone.

To the south was the other extra-remarkable stone. The German sorceress skimmed some of the water off the side of the Water Stone and brought it to the south stone, and emptied her hand atop it. The water sizzled, popped, and steamed immediately.

That thing has to be boiling hot to the touch.

"The Fire Stone is boiling hot to the touch," the German woman said.

Abe sighed.

"There seems to be an elemental correspondence to the stones?" Oliver asked in German.

"There is. To the North is the Earth Stone, and to the East the Air Stone."

Abe looked at the other three stones arranged about the circle. One was the dead amethyst stone. The other two were the golden and amber filled stones. Something very strange rang in Abe's mind about that trio of stones mixed into the seven. Something about their placement made his mind buzz, like seeing an unsolved puzzle for the first time.

Very strange.

The rest of the interview gave more back-story to the forest and the group of people who had protected the circle. Abe listened intently, but found nothing in the interview that made his brain click.

Facebook changed that.

Abe was assaulted immediately when he logged in. He had three new friend requests from people he'd met at the Friday Night Magic card tourney the week prior, and he accepted all of them once he recognized the names.

Nerd unity.

He had two messages to read as well. One was from a former coworker asking how he was doing since quitting, and the other was from a girl he'd been flirting with for months. She almost seemed interested, and that was a great sign for Abe.

I wish I had the balls to just fucking ask her out. Abe took a sip from a near empty can of Red Bull.

He had several notifications as well, and most of those were people liking something he posted or commenting on a status where he'd added his two cents already.

Inane bullshit.

Death Cab for Cutie transitioned into Porter Robinson, but after a couple songs he switched to Lynryd Skynryd.

One of the notifications did manage to catch his eye. A local friend he'd gone to BC with had tagged Abe in a post.

Naked Vigilante Hobo, eh?

Abe grinned and clicked on it.

In the status update there was a link to one of the local news stations. Abe read the brief article speaking about a man who'd intervened and stopped a potential rape, and then clicked on the triangle and started the video.

He laughed at first, but as the dark video came near to closing, something made Abe pause the video.

What the…?

Abe rewound a few moments of the black and white video and watched it again.

No way.

He repeated the process once more. Then twice.

"Mr. Doyle!" Abe yelled as he pulled his headphones off. The loud southern rock escaped into the study, and within seconds Mr. Doyle was yelling back.

"Turn off that infernal racket, Abraham! That music is likely rotting both our brains right at this very moment!" Mr. Doyle was pissed.

"Sorry! I've got something Mr. Doyle. I think this might be something special. You need to see it."

"I'm coming!" the older wizard hollered back from the hall.

Abe reopened browser windows pointed at Oliver Douglas' articles on The Delphinian Covenant, and left the video feed of the naked man open as well. When Mr. Doyle arrived, he had turned off the music, and was ready to make his presentation.

"What is it?" The British man asked as he leaned over the back of the expensive leather chair.

He smells like old books.

"I've been researching all day, as you asked," Abe said confidently.

"Good. You've found something?"

"Yeah. I saw this video about The Seven Stones of the Black Forest earlier. Have you heard of them?"

Mr. Doyle nodded knowingly, "Yes. I've been to them once. Right as the Second World War came to a close. I was in Germany with the Allied forces working against Hitler's occult teams. There is nothing new about the stones."

Once again the man shows his true age.

Abe sighed again. "Well, if you recall, only six of the stones have vibrated continuously, and about ten years ago, when the magic began to fade, one of the stones stopped vibrating right?"

"Yes, that seems so." Mr. Doyle seemed irritated by the old news.

"Well, the very same day that I cast my Commoveo spell we had that earthquake that fucked up the Green Line, and you asked me to quit my job, it appears that the seventh stone, the one that has never vibrated ... began to vibrate."

Mr. Doyle leaned forward, suddenly very interested. "Continue."

"The Seventh Stone is the gold stone," Abe said as he brought up the video of the naked man from the other night. "I just saw this on Facebook. A friend sent me the link. At first it seemed like nothing, but watch."

Mr. Doyle leaned in even closer to get a good look at the small video. Abe made it full screen, and the older man seemed satisfied. Abe watched Mr. Doyle's face as the security camera footage played on.

The British man's eyes went wide.

"Play it again."

Abe did as he asked.

"Play it again."

Abe played the video a third time.

"This is a black and white video, yes? Absent of color?"

"Yes. It was taken from an ATM machine across the street. Pure happenstance really. I think it's connected, Mr. Doyle. I've got a very strong feeling about it."

Mr. Doyle nodded, slowly at first, but then emphatically. "Yes, my apprentice I do believe you are on to something. Please, continue your search, but focus it on the naked man exclusively. I believe he might be very, very important. Fine work Abraham. Bloody fine work." Mr. Doyle stood straight and walked from the room.

He's walking really hard.

"Mr. Doyle, are you alright?" Abraham asked, concerned.

The old man turned, and looked far older than he

ever had before. "The spells that have sustained my life for so long are failing, Abraham. The years will be catching up with me before long I suspect. Hopefully, we can sort this out and I am able to refresh the spells. Though I feel that my time here is near its end no matter what comes of the magic." Mr. Doyle looked sad.

"What are you going to do now?" Abraham asked.

"I'm going to research the Seven Stones. I have a few Germanic texts on them that might shed more light on the vibrations and their meaning."

Abe nodded.

"Bloody, bloody good work Abraham. You'll make a fine mage one day," Mr. Doyle said softly before turning and walking out of the office.

Abe sighed for the hundredth time and turned back to the computer monitor. *You know, that was the biggest compliment he's ever given me.* With a fresh smile, he hit play on the video once again and paid very close attention to the naked man's eyes.

They were gold. Despite the fact that the video was black and white, the man's eyes shone through as pure flecks of gold.

Just like the seventh stone.

"Fuck yeah."

Chapter Ten
Tesser

I appear to be a bit of a celebrity. I'm somewhat accustomed to this. As a dragon, everything ran before me and told tales of my coming, my generosity, and my anger. In my human form, they told tales of my prowess in war, my skill as a leader, and of my ... virility.

This is very different. Now, I appear to be a bit of a cultural attraction. Dare I say some think of me as a form of hero? When the two young girls came into the restaurant several nights ago, they brought a large amount of attention my way. They bought me some of the pizza served here, which was very tasty, and then took several pictures of me using their cell phones.

Cell phones. Delightful devices that use science to transmit both voice and images through the air. It is a tremendous thing to see a non-magical means to communicate over vast distances. Apparently these devices are able to transmit entire conversations across oceans and continents, requiring only the effort of a few movements of a thumb.

The owner of the pizza establishment has granted me a job. I work for him keeping his patrons safe from eleven in the morning until he closes at 2 in the morning. I am able to do this because I've learned how to tell time. Humans have created clocks and watches that can monitor the passage of the sun and moon without actually seeing the sun or the moon. Jerry, the owner of the pizza shop bought me a wrist-mounted clock called a 'watch.' It has a large face with a yellow man made of sponge, who goes by the name Bob.

I find it charming.

He has also given me permission to stay in the back of the shop overnight to rest. I don't really need to sleep every night, but I am choosing to. It is what the humans have always done, and when I am with a species, I match their habits. It allows for the most amount of consistency, and I stand out a bit less.

Keeping the patrons safe has been an easy task. For the majority of the day I stand or sit near the front entrance and have my picture taken with women. I don't need to ask them to leave with my shitty English, they are simply delighted to be in my presence. I've decided to not have sex with any of them.

Yet.

The nights have been a bit livelier, though primarily for the same reason.

Fermented beverages. Beer, wine, and liquor. I've had beer before, or at least what the humans would've called what they drank then, beer. Wine, or fermented grapes, has a history almost as old as I am, and I enjoy a sip or two when I can. Liquor is a newer innovation. Fermented grains and strange fruits concocted to be much more powerful than beer or wine in terms of intoxication.

Many humans act like complete assholes when they drink these beverages. Some nights, it seems like all of them are assholes.

I've learned enough English to understand that most of what they say is nonsense when they are drunk, and most of what they do is also utter bullshit.

I like that expression: bullshit. It doesn't actually refer to male cow feces, it means to be flagrantly wrong or false. For example, saying that I am a mere human is bullshit. I am actually a dragon. Humans call this kind of humor sarcasm.

I think I will use it extensively. Sarcasm. I like to laugh.

When the drunkards come in later in the night I need to be a bit more aware of what is happening. I've had to intervene in several fistfights in just the few days I've been doing this task, and while relatively easy work, I need to be very careful to use minimal strength. Human bones are very strong, but I am a dragon, and breaking bones comes very easy to me. I still don't want to play my hand too early.

The women, drunk or sober, all seem to want me sexually. Almost every female that comes in either has already seen the video from the alley and knows what my naked body looks like, or they can simply sense that I am the alpha male in the room. It's part of who and what I am. Life, in all its forms here on this lovely world, has come from or been sculpted by dragon kind in some form or another. But that's a very long story for another time. Tonight, I protect the young college kids who are trying to get their late night pizza slices.

College is an interesting development. Organized learning. Organized higher learning. It astounds me the level of investment humans have put into education. It certainly explains why they've advanced their understanding of material sciences. Technology they call it. Magic appears to have been forgotten in the shuffle, but this is still quite fascinating. When I was last in their society, creating reliable fire and making boats was the pinnacle of their achievements. They've come so far.

"Hey, gold eyes, you have a name?" a cute brunette with short hair that framed her face asked Tesser.

Tesser smiled, and watched her cock her head to the side teasingly. She was yet another girl who wanted to flirt.

Another adventure in spoken conversation. Here we go. "My name is Tesser. What's yours?" He replied.

I still haven't got the accent quite right.

"Katelyn, but you can call me Katie. Or just call me later?" The girl extended her fingers with a small slip of paper pressed between two of them.

That's a piece of a menu. Shame she tore one up. Jerry

spends good money to have those printed for his business I'm sure.

Tesser smiled and took the slip from her. "I don't have a phone yet."

The girl looked overly sympathetic. "You're getting back on your feet right? You were homeless before?"

Tesser nodded, understanding the basic idea of what she was getting at. "Yes, I am not from around here."

"Where *are* you from? You sound European," Katie asked pleasantly as she rolled her head to the other side in a calculated gesture. A stray lock of her hair drifted across her cheek.

Shit.

"You probably haven't heard where I'm from," he replied.

"Try me. I'm an anthropology major." Katie smiled again as she traced a finger on her cheek to tuck the hair behind her ear. Another decision made to arouse.

From behind Katie two men started to raise their voices at one another. Tesser's golden orbs twitched past her and watched them as their fingers balled into fists at their sides. This was one of the moments Jerry paid him for.

"Excuse me," Tesser said with a smile. He gently moved Katie out of his way and walked over toward the two men.

"Fuck you dude. BC over BU every day!" one moron exclaimed.

Male pride. Tesser sighed.

"The only major they offer at BC is smoking dick faggot!"

Well, that should be enough to get the other man to –

A punch came out. The thinner man who was freshly insulted put all four knuckles of his fist into the teeth of his adversary, sending him stumbling backwards into a crowd of patrons. Many other voices leapt into the fray, and a massive scuffle was only moments away.

Dammit.

"STOP!" Tesser bellowed. He reached deep, further into his chest than any normal man could've, and his voice carried a note of authority that was superhuman. It was the trumpeting of an elephant on the African plains, the roar of the tiger in the Indian jungle. A primal bellow. The entire crowd of pizza eaters and preparers froze solid, and went silent. A popular pop song played in the background, sounding lonely somehow in the absence of the human buzz.

The man who threw the punch turned, several of his knuckles bloodied by the teeth of his victim. His pain and anger overrode his good sense. "Who the fuck are you?"

Tesser remained calm and took the last few steps to the drunk college boy. "I am Tesser. It's my job to keep the people here safe. And you must leave. Now." Tesser kept at arm's reach.

I don't want him to throw a punch at –

The man threw a punch at Tesser, but it didn't land. Tesser saw it coming long before the man was able to wind up to full power, and the dragon in human form caught the punch in his hand like he would an angry child's.

"Tsk, tsk." Tesser grinned and twisted the man's hand forcefully.

"Ahh!" he screamed as Tesser continued to ply force onto the man's wrist, moving him about as if it were a rudder. Before two seconds had passed, Tesser had the man's arm behind his back at a 90-degree angle and was walking him out the door.

"Eat shit and live BC cock smoker!" the punched man taunted through a bloody mouth.

Tesser let the attacker go with a bit of a shove into the still busy late night street and turned to face the man who had tossed out the taunt. "You sir, are next, and I will not stop him from punching you outside of this restaurant."

The man with the bleeding lip shut his mouth

abruptly as a young woman put her arm around him.

"Good choice. Do not taunt anyone anymore Mr. Cock Smoker, or I will ask you to leave—or much worse." He leveled his golden eyes at the college student. The man was taller than Tesser, but he shrank under the dragon's challenge. When he said nothing in return, Tesser nodded and walked past him into the pizzeria. The couple turned and walked away towards the bathrooms in the rear of the restaurant, face and pride injured.

I'm not sure that was a correct usage of the term cock smoker.

"Whoa. You're a tough guy aren't you?" Katie asked him as he returned to where she stood.

I don't know how to answer that question either. This girl has a skill for confounding me.

"I think that's hot," she said, dragging her expertly painted nails down the front of one of the three shirts Tesser now owned. She leaned in and pressed her young body against his.

I wonder what she'd think if I told her how old I really am.

"I think that's reason for a few questions," said a man behind Tesser.

Hmm?

Tesser turned and assessed the man who'd made the statement. Katie remained against him. He was far shorter than Tesser but carried his body with poise. He had strong dark eyes and light brown, close cropped hair. He wore a buttoned shirt that was tucked into pants Tesser knew to be slightly fancier than those worn by the average man. He seemed professional and very out of place in the late night pizza joint.

"My name is Sergeant Henry Spooner with the Boston Police Department. I'm investigating the alleged attempted rape that occurred several weeks ago near the Pandemonium nightclub. I have some questions for you if you have the time."

Katie shrank away into the crowd like a shadow

fleeing from sunlight.
Well, shit.

Chapter Eleven
Tesser

"So you are the man who came to Ms. Blake's aid that night?" Spoon asked as he put his badge away.

The two had moved outside the pizza shop and down the street to a quieter area. No one was listening to them on their overpass guardrail perch.

Tesser's knowledge of the English language was being tested powerfully.

This man could make my life very difficult if he suspects something is amiss about me. I must tread very carefully.

"I helped the woman, yes."

Spoon nodded. "Excellent. She has expressed a great deal of appreciation to the department regarding your timely appearance, despite your lack of clothes." The cop added a friendly grin.

Tesser understood most of that. "I've only recently come to Boston."

"You said your name was Tesser, right? What is that? Russian? French?" Spoon fished out a pack of cigarettes and a disposable lighter. He fired the cancer stick up and took a drag.

"I am not exactly sure. It's quite old." Tesser was almost nervous.

This verbal dance is irritating. If this asshole gets too suspicious of me he might investigate further, and from what I've learned, the government is quite corrupt. Eavesdropping and whatnot. Oh. I've just sworn again in my thoughts, that's a good sign.

"Never heard of it myself," Spoon said, examining Tesser with a practiced eye. "Where'd you learn to bounce like that?"

"Bounce?"

"Yeah, bounce. Security for a club or a bar. Or in your case a late night pizza place. Throwing out drunks and assholes? You tossed that punk real smooth. You've clearly got some experience doing it."

"Hmm. Bounce, I like that. I uh, don't really have experience bouncing," Tesser said.

"You have martial arts experience?" Spoon flicked his ash.

"Martial arts?" Tesser asked, genuinely curious.

"Tae Kwon Do, Aikido, BJJ, Karate? Any fighting experience? Ex-Military maybe?" Spoon seemed authentically surprised at Tesser's response.

"Oh yes. I understand now. The style of fighting they do in the Kung Fu movies late at night? I've never been taught how to do that, but I've been in many fights. Many, many."

"Would you say you're a violent man?" Spoon asked seriously.

Tesser shook his head. "I would not say that I am a violent man. I am capable when it comes to violence." The literal sense of Tesser's statement flew over the cop's head.

Spoon reacted with a slow, wry smile, "I know exactly what you mean."

Good. I think I like this man.

"You have a last name Tesser?" Spoon inquired.

"Tesser is my most recent name."

"No, no. A last name, uh, a surname. A family name."

A family name? I have a very strange family. We've never shared a common name. I wonder if I should create one?

"No, no family last name."

"Interesting. So back to the case I'm working, the alleged rape?"

Tesser nodded.

"The two men were being aggressive, and you heard them, and came to her aid, is that more or less the story?"

"Yes. The two men weren't trying to make a child with her. It was about violence and aggression. I can't abide rape. I loathe it."

Spoon looked a little befuddled by Tesser's odd response. "Make a child with her?"

"Yeah, make a child with her. The sex they wanted wasn't to make a child. It was about power, subjugation. A show of force and manliness. Or lack thereof. They were scum and deserved to be stopped."

"I see. Did you know that you hurt the one man pretty severely?"

And for that, I have zero regret.

"I am sorry. It wasn't my intent to harm him severely. He needed to be stopped, and the situation escalated to violence."

Spoon nodded. "There is video of the fight. You're pretty clearly off the hook based on a self- defense basis and the whole stopping a rape thing. You're in no trouble, though I can't promise the prick won't try to come at you in a civil case. His medical bills are going to be pretty astronomical. His wrist is jacked the fuck up. You must be strong as an ox."

"Jacked the fuck up. I like that expression."

"Sorry, I cuss a lot. Too much time in the military."

"What military?" Tesser wanted to learn about this man.

"101st Airborne, US Army. 187th Regiment, also known as the Rakkasans. Heard of them?"

Tesser shook his head and looked out over the city of

Boston's skyline. The word airborne caused his heart to ache. He wanted to soar above the metal and concrete buildings, to let his wings unfurl in the warm summer air and glide. He discarded his momentary daydream and refocused on the police officer.

"We are Airborne. We jump out of planes and parachute into combat. Or we ride into battle in helicopters. Exciting stuff if you like getting shot at."

Tesser responded with a slow smile, "You are a warrior."

Spoon exhaled some of the rich blue-white smoke and nodded. "I've gone to war, yeah. I'm not proud of some of the things I've done, but someone needs to do these things for the greater good. America is a wonderful country, and I'm glad I served. Have you served in the military?"

I was wrong about this fellow. I definitely approve of this man.

"I have never been in the Army, but I have served. I too believe in the greater good, as you say. Nothing has ever come without some kind of sacrifice in this world."

Spoon appreciated the comment before adding a solemn nod. He put his cigarette butt out on the metal guardrail and flicked it into the traffic below. He looked back to the dragon and assessed him for a bit.

"You know you have very interesting eyes, Mr. Tesser. As gold as the watch I'm wearing."

"Indeed," Tesser agreed quickly. "A curious thing that makes me, me. Jealous?"

Spoon grinned. "No, not really. Just one more interesting thing about you. It might be a good idea to buy some sunglasses. I also want to let you know that I appreciate you stepping up and lending that lady a hand. There are precious few people nowadays that would put their lives on the line to beat down some random fucks for a total stranger. Everyone is texting with their heads down and afraid of lawsuits and medical bills. I also want you to know that you've got no worries as far as your citizen status is concerned. I won't be letting ICE know about your presence here."

"ICE? Frozen water?"

"Immigration and Customs Enforcement. They kick out the people who aren't supposed to belong here in the States and ship them home. You need a green card to stay here if you aren't a citizen."

"Pretty strange rules you have here in America," Tesser said, watching the cars zip by on the highway underneath them.

So many machines.

"Well, ever since 9/11 America has changed. We're scared now, paranoid. We give up freedoms to try and find safety. Everyone thinks the shadows have teeth."

Tesser perked up. "Some shadows do have teeth, Sergeant Spooner. You only need to be bitten by one once to fear every shadow from then on. The uneducated fear what they do not know, and cannot quantify."

"You are an odd fucking duck, Tesser," Spoon said appreciatively.

Tesser grinned. "Sarcasm. I'm not actually a duck. I appreciate that."

"I rest my case. Behave my friend. If the guy who got away comes back at you, make sure you whup his ass on camera again. Cover your ass and entertain the city once more." Spoon produced his wallet and pulled a business card out of it. He handed it to Tesser the exact same way Katie had given him her number on the torn menu earlier.

"I don't have a phone."

"You're smart, you'll figure it out. Have a good night, Tesser. This was a real pleasure." Spoon shook Tesser's hand firmly and walked off down the sidewalk. In the small of his back Tesser saw his holstered handgun.

I bet he could whup some ass without that weapon. Sergeant Spooner is a good man, a tested and honorable warrior. His soul shines bright. I would like to meet him again.

Tesser stood up from his seat on the guardrail and walked confidently back across the street to the pizzeria. It was slowing down in the late hour, but there were still enough tipsy customers to cause trouble. Tesser looked at the cop's business card and slid it into the front pocket of his only pair of jeans.

Chapter Twelve
Matilde "Matty" Rindahl

This was potentially the most important meeting in Matty's life, and she wasn't even slated to speak at it.

Holy moly I am nervous as all get-out.

Matty's hands were sweating. The door to the massive conference room swung open and a middle-aged executive walked in. The room immediately hushed and focused on him.

Oh boy. There he is. He looks handsome again today. So handsome. Look at those bright blue eyes! He was made for this stuff, not me. I'm a science nerd. Not a highfaluting business executive that sits in on big meetings about huge money.

Alec Fitzgerald pulled out the rolling leather chair at the head of the massively long board table and took the seat with a wide disarming smile. He undid his suit button and opened the manila folder that had been placed for him. The array of businessmen and women and scientists packed into the corners of the room stood nervous and excited as they waited for him to start the meeting.

Alexis leaned back in her chair near the opposite end of the table and whispered to Matty, "Hot isn't he? I would tear that man's suit off with my teeth."

Matty leaned in and replied, "I'd fight you for the right."

Alec continued to smile as he sifted through the contents of the folder. Matty watched as he looked at the first sheet intently, then the second and so on. His eyes were active and bright, and she knew he was absorbing every word, every detail. When he finished, he looked back up and addressed the group.

"Thank you for coming to this somewhat impromptu meeting. I apologize for the lack of notice and want to thank all the department heads who were able to get all their information and staff gathered in time for today."

I would straight up suck his dick off. Jesus, I'm lonely.

"I'm sure you're all really quite nervous, but I assure you there's nothing to worry about. No one is getting laid off today, and I'm about as happy as can be. Everyone can call their husbands and wives and let them know they don't have to pick up that second job to make their mortgage payments."

Everyone laughed.

"I've actually brought this meeting together to share a bit of information about an exciting project that we've kept under wraps for about a decade now. Something my father started that I'm excited to bring to completion with your help."

The crowd murmured with subdued excitement. The Fitzgerald family had built this corporation and expanded science with respect, attention to their employees, and a zeal for making humanity and the world better. Anything that was thrilling to Alec had the potential to change the world.

"We've already seen some results from our first ten years of work. I can't share what exactly is going on with the project until we get the rest of our team picked and in place, but I can say that this project has the potential to make our company a world leader in nearly every market imaginable. What I am about to say is of the utmost secrecy, and I would remind you of your employee contracts and beg you to please keep this to yourselves."

More murmurs of excitement came from the crowd. Alexis looked over her shoulder at Matty and flared her eyes in glee. This could be a very good thing for them.

Alec's voice and cadence picked up in its vigor and pacing. "You might recall that about a decade ago we spent a good deal of money on research in Asia. We'd gotten some reports of a few species of flora and fauna that Fitzgerald Industries might be able to analyze, and I am happy to report that the mission we undertook ten years ago has yielded tremendous fruit. We are calling it 'Project Amethyst.' "

A roar of applause came from the gathered executives and scientists.

These people have no idea what they're clapping for. He might be talking about a new jock itch cream for all we know.

"Hold your applause people, thank you."

The adulation ended, and Alec was able to speak once more.

"We are hand picking people to join Project Amethyst. Most of you in this room will be the first to join the small Amethyst team, but some of you will not be chosen because your current roles are far too important for us to move you at this time. Please don't think this is a slight. I value you, we value you all, and keeping Fitzgerald Industries strong in our current markets and areas of research is as important to me today as it was important to my father before he died. If you are not moved to Amethyst, your responsibilities will be paramount in keeping everything moving along swimmingly."

Man, he's good at this. He just told people they were

getting passed on a promotion, and they're patting each other on their backs in celebration over it. I don't know how this guy could disappoint people. I bet if he pissed on one of these board members they'd tell him how thankful they were to be warm.

"My team of assistants will be handing out your transfer papers to Project Amethyst at the end of the day today. As it is Thursday, you'll be asked to pack up your offices and personal affects to move over to our new facility that's dedicated strictly to the project. All the details will be in the packet you get. If you have any questions, you'll be able to ask them tomorrow afternoon at an Amethyst all-staff meeting in the new facility."

Alexis turned and whispered again, "New facility? Where? When did they build a new building for the company? Talk about hush hush bullshit."

"Yeah, kind of strange," Matty replied.

Or kind of awesome. I feel l like a super-secret agent. I need a cape, or a fedora and a snub nose revolver.

"Again on behalf of my family and all of the executives of Fitzgerald Industries I thank you all for your hard work. We could not have done this without all of you, and we will not be able to keep doing it without you."

This time no one held their applause.

I hope I get one of those transfer letters.

*****

Two hours later a tall man that looked like he belonged in the Secret Service visited Matty at her cubicle and wordlessly handed her a thick blue envelope with a smile. It contained transfer papers for her to join Project Amethyst.

Yeah, bitches.

Chapter Thirteen

Abraham "Abe" Fellows

I have consumed so much Red Bull I think my piss will never be clear again. Nuclear urine for me.

Abe rubbed some sticky cobwebs out of the corners of his eyes. He had been awake for a long time—so long he couldn't actually place when he'd woken up. Everything was a caffeinated blur.

Where the fuck is this guy?

Abe had only just gotten back into Mr. Doyle's massive home. He was still sweaty from the sticky mid-July evening heat, and his Wolverine t-shirt still clung to his back. His mission had been to scour the streets and alleys near the ATM where the footage of the man with the golden eyes had been taken. He went from corner to corner for almost ten hours asking each bum, two dollar hooker, and each store owner if they had seen the man.

In fact, many had seen him, though none had laid eyes on him in the past few weeks. Some of the more helpful shop employees in the area had thought he'd moved on to a different part of the city, but with no solid leads he was at a dead end.

Internet to the rescue.

Abe washed his face of salty sweat in the marble sink in the grand guest bathroom that was outside his second floor bedroom before sitting down to start his electronic search in earnest. He had cracked open yet another can of Red Bull as well.

Alright, let's try WWS again. See if anyone has put this together other than Mr. Doyle and me.

He pointed his browser at Wizards Warlocks and Sorcerers.

Whoa.

The number of threads and replies had increased significantly since his last visit. The amount of new accounts had spiked as well. Each had one of a few similar stories.

Foremost there were the sightings. People across the world had begun to… see things. Small creatures in the woodlands that looked out of place at best and outright bizarre sightings in some cases. Several forum threads spoke of fairies in secluded forests and seeing the semi-human footprints of something gigantic in their gardens. From all the corners of the world there were pictures of blurred things moving in the distance. It was eerie.

Secondly there were the threads that captured the thrill and excitement of someone who had done something special. Something magical.

Lucky fuckers.

These people were able to wield a moment of energy, a second of sorcery, and had no idea who to talk to or what to do next. Some people had done a single miniscule thing before their power had fleeted away, but others were experiencing days of repetitive miracles. One woman shared her excitement that she was now able to mix her pie dough by simply swirling her finger in a circle from the other side of the kitchen.

Big fucking deal. So you can make pie with magic. Can you pee standing up? Huh? Make a spell that does that and get back to me.

But alas, WWS was empty of anything about the golden-eyed man.

The Delphian Covenant was the same. The reporters, especially Abe's favorite, Oliver, were reporting on the sudden spike in paranormal activity. Oliver had put in a short blog update on the Covenant, talking about his arrival in Northern Scotland at an old castle that allegedly was showing signs of an angry ghost's return.

Wow. That'll fuck with my sleep tonight.

But there was nothing of the golden-eyed man.

Shit. Social media it is.

Twitter revealed nothing despite Abe's sizable list of people he followed. Twitter had not yet entered into the magical arena, and none of the celebrities he followed had anything to add to his search. He then went to Facebook where he had prior success.

He was rewarded almost immediately.

Abe's Facebook feed was filled with the same nonsense and drivel that every 25-year-old kids is. Fresh out of college assholes having babies, women screaming about how excited they are to be engaged or pregnant, ten thousand pictures of pets, and the obligatory smartasses posting social commentary via captioned pictures. Abe definitely was more the latter.

Earlier in the week Abe had made a specific effort to friend about three dozen local young girls in an attempt to enter a social circle that might yield results. Basically, he wanted to be friends with people who were obsessed with spreading rumors and gossip.

College bitches.

He chose a handful of girls from each of the major colleges in Boston. Boston College and Boston University were at the top of the list. They were large and in the Back Bay. Right below that were Tufts and Emerson. He then made sure to track down a few girls from Northeastern and Berklee, but he had a suspicion that

Northeastern girls were too high a caliber, and Berklee girls were all into music, and those would yield no results. He kept those friend adds to a minimum.

His BU connection was pay dirt.

Charlene Kearns, a junior at Boston University that had brown hair with blonde highlights, bright blue eyes, and an ass to die for reported in on her feed that she'd, "Seen the naked hobo kick more ass."

Oh … this might be helpful.

Abe clicked on the video in her status and immediately knew he was on to something. She'd put up a cell phone video that had been taken later at night in a pizza shop. Two men a few years younger and a lot dumber than Abe get into a very short fistfight after calling each other's colleges horrible things.

Fucking apes.

The girl, Charlene, had her camera in a great spot to capture the man with the golden eyes as he approached them. Then he loudly barked out a single command that froze the entire place. Charlene's hand trembled at the force of the word, and even through the shitty, smudged video Abe could feel the magical power exuded from the man raising his voice. It was less a command to stop and more a magical compulsion to do so. Had they been deaf, they likely would've stopped fighting regardless. Abe's hair stood on end from the power of the word.

Who is this guy? He's got serious game.

Of course stupidity is hard to compel, magically or otherwise, and the man with the golden eyes had to go hands-on. The college kid who threw the punch was wrapped up in a lightning fast and largely pain free restraint and ejected into the street by the stranger. The man who had been punched quickly went to the bathroom with his girlfriend after speaking to the unique bouncer. The video cut out a few seconds after that.

Well, then. That certainly settles the question of whether or not this guy is magical in some way, doesn't it? Mr. Doyle is going to shit a crumpet and a whole pot of Earl Grey tea when he sees this.

Abe's heart raced faster and faster as he restarted the video, looking for some sort of clue as to which of the umpteenth pizza shops in Boston it could have happened at. The only worst-case scenario would've been if it were taken in a shit Chinese restaurant. He looked for a menu on the wall and paid special attention to the moment when the phone's view turned to the front of the pizza shop. When Abe saw the street view outside, he paused it, and within a few seconds of looking at details in the background he knew exactly where the shop was.

I could be there in five minutes. Ten tops.

Abe powered down his laptop and grabbed his wallet and keys.

Should I tell Mr. Doyle? I should tell him where I'm going. If this guy is dangerous I'm royally fucked. I've never cast a single defensive spell successfully, and I guarantee I can't outrun the fucking guy.

Abe debated it, and then left alone.

Confident and assertive right? Time to shine, Abraham Fellows. Time to shine. I should change my shirt, though. Gold eyes might be a DC fan.

Chapter Fourteen
Tesser

It is quite hot tonight. The air is thick and hard to breathe. Were I a normal human like the rest of the people here, I would be sweating profusely.

Boston had reached sweltering temperatures that day. The sprawl of pavement mixed with running cars, and exhaust, and body heat had driven the temperature up to a solid one hundred angry, humid degrees. The humidity had crept right up alongside it like a conspirator in the crime of mass misery. Tesser had moved out to the street to get what passed for fresh air in the city.

I would think more people would want a salad.

The line to the pizza shop was out the door and extended down the sidewalk the length of twenty people. Sal and Pete, the two men tasked with tossing the dough and making the pizza were working incredibly quickly to churn out pie after pie. Tesser watched them toss the circles of soft dough into the air repeatedly, spinning them larger and larger.

It's almost magical. In fact, I'd bet anything there was a tiny trace of the mystical inside each pie.

Tesser turned his attention to the passersby on the street. The sidewalks in that area of the city were wide;

six or seven people could walk side by side easily, so long as they took care to walk around the city trash barrels, signposts, and bicycle stands. Tesser had his heels on the curb as the cars slowly crept by in the rush hour traffic behind him.

So many young people here. That speaks of growth. A civilization filled with youth is a growing and safe culture. But when I watch the television it seems like so many other areas of the world are aging and not growing. The new human invention of the economy seems to be crushing people under the weight of false debt.

Tesser let the negative thoughts drift away. He had a book to read. Reading languages had always come easier to the dragon than speaking them. Tesser had taught himself innumerable rudimentary tongues in centuries past by listening and looking at crude paintings on cave walls and reading etchings in clay tablets. Presently he held a middle school science textbook he'd found at a dusty discount bookseller. It fascinated him.

Particularly the section on biology and reproduction.

"Hey, gold eyes!"

"Hey, Tesser!"

Two more of my lady dominated fan club.

Tesser smiled seductively. "Good evening, ladies. Enjoy the food."

"We will!" they shouted back in unison.

Tesser smiled at the rest of the young crowd standing in line or exiting the shop, pizza in hand. They were young and foolish in the way everyone wished they could be their whole lives. Tesser wondered how it was to grow up in a world dominated by so much technology and so little magic.

It must be strange. But to be truthful, so much of this science and technology achieves what magic used to. To contact someone across the sea one would've sent a missive spell filled with words and thoughts powered by the ethereal energy of the universe. Now one simply uses their cell phone. What is so different about that?

Tesser watched the duo of pretty college girls tap away on their iPhones, sending text messages with practiced grace. One of the girls lifted her phone ever so slightly and took a picture of him. Tesser smiled knowingly.

Tesser inhaled the dirty city air as he leaned his head back, forgetting again the textbook he had been devouring all day. The sky was hazy today, filled with the threat of an evening thunderstorm.

Oh, I wish I could shed this body and fly above these clouds, far from the prying electronic eyes of this society. Not being able to see blue sky makes my skin crawl. It would be such a joy to soar and twist between these tall buildings, to plummet to the ocean's surface, and feel the spray on my scales. I would devour a seal, or a tuna, or a –

Tesser's nose caught something in the air. Something familiar. Something old.

Something magical.

I smell … a wizard.

Tesser's eyes were down at street level immediately, scanning from left to right up and down the sidewalk. His head unconsciously rocked side to side as a hunting cat's would during a stalk. It gave his eyes a better sense of depth should he see what he smelled. It was a decidedly inhuman gesture.

I would not have caught that scent had magic not been so rare. It's incredibly faint. Almost nonexistent. It smells like the scent of a newborn, fresh from the womb. A baby mage.

Tesser turned around and looked across the street where the edge of the overpass was. Leaning against the guardrail was a young man no more than a quarter century old. He had short brown hair and a slight build that spoke of too much time sitting, and not nearly enough experience being active and tested by all the world could offer. He wore shorts that were one size too large and showed off stick thin legs that were practically luminescent they were so white. The young man stood erect, startled when Tesser caught his eye.

It's him.

Tesser sat his textbook down on the magazine stand he'd been standing next to and started walking across the street slowly with a hunter's purpose.

The young man panicked, and started to run.

A chase. I love a chase.

Tesser picked up his pace as the man started sprinting away from him. The young man was fast but kept his pace for only a city block or two.

He's a smart runner. He isn't looking over his shoulder at me. You lose speed that way.

The man slowed and looked over his shoulder at his pursuer. He had no idea it was a dragon in human form.

Never mind. I wonder when he'll try and cast a spell. He's clearly frightened by me. Strange, though, he was obviously sitting there observing me. I wonder what he wants or what he knows? I wonder if he knows why I slept so long?

Tesser's heart was barely picking up its pace in the run, but he could see the young man's chest heaving heavily, and he could practically hear the tiny heart hammering away inside as he dodged slow moving cards plugging up traffic. Like a laughing gazelle Tesser gracefully leapt over the hood of a yellow taxi as the driver screamed amusing profanities at him.

Then, very suddenly, the young spell caster dipped into an alley out of view.

Ah, it comes to a head.

Tesser slowed to a jog, then a walk as he rounded the corner into the alley.

This alley is a dead end. I don't know if he realizes it. I wonder if he has a teleportation spell? Or could this be a trap?

"I don't know who you are, but keep your distance. I may not have a weapon, but I am still quite dangerous!" The skinny young man yelled.

His voice trembles. He is very much afraid of me. He must

know what I am. "I am not here to harm you mage. I sensed your presence, and I know you were watching me. I deserve an explanation for your intrusion."

"I…wait what? Mage?" The fledgling wielder of magic was taken aback by the title.

He is so very new. He looks proud. Maybe he doesn't know what I am. Maybe he's just a pawn. Let's press him and see what he can do.

Tesser dipped his chin and put on a face that seemed sinister. "Tell me why you are watching me, or I shall do what comes very natural to me." He took a step forward deeper into the alley.

The man took a step back to match. "I came to meet you. The world…something…since you appeared…Ah, shit. I have no idea what to say to you."

"You are buying time. You are lying to me," Tesser said in a darker tone as he took another step forward.

"Stop! Stop or I'll cast a spell on you. You won't be so happy after I fry you with a spell, Goldilocks!"

My hair is gold. I don't feel intimidated or insulted by his comment. Maybe pointing out the obvious is an insult? I'll continue to press. Tesser took another step forward. "Tell me or cast your spell mage. My patience thins."

The man panicked. "Commoveo!" The man howled in combination with a sweeping gesture across the alley. Microscopic motes of arcane energy sprouted from his fingertips, but nothing more happened.

There we go. "Try again!" Tesser yelled, taking another step forward.

"Commoveo!" the man repeated as he stepped backward again, only this time a little louder. Similar sparks of lights fell from his fingertips, but the energy of the spell failed to come together.

"Stop saying the damn word and cast the DAMN SPELL!" Tesser grumbled in a near deafening tone, shaking the barrels of trash and sending the debris scattering down the dirty urban pathway.

"Commoveo!" The cornered man said, but this time his tone and inflection was different, as was the motion of his arms. No sparks of light came from the tips of his fingers this time, but Tesser felt the sudden wave of energy pour out from the young mage like a ripple in the essential fabric of the universe. The mystic power of the spell sent the barrels of garbage flying about like puppets on strings, upending them and dropping rancid trash all over the ground. Several soda and beer cans flew up like shrapnel and pinged off of Tesser's body, irritating him ever so slightly. But more, he was pleased at the show of sorcery.

Tesser smiled at the mage as he congratulated him. "There. Much better."

The sweating, frightened man showed a face of exultation as he looked at his hands. Tesser had seen this look many times in his life.

He looks like a father standing over his newborn child.

"I've never done anything that powerful before. Holy shit. Fuck me in the ass wow." Tiny traces of electrical energy dashed along the length of his fingers, dissipating into the air as the spell's power faded from his body.

"You have the distinction of being the first person to ever ask for anal penetration in my presence after casting a spell, stranger. I do hope you are not serious in your request." Tesser grinned, having dropped his façade of menace.

The young man looked up from his hands and shook his head back and forth rapidly, "Fuck no, no corn holing please. I…I'm sorry I threw garbage at you. I didn't mean anything by it. I was scared. I did this...all fucking wrong."

Tesser smiled again. *I like this young man. He has genuine innocence to him.* "You meant to defend yourself with what you had available. It is natural, and it is exactly what you intended and meant to do. There is no need to ask for my forgiveness."

"Are you gonna kill me?"

Let's try this. "Fuck no."

The young man sighed in clear relief. "What's your name?"

"I'm Tesser. Pleasure to meet you, mage. What's your name?"

"Tesser, huh? Weird name. I'm Abraham, but my friends call me Abe. You can call me Abe if you like," Abe said, brushing off the garbage his own spell had strewn on his shirt.

Tesser smiled warmly. "Abe. I like that name. If you would consider me a friend, I would be honored to call you Abe."

"Abe it is, friend." The young man took a deep breath, steeled himself, and walked directly to Tesser, extending his hand bravely.

Tesser took the hand and shook it firmly. "What language were you just speaking? It sounded familiar to me."

"It was Latin. It's old. Many mages use it as a base for their spells. Have you never heard of Latin?"

Tesser shook his head. "Old is very relative, Abe. Can you teach it to me?"

Abe shrugged. "I'm not much of a teacher, but I can give you my college textbooks on it. So I gotta ask, what's the deal with the gold eyes, Tesser?"

"What's the deal with all the magic fading away, Abe?"

"Buy me a slice of pizza?"

"I don't really have any money, Abe," Tesser replied.

"Okay, I'll buy you a slice, but you gotta get me some phone numbers. You are a handsome fella. The girls are smitten with you, huh?" The man and dragon turned and started to leave the alley, side by side.

"The phone numbers of women? You are having a hard time finding a woman? You're a mage, women should be very interested in finding someone like yourself."

"Yeah, I wouldn't be like, advertising that in public man. Magic is sort of a not cool thing. Most folks don't believe in it anymore, especially since it all started to fade a decade ago. Bring that up to a girl in the wrong place and they lock you up with a padded room in the nut hut. I'm just a nerdy accountant that grew up on Pokémon and jerking it to Miley Cyrus. You must be new. Are you new?"

"I'm really quite old, Abe, but I've only been up and about a bit lately. What is this Pokémon you speak of?"

Chapter Fifteen

Sergeant Henry "Spoon" Spooner

Watching the hobo-turned-bouncer had suddenly paid off.

Henry Spooner followed Tesser as he ran after the man who'd been watching him outside the pizza shop. It was fairly easy to keep up with the two as they played their strange form of tag. Tesser had no trouble keeping up with the geek wearing the Bazinga shirt. In fact, he made it look laughably easy.

This is really weird. First the nerd is stalking Mr. Gold Eyes, now Gold Eyes is chasing the nerd. I wonder if the kid has something to do with the rapist that got away? Little brother maybe?

Spoon slowed his pace and kept his distance as the kid ran into an alley with Tesser no more than a dozen paces behind.

Tesser isn't pissed at this kid. At least, he doesn't seem pissed. What the hell is going on here?

Spoon trotted across the street and slid up to the end of the alley, thankful for the car horns and the city noise that was masking his movement. He heard the young man yell something in a foreign language from the end of the alley. Tesser yelled something back. From the tone of the voices, Spoon knew a confrontation was moments away. The compact police detective crept to the edge of the building and crouched low, his gun hand drifting to the grip of his service SIG. Spoon preferred the 1911 clone GSR to the Glocks that his fellow officers liked so much.

"Commoveo!" The cop heard the young man yell.

Tesser replied, but his voice was different. It echoed, resounded, casted out of the narrow alley like the trumpeting of a college band marching, "Stop saying the damn word and cast the DAMN SPELL!"

Spoon watched, frozen in time as the young man did exactly what Tesser told him to do.

In that moment, Spoon's entire existence changed.

The alley and everything in it was hit by an unnatural force as the kid swept his arm through the air. Dirty recycling bins tipped over or flew up into the air and disgorged their contents all about. Cans and newspapers flew about like missiles through the air, and all the while Tesser stood in the center of it, grinning ear to ear like a jovial orchestra conductor being pelted by rotten garbage. After a few seconds, the debris dropped to the ground as if all that had happened was a gust from a strong breeze. But Spoon knew different.

He had seen, and it threw into doubt his entire Catholic upbringing. It violated everything he knew about the natural order of the universe, and deep in his quivering heart, he was confused. War and death was one thing, this was another.

What. The. Fuck.

"There. Much better," Tesser said calmly, as if the miracle that had just happened was the most normal and likely thing that could've happened.

Spoon rolled away from the corner of the building and stood. Somehow, he'd drawn his sidearm. He started walking away from the alley, but could only manage the slow pace for a few steps.

First he jogged to get away.

Then he started to run. He couldn't escape his fears that day, no matter how fast he ran.

Chapter Sixteen

Mr. Doyle

Mr. Doyle sat in a leather armchair that originated in the sitting room of a British king from a different century. Antique collectors would've salivated at the provenance of the furniture, but to the aged and aging wizard it was simply a gift from an old friend. He ran his fingers along the brass beads at the edge of the arm and allowed his mind to wander.

I can feel it. Whatever it is. Something different in the world – something new.

Mr. Doyle was in his third study where he went to think. It was adjacent to the room where he kept many of his fading magical treasures and beside his office where he did all of his reading and writing. Mr. Doyle felt that each room should have a singular purpose. To mix was to dilute purpose. And purpose was the heart of everything.

It has brought magic with it. A pulse of energy, a hole in the proverbial dam.

He reached over and lifted a small glass goblet of deep red wine. He swirled the rich French Bordeaux and allowed the liquid to coat the sides of the glass. It was magical, the glass. It was the delivery vehicle for the magic that he'd used to stretch his life. It was how he'd skipped so many years of aging. But the magic was fading, and Father Time was collecting all those avoided years, post haste.

He sipped from the glass gently. The alcohol coupled with the enchantment gave his throat the tiniest of tingles.

So little of the burn I need. I won't last more than a few more years more at this rate. Less, likely.

Mr. Doyle heard the front door of his substantial brownstone home open and shut. Inside his chest he felt the magic barrier the door represented open and close as well. The door was wide and thick; it was made of stained and carved ash. Ash had power. Ash had purpose.

That must be Abraham. I wonder where he's been.

Mr. Doyle hadn't had a proper cohabitant in over a decade. He abhorred servants, and previous apprentices had either gone off to study the world on their own or had perished as a result of foolish decisions or ignorance of his advice. But he had grown very fond of Abraham. He represented the next generation of mages; those who wielded technology and science more proficiently than the arcane arts. It saddened Mr. Doyle to think like that.

Is that two sets of feet I hear ascending the stairs?

Mr. Doyle got to his feet with a grunt and several painful cracks of the back. He sat his wine glass down and grimaced from the aching arthritis that had set in fiercely over the past two years.

Growing old is the work of evil.

"Mr. Doyle? Are you home?" Abraham's voice called out from the second floor landing.

"I'm here, Abraham. Did I hear you return with a guest? I don't think I've spoken to you about how I feel about guests yet."

Youth never respect the sanctity of a home until they own one of their own.

"I'll apologize after," Abe said as he walked into the thinking room alone.

"You let someone into my home unsupervised?" Mr. Doyle said, a hint of anger creeping into his tone.

"I found the man with the golden eyes."

Mr. Doyle's breath escaped his lungs and he sat down suddenly in the chair, all his strength drained away. He felt his heart flutter unhealthily.

"I uh— I didn't know what to do with him. I don't think he would've let me come home without him either. He's…insistent on speaking with you." Abe looked guilty. Very guilty.

Idiot. This could get us killed. I've been so remiss in my training of this poor boy. It's inexcusable.

"What can you tell me of him?" Mr. Doyle sputtered as his heart tried to calm itself.

Abe switched gears. He was clearly animated and excited about the golden-eyed man. "His name is Tesser. He's…funny. He also said he's really old, but he doesn't look much older than I am. I think he's some kind of magic user. A powerful one."

"Apparent age means nothing. I look old, but am far older. How do you know he's a magic user? Has he been able to cast a spell in your presence? You're not geased are you?" Mr. Doyle stood again, grimacing again, and started to dredge up the memory of how to test a subject for magical compulsions.

Abe shook his head, "No, no. No spells. I don't know how to describe him. Just being around him you can…I can feel the magic. I feel stronger. More capable. It's really crazy."

Mr. Doyle wrung his fingers, anxious, and a fair bit excited.

This is not how we bloody do these kinds of things.

"Well, if he's here, I suppose it's a bit too late to change the course of history in this regard. I will tell you this; I am fetching one of my most powerful wands from my collection, and should this man strike me as dangerous, it may come to a confrontation, Abraham.

Prepare yourself."

Abe smiled. "I don't think that'll be necessary. I'll bring him to the dining room. He said he was hungry. We just ate pizza too."

"Fine, feed this Tesser character while I fetch my good wand."

Abe simply nodded and left the room.

I hope the wand still has enough power. I know I don't.

*****

Mr. Doyle rounded the entrance to his dining room and steadied his breathing. Concentration would be paramount should danger arise.

I'm actually nervous. Scared. Who is this man?

"Good day sir, I am told your name is Tesser," Mr. Doyle said as he laid eyes on the man sitting at his dining room table.

Tesser stood from the dining room table, and Mr. Doyle was able to assess him.

He is nearly perfect. A shade over six foot, slim but very well muscled. His hair, blonde and well styled, though in a way that looks accidental. He is dressed strangely, though. He wears shorts that are clearly a size too large and a shirt with stains on it. So strange that a man so physically well put together would wear ill-fitting, ill kept clothing. And his eyes! So golden! So deep and true. His smile is disarming. Abraham is correct. This man exudes some strange power.

"You are Mr. Doyle?" Tesser asked, a friendly expression on his face.

"I am indeed. I am intrigued by your visit young man. Return to your seat, you need not stand for an elder such as I," Mr. Doyle said as he pulled out a chair across from Tesser's. As the guest sat, the mage pulled out a thin mahogany wand and sat it on the table. The simple stick of wood carried a vague menace.

Tesser looked at the wand briefly and sat as well.

"Your apprentice here," Tesser gestured to Abe, "is a good man. You've chosen wisely in spreading your art with him. Well done."

Mr. Doyle nodded. "Thank you. Though I am feeling as if bringing such an unknown quantity such as yourself into the comfort of my inner sanctum here was a bit of an error on his part."

Tesser grinned and nodded. "I understand. My bad."

Strange use of the phrase. It seemed... inexperienced.

"Nevertheless, you are here and at a quite auspicious time. Abraham has done some valuable legwork and has discovered several strange connections that we felt might have been connected to you. Are you here to discuss these things?"

Tesser narrowed his eyes before responding. "Mr. Doyle, I want to know where all the magic went. That is why I am here."

Mr. Doyle's heart fluttered again. Tesser's statement sounded a fair amount like an accusation, "Mr. Tesser, your statement is difficult to answer."

I sound guilty. I feel guilty.

Abe chimed in, "We aren't responsible for this, if that's what you think, Tesser. I told you about a lot of this earlier—when we ate pizza?"

Tesser's eyes never left Mr. Doyle, though he spoke to the apprentice, "Abe, you have your answers, and your mentor has his. I would like very much to hear his answers now. I'm not trying to be a dick Abe, but you clearly know jack shit about what's really going on in the world."

"Dude, that hurts."

Tesser finally looked over to Abe. "I'm sorry, but I need to hear what Mr. Doyle here has to say. I suspect he is aware of far more than he's let on."

Tesser might be surprised how bloody little I do know about this.

"I'm sorry if this seems accusatory Mr. Doyle,

especially after your offered hospitality. But I've been a bit bamboozled by the state of the world of late, and I would love some answers." Tesser leaned forward.

Mr. Doyle caught the scent of brewing coffee in the air.

A hot cup of coffee does sound good.

Mr. Doyle spoke, "Just over ten years ago magic began to fade from the world. Beyond that, there is little I can offer you other than specific knowledge of how my own magical abilities has abandoned me."

"Others have experienced the same in the past ten years?" Tesser asked.

"It appears to be universal. All continents, all kinds of magic."

Tesser sat back in his chair, deep in contemplation. Abe stood and left for the kitchen.

I hope he's getting the coffee.

While Abe was away, Mr. Doyle's courage found him. He leaned in and whispered a question to the enigmatic man at his dining table, "Who are you? Who are you really?"

Tesser's eyes wandered the room, deep in thought. After a few awkward moments he pointed his golden orbs at the elder wizard. "I am Tesser. Really."

"What are you then? You're a wizard, aren't you? Some kind of foreign spell caster I've never met before. Are you Roma? You don't have the hair or complexion for it, but that slight accent makes me wonder…"

"Roma?" The man with the golden eyes looked confused.

"Eastern European descent. A gypsy."

"Ahh. I've read some about them. No, I am not a gypsy. I am…" Tesser stopped as Abe returned holding a fancy silver platter. He had several coffee cups, as well as sugar and milk.

"Coffee, gentlemen. Sorry it took so long," Abe said as he sat the platter down.

"Thanks, Abe," Tesser said as he picked up a cup of the strong brew.

"Thank you Abraham," Mr. Doyle said as he too picked up a cup. He added a slight pour of milk to the cup, as well as a single cube of sugar.

I love sugar cubes. Perfect doses of sweetness that are error-proof. Pity they aren't as prolific as they once were. Might help with the gluttony epidemic.

As he stirred, he pressed the man, "Tesser I asked you a question. What exactly are you? Who do you represent?"

"The second question is far easier to answer. Mr. Doyle, I represent life, in short. The persistent, clawing, slithering, growing, fucking, and birthing forms of life that shall inherit this Earth long after man has evolved into something unrecognizable. I wish for the world to be in balance, and I represent one of the forces that maintain that balance."

Mr. Doyle sat his spoon down on a napkin and looked up at Tesser utterly perplexed. "What group represents balance? An order of mages I've never heard of?"

Tesser shook his head. "No, Mr. Doyle. There are no mages I can call my true peer in this regard. Only my brothers and sisters, of a kind."

He looks sad. And what does 'of a kind' mean?

"Who are your brothers and sisters?" Mr. Doyle sipped his hot drink. It was good.

Tesser sipped his own coffee and nodded at Abe in approval. "Mr. Doyle I have six…siblings. Six equals. Six allies the birth of whom I cannot recall, as we came into existence simultaneously."

"Seven children at once? All gifted with the skill to wield magic? That speaks of epic sorcery almost beyond reckoning. What spells brought about your family? Who are your parents? Tell me please; I must know."

"Magic did not exist *until* we were born. More specifically, until Kaula was born. My dearest Amethyst."

Tesser looked down at the center of his drink. He swirled the cup with a sad expression in his eyes.

"Wait, what did you say?" Abe interjected. "Amethyst?"

"As my eyes are gold, her eyes are amethyst. We were close, Kaula and I." Tesser sipped his coffee again.

They were in love. Or at the very least, loved each other very deeply as a brother and sister might.

"Tesser, do you know about a circle of seven stones in Germany?" Abe asked excitedly.

"I do not know where Germany is. But I do know of a circle of seven stones. The humans of the day referred to them as the Origination Stones. One for each of my brother and sisters. Quite unique artifacts. We believe they pre-date our births."

"A golden stone in that circle started to vibrate the other day. And ten years ago one stopped vibrating. That stone has amethyst in it," Abe said testing the waters.

Tesser's face lost some of its color. He looked oddly pale.

Mr. Doyle quickly took over the conversation. "I thought you said these people were your brothers and sisters. You speak of this Kaula like she was your lover. I don't think our definition of siblings or what is appropriate to do with them is the same where I am from." Mr. Doyle tried humor.

The sudden spark of hatred in Tesser's eyes spoke clearly. "Mind your comments about Kaula and my kind Mr. Doyle. You tread on very thin ice when I speak of this, and I assure you there will be no one strong enough to pull you out of the frigid waters of my anger."

Abe and Mr. Doyle swallowed nervously. The golden-eyed man's threat carried considerable weigh in the quiet room. Only after a car horn in traffic honked outside did anyone dare to speak.

"I...I'm sorry. It was not my intent to offend."

Tesser kept a scowl for another few moments before

relaxing. "Thank you, and I'm sorry. Your news has disturbed me. I must contact Kaula immediately, and I don't think I can do it alone. Have you a spell of distant communication? Something that can connect two minds over great distances?"

Mr. Doyle leaned forward, afraid no longer. "Yes, I do, but it hasn't worked in nearly three years. I've been forced to use only the telephone. I fear the government has been eavesdropping on my most private of conversations."

Tesser sat his cup down. "Your spell will work with me helping, of that you can be sure. Begin your preparations please. I have put this off far long enough. Abe, I need to return to the pizzeria to let them know I can't work tonight. Will you accompany me?"

Abe nodded without thinking.

Mr. Doyle stood, leaving his half-drunk cup of coffee on the table. His joint pain was long forgotten. His heart was filled with a youthful enthusiasm.

I haven't been this excited since the summer of 1936 when we hunted down that werewolf in Belgium. Now THAT was a rush.

Chapter Seventeen

Matty Rindahl

Matty's left forearm burned.

Fucking commute is going to burn me to a crisp. Man I hate my skin tone. I need to get some SPF one gazillion on my way home tonight.

The Project Amethyst facility was north of Boston, just off Interstate 93 and just short of the New Hampshire border. Matty rarely drove, so the adjustment to a commute had been an unpleasant one, despite her brand new car. She and her ex, Max, had driven up to the lakes in central New Hampshire several times, but that had been the extent of her I-93 experience.

It'd also help if I didn't put my damn arm out the window to surf the air all the time either.

Matty sat down in her own office. Her first office. Ground floor, with a view of the small pond in the back of the building. The transfer from the main labs to the Amethyst project had been good for her. She'd received a promotion from Lab Technician 2 to Senior Project Analyst. The title came with another 15 grand a year, a large office, a company phone, and a ton more responsibility.

So far, all she'd done is organize her large office, at an

additional seven bucks an hour.

"Miss Rindahl?" A man's voice called out from her office door.

Matty had her back to the door, filing away blank forms that she'd need at some point in her near future. "Yes, can I help you?"

"That is why you're here," the man replied.

Oh shit. I know that voice.

Matty turned and immediately recognized the man standing in the frame of her open door. It was Alec Fitzgerald. Multi-millionaire, genius, male model, and most importantly, her boss. "Oh, I'm so sorry, Mr. Fitzgerald. That was a bit unprofessional of me." Matty straightened out her slacks and put on her best smile.

"I didn't hire you for the smile, but I'm certainly glad it came with your talents," Alec said, walking into the office. He wore a crisp blue button down shirt with a navy tie. The crease in his slacks looked sharp enough to cut your finger on. He was impossibly handsome.

"Well, some days I think my smile might be my only redeeming quality."

"Nonsense. If that were the case you wouldn't be in this office right now. You're a gifted scientist. Your eye for detail is impeccable," Alec said as he sat in the chair opposite her desk.

"You know an awful lot about me. It's an understatement to say I'm flattered," Matty said as she took her seat behind her desk.

"Can I tell you a secret?" Alec asked as he leaned forward, snagging a Hershey's Kiss from a candy bowl on her desk.

Holy shit, he just took one of my candies.

"Of course. I signed an NDA."

"You're funny. Miss Matilde, I personally oversaw your hiring, knowing you would eventually be transferred to Project Amethyst. Let that one sit on you for a bit." Alec sat back and unwrapped the chocolate, popping it in his mouth with satisfaction.

"That borders on creepy," Matty said with a grin.

Alec grinned with her. "See? Funny. Fringe benefit of hiring you. Can I tell you another secret? The one I actually intended on telling you when I came in here?"

"Ooh. The suspense. Well, I do suppose that I can keep a secret. You are paying me a fair amount of money to do so." Matty rubbed her hands together greedily and leaned forward on her desk.

"I sign off on your salary Miss Rindahl, it's more than fair. But you deserve it, especially after today." Alec flicked the wadded up metallic wrapper of the chocolate across her office and into the small round trash bin.

Geez, even his aim is perfect.

Alec's voice lowered, and took on a more intense tone, "You recall the conversation from the meeting about the discoveries we made in Asia a decade ago?"

"Of course."

Alec leaned in, and peered out the office door before continuing. "That story has more details to it, as you might imagine. Chief among those details is the fact that we did not discover or collect many species from Asia. We collected a single creature. An entirely new species undocumented by modern science, known only from the myths of dead civilizations."

Holy shit, I'm tingly. This is like an Indiana Jones moment. He found the Ark of the Covenant. The Holy Grail. The Missing Link. Nessie.

Matty cleared her throat, "What did you find?"

Alec stood. "Walk with me." He gestured to the door.

Matty stood and the two left her office, heading down a window-lined hall. They walked in silence side by side for many minutes, Matty looking out at the lush greenery that Fitzgerald's money grew and maintained. There were dozens of tall, thin birch trees. They looked like spikes of silver and black covered in greenery. Several coworkers nodded at her and greeted Alec as they walked.

I feel like a rock star.

They turned down a hall she'd never been down.

"This campus is very secure as you probably have realized," Alec said idly.

"Yes. Fences and guardhouses and all the electronic card locks."

"Not to mention the security teams that are on the roof, as well as staffing the exits, and roaming the campus."

"I— I haven't seen the men on the roof." Matty was suddenly a bit nervous, and it carried in the tone of her voice.

Alec stopped and turned to face her. "Don't fret, Matty. It's a precaution. There's far, far too much money to be made here for me to not employ such a robust form of insurance. These people are here to protect you just as much as me, and just as much as Amethyst."

I'm gonna die.

"That's reassuring."

Alec turned and continued walking. They took another turn and stopped at the elevators. She'd never seen the building's elevators.

"You'll be issued one of these at day's end," Alec said as he produced a small identification card from his front pocket. It was thicker than a normal ID and had numerous, strange looking barcodes on the back. After twirling it in front of her eyes, he slid it into a tiny card reader just below the elevator call button. Matty heard the hum of the elevator moving to their floor before the 'ding' signaled it was there. The two entered the elevator, and it began to descend automatically.

We have basement offices?

"Quite a distance below the ground level facility is a two story containment structure that we spent nearly thirty million dollars on over the past five years. The real trick was getting the subject inside the main holding room before sealing it and putting all the earth on top with no one noticing. Building the surface facility was cake after that." Alec made it sound like a task no more challenging than knitting a scarf.

"The things you can do with money," Matty mused.

"Indeed, Miss Rindahl. And make no mistake, Project Amethyst is our equivalent of the printing press for money should we do this right."

Matty let that sink in before asking her next question, "How far down?"

"That's a secret I can't share Matty. But the good news is, you get the big secret today." Alec smiled at her, clearly excited to share whatever it was he intended to.

"I gotta admit, Mr. Fitzgerald, this is putting me off. Armed guards, secret underground bunkers, decoder rings..."

He laughed and flashed that million dollar smile again. "Reserve judgment. Wait until you meet her."

The elevator doors opened with a hiss before Matty could press for more answers, and the two stepped out into a sterile, fluorescent-lit hallway. It extended forward for a short distance and then terminated in a vault strong lab door. Glass windows to both sides revealed several uniformed armed guards that stood in waiting. They held weapons that bristled with extra gadgets and looked to Matty like they belonged on a Middle Eastern battlefield instead of in her place of work in suburban Massachusetts. The security guards inclined their heads respectfully as Alec and Matty approached the main door.

"Your ID card will also grant you access to this door," Alec said as he slid the card in a wall mounted reader. After a few moments wait, a series of small red lights blinked green, and the vault door slid in and opened with a mechanical hum. A second door awaited them inside the airlock. Once they had both stepped inside and Alec hit a button, the outer door shut behind them and the inner door released. Matty felt a strange change in the air pressure, and her inner ears popped.

"Matty, keep an open mind," Alec said as the door removed itself from their way. He waved her to go through and let her past.

The room was massive and made of industrial concrete that reminded her of a Bond villain's lair. There were a dozen men and women scurrying about, some in head to toe clean suits, others in regular clothes. Banks of computer terminals were everywhere around the edges of the room, all churning away at collecting and processing mountains of data—machines dedicated night and day to contemplating dark secrets thanklessly. She fully expected to see people wearing name tags that said 'minion' on them, but there weren't any. Just dedicated coworkers who were busy getting things done.

But the center of the room was the true reason for coming here. End to end the room was long. Perhaps as long as the football field she'd watched her beloved BU Terriers play on. The center of that space, nearly half the width of it and half the depth of it, was owned by an expansive clear room with walls that were twenty feet high or more. The ceiling to that transparent room was arched and clear, as well.

Glistening, glimmering, pearlescent in a way she'd never be able to describe adequately for the rest of her life, was something that resembled a reptile nearly a hundred feet long. Its scales weren't green, or red like the dragons she'd seen portrayed in movies and on the covers of fantasy novels. Each individual scale looked a singularly massive chip of luscious purple Amethyst. There were a million scales in a million shades of purple.

The tail was thin and fine, tipped with a large shard of the violet stone-made-flesh. It ran to the back of a thick and powerful body, complete with four limbs. The two limbs nearest the tail were clearly legs, and the two towards the neck and head were clearly the arms. The hands were equipped with thumbs the size of a Saint Bernard, denoting possible tool use. The claws were equally mammoth. The neck was long as well, nearly a quarter of the beast's length and the head that rest on the gray floor was the size of a pickup truck. Gargantuan teeth made of the amethyst bone-stone poked down almost elegantly from what she could only imagine was an upper lip.

Tubes ran into the creature from a dozen directions. They sprouted from the floor like mechanical vines and pumped fluids into the monster as well as out. Its snout was covered in a clear massive breathing mask that pumped some kind of oxygen mix for it to breathe. She watched as the creature's exhalation caused a faint condensation on the side of the breathing apparatus. On its body there were patches of scales that had been surgically removed revealing what appeared to be normal, pink flesh underneath.

I wonder what they do with the scales?

But of all the things to remark over, of all the things her eyes could not look away from, the butterfly-like gossamer wings were the most incredible. They were transparent. And despite the flaccid fluorescent light offered by the bulbs high in the ceiling of the room, they were transcendent, glimmering, and gave off a glimmer that made her stare and brought her back to dreams of things she'd long since forgotten. Memories of invisible friends from her childhood rose to the surface of her mind, as well as the chills of scary campfire stories that kept her awake at night. She remembered tales her father told her of giant Norwegian Trolls that turned to stone in the day, and of the vampires he said stalked the dark forests and empty villages of eastern Europe. Suddenly, everything she knew was tossed up in the air, and she wasn't sure what would fall and become the truth again or what would stay floating in the air and be myths reborn.

"It's normal," she heard a new voice say suddenly.

Matty snapped back to reality. "What's normal?" A middle-aged man with glasses perched on his nose with lenses a foot thick was standing next to her with an awkward smile on his face. His facial hair was growing in unevenly. He held a touch screen device that at a glance she knew monitored many things that happened in the room all at once.

"The strange wanderings of the mind. There's a face we all get when it first hits us. Memories? Sudden doubt of what's real and not real? Was that really the boogey man under my bed when I was a kid? That's normal the first time you see her. It'll happen again every once in a while. Try not to stare at the wings. We're pretty sure it's her wings that cause it."

"Her?" Matty asked, looking at the massive creature's body for signs of breasts or a vagina.

"Yeah, the anatomy department says it's a she. We just call her Amethyst. Beautiful, ain't she?" The man turned his binoculars towards the tent like center building that housed the magnificent creature.

Matty had to dig deep to find any words. "She is."

Suddenly Alec appeared again, and the lab guy melted back into his work. The multi-millionaire stood simply with his hands in his pockets as Matty scanned around the room, her eyes always returning to the body of the creature. To those incredible wings.

"Is it dangerous?" she managed, looking at the teeth and claws that looked like they could tear an elephant apart.

"Incredibly so. We lost many men when we first encountered it. Good people. Scientists, scholars, soldiers." Alec sounded sad.

"Can it fly?"

"When we managed to capture it, it had flown. Scientifically we're told flight with those wings at that mass is impossible, but we knew it was airborne at one point."

"How did you capture it?" Matty asked.

"Sorry, but that's another secret you don't get today."

Matty sighed. *I want to ask a million and one questions, and I know he won't answer them. Maybe he'll answer this one.*

"What is it?"

"Miss Matilde Rindahl, I would like to introduce you to Amethyst. The world's first and only Dragon."

Dragon…

Chapter Eighteen
Tesser

Tesser had quit his job, much to the dismay of Jerry, the pizzeria's owner. Having the pseudo-celebrity work at his late night restaurant had brought him a fair amount of extra business, and he would miss it. Tesser apologized to Jerry profusely and thanked him for the opportunity he'd been given. The two men parted ways graciously.

It took Mr. Doyle almost 48 hours to prepare his spell and nearly 10 hours of that time was dedicated solely to calming Tesser's patience.

"You said it would be ready by now, Mr. Doyle. Why is it taking so long?" Tesser asked the old man impatiently. Mr. Doyle was sitting in a high backed leather chair and was grinding a previously alive exotic insect into a mush with a glass pestle over an open granite work surface. The smell the dark pulp gave off was acidic and stung the nose.

"Tesser, I realize you are in a hurry, but you need to understand two very important facts; primarily, magic has been neutered of late, and a near second, the more you bother me, *the slower this goes.*"

The dragon's chastising began immediately. "In

previous times, wizards less powerful than you..."

Mr. Doyle cut him off, "Had far, far more magic to work with. I needn't remind you that working glamours and casting spells right now is the literal equivalent of wringing blood from a stone, or swimming in the Sahara. While not as impossible as I frequently feel it is, it takes a bloody good long time to achieve anything worth doing with sorcery, and it is rather difficult. I would thank you kindly to go away, and leave me be so I can ready this ritual."

Abe had slid in behind Tesser and put a calming hand on the dragon's shoulder. "C'mon bud. He's right. You're pushing him too hard. Especially at his age."

Mr. Doyle glared at Abe.

Tesser turned almost angrily, but after a deep breath, he settled his temper. "I'm sorry. Kaula is incredibly important to me, and far more so to the world. In *her* absence, things have come undone far worse than in *my* absence."

"You're going to have to explain yourself pretty damn soon, Tesser. All these riddles are pissing us off," Abe said as the pair moseyed their way back to the young man's room. Abe had his laptop flipped open and was streaming Mad Men. He was in search of the elusive Christina Hendricks topless moment, but had seen nothing.

Yet.

"After tonight, I think you'll be quite aware of what's going on." Tesser's body stiffened, and he flopped onto Abe's bed with dramatic effect. He exhaled a powerful rush of frustration and rolled over to watch the television show. Abe sat down in the office chair he'd been sitting in when he first laid eyes on Tesser online.

"You like this show?" Abe asked idly, pointing at the laptop screen trying to make small talk.

"I've never seen it before. Everything seems strange. The clothing and hairstyles don't match what I see on the streets. Why is that?" Tesser asked.

"This show is set in the 1960s. About fifty years ago. Styles change my friend."

Tesser rolled onto his back. "I don't think I want to watch a show about fifty years ago unless it will help me learn more of your culture today. Can you put some music on? Something I don't have to watch?"

"What kind of music are you into?" Abe leaned forward in the chair and grabbed his mouse. He shut down the television show and started to search for music to entertain his guest.

"I thought the stuff they played at the night club was catchy. I enjoy heavy beats. The vibration in my chest is kick ass."

"You speak funny," Abe said with a laugh.

"Your face is funny," Tesser retorted.

The two shared a laugh.

"How about some Skrillex? He's pretty popular online, and has 'dropped the bass' a few times."

"Is he the one who makes music that sounds like change being sucked up into a vacuum cleaner that's about to explode?" Tesser rolled back over, excited.

Abe grinned ear to ear. "Yeah, I mean that's one way to describe dubstep."

"He'll do. Please play it loud," Tesser said as he flopped onto his back once more.

"You're a strange man, my friend," Abe said as he hit play on Scary Monsters and Nice Sprites.

Tesser looked up at the high ceilings of the pricey home and let the electronic cacophony take him away.

Dear Abe, I'm not really a man at all.

*****

At an hour before midnight Mr. Doyle fetched the boys. Not before reaming them out politely in his British accent thoroughly for their loud music and general levels of disrespect, of course.

Tesser and Abe were humbled and a bit impressed by how much shame the man could dole out, all the while refusing to use curse words, insults, or raising his voice.

The man has a strange gift.

"We'll need to link hands on the floor inside the inner circle of ground feldspar. You'll notice the outer circle of salt and mashed insect. That's to keep the demons at bay should we draw their attention. Take care to not disturb the circles."

"There are no demons that can cross the threshold without being first invited. None that would be interested in interfering with this, at least," Tesser said flatly.

Mr. Doyle started the argument, "My son, there are thousands of years of documentation showing clear evidence of…"

"Creatures from other planes of existence cannot pass through the threshold unless brought across intentionally. It has never been done and never shall be done. If you fear ghosts, spirits, eidolons, poltergeists, gremlins, brownies, seelie or sidhe, that is one thing. Your barrier has value, but not against what you think it does," Tesser said with finality.

"How do you know all that?" Abe asked as Mr. Doyle stared at the gold-eyed man, experiencing his own frustration again.

"Experience. Can we begin? I'm not getting any younger," Tesser said as he took a seat inside the circle. *Though I'm not getting any older, either.*

"You need to move over there," Mr. Doyle said, pointing at a different spot inside the circle. Tesser slid over immediately.

I'll have some answers soon. Finally.

The two mages sat down in their own designated areas of the floor, and all three took each other's hands at Mr. Doyle's insistence. The aged wizard took a deep breath, and after visually confirming that the two men were still in fact with him, he began his chant.

I think some of that is the Latin language Abe mentioned.

Mr. Doyle's chant drifted from one dead language to the next fluidly, as if the words belonged next to one another. Tesser tried to listen to each word, to pluck the meaning of the spell from thin air.

“Loquor—Clara Voce—Nulla Timor—Veritas—Duo Magus—Kaula—” and it went on and on. Disjointed phrases strung together smoothly somehow, with a tenor that alternated between whispers and shouts that at times felt so right, Tesser couldn't help but smile at the beauty of it all. Hair stood at end.

This man used to be powerful. His skill is admirable, though he is unable to tap into so much of the energy that is gone. I see now so clearly what he meant when he said wielding magic was like drawing blood from a stone. There is so little of Kaula left in the world it is a surprise the sun is even shining.

Mr. Doyle's voice was stringing together sounds now. He spoke syllables and consonants that couldn't possibly *be* words, but sounded to the ear like the turning of a gigantic tumbler inside the lock of reality. His words, his mouth, were recreating what was possible.

“Ga—Ro—Re—Chal—Vo—Tem…”

Then, silence.

Everything has gone dark.

A dome of blackened energy had formed around the outer circle of salt. It cast an absence of light that seemed infinite, and reminded all three men of the vast, endless night sky full of mystery. Rather than drawing out primordial fear, the blackness drew out childlike wonder.

"Speak to Kaula, Tesser. Our minds are drifting in a void of the universal subconscious. We are connected to a billion minds, and a billion souls. Maybe more. Speak out firmly to Kaula, and if she can, she shall respond to you," Mr. Doyle said, his voice a breath above a whisper.

"This is amazing," Abe said under his breath.

Tesser closed his eyes and shifted his body. He kept the changes internal, altering his vocal cords and lungs to enable an entirely different mode of sound. He might be saying words, but the sounds he would be making would carry meaning to only a select few.

My dragon kin.

"Kaula," Tesser said softly, beckoning to his long lost love.

I can still see your face.

The void returned nothing.

"Kaula, please. I must speak with you," Tesser said.

I want to hear your voice.

Abe turned to Mr. Doyle, "Can you hear that? Something different with his voice? A vibration? A tone? Like he's speaking twice, or something?"

Mr. Doyle could only nod as he motioned for Abe to stop talking.

"Kaula?" The trio let the plea sit in the darkness for several minutes, but nothing returned. No answers, no salutations, no faces, and no satisfaction. Tesser felt a hot tear streak down his cheek.

She mustn't be dead.

"Tesser, the spell will end soon if we do not forge a connection with someone. Are there others you can reach out to? You said there were six others of your organization?" Mr. Doyle suggested.

"Six others of *my kind.*"

"Try for one of them. Better to reach a different person than no one altogether." Mr. Doyle sounded conciliatory.

Tesser wiped the salty tear from his chin and licked his lips.

A Dragon's tear. Purest salt.

He spoke again, his voice reaching out far across the world, "It is I, Tesser. Speak to me my brothers and sisters."

The void remained black and endless for a painfully long span of seconds before several specks of light appeared in the depths of the darkness far above. Pinpricks of color grew and swirled about, approaching the men where they sat, covering distances so vast they were unimaginable. Eventually the motes of color buzzed between the men, dancing about like a child's sparkler on a midsummer night. Each was a different color. All of the streamers escaped away suddenly, sans one, a blue like the azure sky.

"Kiarohn," Tesser said with a rapid breath, on the verge of tears of joy.

The mote swirled again, and a soft voice, neither male nor female could be heard by all present, "Tesser. It is good to finally see you again. We have mourned your loss, but now we celebrate your return."

"I have not died," Tesser said defiantly, proudly.

The mote twisted in the air acrobatically. "That much is true, though we were beset with sadness when you left this world. Well, most of us. What say you of your story?" The color called Kiarohn asked.

"I was forced to sleep."

"Forced to sleep? You were never one to conjure excuses, Tesser. How does one make our kind fall asleep for so very long? Sorcery? Poison?" The whirl of blue energy changed its tint inquisitively.

"I do not know. Both perhaps. My last waking memories are of a time very long ago. Wooden castles, men starting fires, and the first kings. Magic was abound with the humans, and mathematics was no more developed than the wheel. I have no memory of how I came to be asleep for so long. You know my word to be true. My soul is open to you." Tesser emphasized the point by pulling his shirt apart, busting the buttons and sending them skidding across the hard wooden floor. One stopped and spun dangerously close to the circle of ground feldspar.

The mote danced near Tesser's chest, as if proximity would assure veracity. "You tell the truth. I am sorry for my interrogation friend. Ever since Kaula..."

Tesser leaned forward, almost letting go of Abe and Mr. Doyle's hands. The two mages gripped the golden-eyed man's fingers strongly, and he tilted back. "What of Kaula? Where has she gone?"

"She searched this world from pole to pole for a hundred years when you disappeared. Even *her* magic failed to find you. She hasn't been the same since. Distraught, depressed. Reckless at times even," the blue said.

"What. Of. Kaula?" The unmistakable sound of anger had crept into Tesser's voice.

"Always so short tempered. You were the hottest of our kind."

"Zeud is the *hottest* of our kind. Yet she is calm, where I am anger. What of Kaula, Kiarohn? I'm begging you." The anger had given way to sadness.

"A decade past she was in Asia. That was her region of the world. Since your slumber we've divided it. Seven continents, seven stewards. A simple plan, though North America was left orphaned in your wake. Then one day, with nary a spell cast or shout issued forth she simply disappeared. Try as we might, the seven became five. And ever since, what she brought to the world has faded away. But that you've already experienced, I'll wager."

"Kiarohn, you're not the wagering type."

"So true my friend. That has not changed since you've been away. Where are you?"

"Boston. I awoke under the ground, and fell into a subway tunnel when I stretched my muscles. It has been a challenging adjustment. This world is near alien to me."

The two mages were wide eyed with the conversation. Neither had experienced anything quite like it.

"I can only imagine. The world has changed much since your disappearance. We fear the world will change far faster and for the worse without Kaula's essence." The blue color darkened, sad.

"Has Ambryn…?"

"No. He has not died." The color said confidently.

Tesser's head drooped in slight relief, matching the color's change, "How long was I asleep?"

The mote of energy moved up and spun in rapid circles, thinking. "I do not recall the exact number of years Tesser, but I would guess it at around twenty thousand trips around the sun."

"No," Mr. Doyle blurted. "That doesn't add up at all."

The blue stream of color twisted, suddenly aware of the presence of the elder wizard. It drifted accusatorially between Tesser and the British man, its colors flickering in intensity rapidly. "Who is this? Has he been here all along?"

"Yes, I'm sorry Kia. Meet Mr. Doyle. He has been very helpful to me. This conversation is occurring due only to his and his apprentice's assistance. I owe them a debt of gratitude."

The storm blue color lightened steadily to the color of clear sky. "I thank you then Mr. Doyle. And you are most correct in your statement. That does not add up."

"What does he mean?" Tesser asked no one in particular.

The Brit ex-pat answered, "You said you remember castles and fire. Kings and the wheel. The wheel was invented seven, or perhaps eight thousand years ago. You speak of a history that doesn't exist. Humans were not where you say they were twenty thousand years ago."

The color spoke, "Mr. Doyle, humans are only aware of the history we want them to remember. In Tesser's absence, we have had to take drastic measures to steer the course of humanity. Ultimately, we were unable to do what we wanted to, and had to.... start you over. It is his task, and his art, *not ours*, to manipulate life."

Abe was the one who asked the ultimate question,

making the boldest statement. "Alright, fuck this. What are you? Kiarohn, Kaula, Tesser, Ambryn, Zeud? Coleco? Atari? Four names of the seven, that much I get. Each tied to the Origination Stones right? The only thing older than you?"

"You speak these words like you know them young one," Kiarohn shot back.

"I'm pretty much making it up as I go here," Abe shot back honestly.

"Well, young mage, if Tesser hasn't told you perhaps I should not either."

Abe pleaded, "Tesser, come on. This just the tip bullshit is killing me. I've been waiting my whole life to see something amazing, and here I am, on that threshold. I want to see spells. I want to see gnomes, and ghosts, and magic, *real magic*. I want to tell my grandchildren that I had tea with a troll, and watched a giant fell a tree so he had something to pick his teeth with. I want to tell them I snuck into a dragon's lair and stole his treasure. I want to *live* Tesser. I'm sick of being an accountant that dabbles in wonder part time. And I *know* you can show me what I want. I can feel it deep inside me, and you can give me my dream right here, and right now."

Hm. Well, if only for the speech.

"I do not know if there are any gnome hills left to take you to, Abe. I am sure with some searching we can find a trapped soul somewhere, and then you can see your ghost. Here we sit, practicing real magic. Trolls? I haven't seen a troll since I slept, and they are wondrous creatures, though the sunlight hates them so. And should we find a giant, you'll find they are not nearly as large as you'd hope. A tree would be more cane sized for a proper sized titan, though an angry one would pick your flesh from his teeth using your bones."

Abe's eyes were alight. Mr. Doyle's as well.

"And as for stealing a dragon's treasure…"

Both men held their breath.

"I have no treasure for you to take. But one day, I shall breathe fire, and you shall see me for what I am.

I am Tesser. And I am Dragon."

Chapter Nineteen

Sergeant Henry "Spoon" Spooner

Spoon looked down into his whiskey tumbler. It was empty again.

That makes me angry.

Spooner sat in a bar near the north end. He'd gorged on oysters, called a fellow cop buddy of his, and walked over to start drowning his concerns in watered down whiskey. The bartender knew him, and with it being the afternoon and the bar being mostly empty, there was no reason to simply not hand Spoon the entire bottle.

It could wind up being a mistake.

Fuck Bobby, where are you?

As Henry was expressing his turmoil in his mind to no one in particular, his friend Bobby came into the bar. Bobby served with Spoon in Afghanistan. Both men had been in different units but assigned to the same FOB for a stretch, and they were still close. They'd shared more than one bottle of Scope that had been dumped out and filled with dyed vodka. Bobby was tall and thick like a linebacker for the Patriots, and had long hair and rough beard. He worked for the narcotics division of the

Massachusetts State Police, and frequently worked undercover and had to drive a couple hours to meet Spoon that day. He was one of the only people Spoon trusted completely.

"Spooney, brother," Bobby said in his gruff, thick voice.

"Shit, Bobby, all those Parliaments are crushing your voice. You sound like a Broadway two pack a day whore," Spoon said as the two men gripped hands in a rugged handshake.

"Hey, it's nice to see you too. You got cum on your face."

Spoon shrugged. "Hey, it happens. Thanks for making the trip. I got us a bottle."

Bobby nodded and waved to the bartender. "Glass please." A few seconds later a tumbler identical to Spoon's slid down the counter and Bobby scooped it up gracefully. The bar was covered in cigarette smoke stained photos of familiar Boston entertainers and athletes. Larry Bird, Bobby Orr, Paul Pierce, Red Auerbach, Bob Cousy, Robert Parish, Carl Yastrzemski, Ted Williams, Aerosmith, and a hundred more. There was a history of the city here, right down to the nicotine and booze ingrained into the walls, and Spoon liked it. It felt comfortable, like a worn in recliner.

The two men made their way back to the tired booth that Spoon had claimed. The shorter ex-paratrooper slid into the booth easily, but the massive Bobby had to suck in his belly to squeeze in.

"Bobby, I forget how big an ape you are. Christ man, what do you eat to stay that large?"

"Just ate ten bananas and a blonde on the way here. Feed me a few drinks, and the pain of this table in my spleen will go away." Bobby pushed the glass towards Spoon, and he filled in. Bobby took a mouthful and winced from the burn. "God that's horrible. Like piss and diesel. Hey, congrats on making Detective Sergeant. You deserve it. Good man, good cop."

"Yeah, well the papers aren't in yet, just all the extra work. Easy way for them to get me to do the job without adding what I'm owed into my paycheck." Spoon took a mouthful of the whiskey and let it slide down his throat. It burned, but it was a cleansing fire.

"Ha. City job, state job, they fuck you somehow. Either way man, good on you. You'll get what's coming to you. What brings me out here? You need help on a case?

"In a manner of speaking, yes. I uh…I don't even know where to start on this, and I know you're not going to believe me. But you gotta gimme the benefit of the doubt on this?"

Bobby drained his glass with a wince and a cough and pushed it forward again. Spoon filled it. "You got it."

"Okay, so I was assigned the attempted rape near that new nightclub near Chinatown, right?" Spoon started.

"The one with the naked dude that came to the rescue?" Bobby asked, wrapping baseball glove sized hands around the tiny glass.

"That's the one. So I get a tip that leads me to the dude, the naked dude, and I track him down to a Back Bay pizzeria where he's working as a late night bouncer for the club drunks. He's got clothes, and he and I sit down for a chat. He's foreign, got an accent I still can't place, and I immediately get the feel off this dude that he's on a different level, if you know what I mean?"

"Like Stephen Hawking on a different level? Mila Kunis on a different level?"

Spoon laughed. "No. Remember when the Special Operations guys would come through the base? Or when we'd deploy with them? You know how some of them just…exuded that air of 'I wipe my ass with the enemy?' That subtle arrogance? A healthy cockiness that only comes with being through the fire? The good kind of cocky?"

"Yeah, like a fifth degree black belt. I think I know what you're saying."

"Yeah, so this guy is like dripping with badass, but he's soft spoken, and patient, with a good sense of humor and I know that he's going to be snapping drunk college kid collar bones within a month at this pizza shop, and I just get that fucking itch that there's something deeper with him going on."

"Like Russian mafia shit?" Bobby sipped the whiskey.

Spoon sipped his liquor. "At the time, I dunno, maybe. Sure. Something. So get this. I decide I'm gonna keep an eye on this dude; his name's Tesser by the way. I forgot to say that. I get my ass a magazine, a smoothie, and I sit on a bench down the way watching the pizza shop for a few days. One evening, Tesser, still wearing clothes, is out reading a book on the sidewalk. Then he gets this 'I just smelled shit' look on his face, does a 180, makes eye contact with this kid that had been standing on the opposite sidewalk fifty feet away, and the kid squirts, running for his fucking life."

"Nice! Is that your second perp from the attempted rape on the girl?" Bobby was getting into the story.

"No, he didn't match the description. But seeing as how I love to protect and serve, I set my six dollar smoothie down and run after them. The kid is running for his life okay. *For his life*. Horror movie style, and Tesser is like jogging in the fucking park, running this kid down like it ain't no thang."

"Nice. Should have this Tesser guy put in an application to be a trooper." Bobby gulped some whiskey down and poured another finger's worth.

"Yeah, fuck that, listen to this. So the kid turns into an alley, and Tesser follows. When I get to the damn alley, I lean around the corner for cover, and the Tesser guy is saying something like, 'Cast the damn spell dude!' Right?"

"Cast the spell? Like World of Warcraft? They role-playing or something? Live action Skyrim? You doing a stakeout on a bunch of basement dwelling gamers?" Bobby taunted his friend.

Fuck you pal. Chew on this.

"And then the kid does this like, Gandalf thing with his hands, and says something I think in Latin, and all the shit in the alley starts flying around like the end of fucking Ghostbusters or in that movie Poltergeist. Or Twister! Yeah, Twister! I shit you not Bobby. My hair was standing on end, and I think I might've pissed myself. That fucking kid used magic in that alley, and Tesser *knew it*. Knew he could do it. Asked him to do it."

"How much whiskey have you drank today?" Bobby said flatly, unsure of what to think.

"Not nearly enough Bobby. I'm telling you. Right after that happens, I realize somehow during it all I drew my service weapon, which I don't remember doing by the way, and it was everything I could do to run away as fast as I could. I have never been more scared. More… more disrupted by anything I've ever seen. I still ain't right. What burns my ass is I don't know why I'm so fucking on edge about it. I seen a lot brother, you too, and this is nothing compared against some of that. But Bobby. I felt something watching those two. Remember when the towers came down? That sinking pit of the stomach clench? That realization that something has changed? It felt like that."

On the other side of the bar a middle-aged woman with peroxide blonde hair started up some music on the bar's antiquated jukebox. The classic riffs of Led Zeppelin started to fill the bar with precious filler noise.

"I went back to the alley. I've been back four times. I've looked for wires, fans, signs of any kind of Hollywood special effects bullshit, but nothing. The alley is clean and clear. No tricks, no nothing. I'll do you one better, Bobby. I sat there for hours checking through shit, and no matter how bad the wind picked up, it never once stirred the trash in that dead end. Even when we had that shower the other night. That alley man... Tesser and that kid. Something real strange I cannot explain. And I'm trying. I haven't slept for more than an hour since."

Bobby sat the whiskey down and looked long and hard at Spoon. Spoon had sat his own glass down and was staring down into it. Bobby could see the conflict in his friend's eyes.

He probably thinks I'm fucking crazy.

"I think you're fucking crazy," Bobby said flatly. "But that ain't new. You got years of being crazy under your belt. But I can see something in your eyes Henry. Something I haven't seen in someone since Afghanistan friend. And it chills me. Brings back some darkness."

"I'm sorry, Bobby. I didn't bring you here to bring that out again. I just needed to talk about this. You're the only man I trust right now, and I was hoping I could talk and not feel quite so motherfucking lost on this."

Bobby chewed on his lip and shook his head. "Spoon, you are never alone on anything. You're part of a brotherhood. I can't say all of the rest of our blue family would take this story as well as I have, but you are never alone, don't ever forget that."

Yeah, he's right.

"What now?" Bobby asked bluntly.

Spoon shrugged, lost. "I don't know. I know if I take this up the chain to the brass I'm gonna get either fired or sent in to the shrink to have my head examined. I don't know if I keep tailing this Tesser character, or if I just fucking walk and try to pretend like there aren't motherfuckers out there that can do magic and shit. Pretend like the world is as boring as it always has been."

"That's some serious rabbit hole shit, brother."

Spoon agreed. "Yeah. I don't know what to do. I was hoping you had some ideas to share."

"Assuming you are telling the truth, and I'm being real generous when I say that I believe you on this, how does any of what happened in that alley change you being a cop? A pretty good cop I might add."

I hate having friends that give good advice.

"It doesn't change anything I guess," Spoon said as he pushed the whiskey glass away.

"Right. You still have a case to work, and if anything, you stay on this Tesser dude and ride that until the other perp comes at him or you get a better lead, which by the way, you should be working on. And if while you're following Tesser you see more of this spell bullshit, or you see a dwarf running down Comm Ave., and you can get evidence of it then you go up the chain of command. But *not* before you have proof, understand?"

"Yeah."

"You do it too soon, and it's career suicide. You won't be able to get a job this side of the Mississippi." Bobby tipped his tiny glass up in his bear like paws and drained the last of the whiskey.

"Thanks, Bobby. I don't know why I didn't reason all that through on my own. I'm swimming at the bottom of this mire looking up through the shit and not thinking. I'm sorry to drag you into this." Spoon put the cap on the bottle of the whiskey. The drinking was done.

"When you're in too deep sometimes you need a hand getting out of the hole man. You were there for me once. More than once. High time I put out my hand for you. Spoon you're a hard man. You've been through the ring of fire the same as those Special Operations guys and the same as this Tesser guy. Never forget, Spoon. In the valley you fear no evil because you're the baddest motherfucker in that valley brother. It ain't no cliché with some people. Never forget."

"You say such nice things, Bobby. I think we should go steady."

"You would like that, wouldn’t you? I don’t think Susan would approve. But I'll let my wife know she's on notice. I've got a plan b now."

The two men exited the booth and embraced like brothers should. It might've been the whiskey, but Spoon caught a sniffle in his nose, and wiped some moisture away from his eyes.

"If this shit is real Henry, you play it smart, and don't get in too deep alone. Horror movies start this way, and you're too pretty to survive."

"Ha. My mom pay you to say that Bobby?"

"Your mom pays me to bang her. Be safe."

"Will do." Spoon watched Bobby leave and then took a seat in the booth again. He closed his eyes and took a deep breath, clearing out the unnatural anxiety he had been fighting. It didn't make it all go away, but it helped some.

Baddest motherfucker, eh? Yeah, sure. God, I'm in for it, aren't I?

Chapter Twenty
Abe Fellows

For better or for worse, life had changed for Abe, and if Abe suddenly went blind, deaf, and dumb the world would still be vibrant and different.

Better.

I still don't think he's a dragon. He is refusing to shift forms, despite saying he can shift whenever he wants to, and ever since his big announcement all he's done is patrol the internet, read books, and eat our food. I mean, I suppose he could be telling the truth. Mr. Doyle said that the defero spell we cast would've never worked unless Tesser had been there. If he isn't the dragon of magic, I wonder what this Kaula is like to have around.

Abe had left Mr. Doyle's home to head back to his apartment for a bit. It was mid-evening, and the sun was hidden behind the buildings of the old city, yet its light kissed soft yellow streaks across the blue sky. Despite the wonderful accommodations, Abe felt it prudent to keep his lease. You never know when a relationship will shit the bed. The presence of the consumed dragon in man's form in the brownstone and the overbearing and bossy British mage had driven Abe away for a bit. He also needed more underwear.

Shit, it is hot again. Late heat this year is fierce. It's almost mid-August and we're still pushing a hundred. Damn humidity too. It's like walking through a fucking hot tub all the time. Sweating awful.

The temperature in Boston had been brutal. Temperatures across the whole world were up on average. Global warming was blamed, as was the presence of GMO foods, but after the discussion Abe had been a part of he wondered if the disappearance of this Kaula dragon and sudden awakening of Tesser had something to do with it. But Abe was also a wee bit stuck on the idea that dragons ran the world.

Kaula as a word had Indian roots, which had some traction since the dragon named Kiarohn said that was where she lived. Asia. Likely, the name Kaula long predated the use of the word now, but still it was something a quick Google search helped with.

Abe wiped sweat from his brow and made the turn onto Mr. Doyle's opulent street. It was in perhaps the best area of Boston to live in if you could afford it. The four and five story tall brownstone homes were centuries old and immaculately maintained. Most were single family it seemed or had been renovated into condominiums. Mr. Doyle's was his and his alone, and it was filled with remnants of a long and glorious past.

The streets were lined with the vibrant green of hedges, small trees, and speckled with the colors of flowers. On Beacon Street the scent of the gardens nearly overcame the pervasive smell of car exhaust. It was like escaping into a different century, one with less concerns, and a dragon named Kaula.

Not that having Tesser around was bad, of course.

Abe wasn't a fan of joggers. In fact, he wasn't a fan of anyone who did anything physically active. If he could do everything from his bed, he would. When a married pair of middle-aged double income snobs pressed him against the fence in front of a house as they ran by, Abe sneered.

Dickheads. Spandex is a privilege, not a right, douchenozzle. Though she does look good for a lady pushing forty. I'd hit that. I wonder if she's into nerdy wizards. Wait. Was that tree there before?

As Abe returned his gaze to the forward position from the spandex bottom of the woman jogging his eyes lingered on a tree growing in a garden two houses down that he swore wasn't there a day ago.

I don't think that tree was there when I left the house. In fact, I KNOW that tree wasn't there.

The tree was a tall and slender birch with a trunk no bigger than a cooking pot at its thickest point. The tree's top reached the full three stories of the houses along the row, and it grew in a garden where it was surrounded by thick hedges.

Who the hell would plant a tree right there?

Abe approached the tree cautiously, as one might walk toward a growling dog.

This is absurd. I'm scared of a fucking tree. I hope I get over being such a chicken shit. I'm seeing ghosts everywhere, and I'm like 99% sure my shadow has it out for me right now.

The tree was pretty, though not in the way a flower was. It had a silvery paper look to it and seemed old and strong, though it didn't look decayed and rotten as some old trees can look. It almost seemed fresh and rejuvenated, like the grass after a warm summer rain.

Abe played dumb and tied his shoelaces as two neighborhood locals walked by. They looked at him as if he were a vagrant.

Yeah, fuck you. So what I like to wear Chucks? We don't all have 'earning money' as our purpose in life. Fuckfaces.

When they safely passed and were a distance away, Abe built the courage to reach over the wrought iron waist high fence and touch the tree.

It feels papery. Birch bark is so strange.

Abe stepped away and looked at the tree, relieved that it was normal.

Then the tree looked back at him.

Two small knots in the tree's side spread open revealing eyelids and two glassy orbs that looked far too human and too wise for Abe's sanity to stay firm. As a tiny mouth appeared in a crack of the papery bark below, Abe let loose a shriek that rattled the old glass windows of five homes, and he ran away as fast as he could straight to Mr. Doyle's home.

"I guess I'll introduce myself later," the tree said softly to the hedge.

It took Abe somewhere between eight and ten seconds to reach the top of the stone stairs leading to the wide ash door and get his key in the tumbler. Five more seconds saw him reach the top of the second floor landing, screaming for Tesser all the while.

"What? Abe are you okay?" Tesser asked as he stepped out from the bedroom Mr. Doyle had allowed him to stay in. Tesser was wet from a shower. His dirty blonde hair was darker from the water, and his muscle-etched body was still covered in moisture. All he wore was a plush white towel.

"A tree!" Abe gasped. "Just fucking!" He gasped again. "Looked at me!" He folded over hard at the waist and put his hands on his knees. He heaved hard for air. Covering the thirty yards of sidewalk had obliterated his entire reserve of stamina.

Mr. Doyle appeared suddenly at the top floor's landing, "What is he speaking of? Abraham, what did you say happened?"

Abe swallowed and tried to eke out an answer, but his lungs just wouldn't cooperate.

Goddamit, I am out of shape. And look at Tesser. He's a fucking Greek statue over there. He could run a marathon twice and then recite poetry. I gotta cut back on the sodas.

"Here," Tesser said as he offered a fresh glass of water to the exhausted man.

Thank God.

Abe greedily swallowed down a gulp, then spoke, "I saw a tree outside that looked new. A tree that wasn't there earlier tonight. Or yesterday. I walked over to check it out, and after I touched it two, like, knots in the wood opened up, and I swear to God, Mr. Doyle, there were eyes inside. It had a face. The tree looked at me. You guys gotta go look."

"I highly doubt God had anything to do with your eye-tree Abraham."

Tesser turned and looked up at the mage. "And what would *you* know about God, Mr. Doyle? I don't think you're old enough to have an informed opinion on what God does and doesn't have a hand in."

Mr. Doyle scoffed, but came down the stairs nonetheless. "Abraham, please take us to your talking tree."

Abraham led the old wizard and Tesser out the front door of the massive home. Mr. Doyle walked cautiously using a cane made of wood he claimed originated from a tree that grew on a Tibetan mountainside where a monastery dedicated to the pursuit of ethereal travel was. He'd claimed the cane allowed him to avoid unseen obstacles. Tesser was still dressed in just a towel.

They reached the sidewalk as the two middle-aged joggers were returning. The husband of the pair looked at the semi naked Tesser and gave him a bluntly dirty look. Tesser's simple response was to smile at the pretty wife with the tight spandex. She smiled back so enthusiastically she nearly ran straight into a parked car's side view mirror. The husband said something angrily to her as he gave the towel wearing man another angry glance. When Tesser turned back, Abe was smiling. Tesser winked.

I really like this guy.

"It's right there. The birch looking tree." Abe pointed at the metallic barked tree that was sitting where it shouldn't have been.

"That is a paper birch tree, Abraham. And you are most definitely correct. That is a very new tree." Mr. Doyle took a slow step backwards towards the curb, unconsciously backing away from the invading plant.

"Hm," Tesser said as he walked past both men towards the tree, unafraid. He kept one hand on the fold of the towel at his waist to ensure it wouldn't fall off in public.

"Does anything scare you?" Abe asked as Tesser walked towards the birch.

Tesser stopped and considered the question. "I am a little concerned about whatever brought about the disappearance of Kaula. But other than that, no, I fear precious little. It becomes tedious after a fashion. Being scared can be fun."

God, he's crazy. I gotta stop thinking the word God. Mr. Doyle is gonna find out.

Tesser approached the short metal fence in the fading sun of the evening. Behind them, a few scattered streetlamps were starting to warm up their odd orange glow.

"Hello, tree," Tesser said in tone so friendly it was nearly absurd.

He reminds me of Barney.

The twin knots of the tree slid open again, this time a little slower, like a sleeper awakening. The slit in the bark cracked open once more, and this time the three were able to hear the tree's feminine voice.

"Hello, person," the tree said back to Tesser.

"It's nice to meet you. I'm Tesser."

"I know that name. You're very old. Much older than I am, and that's saying something," the tree said in a cadence that was as whispery as a smoke filled wind moving through a chime.

"You're a hamadryad aren't you? Do you have a name?"

The tree's massive collection of leaves and branches

high above tilted forward strangely.

Holy shit, that tree just nodded at him.

"I've been called Ellen by people before. A very long time ago."

Tesser smiled happily. "I'm so glad to find out your kind still exists. I've been asleep a very long time, Ellen, and I'd thought all of the special things such as yourself had faded from this world."

"My kind began to get quite tired forty two seasons past. Like the sun had set for good, though the light above kept shining."

Tesser nodded knowingly. "I know exactly what you mean. I'm sorry your life has been so strange of late."

The tree hummed softly before speaking again. "It has gotten better. I've been moving closer to this street for many days now. There's a different light coming from here. Coming from you, I think. I wanted to be near it. It feels good to be warm again."

"I'm glad I could help, Ellen. Can you speak with other dryads? Other hamadryads?"

"I could get them a message, though it is very hard for me. I will need to sleep for many days and nights to recover. But if it is important, I will do it for you, Tesser."

Abe looked around, waiting for someone to walk or drive by as the three men stood in the middle of the sidewalk openly talking to, and listening to a tree, but no one came. An empty street at this hour was a freak moment of chance.

"Can you ask the treekind what happened to the amethyst dragon? And can you tell them to be patient? I think the world is about to change again and this time for the better of all." Tesser spoke with conviction.

"Of course. Can I sleep right here? Is this safe?" Ellen the paper birch tree asked.

Tesser turned half-naked to face his friends. "Mr. Doyle, do you think it would be prudent for Ellen to move into your garden? I think she's far less likely to feel the scrape of an errant saw blade if she were safely behind your small fence."

Mr. Doyle was standing slack jawed.

Ha. He has no idea what's going on right now. Arrogant old fuck. This is awesome. I saw this thing before him. I'll never let him live it down!

"Mr. Doyle?"

"Yes, Tesser!" Mr. Doyle blurted. "She, Ellen, may move to my garden, though I don't know how long she plans on staying."

Ellen's paper mouth cracked into a happy smile, "I would live there as long as you would have me. Having a hamadryad as a neighbor has many benefits."

Mr. Doyle stepped forward. "Despite my raving paranoia regarding all things supernatural, I shall grant you your wish and be honored to do so. Please Ellen, move into my garden, I would love to have you as my neighbor."

God, he looks nervous and freaking excited all at the same time. What a relief to know I'm not the only one.

"Then it's settled," Tesser said, clapping his hands together.

"Let me send your message, and once the night has fully dropped down upon us, I will move over to where you wish," Ellen said, her voice trailing off into the sound of a breeze between her branches.

"A dryad's sending. This will be in your memories for a very long time, I think," Tesser said as he backed up to where Mr. Doyle and Abe stood.

The tree's top swayed to and fro as if a gale force wind was building in the air, though there was none. One by one the branches rippled, turning the leaves of the tree up and over. Were it not for the humidity and stale wind all around them, they could be fooled into thinking a tornado was swirling right over the magical birch just feet away. Then suddenly a real wind picked up. The air started slowly at first, moving just enough to cool the sweat on Abe's brow, but then more, much more. The leaves of the tree flickered back and forth, and suddenly, giving off a faint plinking noise, they all snapped free, and hovered in midair, frozen like a painting.

The gust exploded upwards and wicked away all of Ellen's leaves into the darkening night sky where they scattered in every imaginable direction high above, unseen by the millions of people below.

Tesser, still wet and wearing only a towel in the street stood happily. "Thank you, Ellen."

The tree tilted forward, inclining itself humbly.

"That might've been the coolest thing I've ever seen," Abe said softly.

"How many trees will that…message reach?" Mr. Doyle asked.

Tesser shrugged. "It's hard to say. It depends on how many dryads there are near here, and how many of them are still awake and capable of receiving her sending. When I roamed the earth long ago a sending like the one we just saw would reach a hundred dryads, maybe two hundred. Now, it is hard to say."

"What do you hope to accomplish sending that message?" Abe asked.

"Just that, Abe. Hope. It's one of the most magical things in all the world, right up there with love, faith, and wonder. Without it, there's very little reason to go on. I have hope, and it's important that all the special things in this world that have faded away have hope too."

The three men left Ellen to rest before her move and returned back to the brownstone. Tesser left wet footprints on the sidewalk as he went.

Chapter Twenty-One

Matty Rindahl

So. Much. Data.

Matty was at her desk, eyes locked onto the monitor where spreadsheet after spreadsheet tantalized her with hidden details. This was something she was good at; finding the needle in the haystack. This was a large haystack.

She'd been stuck at this desk, many stories above the underground containment facility where the world's only dragon was kept in a medical coma for experimentation purposes. It sickened her if she thought about it, so she tried to bury herself in the research.

It was proving to be a momentous task to isolate usable information from the batteries of tests they ran. It was almost like the purple beast below was shifting about the answers its very body gave to elude being quantified.

DNA tests had revealed not one, but eighteen different results for the dragon. A different result for every test they had run. Some of the tests showed a male result some a female, though the evidence pointed that the creature was female.

Blood panels came back with numbers that made no

sense either. Blood types changed daily, and as soon as they tried to start predicting what the numbers would be on cholesterol, potassium, protein, phosphates, and sugars, the numbers would go whacky on them. The lab geeks were going gray.

It's like she's defying us in the only way she can.

Matty was on the fringe of the development departments related to Project Amethyst. They were taking the multitudes of samples and finding applications for them. Two such sub projects had sent out emails earlier that day, and Matty took a break to read them.

The first was titled "White blood cell tests— phase thirteen."

Phase thirteen? Shit, this has been going on for some time now.

The email contained enormous amounts of scientific data. Control information, dates, trial codes, tests and retests, and summaries. It was a mountain of info, and Matty skipped directly to the cause for Phase Thirteen. The hypothesis. The researched believed that when the dragon's white blood cells were applied to cancer cells, the dragon's white blood cells would eat away at the cancer, eliminating it.

The email's tone seemed to support that idea, though the blood cells needed a fair amount of time to star their work, and if done wrong, the dragon blood destroyed the cancer-ridden patient faster than the cancer.

Jesus. Her blood can cure cancer?

The face that of that impossible thought, she closed that email and went on to the next one. It carried the heavy titular question of; 'Possible names due to Dragon Skin patent.'

Dragon Skin?

Apparently Fitzgerald Industries was working on using the dragon's scales to create body armor for the military. And according to the ballistics data that Matty had no idea how to decipher, the armor was performing very well. The email went on saying that the basic armor design incorporating small scales from the dragon's body were coming in at "Class Four," and the heavier armor that used only larger, thicker scales was "clearly Level Five."

Level Five. That sounds really intimidating.

A quick Googling of body armor told her that Level Five armor was cutting edge, and could stop most high velocity military rounds. It was still classified and highly secretive, and the government wanted it developed very badly. When she returned to the email she saw multiple mentions of how much the State Department wanted lightweight Level Four and Five armor.

Prices of three to five thousand dollars per suit of the Level Four seemed to be reasonable. The discussion of raising the price to six thousand for the government was had as well.

Sticking it to the Feds.

The email went on to calculate the rate at which the scales regenerated after being removed, and the overall number of scales the dragon could be harvested for within a given calendar year. The gross dollar amount was in the mid eight-figure range at the lowest end.

Christ that's just armor. How much money could we make if we could cure cancer?

Matty closed the emails and sat back in her chair. It was a very expensive office chair, and was very comfortable. She spun in a circle, feeling waves of confliction wash over her.

I don't like this. I feel like keeping that creature alive down there is somehow wrong. After seeing those wispy, beautiful wings, I can't stop thinking about what it would look like soaring in the sky, free and beautiful.

Matty closed her eyes and tried to envision it. The image came to her quickly and freely, bringing a smile to her face.

But if we can cure cancer? And if this body armor project pans out, how many lives could be saved? Soldier's lives. Police and politicians alike. Well, maybe not the politicians, but still. We're talking about millions of lives saved. Maybe more if we don't give the body armor to the politicians.

She needed a break. Something to cheer her up and get her mind off of the entire Project. She picked up her phone and dialed the Boston office. A few prompts of the menu later, she was talking to her old boss, Alexis. She couldn't say what she was doing now, but she could vent about how much stress it was putting her under.

"Girl, I totally understand you. The more money they pay you, the less joy you have in life. It's an inverse ratio, hun," Alexis said.

God, I love her. I should've stayed in her department.

"Yeah. I don't know Alexis. This project is great, my office is great, and I know I'm doing good important work, I'm just feeling it. I need to buy a new vibrator or something. Watch some Twilight movies and cheer myself up with a bottle of Moscato."

Alexis laughed. "Well, if you're gonna go that route, I'd suggest boxed wine. But a smart girl would realize that she cannot find happiness with cheap wine and some C batteries. You need to get out girl. You're a cat away from a cliché."

It was Matty's turn to laugh at the redhead. "What are you suggesting? We get dressed up for no good reason and go out to dinner?"

"That's just the start lady. After you and I eat a salad, wishing we were eating a burger, we are going to out to a nightclub frequented by young men that we will not care about and proceed to make real bad decisions that will feel real good in the moment, and we *will not regret* those decisions in the morning."

"Alexis, when was the last time I told you I loved you?"

"Say it. It'll make you feel better."

"Alexis, I love you." Matty giggled.

"And I love you too. I'm free Friday. Hey, we can celebrate the arrival of September! That's a good enough reason to drink fruity cocktails and hope we remember condoms. You can't trust these cubs nowadays, they're all into going bareback on ya."

"You're filthy."

"I'm not getting any younger, my dear. The urge to make a baby is clawing at me like my need for dark chocolate. Cutting to the quick gets me what I want sooner, and that means I get more of it in the long run. I'll see you on Friday, at your place, promptly at eight o'clock. Wear something slutty."

"I don't think I own anything slutty." Matty had to think on it.

"Fine then. I'll be by your place tomorrow night at six. We'll go shopping and form a battle plan for Friday. When I'm done with you, all the boys will want a piece."

"But what if I want to meet a nice guy, Alexis? What if this is about settling down?" Matty baited.

"I'm just going to go ahead and hang up on you. See you tomorrow night, sweetie! Muah!"

Alexis hung up the phone, and Matty did the same. It was actually exciting for her to think about going shopping and going out. She hadn't even attempted to make herself look pretty since the miscarriage and break up with Max.

I'm long overdue to feel wanted. I want to be wanted.

A rejuvenated Matty spun her chair round in circles and tried to imagine what the boy she'd make a bad decision about would look like. The image of the naked hobo strangely kept coming to the front of her mind.

Chapter Twenty-Two

Tesser

I am thankful for all the resources here. Mr. Doyle and Abe have been gracious hosts, providing for whatever I've asked of them. Daily, Abe presses me to reveal my true Dragon form, but this is not the time and certainly not the place. My sudden appearance in this city in full form would throw everything into a tailspin. Amusing saying. Tailspin. A species unable of achieving flight has invented a dozen now well-known sayings based on the science of taking to the air in technological contraptions.

Good for them.

Abe was sitting in the living room on the first floor of Mr. Doyle's home. They'd been sitting in silence for hours together as Tesser searched diligently online with a new laptop for signs of his lost companion, Kaula. He had already been introduced to The Delphian Covenant, as well as WWS, and while he'd been able to learn a fair amount about the goings on of the recent modern world, there was an utter and total lack of anything meaningfully draconic. Accurately draconic that is.

"In a world so connected, I am surprised that all of the other dragons have remained out of the media," Tesser said to Abe.

Abe looked up from his B.P.R.D. comic somewhat surprised by the statement. They'd both been quiet for a long time. "You're incredibly intelligent creatures, Tesser. You can shape shift, fly, and I'm sure even with Kaula missing, many of you can work some impressive magic. It's no surprise to me."

Tesser shook his head. "Some of us can't shape shift."

"Really?" Abe sat the comic down in his lap.

"Yeah. Kiarohn? The dragon who spoke to us in the void. The blue? Kia can't shape shift. Also can't land."

"No shit? Like he has no legs?" Abe was fascinated.

Tesser laughed a bit. "Actually Kiarohn doesn't have any, that's true. Kia is the dragon of wind. If Blue were to land, the air all across the Earth would stop blowing. Weather would be affected, droughts would happen, all manner of bad things."

Abe laughed. "You're telling me the only reason we have breezes and rain is because of a legless blue dragon that can't ever stop flying?"

"Well, Kiarohn isn't the only reason, but the most pertinent one."

"You gotta be shitting me. Scientists have all this crap figured out man. I took environmental science in college. Moon phases, global warming, ocean currents. There's a bunch of things that contribute to how weather and wind happens.

Tesser couldn't help but agree, "Yes, but what exactly contributes to those powers? You think the currents stir themselves up? You think the wind blows in a pattern over and over due to luck? Chance? Maybe, I suppose. Or maybe it's that your science sees what it can find, and the more we believe in a thing the more real it becomes."

"Belief defining reality?"

"Well said," Tesser muttered, turning back to his laptop.

"I would've thought a blue dragon would've been in charge of water. Water is often characterized as being blue."

Tesser shrugged and muttered, "The dragon of water is also a shade of blue. More of a blue-green however. She has legs."

Abe shook his head, smiling at the absurdity of it all. "No word from Ellen's sending yet?"

Tesser shook his head, never looking up. "No. She's still resting. The amount of effort that a hamadryad puts into a sending is off the charts. To give up all your leaves? It's the equivalent of a long fast for you and me. Hopefully, she'll have something to tell us in a few days."

Abe watched Tesser for a moment. The dragon was focused, no, obsessed with searching. It was becoming a detriment. The dragon hadn't stepped outside in days, and Abe was convinced Tesser would lose some of his innate essence if he poured too much effort and hope into the internet. It was time for action.

"Get up, we're going out to dinner."

Tesser looked up, just a smidge confused. "What? Why would we do that? We have plenty of food here."

"Because we're men, and men need to go out and eat food. Meat cooked properly, if possible. And you've been cooped up in this place for days on end, nose buried in the internet with nothing to show for it, and I want to go out to eat, for the sake of Pete."

"Who is Pete?"

"Ever seen Short Circuit?" Abe stood up.

"I've been asleep for a very long time Abe."

"Oh yeah. We'll watch it sometime. I own the DVD. Come with me. There's got to be a nice suit in a closet upstairs somewhere."

The two men got off the couches and started towards the massive staircase. "Will Mr. Doyle come along? I would think an invitation is in order."

"Fuck him. Curmudgeony old shit."

This might be fun.

*****

Three hours, and a pair of almost matching, classy vintage pinstripe suits later, Tesser and Abe were sitting in the North End at a fairly pricey Italian restaurant. The hustle and bustle in the establishment was electric. People young and old, vintage and cutting edge, sat in every chair and stood at every stool at the bar. It was a cross section of city life, and it was thrilling to be amongst it.

I love gatherings. You can see the speed at which the human society moves when there are so many of them gathered around here. I always was the social one of my kind.

"Nice place right? How was the mushroom appetizer?" Abe asked, having to speak loudly to be heard over the restaurant's chatter.

Tesser could hear him fine. "The portobello was very good." The dragon felt a stirring somewhere inside him. The presence of so many people, all their scents and body language, was triggering an emotion he hadn't felt in a long time. A hunger. A need to hunt.

I have been contained for far too long. No flames have passed between my teeth and over my tongues in more years than I can remember. I haven't stretched my wings properly, and I haven't felt the kiss of the winds underneath me in so long it hurts. And the last time I felt the comfort of a woman…

"Hey, you in there? I asked you a question." Abe had leaned over the table, snapping his fingers.

"I'm sorry Abe, I was just enjoying the moment. Reminiscing. Thank you for making me come out tonight."

Abe let loose a pleased sigh and rubbed his tummy. "Hey, my pleasure. Mr. Doyle pays me well, and you need the culture. Besides, lightning could strike and we could get lucky."

Oh, now there's an idea. I should spend more time looking into women. After all, it is what I've done best for so very long.

"You want to be with a woman tonight?" Tesser asked the question more as a statement.

Abe's awkwardness sprouted like a mushroom in the dark. He shrank back into his seat, his lack of confidence showing dramatically. "Oh, I was just kidding. I'm not really looking for a relationship right now, Tesser. Far too much on my plate. But hey, thanks for looking out for— "

"Shush. You are a handsome young man, and I resemble one as well. We have needs Abe, primal needs. A need to hunt."

"Yeahhh...I don't really need a girlfriend..."

"Shush. You need to get your dick wet tonight, as do I."

Abe was speechless, but couldn't stop from grinning again.

He's excited.

Tesser took a sip from his whiskey and ginger and assessed the people in the restaurant for this new purpose. He was hoping to find—

Two women.

A redhead and a brunette sat together at a table off to the side. Both were dressed in short but classy dark colored evening dresses and were very attractive. Tesser closed his eyes and inhaled deeply, sorting through the aromas of food, the colognes and perfumes, and the musky scent of each person in the room. He caught the tiniest caress of the redhead and knew she was prime. He caught a vague scent off of the brunette, and through all the other scents of the restaurant it reminded him of clean river stones, and snow.

That scent is SO familiar. I must talk to her.

"Get up," Tesser said as he got to his feet.

"Um...Tesser, I am not really 'gifted' with women per se. I don't think you need me as a wingman on this mission Captain."

Tesser picked up his glass and gave Abe a look showing he wouldn't take no for an answer. Abe stood and grabbed his beer.

The thrill of the hunt.

The two men crossed the busy restaurant, people unconsciously getting out of Tesser's way. He was pushing his charisma out with experience, forcing the people he didn't want to interact with away from him. It was an old trick that worked frequently. Scientists might call it the work of pheromones.

Mr. Doyle would call it magic.

"Hello," Tesser said to the two women. He had a disarming smile on immediately, one that said he was someone people wanted to talk to.

The redhead looked up first, and her eyes flared happily.

She's attracted to me. Excellent start.

"Hello, handsome. What can we do for you and your friend tonight?" She lifted a glass of wine and sipped at it seductively. The gesture looked just shy of desperate.

Tesser looked over at the girl that carried the clean scent. She was very pretty. Smooth skin that avoided the harsh caress of sunlight, and dark hair that she'd pulled back into a ponytail. She wore minimal makeup, and she looked innocent, just a breath out of place with the vivacious redhead with the red lips. She still hadn't looked up at Tesser yet.

She looks uninterested – or is that intimidated? I must learn more about her.

"Well, this is my friend, Abraham. He prefers his friends to call him Abe. I think you should call him Abe. My name is Tesser." The disarming smile stayed steady as he switched his drink into his left hand and extended his right towards the redhead. She took it as she answered.

"I'm Alexis. And this beauty is Matty."

"Beautiful names, hello Matty. Is that short for something?" Tesser let go of Alexis' hand and presented it respectfully to the brunette.

"Matilde. My father is Norwegian," she said, finally

looking up at Tesser. Her eyes froze in recognition of him.

Her eyes. What a pretty green. And Norway…I'm missing something here.

"Norway. A pretty place. It's a true pleasure to meet you two ladies; I hope you don't think we're being too forward," Tesser apologized as Abe introduced himself to Alexis. Tesser listened to Alexis' replies to Abe and heard that her tone hadn't changed from when she spoke to him. She was attracted to the much younger fledgling mage.

"Have you...been?" Matty asked, something clearly on her mind. She was still staring at Tesser.

I can finally smell her. Well, smell something about her state of mind and a special area of her body at least…but she's also nervous. Adorable.

"I visited a very long time ago. When I was younger. Matty, you've a look on your face like you want to say something. Speak freely." Tesser had a feeling he knew what she was thinking, and his tone told her so.

The girl named Matty blushed, and it looked ever so pretty on her pale skin. "I recognize you. I think. Are you the man from the video near the nightclub?"

"Oh my God!" Alexis said.

Tesser smiled again, a little bigger this time. "Ya caught me. I did manage to put some clothes on tonight. I'm learning some manners."

Matty's mouth opened and closed but said nothing. She looked unsure of quite how to respond to Tesser's baiting. Finally she got something out. "I feel like there's a really embarrassing story behind that video."

"I don't get embarrassed easily. Matty, Alexis, it's an awfully long way back to our table over there, and you two look like you're interested in meeting pleasant new people tonight. Are these two seats taken?" Tesser pointed at the two empty chairs.

Matty started to answer, but Alexis didn't give her the chance to reply. "Of course not, Thomas! Have a seat."

"Ha, it's Tesser. But you can call me Thomas if you keep calling him Abe."

This could be a really good night.

Tesser was right. It turned into a really good night.

Chapter Twenty-Three

Matilde

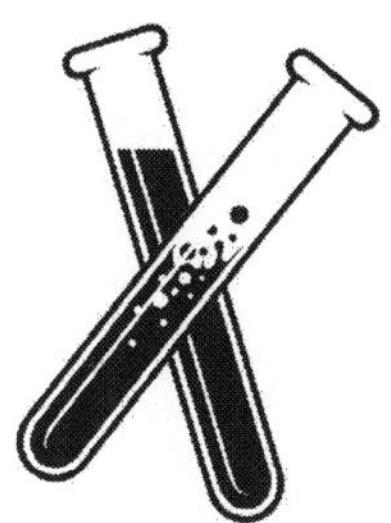

This is turning into the best bad idea I've ever had.

Tesser had one hand on her hip and the other nested firmly around the back of her head, pulling her into his kiss.

This guy can kiss. He can really kiss.

She was tearing at his suit, ripping it off of his shoulders, and yanking it downward, disrupting the eager placement of his hands. As soon as the fancy striped suit hit the floor, his hands were back, expertly exploring her body with surprising firmness. He was incredibly strong.

This was such a good bad decision.

But it was an incredibly difficult decision to make.

*****

Earlier that night Matty had nervously asked the handsome man what his story was.

They'd been standing at the bar in the same nightclub near where Tesser's naked fight had happened. Club Pandemonium. The music had been loud and deep, pulsating at a breakneck rhythm, and Tesser looked at home, his head nodding to the beat ever so slightly.

Every girl in here is staring at him and glaring at me. This is awesome, and just a little horrifying. How am I even entertaining his attention?

"It's pretty simple and not that interesting really. I'm not from around here, you see," he'd started. "English isn't my first language, and having just arrived here, I didn't have any money. That night when I saw those guys trying to work that girl over, I said enough is enough. I don't like rape. You saw the video. You know the rest."

Matty nodded, straining to hear him over the loud club music. "I definitely saw the video. You've become a bit of a celebrity."

Tesser shrugged. "Do what's right. Celebrity is quite secondary. I'm thankful, though. Because of that night I was able to get a job and get some help learning the language. I was able to meet Abe, and he's been an incredible friend."

Matty leaned in, more than a little skeptical. "Learn the language? You speak *perfect* English, Tesser. Perfect."

Tesser grinned in that way that made her tingle. "Well, dear, I am a very fast learner, and Jerry, my boss, allowed me to watch Jay and Silent Bob movies until I got the language down pat."

Matty swooned, sipping at her fruity cocktail. "I LOVE Kevin Smith movies!"

Tesser nodded in agreement. "Yeah, me too. I learned a shitload about America watching his flicks."

The two watched as throngs of college aged men and women moved about. Some were on the dance floor, dancing to the beat of a trance song that had been going for what seemed like forever.

Then again, all of these songs are long and sound the same.

"What do you do for a living?" Tesser asked loudly over the music.

"I'm an analyst at a biotech lab. I basically pore over

huge piles of experiment data and mine for trends and results that we should investigate further."

"That sounds really...boring," he said back.

Matty laughed. "It is. It's like, watching paint dry some days. But I've got to say Tesser, the company I work for does really good work. Important work, and it makes all the bullshit worth it. I think."

"You think?" Tesser gulped down a big mouthful of his cocktail.

He can sure drink. That's easily his fifth.

Matty looked over Tesser's shoulder into the crowded dance floor. It didn't take much effort to locate her fire-haired friend. Alexis was strutting her stuff, surrounded by young men and women half her age. Perhaps most remarkably, Tesser's friend Abe was grinding on Alexis' ass, his hand wrapped around her hips, pulling her onto his groin. It was tacky, juvenile, and the look of sheer joy on both of their faces was priceless. Matty envied her and felt incredibly out of place.

She finally got back to their conversation. "Yeah, I think. Hey, I just, you know...I wasn't sure what I wanted this to be tonight. I thought I could just forget about the past and forget about who I really am and just have fun, but here with you, I feel like a fish out of water."

Tesser leaned in as if to ask her a question, but instead took her hand and led her away from the dance floor. They walked hand in hand to the back of the bar where there were fewer speakers and far less commotion. When they reached the back, Tesser pointed at a barstool next to the one he chose for his own seat.

This is...weird.

Tesser somehow managed to catch the attention of a female bartender on the other side of the square bar, and after a wave of his hand and a smile, she brought over another whiskey for him and another fruity drink for her.

"How do you do that?" Matty asked impulsively.

"Do what?"

"Get people's attention like that? Get people to do things for you so easily? First the random video that looked so good it seemed staged, then the restaurant…I saw everyone looking at you before you even came over to us. And Alexis? Boy, Tesser, she's in love with you. At least the kind of love that makes you wake up in strange beds the next morning covered in bodily fluids. And when we got to the club, you just waved at the damn doorman, and all four of us were let in. And just now, there's a hundred people on the other side of this bar trying to get a drink, and within ten seconds you're able to catch the attention of the hottest bartender in here and get us our drinks. It's weird. You're famous— no, you're notorious."

Tesser grinned sheepishly. "You catch on quickly. It makes you uncomfortable to be with me, doesn't it?"

"Don't change the subject on me. What gives?" Matty slurped a mouthful of her Caribbean living inspired drink and lowered her eyes at Tesser. She wanted an answer.

After sipping his drink he gave her the answer she pried for. "I'm charismatic, what can I say? I exude a certain aura that I have figured out a way to use and abuse for the benefit of myself and those I care about."

"You exude an aura?" Matty rolled her eyes and sipped her drink again.

God, this drink is delicious.

"Can you argue with the results?" Tesser reached a hand across the bar and left it uncomfortably close to her hand. She slid her own hand an inch or two away from his simple advance. It was a reflex. Echoes of Max.

"It's weird, is all."

Tesser couldn't help but agree, "It is weird. And you never answered my question. It makes you uncomfortable to be here with me."

Matty looked away, feeling very revealed and vulnerable. She didn't like to feel that way.

"It's pretty obvious, Matty. I'm not hurt. I just find that fact very intriguing. Tells me there's a story to be told. There's an army of women here who are all giving you profoundly dirty looks because you're sitting here with me. Some men in that platoon as well, and you look like you'd rather be walking on hot coals than having this conversation and getting some positive attention from me."

"Yeah, well..."

"Yeah, well, what? Talk to me. You're only a few seconds away from telling me you want to go to the bathroom to slip away anyway."

Matty took a tug on her straw and nearly emptied her entire drink in one fell swallow.

Fuck it. He's right.

All in one exasperated breath, she let it loose, "My last relationship ended shitty. I haven't seen anyone in a really long time, not since Max. I wanted for tonight to be a wild, let loose, and take off my shoes kind of night. I wanted to make bad decisions about boys, and here I am, scared out of my mind and feeling incredibly inadequate, and of all the boys in all of Boston to show me any kind of attention tonight, I wind up getting you. The guy I nearly masturbated to a grainy security video of, who every woman in his presence wants to bear his children, and who I feel like a grain of sand sitting next to. You're ungodly hot Tesser. It's not fair. I needed a layup tonight, not a slam dunk."

Tesser listened like a champion, allowing her to vent it all. When she finally finished and emptied the rest of her drink, he spoke. He chose his words carefully. "Matty you have a right, a basic human right to be happy. I haven't known you all that long, but from what I see, you've let a piece of your past define your entire future and that's making you unhappy. I'd bet work has become your life, and that's rarely enough for anyone's soul to thrive on. I can't tell you to take off your shoes and dance tonight. I can't tell you to let loose and make bad decisions about boys, or about me, but I can tell you that you are more than adequate. You're more beautiful than the dyed hair trollops that are staring at us and a better person than they could ever hope to be. If you think that you're inadequate sitting next to me, that's an old feeling you're having, and it has no place inside you anymore." Tesser leaned in closer, very close, and rested his hand on hers. This time she didn't pull away.

"Trollops?"

"Trollops. There are a million women in this city. Two hundred pretty ones in this room with us, and the only pretty girl I want to be with is you."

You only live once.

Matty leaned into him, letting the liquor fuel her courage. Tesser leaned in as well, and their lips met softly, then their tongues.

The world only stops for a few moments in a person's life. Matty oddly thought of a few examples: the birth of a child, the vows at your marriage, the moment you hear a loved one has passed, and if you're lucky, at the moment of a great first kiss.

He tastes good. A little like liquor, and a bit earthy, in a masculine way. I forgot how good it feels to be kissed.

Tesser broke it away at a sweet moment, having just nibbled on her lower lip. He made eye contact with her, and she felt her heart flutter.

How did I not notice his eyes were that gold? They don't even look real.

"Matty, I don't want you to make a bad decision you don't want to make, but ever since I saw you at that restaurant earlier, I haven't had a single different thought other than being with you. Being alone with you."

He wants to have sex with me. God, I wish I had another drink. I don't know if I have the guts to make that decision. Oh I know. Sarcasm. That usually works.

"I don't know how to answer you. All I know about

you is that you beat people up in alleys." Matty leaned in again against her better judgment and nuzzled into the nape of his neck. He smelled good, despite not having any cologne on.

"You also know that I beat up men who try to harm women. I'm so chivalrous it's disgusting sometimes. There's an era I wished I'd spent some time in."

"Are you a white knight? Are you here to rescue me, good sir?" Matty asked, her eyes getting wide and her nerdy inner nature surfacing again despite her better judgment.

"I am no knight my lady, but if you need rescuing, I'll gladly risk life and limb to deliver you safely from harm. Was that too cheesy? It felt really cheesy."

"Yeah, it was cheesy. But kind of cute."

Tesser looked relieved. "I haven't talked to a girl in a long time. I would be lying to you if I told you I wasn't a little nervous right now."

"Nervous about little old me?"

"You're an incredibly interesting woman, Matty. Beautiful, intelligent, funny, and you've got a quality about you that I find…fascinating."

"We'd better leave before I change my mind about having sex with you. This booze won't last forever and if I sober up, there's no way I'm having sex with you tonight."

"Do you want another drink before we go?

Matty sucked the water from the melted ice in the bottom of her plastic up and slammed the empty down on the bar. "Hell, yes."

Tesser waved for the female bartender, and like magic two new drinks appeared.

*****

They'd left in a cab after saying goodbye to Alexis and Abe. In order to say goodbye, Matty needed to pry

Alexis' face off of Abe's in the corner of the thumping nightclub. The fiery cougar looked invigorated beyond description with her red lipstick smeared half across her face. Abe looked the same, right down to the smeared lipstick.

In the back of the yellow taxi they made the decision to go to Matty's place.

At her front door she'd made the decision to start kissing him, and in her kitchen, as they headed to the bedroom, he'd made the decision to undo the zipper on the back of her evening dress. It fell to the tile floor soundlessly, inconsequential and forgotten in the moment. She stepped out of it, her mouth still on his, both of them moving towards her bed.

His shoes came off, and then hers, all four items kicked about the small bedroom haphazardly, without concern. He fumbled a bit, then his hands feeling at her breasts through the bra she wore. He tugged at the undergarment, attempting to get it off her without undoing the hooks in the back. She pushed him away and reached around, freeing up the bra, and tossing it away. His hands immediately returned, cupping both her breasts as they kissed again. Within a moment she'd undone his shirt buttons, and had tugged it off his back, his fingers gently pinching her nipples.

My God, he's almost all muscle. But in that good way.

She bit his collarbone for no reason she'd be able to describe later, and he let slip a satisfied laugh. She then reached down to his slacks and undid his belt, noticing he had a girth pressing against his zipper that could only be an erection. She undid the zipper and before the man could do anything about it, she yanked down his pants and underwear, letting his cock pop out.

It's like a sexy Jack in the Box. Nice dick.

Tesser pushed her flat on the bed and pulled her underwear down as she stroked him. He was ready, and when his fingers reached between her legs at the freshly trimmed area she'd spent time on in the shower earlier, she felt how ready she was.

"Wait."

Tesser froze immediately. "Is everything okay?"

"Yes, silly, but we need a condom." Matty squirted out from under him and rolled over, pulling out her bedside drawer. After rummaging around in a completely unsexy way, she produced the small square foil wrapper, and tore the corner with her teeth.

"What's that for?" Tesser looked intrigued. Horny, but intrigued.

"Um, for real?" Matty looked at him, slightly drunk and amused by his apparent newness.

There's no way he's a virgin.

"Yeah, for real. I've never used one before. Where I'm from. Does it make sex better?" Tesser watched her as she pulled out the condom. He sniffed the air.

"Well sort of. You'll probably—hopefully—last longer with it, which is good. But really, these help prevent girls from getting pregnant, which isn't a real problem with me, but they also prevent the spread of disease. I can't believe I'm explaining this to you." She scooted down towards the foot of the bed where Tesser stood naked, dick standing proudly at attention.

"You can't get me sick. And as for having babies…"

Before he could say anymore, she put the condom on her lips, and used her mouth to slide it down on his cock. It was a maneuver she'd done more than once in a happier time. She rested back on her bed and spread her legs, one hand finding its way to her clit, the other finding a nipple. Her heart pounded happily.

"I guess we'll make it work," Tesser said breathlessly as he climbed onto the bed, then on top of her.

A moment later Tesser slid inside her, and for Matty, the world stopped moving again. It didn't start moving until they were done, quite some time later.

Chapter Twenty-Four

Mr. Doyle

The telephone would simply have to do.

Despite my efforts, and a throbbing, aching head as a result, I simply cannot make long distance communication spells work without the presence of Tesser. The man confounds me. A Dragon? I think not. Someone strange who possesses a set of unique powers, sure.

Mr. Doyle sat at his desk and looked at his telephone with disdain. Technology in any form made him sad. A reliance on something unnatural seemed...unnatural. It was an old phone, with fine brass finishing and an antiquated rotary dial. It was from another century. It relieved his distaste a small amount to use antiquated things.

Well, it's overdue and needs to be done.

Mr. Doyle reached out and picked up the receiver. Holding it to his ear, he reached out with his other hand and spun the phone's dial repeatedly, having to stop and slow his wobbly fingers more than once to guide them into the small brass rings accurately.

Damned arthritis is flaring again.

After a long hissing pause and several clicks indicating the transatlantic call was being connected, the phone started to ring on the other end. After a few tones, it was answered. The gruff male voice had a familiar Russian accent.

"This phone has not rung for me in many years. Does it ring now with the good news or the bad?"

Mr. Doyle couldn't contain a smile. "It rings with tidings neither good nor bad, merely compelling and in need of sharing."

A laugh was given in response. That too had a Russian accent. "For an old Limey, you are still a good man, Doyle. Kak pazhivayesh?"

Mr. Doyle's smile persisted. "Nice of you to ask, Belyakov. I am getting older faster than ever, and the world seems to be changing right before my eyes, I've no idea why my spells are still failing, and I haven't the energy to keep up with any of it. In short, I am shite."

Another Russian laugh came back. "Your spells are failing, warlock. You should've expected this. All the magic in this world bleeds away. Our time is faded. You need to move to an older place where the magic has not faded so much. Come to Russia. And soon is best."

Mr. Doyle leaned forward on his desk. "I'm not so sure, Belyakov. Things are happening where I am. I've come into contact with a strange man who claims to be a dragon. He calls himself Tesser."

Belyakov snorted, "A dragon? Taking the form of a man? Tesser? Such a silly name. Dragons are myths. Tales told by ancient wizards to scare their children into being cobblers and bakers. They don't exist. Dinosaur bones and active imaginations."

"I'm not so sure. My thoughts are this man might be something special. Something very new to us that we've never encountered before. I've searched all my texts for mentions of the name Tesser and nothing has come up. Dragon or not, true or false, the man has brought arcane power with him that I haven't seen in well over ten years."

"Arcane power?" The Russian said, his skepticism

lost.

"Arcane power. I was able to cast a defero spell easily with his assistance, and our kind haven't been able to perform that act in far too long. He has access to a different reservoir of power, some kind of essence that is internal, special, and far larger than anything we have access to now. Something I can't tap without his presence. Even when he is nearby material things work better. Many of the relics in my collection regain their properties when he is in the house. I can't say if he truly is a dragon or not, but he has a quality about him I've never seen before."

The Russian chewed on that thought for a bit. "Are you watching the world? There have been stirrings all about. Things we thought were extinct are moving again. Our old friend in Romania sent me a letter the other day. He has said that the dhampyr have returned."

"Ah, letters. A lost art of communication. Is he certain?" Mr. Doyle asked.

"You doubt the Romanian?"

"No, I suppose I don't," Mr. Doyle said, rubbing his chin in thought. "I've noticed some things. I haven't heard of the dhampyr yet, though. Very worrisome. You know what follows in the footsteps of the dhampyr. Other friends around the world are saying more or less the same. Belyakov, tell the Romanian a hamadryad has moved into my front yard. I've never encountered one, and here I sit, looking down at it as it stands in my front yard. I had to look at a book to realize what it was. It claims it came to us because of this Tesser character. I know this is optimistic, but I think he might be the key to returning magic to our world. He claims another of his kind, a dragon named Kaula, has disappeared and that her absence is why our talents are failing."

"Bullshit, as you say. Magic does not come from dragon."

"But how do we know that, Belyakov? Truly? None of

us knows where our gifts come from, we merely speculate and postulate over brandy and insults. Is it that hard to imagine that there is a single creature out there that allows for the miracle of our spell craft?"

"You are drinking too much of your ensorcelled wine, my friend. Soon you will tell me you are marrying a stick thin woman without breeding hips. When are you having a child? Tell me of your apprentice. Does he progress as you would like? Is he still alive, unlike many of your others?" Belyakov provoked.

"Funny, you old bastard. It's times like these I recall why I don't ring you more often. But I still miss some of my former students dearly. Yes, Abraham is still alive, and he's doing as well as you would imagine in a world gone cold. I find him refreshing. His youth reminds me of my insolence and wonder. Having him around is akin to pulling out my fingernails at times, but I do love him so."

"You are foolish to try and teach magic to this generation, Doyle. No honor or work ethic, just video games and internet sex videos. You waste your time. Focus on keeping yourself alive another decade, that is what is important for you now, "the Russian chastised.

"I love magic far too much to let mine die with me. If all he manages is a single spell, I'll consider my efforts to teach him to be worthwhile."

"You're a strange man, Doyle." The aged Brit heard the Russian sip heavily from a drink. He wondered if it was a life-extending brew like his own.

"We live in a strange world, Belyakov. Watch the news; talk to our old friends. Something is very much important about this Tesser, the so-called dragon man. I'd wager that he does something very noteworthy soon. I don't want us all taken by surprise like Iran in '67. Or Peoria in '82."

"No, we wouldn't want that. I'll keep my ear to the ground for you friend. It is good to hear your voice again. Be wise. Da Sveedaneeya."

"It is good to talk to you as well. Until we speak again, old friend." Mr. Doyle hung up the phone with a sad smile and picked up his enchanted wine glass once more. He assessed the level of shake in his hands and reminisced as he swirled the wine.

I'll be dead soon if something doesn't change.

He took a long tug from the rich wine in the glass and set it down on the heavy desk. The life-extending tingle on his tongue was miserably faint. He reached for the phone once more and recalled the number of his old friend in Romania.

If dhampyrs are coming back, I want to know more – and for this, there is no time for a letter.

Chapter Twenty-Five

Tesser

Try as hard as he might, Tesser couldn't clear his mind of Matilde. Matty. He sat down the world almanac he was reading and let his mind wander.

Such a beautiful creature. Soft skin, intense eyes. And her scent. I know it from somewhere. Why can I not place it? Ahhh, she antagonizes me.

"Man, I feel like a million bucks, Tesser. Alexis is one hot woman. I do not know how you did it, but Tesser, you're the fucking man. Best wingman ever. Must be because you're a dragon, right? Get it? Wingman? Dragon?" Abe quipped. He collapsed happily into the luxurious couch in the lower sitting room of Mr. Doyle's opulent home.

Tesser smiled at his friend. *It is good to give you confidence, Abe. You are a beacon that is as yet unlit.*

"I'm glad."

"You're glad? I'm fucking ecstatic. I went back to her place, Tesser. Do you understand what that's like for a guy like me?"

"Language Abe, you wouldn't want Mr. Doyle to hear you." Tesser picked up the almanac once more.

"Ah, fuck him. I'm too happy still." Abe grabbed the

remote and popped the television on. The sounds of reality television and news that pleased no one flooded the room. Both men's eyes drifted up to the widescreen television and immediately became entranced.

I think the television is evil. "There is something strange with Matty," Tesser said before he realized it was a thought.

"Strange how? Dangerous strange? Or like, exotic and sexy strange?" Abe asked.

Tesser shook his head, unable to find the descriptive words needed. "She carries a scent. An old scent. She reminds me of snow, and running water, and long nights. I cannot place where it comes from, but it is familiar to me somehow. She perplexes me. It's going to drive me insane if I can't figure it out soon Abe."

"You're crushing on her *hard,* bro," Abe teased.

Tesser gave Abe a hurt look. "My feelings for the lady aside, there is something quite incredible about her. Something old. It could be important."

"Well, buddy, you should definitely stay in touch with her. If you're that interested in her scent, that is." Abe flipped the channel again. He found more news that depressed. "Does Alexis have a strange scent?"

"She smells of a woman about to pass her time of fertility. And I *am* that interested in Matty's scent. And I thank you for showing the appropriate level of concern over my challenged state regarding Matty. Typically when a dragon takes interest in something, it is worth putting some of your own time into that thing."

"You sound butt hurt, bro."

"You are taunting a dragon."

"I am taunting a man that says he is a dragon. There's a difference." Abe didn't even look over at Tesser. The magic of the television was in full effect.

"I could breathe fire on you and show you what's up."

Abe lolled his head to the side, completely unimpressed by the threat, "Whatever dude. Come at me, bro. Breathe away. Kill your wingman."

Tesser sighed. *I want to see Matty again. I should've gotten her phone number. I should get a phone too. I suppose that should come first.*

Chapter Twenty-Six

Alec Fitzgerald

Alec Fitzgerald sat in his corner office at the Amethyst Project facility. The office was lavishly appointed with mahogany bookcases, a desk to match, and plush leather chairs and couches. The rug was thick and felt pleasant under the shoe, and the large walls made of smoked glass looked out into the green suburbs of northern Massachusetts. If you looked high enough and the sky was clear, you could see deep into New Hampshire and see the White Mountains. The walls were covered with awards and plaques that showered praise on Alec's achievements in the biomedical field as well as with the word at large. He'd given hundreds of his own hours to charity and millions of dollars. Fitzgerald Industries was the model of what a good company should look like, and Alec himself was the model of what a good man should be. Alec was handsome, successful, philanthropic, witty, charming, and motivated. He was the full package. Some of his college friends from Yale used to call him that. The Full Package.

Alec was poring over a report that a close aide had handed to him earlier in the day. It was a short assessment of the amount of effort and energy it required to keep the purple dragon contained in the vault far below. It was staggering.

The electricity required to maintain the subterranean complex each month was over $75,000. Alec required a rotating staff of thirty-seven specialists with a combined monthly salary of just under $200,000. Maintenance on tubes, wiring, air conditioning, hermetic sealing, security weapons, cameras, and such was over $10,000 per month as well. The true monetary costs were hidden in the exotic cocktails that were pumped straight into the bloodstream and airway of the massive dragon. Some of them weren't commercially available anywhere and needed to be manufactured from scratch by other Fitzgerald industries companies. The legality of the powerful mixtures was dubious, but the FDA wasn't paying attention to the safety of drugs for dragons yet.

All told, it was costing Fitzgerald Industries nearly a million dollars a month to house the slumbering dragon. Alec and company had been doing this for almost a decade in this way. If Project Amethyst yielded the fruit he expected it to, he'd make that money back in year. There were other costs associated with keeping the dragon still, but that price had already been negotiated.

Alec sat the report down and spun in his chair, happy that everything was going according to his plan. *It pays to be King.*

The phone on his desk toned an internal call. Alec spun around again and looked at the name on the call. It was Samuel Host, his head of security.

This can't be good.

Alec snatched up the receiver, "Yes, Sam?"

Samuel's voice was low, and layered. He sounded like a three pack a day soldier that had seen it all and couldn't care less about what had happened to him. Samuel was the only person in the world Alec feared.

"The sniffers have picked up a strange alert on the first floor. Dragon scent."

Alec sat forward in his seat. "Someone trying to steal something from the vault again?"

"No. The sniffers caught the alert at the main entrance coming in." Samuel didn't sound alarmed despite the incredible strangeness of the situation.

"Wait, coming in? As if someone were bringing parts back in? How did they slip the parts out in the first place? Is the inventory accurate? Are we missing scales, or blood? Anything?"

"Inventories are tracking as accurate. There's something else."

Alec felt his temper start to flare. "What else?"

"It's a different signature."

"I'm sorry, signature? Speak science to me, Sam." Alec's heart was racing. He was getting furious.

Sam explained the matter flatly, "A different signature. A new signature. A new scent. A different dragon, Mr. Fitzgerald."

Alec's heart stopped beating and he was instantly covered in a cold sweat. *A different dragon? A second dragon? Here in the building? Here in America? This could be an incredible opportunity…* "Are you familiar with this dragon, Samuel? Are your…people familiar with it?"

"We had taken care of it, but it appears to have resurfaced, quite literally. This could be a significant issue."

Alec's blood slowly started to congeal inside his body. *A meddling dragon could be the end of me, the end of everything.* "Why didn't your people kill it?"

"Killing a dragon isn't the best idea, Mr. Fitzgerald. Our reports indicate that destroying one of them would cause…issues. It is better to incapacitate it if you have the means. We've explained this at length already. Should I forward the memo again?"

I don't even want to know what he means by that.

"The alert came from Matilde Rindahl," Samuel said.

"Matty? We had her vetted; she's clean as a whistle."

"Nonetheless, the alert came from her and continues to trigger in her office. Would you like us to speak with her?" Samuel sounded…blunt.

"No. Not yet. Put a tail on her. See where she goes and who she speaks with. I want to know everything about her from this point forward. What she eats, where she shits it. Tap everything she owns."

"We've already started the process. Mr. Fitzgerald, you realize I'm required to pass this along to my superiors?" Samuel spoke the words as a warning. A dark courtesy.

A bead of sweat ran down Alec's cheek despite the cool environment in the air-conditioned office.

Shit. "Of course, Mr. Host. Pass the information along. Assure your superiors all will be taken care of."

"I'll tell them you're working diligently on the issue." Samuel hung up.

On an impulse, Alec stood up and left his office.

*****

"Hey, Matty?" Alec asked from the hall.

"Yes, Alec? Matty replied. She was sitting at her office desk behind a pile of printouts. She had been combing data.

She looks great. Some color in her cheeks, a little bounce in her voice. I think she's working out – or giving herself dragon blood transfusions.

Alec seized a thought out of thin air, and started to speak it. "I was being a little nosy earlier today Matty, and I noticed that your name was at the top of the list of people printing hardcopy information out." The lie gave him reason enough to be in her office.

Matty looked guilty as her eyes drifted across the small mountain of computer reports. "Yeah, about that. I think I'm just more effective when I can spread papers across a desk in front of me. My eyes get really strained when I sit and stare at a monitor."

Alec nodded knowingly. "I understand completely. I guess I'd just ask you to be judicious in what you're printing. We already spend a small fortune on this project, and if we can shave even a few dollars a month off our budget it'll help the company in the long run."

"Alright, I'm sorry. I'll try to be a little more under control when I hit print from now on," Matty said sheepishly.

"No worries. How have you been by the way? You look great."

Matty's body perked up. "I'm doing wonderful Alec, thank you. Work is good, I'm very happy."

She's getting laid. That's what it is. Time to go for the throat.

"Are you seeing someone?" Alec teased playfully.

Matty responded less awkwardly than he'd imagined she would. "I may have seen someone. Nothing too serious. Is that a problem? I can assure you my private life won't interfere with my work responsibilities."

Alec made a grand apologetic gesture. "No, no, no. Nonsense, Matty. I wouldn't dare to tell you what to do with your love life. That's not the kind of company I run nor the environment I want to work in myself. I was just commenting because you look terrific, happy. I'm just being nosy and I took a stab in the dark. Truthfully, I was hoping you'd blush."

Now she blushed. "Okay, good. And uh, yeah I saw a guy; he's really sweet."

"Going to see him again?" Alec asked, playing the role of the supportive, platonic male friend. For every situation, a new face.

Matty shrugged hopefully. "I'd like to. But I didn't get his number. I think I could get it through a friend, though."

"Well, if seeing him makes you look as happy as you look right now, I think getting his number is a smart move."

Matty looked up at the office tile ceiling and spun in her chair, daydreaming. She looked like a teenage girl lying in a summer hammock, staring at the clouds, and thinking of a boy.

"Take care, Matty. Watch out for those print outs, please."

"I will Alec; sorry for the bother."

Alec smiled in his charming way. "It's no bother. It's always nice to see your face. Keep up the good work. You're appreciated around here."

"Thanks!"

Alec left her doorway and strode down the hall. He fished a secure, encrypted office portable phone from his slacks pocket and dialed Sam Host's number. The solemn guard answered on one ring.

"Host."

"Samuel, I spoke with Matty. She's seeing someone. I'd bet the comatose dragon in my basement she's getting that scent from him. That's the new variable in her life. Home in on that. That's the key."

"As you wish." Samuel hung up.

Fuck yes. Another dragon. Of course, that'd mean he'd be pushing for more…outside support, but in the quest to better humanity and make a fortune in the process, you need to make compromises. Big ones. But that means dragons could take the form of people… How is that even possible? If they can shape shift, I wonder if we could extract that quality and synthesize it for plastic surgeons?

Alec strode towards the elevator and attempted to hide his excitement. A second dragon could mean untold riches and leaps forward in medicine and science. It was a delicious thought.

Chapter Twenty-Seven

Sgt. Henry Spooner

Spoon had gotten into the habit of having his M4 in the front of his unmarked cruiser. It rested on the floor in front of the passenger seat just under his unworn sports jacket. It was against department policy and could get him fired if he was caught with it as such. He kept a loaded magazine in the weapon, but no round in the chamber.

It was irrational how he felt, and he knew it. His behavior was illegal and more than a little crazy.

I am scared, and I don't know why. I haven't been this nervous since my first deployment. I am a combat veteran and an experienced Massachusetts State Trooper. I have been shot at, bombed, flown in planes and helicopters into combat, arrested armed felons, and I've been through some shit. I am analytical, and rational, and here I am, sitting in my cruiser staring at an expensive home in the Back Bay; I'm waiting for either of two strange young men or one old man to come out for very little valid police reason because I'm fairly sure one of them is possessed by the Devil. Or something worse. I've lost my shit.

Spoon downed a mouthful of Dunkin's. On the seat perched above the M4 was a full Box o' Joe and a bag of sugar and creamers, all strictly for his own use. It was midday, and the last of the summer city heat was fading away. Spoon had his cruiser's window down and was letting the fresh air in to cool off. The back of his dress shirt was slick with sweat from the late summer sun.

Spoon had been led to the massive brown brick home in the upper crust neighborhood of Boston by the young man he had seen in the alley with Tesser the night of the strange occurrence. Spoon had seen him wandering in the Back Bay near the Berklee College of Music and tailed him to the fancy home here. He'd seemed ordinary as he walked, giving away none of the strange power Spoon felt he possessed. *Knew* he possessed.

Commoveo.

I'll never forget that word. I know what happened in that alley was supernatural. I know it. I could feel it in my bones, in the pit of my stomach. I still feel it even now, weeks later. I checked that damn alley out for hours. Four times now at different times of the day, in different kinds of weather, and not once has the wind swirled the way it did when those two were there. Not once did it feel the same as when those two were there. Maybe it's that sixth sense they say cops have? Maybe I'm tapping into a subconscious awareness of God or the Devil? It's like a compulsion I can't shake.

And where the FUCK did that tree come from?

A strange looking birch tree had appeared in the front yard of the brownstone where Tesser and the young man had been living together. It was weird enough that after the alley confrontation where the debris flew about as if possessed, the two had simply moved in together as if all were utterly and completely mundane and normal. And then suddenly, the tree appeared. Fully grown, overnight. No gardening crew brought it there, no grounds workers dug the hole and planted it, and the two younger men acted as if it had been there all along. The older man, however, he seemed to act somewhere between scared and excited that the tree had appeared.

He looked surprised by it. And I'll be damned, but I think he talks to it.

The old man, who appeared a little worse off each time he stepped out of the home, often sat on the stoop when the two other men had left and gazed at the tree as if he had no idea what to make of it. When he took a seat at the top of his fancy stone stairs he would sip at a fine china cup of what Spoon guessed to be Earl Grey tea, and he'd mutter to himself and look to the tree for answers. Sometimes the old man would respond as if the tree was talking back.

Of course, when I tried to walk by innocently he stopped talking to the tree. Strange thing that was. A crazy person wouldn't stop taking to his friend, the tree. A sane person with something to hide goes silent. What weirds me out even worse than an old man talking to a tree that apparently teleported into his yard, is that it wouldn't strike me off in the least if the fucking tree was talking back to him. What passes for weird in my imagination lately is starting to alarm me.

The tree had no leaves, but they were appearing haphazardly and fully grown every day. No buds had started, just fully grown leaves appearing on branches overnight. It was as if the impending autumn had come early and in reverse.

Such weird shit is going on. And who the hell is this Doyle character? Sketchy old fuck.

The old man had been easy to investigate. With an address in hand, finding out the owner of the home had been basic investigation. A Mister Mycroft Rupert Doyle was the owner of the home. Originally a British citizen according to some ICE records he dredged up, he came over to the States sometime in the late 1940's a few years after the end of the Second World War. That's when things went amiss.

The math doesn't add up on this guy. If he came over as a young man in the 1940's, and he was of an age where he could buy a house at that time, that'd put him at well over 90 years of age. He looks like he's getting up there, but he can't be over

70. It doesn't add up at all. Doesn't pass the sniff test.

Spoon finished his paper cup of coffee and poured another from the spout in the box.

My Captain thinks I'm sitting here in the hopes that I'll find the second attempted rape suspect. I sold him on the idea that Tesser might be tracked down by the guy and that I wanted to tail him until I felt he was safe. Of course, now all I want to do is figure out what the hell happened in that damned alley. The rapist…to hell with him. He learned his lesson. So did his pal. Tesser was all the justice those two pricks needed. All I want to know now is what the hell is up with these people. Are they dangerous? I can't put my finger on the truth of it all.

Not yet.

Spoon's department phone rang. He picked it up off the seat from its hiding spot under the box of coffee and looked at it. He couldn't tell who was calling inside the department, but he knew it wasn't from his district. He answered it.

"Sergeant Spooner."

"Henry. Hey, buddy, it's Paul. How you been?"

Paul. The SWAT officer Spoon had been with in that Dorchester raid. That seemed like forever ago. "Paul, man I'm good. Busy trying to track down my errant alleyway pervert. When these pricks go to ground they go deep my friend."

"No doubt brother, but hey, they gotta come up for air sometime, right? Speaking of which, I got a guy who just walked in here at D4 on Harrison saying he's your man. Turned his own ass in. Guilt is just tearing this prick up. He matches the video frame we've got on him. You should probably come over. He hasn't lawyered up yet, says he wants to confess. Figured I'd call you direct."

Fuck me in the ass. Shit. "Yeah, buddy that's great news. I'm on a stakeout not too far from there. Gimme an hour or two. Give him a cup of shitty department coffee, a roll of BPD sandpaper, and watch him get the shits. That'll keep him busy 'til I get there."

Paul laughed. "For sure, buddy. Congrats on the close. See you soon."

"You bet." Spoon hung up the phone and immediately started hammering away at the steering wheel of his department car with his fist. He pounded on it until his hands hurt.

"Fuck!" He roared into the air, startling some birds and a few people walking by on the sidewalk nearby. "Sorry, bit my tongue," Spoon said out the car door. They gave him a conciliatory face and kept walking. Everyone knew the pain of a bitten tongue. It created immediate sympathy and frequently led to a quick dismissal. He'd used that excuse several times in the past to encourage strangers to overlook a slip in language. Spoon backhanded the headrest of the passenger seat a few times for good measure once they were out of earshot.

This fucks everything up, closed case or not. A walk in suspect doesn't make me look like a good cop. But I'll take the closed case. I'll need another reason to keep an eye on this house, though. Something legit. Maybe I can turn the Captain onto Tesser as a suspect in something. But shit, he seems like a decent person. Ah fuck, I can't do that. What the hell am I doing?

Spoon backhanded the headrest once more and heard something crack inside the seat. He downed his fresh, still-too-hot cup of coffee and tossed the empty paper receptacle out the window, his mouth and throat burning. Littering in the rich neighborhood made him feel better. Spoon started the cruiser and slid the shifter into drive. He pulled out into the street and made his way towards Harrison where the District Four headquarters was.

I'll need to stow the M4 away in the trunk before I get there. I don't need that kind of shit.

Chapter Twenty-Eight

Matty Rindahl

Matty was driving to work. It was getting towards the latter half of September.

Cowardice is a terrible thing. Matty had picked up her phone ten times a week for three weeks since the night she'd had with Tesser, each time bringing up the dialer and each time not having the courage to hit 'call.' Of course, she wasn't even calling Tesser. She didn't have his number. She was only attempting to call Alexis.

Because Alexis was still seeing Abe, and Abe could get in touch with Tesser.

But calling Alexis meant having to *tell* Alexis that she liked Tesser enough that she needed Abe's number. And, of course, getting Abe's number meant she'd then have to call Abe (which, in and of itself was tantamount to climbing Mt. Everest) and then having to ask dear Abe for Tesser.

And sweet, baby Jesus, that would mean having to talk to Tesser himself. Matty couldn't even imagine a scenario where that conversation went well for her.

Hello, Tesser. I just wanted to call and tell you that I haven't really stopped thinking about you, and how I really enjoyed our sex, and that it was pretty much life changing, and how I haven't stopped thinking about you, and how I really wish I'd gotten your last name because it's really hard for me to imagine us married when I don't know your last name, and how I still have that song stuck in my head from the club when you leaned in and we kissed and how I want your babies but I can't have babies, and how much I missed you, and I was wondering what you were doing this weekend because I think you should take me out for a cup of coffee, or tea or a scone, or whatever it is I can ask you to take me out for because I really want to see you again, and I'm not sure I'll ever build up the courage to ask anyone else to kiss me.

Ever again.

Matty knew why she was scared to call. Being vulnerable wasn't her strong suit. Neither was taking big risks.

She parked her car in the parking spot that had her employee number on it and locked the door with her key fob as she walked to the building. The day was beautiful. Cool crisp skies and a gentle early autumn breeze had cut away the humidity that had plagued the New England summer. The sun had toned down its assault on Matty's skin as well, and she walked into work with a forced bounce in her step. *Fake it 'til you make it, as Alexis would say.*

She pulled open the glass doors of the main building and passed through the security corridor. Going to work here was like traveling on an airplane, only worse. Shoes came off, jackets came off, and everything passed through an X-ray detector. The security personnel all carried pistols, wore bulletproof vests, and looked like soulless automatons. It was worse trying to leave work. No one wanted to bring anything in, so they focused on people trying to bring things out. Everyone was subject to search at any time. It was part of your lengthy employment contract.

The nameless security officer who intently looked at the out-of-sight x-ray screen paid her no attention. She might've been the President or a dancing clown, but he didn't care. His sole concern was her briefcase and her laptop. The armed guard awaiting her at the end of the metal detectors wanded the areas where she was wearing metal, and after making a sour face at her for wearing a belt with a metal buckle, he allowed her to gather her things and head to her office.

Matty rounded the corner and was taken by surprise by the sight of three people standing in the hall. Alec, the handsome man who ran the company she worked for, a lab technician, and one of the more high-ranking security officers stood outside her office door. They looked at her, and as soon as she saw their faces she knew they were specifically waiting for her. The security guy gave her the creeps with his chromed pistol bulging from the holster at his hip.

"Matty. So nice to see you this morning," Alec said.

I don't like the way he said that. "Hi, Alec. What can I help you with this morning?" Matty tried a smile.

"Let's step into your office for a second and chat. There's something we need your help with." Alec gestured at her doorway, and Matty entered. All three of the others followed her in.

I'm nervous. Like, really nervous.

Alec sat down. "Matty, there's something that's been going on of late and it has a few of us just a little confused and a lot concerned."

"Okay. I'm to assume it has something to do with me?" Matty powered on her desktop machine and sat down her brown bag lunch as the computer started to hum to life. She gauged the odd lab technician standing in the corner. Matty noticed the ends of a stethoscope sticking out of a deep pocket in his white lab coat.

He isn't a lab nerd. He's a fucking medical guy.

"Well, we think so, but it's complicated. One of the things about the Amethyst building Matty is the security. We check everything going in as well as out, right?"

Matty was instantly defiant. "Do you think I've stolen something? Because I haven't."

Alec put on a charming face that she immediately knew was designed to disarm her. "Well, at first we thought you'd stolen something, but the evidence points out you haven't. We've been keeping an eye on the security data for about three weeks, and we're confident now that you're not a thief. In fact, the sniffers are indicating that you might be bringing in something new to the facility. Something next-gen we need to investigate further. Something that we need to rule out quickly."

"Next-gen? Sniffers?" Matty felt turmoil in the pit of her stomach. It wasn't a new feeling. She'd had the bubble guts since she saw Tesser.

"We've got security devices that can smell the air placed all over the building. If someone tries to bring out a piece of miss purple downstairs the sniffers will alarm and we'll know about it. Matty, you're triggering the sniffers on the way in, not the way out. This is very, very interesting to us. Even more eye brow raising Miss Rindahl, is that the sniffers are reporting a larger trigger from you as time goes on. We think there might be something wrong with you. Some kind of reaction to the presence of the dragon. Perhaps some kind of growth. Or at the very least, something interesting happening with your biology. We'd like to run some basic medical screens on you to make sure everything is alright."

Matty was worried. *What could be wrong with me?* "Growth? You mean like a tumor?"

"It's hard to say, Matty. We've never seen this kind of thing outside of testing with direct applications, or infusions of dragon tissues, or derivatives of dragon tissues. It doesn't make sense that you're sick, but all the signs point to you being in a very precarious situation. I don't think I need to remind you that your employment contract requires you to submit to a medical examination in the event of a contamination event?"

Matty felt sick. Really sick. "Of course, I guess. When? Now?"

Alec nodded. "Time is a factor, yes. Ron here, sorry, Doctor Wooster, is a company doctor that we keep in our employ for internal medical issues just like this. He takes care of my personal needs, and I trust him implicitly. He's got an office on the third floor and if you're okay with it, I'd like you and Ron—sorry, Ron—Doctor Wooster, to spend some time together trying to get to the bottom of this. For your safety and for everyone else's safety."

Matty stood without even thinking about it. Bile churned in the pit of her stomach. It hurt.

"Matty, if you will, come with me," the doctor said.

She let him lead her out of the office, leaving the security officer behind.

I wonder what would've happened if I said I only wanted to see an outside doctor? I bet that's why that creepy fuck with the shiny pistol was there.

*****

The medical exam had been extensive, but Doctor Ron Wooster had been great. That almost made it worse. He was gentle, caring, and clearly genuinely concerned for her well-being. He even made some jokes that were well timed and helped to break the tension of the moment. There were x-rays, blood draws, mouth swabs, and more. Near lunch time Matty was able to return to her office.

She didn't even bother to sit down at her desk, she just scooped up her purse and went out for a sandwich. She'd forgotten to put the lunch she'd brought that morning in the refrigerator in the break room, and it had gone bad. At the sandwich shop down the street she ordered a turkey with

Muenster, topped with romaine lettuce, and honey

mustard. It was her favorite sandwich.

She ate it emotionlessly at her desk. The normally bright flavors felt numb in her mouth and made her stomach churn again. There was no escape from the anxiety. When she finished, she spun her chair to face her monitor and keyboard and fired up her actual work.

If I look at the bright side of this, I haven't thought of Tesser at all today.

Her phone rang, jolting her. She answered it.

"Hey, Matty, this is Ron upstairs. How are you doing?"

He sounded pleasant. Matty was starting to be thankful he'd made the whole exam process easy. "I'm okay, all things considered. You have more questions for me, doctor?"

"Yeah, actually. I wanted you to know your blood numbers are great, as are your urine numbers. Great news is that if we did random drug testing, you'd ace it," he said with a laugh.

Matty knew he was trying and forced a small laugh. "Thanks. I think all that proves is that I lead a boring life. What question do you have?"

"Not that boring a life, Miss Rindahl. I was wondering when your next ob-gyn appointment was? And are you taking prenatal vitamins yet?"

Matty nearly dropped her phone. *The fuck?* "What? I'm sorry?"

There was an awkward pause. "I uh...Were you aware that you're probably pregnant? I say probably and mean definitely. All your screens are showing positive. Have you had an ultrasound yet? Gosh, I'm sorry Matty, I thought you might've known and just kept it quiet."

Matty's heart started to race. "I can't be pregnant. I had a miscarriage. A bad one. My doctors told me that I'd never be able to have a baby again. I can't be. I can't be pregnant."

"Have you had some stomach issues the past few

weeks?"

That's nerves. And I'm not eating well. "A little."

"Mostly in the morning?"

Fuck. Shit. "Sometimes."

"Are you late for Aunt Flo?"

"I'm frequently late. I used to take birth control just to regulate when my period came. I think I'm okay, though. Not too late." *Doctor Ron is starting to piss me off.*

"Well, Matty, I highly suggest you avoid alcohol and smoking and get yourself an appointment to get it checked out by a specialist. I'm wondering if Mr. Fitzgerald's equipment is getting a false flag because your hormones have changed noticeably."

"Yeah, maybe," Matty said lifelessly.

"Well, hey, exciting right! Turn that frown upside down! Go call your boyfriend and have a large glass of grape juice tonight and figure out the next step. If anything else comes up, I'll give you a call."

Matty nodded, and realized she had to say something for him to go. "Okay thanks." Then she hung up.

Matty looked at the inanimate phone as if it were a cobra coiled and ready for the kill. Touching it or even moving an inch could be lethal. But now it needed to be done. She picked it up and dialed a specific number at the Boston office. Alexis answered.

"Alexis here." She was chewing on some food. She was eating her lunch. Matty wondered if it was take-out.

"Hi, Alexis. It's Matty." Matty couldn't hide the anxiety in her voice.

"What's wrong? Did a man treat you wrong? You sound pissed." Matty imagined Alexis sitting forward in her office chair, ready to bite someone's head off.

"No, not really. Do you have Abe's number? I need to get in touch with Tesser." Matty grabbed her small Hello Kitty notepad and a pen.

"Yeah, baby, hold on." Alexis put her on hold for nearly a minute, and returned. "Got a pen?"

Matty said yes, and Alexis gave her a local Boston number. "Thanks, Alexis. I really appreciate it."

"Did he hurt you? Do I need to talk to Abe? You know Abe says Tesser still wants to see you. Talks about you all the time."

I don't know what to make of that. "Well, good, because I'm calling him."

"Alright babe. Keep me in the loop? Work going okay over there in Area 51?"

"Of course I will. Work is fine, thanks. Sorry I haven't been in touch much lately. I've been sort of scared to take the next step."

"I figured. Good luck, hun. He's a catch. I think."

"Yeah, he seems that way."

They ended the call with a pair of goodbyes.

Matty dialed the number that would put her in touch with Abe.

Far down below her office in the bowels of the underground facility that surrounded the vault containing the purple dragon, Mr. Host sat in his own office. It was the nerve center of the entire security complex.

He'd heard the entire conversation. He smiled.

Something else in the room smiled with him.

Chapter Twenty-Nine
Tesser

Matty wanted to meet Tesser again. This made Tesser quite happy.

That is such good news.

They had very briefly chatted on the phone a few nights before and agreed on a neutral location during the day. Both drank coffee, so they met at a Starbucks in Medford, just off the Orange Line.

Tesser was late to the meeting, and Matty was already sitting, both hands wrapped around a latte. The shop smelled of roasted coffee and baked goods. It was slightly cool outside, and she was wearing a thin sweater under a fleece jacket.

She looks pretty.

"I'm going to get a coffee, can I get you anything?" Tesser asked her when he entered the franchise and walked to her table. *Now she looks irritated.*

Tesser waited patiently in line and bought his own coffee. *I'm surprisingly nervous right now. I can't recall how long it's been since I've befriended a woman who had me this interested in her. Humans are much more complex than I ever imagined them to be. Matty also; she's special. That scent, and there's just something about her. I wonder where this will go?*

Tesser sat down. "I'm glad you called."

Matty didn't look up from the lid of her coffee. "There's something serious we need to talk about."

Tesser frowned. "Serious good or serious bad?"

"Depends on how you look at it." Matty sipped her latte and then set it down. "I'm not entirely sure myself."

She looks like she's unsure if she should be drinking it.

"I don't know how to say this without being super blunt, so I'll cough it out so we can cut to the quick. Tesser, when we had sex the other night you got me pregnant."

Tesser beamed instantly. "That's terrific!" He said in an exuberant tone. Several people in the coffee shop looked over, and smiled. Tesser's mood was infectious.

"Yeah, here's the thing Tesser. We used a condom, and I've been unable to have a baby for a fair bit of time now. I don't know how this happened."

*She looks unhappy. Does she not want my bab*y? "Well, I had an orgasm inside you Matty. It's pretty basic mammalian biology."

Matty looked up, anger flaring in her face. "I know that, you jackass," she whispered. "But the condom is like 99.9% effective at catching sperm, and if you didn't hear me, I am INFERTILE."

Tesser sat back, unsure of how to handle the situation. Human women experienced incredible swings in hormones during pregnancy. Perhaps that was the cause. "Well, Matty, I can't be certain, but when I discarded the rubber thing you put on my penis I think it might've been broken. In fact, I'm fairly certain of it."

Matty's face retained all the anger and added a flush red color that looked unhealthy. "And you didn't think to tell me the condom broke? You're fucking with my LIFE, Tesser. This shit isn't funny."

Tesser shook his hands apologetically. "I'm sorry, Matty, I didn't think anything of it. I've never used one before and I wasn't aware that they weren't supposed to break. I didn't know anything was wrong, and in my own defense, you didn't speak up either. And I'm sorry, very sorry, but you are at no risk of anything from me. Well, save pregnancy."

Her eyes were getting wider. Pretty clearly everything he'd just said was very much the wrong thing to say. "Tesser, how the hell do I know that you aren't HIV positive? Or have the Hep?"

"Because I can't get sick." Tesser said it so plainly it was almost laughable. It was the words of the young child who still thinks they are invulnerable. This, however, was the truth.

"You can't get sick?"

Tesser shook his head. "I can't get sick. Literally. I've never been ill in my entire life. It's impossible."

Matty shook her head and downed a gulp of the latte. She thought on it as she looked into his golden eyes. "For whatever frigging reason, I believe you."

"You should. I'm telling the truth." Tesser sipped on his latte. It was still very hot.

"Look, I'm sorry I'm so angry, but this was a gigantic, enormous clusterfuck surprise. I found out at work, and I've only known a couple days, and you and I are so new, and I have no idea where this relationship is going or if I want to keep this baby, or if you're going to be in its life if I even decide to keep it. I'm completely overwhelmed. Plus, holy shit, I can't stop thinking about my ex all of a sudden. He and I broke off our engagement because I couldn't get pregnant anymore, and here I am, bing bam boom, knocked the hell up. I feel like an ass. Or worse, a whore."

Keep the baby? "I'm sorry, Matty. I think this can be attributed to my…I guess we can call it my nature. I'm quite fertile you see. Super sperm."

Matty looked at him strangely, confused and amused. "Super sperm, huh? That figures. 400cc's of Nitrous Oxide and jizz?"

The dragon-man grinned. "Something like that. Fast and furious. Matty, you mentioned something about keeping the baby? What do you mean? Do you intend to give it away?"

Matty looked at Tesser and assessed his expression, gauging him. *She's not sure how to answer me.*

"I can't be a single mother, Tesser. I've too much on my plate, and I'm still not nearly ready to be a mom. I collect Lego minifigures and Doctor Who memorabilia. You know how many sonic screwdrivers I own? I like to stay up late watching bad horror movies, eating microwave kettle popcorn, and drinking spiked hot chocolates. I don't know if I want to keep the baby or even go through a pregnancy. I might want to abort it."

Something odd caught Tesser's nose and he froze, Matty's words suddenly lost. *What is that smell? Something incredibly powerful. Something old. He* leaned in and smelled Matty; it seemed to be coming from her. *She smells…something like me. Maybe it's the child inside her? I should be less paranoid.*

"You done being a fucking weirdo?"

"I'm sorry?"

"Sniffing me? You just gave me the up and down with your nose like you were a Lab at the shitting park looking at buttholes."

Tesser laughed. "You are so eloquent."

"Another reason for my hesitation in being a mom. Are you in or are you out, pretty boy? If I keep this kid, are you with me? I need to know."

"I would want you to keep it. Carry it to term. If you wish to give it away, I would ask that you give it to me so I may raise it. Typically I don't stick around with the mother, but if you want me to, I will."

"Wait, typically? What the fuck does typically mean? Am I not the first woman you've knocked up? Matty's face started to turn that scary shade of red again.

Shit. "Well, I'm quite older than I look Matty. And as I

said, I'm very virile. Very fertile. More than you can imagine. There have been...many conceptions in the past. Super sperm, remember?" *Shit.* "It was all in the name of good. In the name of life." *Shit that didn't make it any better.*

"How many?" She growled.

Dammit. "I don't know. More than I can remember if you want me to be honest."

"More than you can remember like five? Or more than you can remember like ten?" Matty's knuckles were turning white she was making such tight fists.

"If you count different species, the number could be in the millions." Tesser said before thinking. *This is going very badly.*

Matty picked up her latte calmly, removed the lid, took a tiny sip, and threw the coffee in Tesser's face. He probably could've dodged it, or most of it, but sometimes you just have to take your licks.

"You're a fucking pig. That's either the worst joke you could've possibly told me or you're the worst human being in the history of mankind. Either way, I want nothing to do with you. I never want to talk to you again."

"Matty you don't understand," Tesser said, wiping the pumpkin flavored drink from his eyes. "I'm a-"

"I don't UNDERSTAND?!" She screamed in the coffee shop, drawing the attention of workers and patrons alike. She stood. "I don't understand why you'd joke about fucking more women than you can remember and maybe some animals too? You're an insensitive asshole at best you *dick.* And at worst, you're a whore that fucks animals. Let the bitches in this city salivate over you. You're an asshole and a nut job to boot. Another pretty faced psycho. Go fuck yourself Gold-eyes!" Matty walked out, slamming the glass door behind her.

Tesser sat in his metal chair alone at the table, pumpkin flavored latte running down his shirt and pooling in his crotch. The rest of the shop's customers watched him with a mixture of sadness and revulsion. One younger man in the corner saw the humor in it and was laughing quietly.

At least someone appreciates a good embarrassing. Tesser walked over to the counter and grabbed some napkins. Even though his pride had taken a hit, he was still going to clean up after Matty's explosion. It wasn't fair that the Starbucks people should have to clean up his mess. He was already thinking of what to say to her to explain the situation, when a woman winked and left her business card for him in a dry spot on the table.

Sometimes I hate being what I am. I'm going to need help on this one.

Chapter Thirty

Alec Fitzgerald

Alec Fitzgerald sat in his office. It was long after the end of business hours, and the only light in the room came from a small banker's desk lamp. The green glass shade tinted the light and cast an odd pallor in his massive corner office. Alec was nervous. His heart pounded.

I need to know. Where the fuck is Mr. Host and his motley crew of creeps anyway?

A knock on his door startled him. He cleared his throat and sat up in his leather chair. "Come in." Only a small number of people knew Alec was still in his office, and none would dare to knock before calling other than Mr. Host.

The wide panel door swung in and Mr. Host came through. He had another man on his heels. Both men had that air of military service to them. Alec recognized the other man as one of Mr. Host's closest security officers. He had the same vacant, menacing look to him, though he was much younger in an indescribable way than the leader of Alec's security force. In truth, the two men shared many of the same features. They could've been distant family. The younger guard carried a briefcase.

After shutting the door, the two men approached Alec's desk.

Why am I so scared? Oh, that's right, because I know what these men are capable of.

"Mr. Fitzgerald," Mr. Host said flatly. There was no charisma or familiarity to his greeting. They might as well have been total strangers instead of employer and employee. Of course, that wasn't their real relationship either.

"Mr. Host. I hope you and your man bring me good tidings. It's awfully late."

The younger man sat the briefcase down on the corner of Alec's desk. Had an ordinary run of the mill employee done the same Alec would've reprimanded him, but this was one of Mr. Host's men. You didn't reprimand them. They only listened to Mr. Host.

"Indeed. Mr. Tracker was able to follow Miss Rindahl to her meeting with the man named Tesser successfully."

Alec sat forward, thrilled. "And? Were we able to get proper surveillance? Usable data?"

The younger man, cleverly named Mr. Tracker according to what Mr. Host had said, opened the briefcase quickly and produced a small digital voice recorder. With pale yet strong hands he sat the recorder down and pressed play. The entire exchange between Matty and this Tesser character electronically regurgitated out for all three men to hear. By the end of it Alec was laughing. It was funny shit.

"Fantastic. So he's definitely the father, that's great news."

"Before we continue, you should turn on your computer and search something," Mr. Host said.

Alec turned and wiggled his mouse. His screen came to life and he quickly opened a browser window. "What am I searching?"

"Naked vigilante hobo."

Are you shitting me? How did you say that with a straight

face? "I'm sorry?"

"Search naked vigilante hobo. There will be a security camera video. Load the version that has fifty thousand views."

Alec lifted his eyebrows skeptically and typed in the strange search. Mr. Host was right; several hits on YouTube came up of a black and white video. Alec hit play on the one with the most views and watched as a strangely perfect man came to the aid of a woman who looked to be in a bad situation. The naked Adonis wrecked one man as if it were child's play before the other ran off. Alec watched the video several times, noting the strange glint coming off the eyes of the person.

"What is up with his eyes? They look reflective, like a cat's or something?"

"They appear to be gold to some. Those that are touched with a bit of...specialness."

Alec leaned back, "Specialness?"

"Special in the way that the dragon below us is special. Special in the same way all the other things your family has discovered and taken advantage of are."

"Special like you and, Mr. Tracker?"

Mr. Host nodded ever so slightly. "Yes."

I'm not special. Alec fumed, but choked down his jealousy. It wasn't his lot to be like that. It was his job to walk the line between the two realities of the world. To try and be more than half in either world invited something worse than danger.

"Were we able to confirm that this Tesser character is a dragon?" Alec asked.

Mr. Tracker nodded wordlessly and spun the briefcase to face Alec. He lifted the lid and revealed a startling, fleshy mass within. It was plugged into a tangle of colored wires that led to what appeared to be a battery, several microprocessors, and a small LED screen. A small hole in the briefcase was linked to a tube and a fan, creating a vacuum of sorts. The mess gave off a faint odor of blood, decay, and mucus.

"What the hell is that thing?" Alec asked, leaning away.

"One of your secret projects, Mr. Fitzgerald. We removed one of the dragon's olfactory systems a few years ago. We were able to sustain it outside the creature's body in the lab and were able to run a multitude of tests to determine electrical olfactory responses to stimuli. Your programmers were then able to write a code that told us what the dragon's nose was smelling. This is the current iteration of the system. A portable, refined version of the sniffers we have been using around the facility since the building opened."

"That's goddamn fascinating. Is this marketable? Can it smell drugs or bombs accurately?"

Mr. Host simply looked at Alec in response. He was devoid of emotion or decision on the question, and Alec let his question die in the air.

"The sniffer confirmed that Tesser, who is the man in the security camera footage you just watched, as well as the father of Miss Rindahl's baby, is indeed a dragon. He appears to have shifted into the form of a human being. We believe he has done this to blend in. To learn."

"Holy shit, a shape shifting dragon? The applications are endless. His cellular makeup and DNA must be absolutely off the charts. Can the purple dragon change shape? We never saw her do it."

"The purple dragon is likely able to, though our... sedation techniques are powerful enough to prevent a change."

"Thank God for that. So what now? You go and grab him? Is that even possible? Can you do to him what you did to Purple downstairs? Are we going to need another facility for him?"

"Containment and apprehension of the Tesser is possible, though it might be a destructive event. He is a different animal than the purple dragon. More destructive if push came to shove. More importantly, and certainly less dangerously however, is the unborn child your employee carries."

Alec rolled his eyes in amazement. "Dear me, yes. When Matty comes into work we need to put her on quarantine. That's not in the employee contract, but she'll understand. For the sake of the baby and all that."

"We feel that her retrieval cannot wait," Mr. Host said with finality.

Alec swallowed nervously. Mr. Host's feelings weren't shared with the intention of seeming like advice or the asking of permission. "Okay. I'll send a car to go get her."

"I've already sent a team. They should be there momentarily."

"A team? Is it just me or are we at that 'point of no return here?' We're about to kidnap a pregnant woman because she's carrying the baby of a rogue dragon. If this gets out, Fitzgerald Industries is done. You realize that, right?"

"Your father did things far more risqué than this, Mr. Fitzgerald. The bold control the future. The bold change the world. Are you bold, Mr. Fitzgerald?"

Alec thought of his father. He wanted the company to be ten times what his father left him. His ambition burned in his chest unending. Never satisfied. It was the curse of being a Fitzgerald. You could never be satisfied, not fully. "Grab her. Please be careful though. We can figure it out later, I suppose."

"Agreed. Once the woman is safely below in a secure room, we will consider going after Tesser."

"You know where he lives?"

"My associate, Mr. Follower, was able to…follow Tesser to a home in the Back Bay. He's currently under observation."

"Mr. Tracker? Mr. Follower? Names regardless, you really have your shit together, Mr. Host. I'm halfway between horrified and impressed."

"An accurate assessment of the emotions we frequently inspire, Mr. Fitzgerald," Mr. Host said as Mr. Tracker shut the briefcase and removed it from the desk. The strange younger man had still not said a word.

"We?"

"We indeed. I will advise you when Miss Rindahl is in our custody. We will then move on the Tesser. Get some rest in the meantime. You will be very busy once we have her and the dragon in our possession. The leaps in science that will be at your fingertips will make all this unpleasantness seem idle. I would contact your human resources department and tell them to begin interviewing for more staff." Mr. Host and Mr. Tracker didn't wait for Alec's response. They simply walked away and left the office with a quiet click of the door lock.

What am I doing? Alec turned and grabbed a crystal decanter filled with very expensive scotch and poured a tall drink. *Mr. Host and his men aren't covered by my human resources department. Weird that they are all contactors. Why does that thought frighten me so goddamn much?*

His hand shook as he drank.

Chapter Thirty-One

Matty

Matty sat alone in her apartment at the kitchen table. It was late in the evening after her tragic meeting with Tesser at the coffee shop, the father of her freshly conceived child. Her chair was pulled out on nearly the very spot where her underwear had hit the floor the night she'd conceived the tiny baby growing inside her. One of Matty's hands drifted down into her lap to press against her still flat belly. There was no movement to feel yet. No evidence of the wondrous and unexpected life inside her. The impossible life.

On the table in front of her were an opened bottle of vodka and a freshly opened bottle of prenatal vitamins beside a glass of tap water. The items represented the ultimate choice, placed directly in her path by her own volition. Drink the vodka and commit to visiting the abortion clinic as soon as she possibly could. She would leave behind the risk of abandonment by Tesser and the enormous mountain of responsibility of not only being a mother but potentially being a single mother. Years of soccer practice, PTA meetings, dance recitals, Christmas concerts, wrapping unending amounts of thankless birthday presents, scraped knees, bad first dates, and broken hearts would all be avoided. It was in truth, the easier way out. It was the bottle of vodka. The great goodbye.

The glass of water and the taking of a single pink pill filled with precious nutrients meant that instead of turning away from the storm of all those scary thoughts, she would turn into it. It meant potentially being a mother without support. It meant years of basketball practice, a first step, a first word, the wonder of whether or not the baby's eyes would be green like hers, or gold like Tesser's. It meant buying fun wrapping paper, going to the park, and sitting in the front row at a wedding she couldn't stop crying at. It was the ultimate hello.

Both decisions were horrifying. Should she decide to walk away from the baby she'd be abandoning a second chance to be a mother. Her first chance at creating life with Max had failed so miserably, so painfully. Poor little Aiden. He never had a birthday. This could be her opportunity to make things right. Give someone to the world who deserved to be born.

Matty felt a growing warmth inside her, and she knew it was confidence. It was the feeling of commitment. The primal sense of doing what was right. It grew right beside her baby. Tesser's baby. Matty unscrewed the colored cap to the vitamins and tipped the bottle until a pill fell out into the palm of her hand. Bottle set down, she popped the nurturing medicine into her mouth and downed the pill with the entire glass of water. She picked up the cap to the vodka and screwed it tight.

Tesser or not, this baby will be born. This is a second chance I can't give away.

There was a knock at the door of her apartment.

Who the hell is that? Matty stood up and pushed her chair in as her mother had always asked her to. Some habits last. Her apartment was a nicer place in the Beacon Hill area of Boston, and neighbors didn't knock late. It also struck her as strange that the lobby concierge would come upstairs instead of just calling her place directly. With a shrug, she walked over to the tiny peephole in the door. She put her eye to the hole and looked into the hall.

Her heart stuttered when she recognized Mr. Host, the head of security for Fitzgerald Industries. Her mouth dried up and filled with the acidic taste of chalky bile. There was no good reason for him to be here. His purpose couldn't be good.

Matty checked the chain on the door and turned the deadbolt. She let the door open inwards a few inches, and she leaned over into the space between door and jam. "Hello, Mr. Host. Very peculiar to have you here at my home at this hour. Can I help you?"

Mr. Host tried to smile, but all it did was chill Matty to the bone.

"Good evening, Miss Rindahl, sorry to bother you. I came here at the request of Mr. Fitzgerald. Apparently time is a factor. The doctor discovered something amiss with your pregnancy, and they'd like you to come in immediately for testing and observation."

Something felt very wrong to Matty. "Doctor Wooster told you about the pregnancy? Doesn't that violate some kind of right of mine? Patient-client privilege?"

Mr. Host licked his lips, searching for a response. It took only a flash of a second, but it told Matty everything she needed to know. *He's lying.*

"Miss Rindahl, I can't speak to your rights, but I do know they were very insistent. I'm here to help. They need to see you immediately."

"If I need to go to a hospital, I'll head to one of my choosing. Thank you for the information Mr. Host. I'll see you soon." Matty smiled at the creeper that worked for her boss outside the door and shut it. But the door caught on something. She looked down and saw Mr. Host's foot stopping it from closing. Her heart stopped, and a lump of fear formed in her throat.

"I'm sorry, Miss Rindahl. Your wishes will need to

take a backseat to the needs of your child," he said without emotion.

Matty looked up sharply, feeling her body flood with adrenaline and fear for her life and the life inside her belly. Standing behind Mr. Host were two new arrivals. She recognized them as other security men from the Project Amethyst building. One was the same man who gave her the blue envelope that contained her job offer.

"Fuck off!" she screamed.

I have to get to a phone. My phone.

"Think of the baby, Miss Rindahl," Mr. Host said emotionlessly.

I'm going to die here. They're going to shoot me in the head and scrape my baby out of me. They don't even care about me. I know it. I know it. Matty abandoned the door and scampered over to the kitchen counter where her phone was. She turned it on with addled fingers and started to dial 911. She grabbed a long kitchen knife from her cutting block and held it in shaking fingers. Matty held the phone to her ear, awaiting the 911 operator's calm voice. She watched as Mr. Host's long and fluid fingers reached into the gap between the door and around it, searching for the end of the chain so he could undo it.

"Fuck off asshole! I'm calling 911! The cops will be here in no time!" It was a hollow threat, but it was all she had.

Mr. Host's fingers stopped moving. For a second Matty thought her threat worked. Instead, the trio of men in the hallway laughed in a unison that was unearthly and drained her of hope.

Mr. Host's voice came again, and caused her to shudder in fear. "Miss Rindahl, we're employing a signal jammer downstairs. There is no cell service available to you. Your ruse is clever, but will only delay the inevitable. Once again, I ask you to *think of your baby.*" The man's white hand went back to its work on the chain. He'd have it open in just a few seconds.

On instinct, on impulse, she scampered forward and slashed at the knuckles and fingers with her knife. The sharp carving knife did as it should have, and cleanly lopped off two of the fingers and half severed a third. A tiny squirt of blood (one much smaller than Matty would've expected) shot across the interior side of her door, leaving stark evidence of the violence. Alarmingly, Mr. Host didn't yank his hand away fast. Instead he pulled it around the edge of the door slowly and under control. His foot and hand out of the way, Matty slammed the broad white door with the blood spatter on it shut. She twisted the deadbolt closed.

From the other side of the door she heard Mr. Host again, "Think of the baby, Miss Rindahl."

"Think of the baby," another soulless voice said

Matty screamed. She turned and ran towards the three large windows that framed the wall of her living room. If she were to open one, she could get outside onto the fire escape and freedom on the street below.

I need to tell Tesser somehow. I need to get him a message. He'd know what to do. He'd come to help me. He'd have to.

Matty crossed the room as the phantoms in the hallway knocked on her front door. She could still hear them telling her to "Think of the baby." She screamed again as she sat the knife down on the windowsill. Her fingers clumsily twisted the window latch and lifted the heavy wooden frame and large window. She grabbed the knife and started through the escape as the front door exploded inward. Over her shoulder as she dived through the window onto the cold and hard iron fire escape she saw Mr. Host and his two goons enter the apartment. They moved slowly, with patient intent. They already knew how this would end. They merely needed to suffer through this waste of their time she had visited upon them.

Matty's shoulder popped out of joint with an eruption of agony as she hit the iron grate of the escape. Darkness brought on by the pain nearly overtook her, but she clawed out of it and got to her feet. Her left arm felt numb below the excruciating pain of the dislocation. Matty fought it and ran to the end of the steel platform where the stairs looped around and headed downward towards the safety of the public street. Then from the street below, she heard an impossible voice, a voice from an impossible place.

"Think of the baby, Miss Rindahl."

How?

It was another voice, but the same. "Think of the baby, Miss Rindahl." Then the two voices became four. Then the four became ten. It was an evil chorus. Matty stopped moving down the steel stairs and looked over the railing down into the small back alley she'd hoped meant her escape. Parked directly below her was a large black SUV with tinted windows. It reminded her of the large trucks the Secret Service used to protect the President. For some reason, this vehicle felt sinister. More black. It absorbed the light and gave back no reflections. The vehicle had a unit of Mr. Host's men standing around it, and even though she knew they were all different men, her mind muddled their faces into a single image of Mr. Host himself. They all looked like him. They all *sounded* like him. It couldn't be.

Matty looked up at the window of her apartment and saw Mr. Host leaning out of the window she'd leapt through. He looked upon her as if she were a petulant child. He was absent of malice, and that worried her more than if he'd shown anger. She could understand anger or madness. This was worse.

"Miss Rindahl, please think of your baby, and come with us peacefully," Mr. Host said a final time.

Matty's mind fractured in that moment as her eyes connected to her mind, and she saw Mr. Host's true faces.

His legion of faces.

A kindness came to her as she blacked out.

Chapter Thirty-Two

Tesser

Tesser made it home from the café without having anything else thrown in his face, which he considered a notable win when compared against his meeting with Matty. The expectant father had returned home to the brownstone that he shared with Abraham and Mr. Doyle and had gone straight to his room. He needed time to sort out his thoughts and plan a way to tell her the truth without being bludgeoned or soaked with a drink. Matty and their unborn baby were far too important to him.

Like every other dragon on Earth, Tesser had a singular role that maintained the balance of all existence on Earth. As strange as it had been, Tesser had told her the truth. He had in fact copulated with hundreds of thousands of living creatures over the years. The vast majority of which were wild animals, and now extinct species. It was his mission, his task. It was the very meaning of his existence to propagate life, and in order to assist certain species in their quest for success, Tesser bred with them. He was made for it. Everything about him made his accomplishment of that task easier.

Every creature that gave birth to a baby of the dragon of life had advanced their species, for their offspring were improved in every way. A better size more suited for success was the change at times, but at other times the babies developed more cunning, evolved longer legs, or had a sudden desire to leave the ocean and walk on land. These small, incremental, carnal steps taken over hundreds of thousands of years changed life on Earth. Tesser's cultivation of Earth's life forms was an artistic epic that spanned millions of years, and was still unfinished. Tesser doubted he'd ever finish. This was a journey; a rewarding and orgasmic way of life for him.

Sleeping with Matty had been more than just sex for the dragon. He was entranced with her. She was smart, pretty, interesting, and funny. She had all the physical and mental traits that attracted him to a mate. He knew she was biologically damaged. He knew it the moment he'd sat her down in the nightclub. He could sense it the same way a predator can sense sickness in diseased prey or how a migrating bird knows which way is south. Tesser didn't care that she was flawed. He simply wanted her. Wanted to be with her.

She became pregnant because sleeping with Tesser meant just that. It was an act to make to life, not simply one for pleasure. Biological damage be damned, the primal force of Earth's life would find a way to spread itself.

Tesser reminisced, and a warm feeling came over him. The memories of their night together made him want to shuck his human body and fly high, the mist of the clouds covering his face, forming rivers of moisture down his scales. He wanted to let loose the fire within and belch it into the night sky, turning the dark into light. A draconic celebration not remembered in the oldest of human living memories.

But first he needed to figure out how to make Matty want him in her life again.

Tesser left his bedroom the following morning and trudged downstairs, his mind still full of questions and devoid of answers. Sorting out the modern world had been difficult. Sorting out the modern woman was seemingly impossible.

"Hey, buddy," Abe said from the dining room table. The young man was reading something on a tablet device and drinking a cup of what smelled like coffee.

I feel asinine asking Abe for any kind of relationship advice. In terms of sex and seduction that's akin to a lion asking a tree how to better hunt for gazelle. But I need to start somewhere, and I trust his intentions.

"Good morning, Abe. Is there more coffee?"

Abe sipped his drink. "Yepper. Most of a pot still."

"Be right back," Tesser said, and then walked into the kitchen. Tesser made a large mug of the dark brew and sweetened it with several of the British man's sugar cubes. He poured a dollop of cream in and stirred the drink. A sip told him it was sweet and savory. *Just how I like it.*

"I would've thought a dragon would take their coffee black," Abe said as his finger flicked a page on the tablet.

"I'm sure others of my kind drink their coffee that way. I prefer sweet things when they are available to me. What are you reading?"

"I'm just trolling some forums. Nothing sorcery related, mostly hobby stuff. I need to stay on top of the developing decklists for FNM. Although I'm not sure when Mr. Doyle will let me go to play again. Short leash is the rule lately."

"Boys and their toys. Speaking of sweet things, I would like to… I guess drop a bit of a bomb on you. I need to bounce some thoughts off of you."

Abe looked up with faint surprise. "An ancient and ageless being of incredible power seeks the council of lowly and sarcastic Abraham Fellows? This one is getting marked on the calendar as a life event. I am honored. What can I do for you?"

"Smartass."

"Correct. Again, what can I do for you?"

Tesser cleared his throat. "I've had a bit of a falling out with Matty."

"Oh no. You were totally into that chick too. She was hot shit. What happened? You say something stupid? Tell her you love her? Tell her you didn't love her?"

Tesser grinned. *He may know something about this after all.* "I wish it were that plain. The elephant in the room with her and me is the fact that I've gotten her pregnant."

Abe's mouth drooped slowly open in shock. "You what?"

"I got her pregnant. Natural consequence of sex? How you were born? Pregnancy?"

"I'm aware of what sex does, Tesser, thanks. Please tell me if I'm correct in hearing you. Right now, in modern day Boston, there is a woman walking around that is carrying in her womb the baby of an ancient dragon?"

"Can you not say ancient again? It's making me self-conscious about my age. And yes, Matty carries my child. It was bound to happen sooner or later." Tesser took an angry gulp of his coffee.

"How does that even work? Is she going to lay eggs? Will the baby be a dragon like you? How big is a baby dragon? Sorry man, but these are questions that need answering," Abe was on the edge of his seat with interest. His tablet was discarded.

"She'll have a normal human baby via a normal human birth. There have only ever been seven dragons, and there only ever will be seven. We are, for all intents and purposes, immortal, and there can be no more of our kind. The balance must be maintained."

"Fascinating. Wow. Will the birth of this kid make the world cooler? Like how we can do magic easier when you're around?"

Tesser contemplated before answering, "I don't know. There is a strong chance of it."

"Then here-here friend." Abe raised his cup of coffee

in a toast, "May her pregnancy be easy, the birth swift, and the life of your child magnificent."

Tesser raised his cup and toasted with Abe. After taking a sip he continued, "I'm not sure Matty intends to keep the baby. She asked me if I wanted to be a part of its rearing, and I made some… ignorant and obtuse comments."

"Ignorant and obtuse? Can you go into more detail?" Abe had a smile on his face.

Let the humiliation begin. Tesser told Abe all about the exchange, focusing heavily on the joyous errors of telling Matty that he'd slept with an unending amount of females. After spitting up most of several mouthfuls of coffee, Abe held his sides from the pain of laughing.

"I realize my choice of words, and especially my lack of restraint about what I said, leaves me in a bit of a pickle. But it's where I am, and I've run out of good, informed ideas on how to move forward. Any advice you have would be appreciated."

Abe leaned back in his chair, a serious expression replacing his grin. "This does suck. Had you told her you were a dragon at least she'd be less likely to abort the baby. Right now there's no reason for her to keep it. Shit, if I were her I'd be thinking about getting rid of it out of impulsive anger just to get some kind of petty revenge. But then again, I'm not a woman, and I'm kind of an immature asshole."

"Fair statement, that."

"I know my limits."

"Not sure about that one. But seriously Abe, what the hell do I say? What do I do? The last time I had sex with a human all I had to do was woo her with strong, bold words, and drag the carcass of an elk into her village for her family. It's all so different now. I'm too clouded by emotions for Matty as well. I feel like I need to come clean and tell her everything. Show her what I am, and hope she accepts me for *me* and the beauty of what we've done."

"She could also realize that she's had sex with a shape shifting monster from myth and legend that looks like it's related to a flying dinosaur on crack that can breathe fire. And, by the way, I'm still waiting on visual confirmation of that. Bro, you got mad issues."

Tesser swirled his coffee cup. I feel defeated. I don't like this feeling. I am a creature of action, not hesitation.

"I tell you what, dude. I'll call Alexis when she takes lunch and touch base with her. We'll put her on the case. You're a good guy. Alexis likes you. I think I can get her on the case."

That might work. "Thank you."

"You get yourself into the strangest predicaments, Tesser. It's like a gift. No one fucks themselves over quite like you."

"No argument."

Chapter Thirty-Three

Alexis

"No shit? Pregnant?" Alexis asked. She was on the phone with her young man and was hearing for the first time the details behind Tesser and Matty's drama. It was delicious stuff, but Alexis was genuinely concerned for Matty.

"Yeah. How about that luck, right? First time and they get the recipe just right. Bun in the oven," Abe said to her.

He's so cute with his silly expressions. "So what happened? Huge argument at the Starbucks? He said some dumb shit and now what? He needs help sorting it out?"

"Yeah, really dumb shit. Like, were you born in a different century dumb shit," Abe said laughing. "It wasn't his fault, really. It was numbskull stuff."

"Alright, alright. I'll give her office a call in a few minutes. Tesser just wants to talk to her? Or does he want to see her again?" Alexis asked. She took a small bite of her bacon cheeseburger and relished it.

"Both, I'm thinking. He just wants to apologize and explain the real story behind what he said. He said some stuff that really, really doesn't make sense unless you know some of his, well, some of his really old history. Alexis, Tesser is a special person. Unique. Sort of a one of a kind. He's really new to American culture and our language, and I think he muffed it up like a boss with Matty. He likes her a lot. I think he might love her."

Alexis sighed softly while chewing. *Love.* "He seems really nice. God, he's handsome too. The things I would do to that man's body."

"You said that out loud," Abe said regretfully.

"Oh babe, it's nothing against you. You're a handsome devil. My handsome devil. He's just... well. They don't make guys like him much."

"You have no idea, but I get it. I live with the guy; it's infuriating. You know he doesn't exercise at all? Sits around reading all damn day, learning about the world; and he's cut like an MMA fighter."

And smart too? Lord have mercy. "Interesting. Look, I'm gonna give Matty a call. You tell your buddy he owes me one. And you sugar, you owe me one too," Alexis teased.

"Just one? Can't I owe you two?" Abe pleaded.

"Well, we'll see if you've been a good boy or not. Play your cards right, and it won't matter which you've been. Muah, baby, I'll call you later with what I find out," Alexis smacked her lips making kiss noises repeatedly as Abe said goodbye. She then end call icon and sat her phone down.

I'm gonna power through this greaseburger and give Matty a call in her office. Hopefully, she listens to the sense I'm gonna make. Men like Tesser only come along so often, and she'd be a fool not to jump all over it. For my sake, at least. Plus if she's pregnant...gotta make that work, baby.

Alexis bit off a mouthful of her burger and chewed the smoky, cheesy, meaty goodness.

*****

It was nearly time to go home. The afternoon sun was heading towards the horizon at a good clip, and the yellow-gold line on the wall of her office told her exactly how long it'd be before night. She'd be stuck in traffic on the way home before the sun set, but she still needed to get in touch with Matty.

I keep getting her voice mail. Alexis dialed the number for Matty's office again and let it reach Matty's voice mail. The recording of Matty's voice sounded hollow and old.

—Hello you've reached the voice mailbox of Matilde Rindahl in research assessment. I'm sorry I couldn't take your call. If you'd like, please leave your name and phone number or extension and the reason for your call, and I'll get back to you as soon as I am able. Thank you and have a great day.—

There was a tone, and Alexis left a message. "Hey, Matty this is Alexis. I'm just calling to touch base with you about some stuff. I talked to Abe earlier, and he was passing the message along that Tesser was worried. Your man wants you to call him or meet up. Give me a shout when you get this message. I'll try your cell after work hours. Love you, muah!" Alexis hung up her office phone and went back to the process of closing down her desktop. Each application was saved and closed independently, and all the pens and papers on her desk were placed in their overnight homes in her desk drawers.

This doesn't feel right. I wonder if she called out sick? It's Tuesday, and no one uses a sick day on a Tuesday. Of course, if she's preggo, there's a damn good chance she's sick as hell. Wait, I got an idea.

Alexis had her purse in one hand, and she snatched up her phone with the other. She dialed Matty's number again, but when she had the chance, she dialed 0 repeatedly to get to the operator. After a few second's pause, someone picked up.

A young woman's voice spoke, "Thank you calling Fitzgerald Industries, how may I direct your call?"

"Hey, this is Alexis Banks from the Boston office. I've

been dialing Matty Rindahl's office all day, and she hasn't called me back. Can you tell me if she's in the office today?"

The operator answered immediately, "Miss Rindahl is listed as out today Miss Banks. Would you like her voice mail?"

"No thanks, dear. I've already left her a message. I'll try her cell phone, thank you; have a great night."

"Same to you, Miss Banks," the operator said back as the call ended.

Okay, that's good. I'll call her when I get out of the parking garage.

*****

The Fitzgerald Industries parking garage was shared with several other businesses in the area. Part of several colleges shared space in the eight story concrete structure as well as many private companies. Alexis had the dubious honor of an eighth level parking spot. It meant she had a commanding view of the Charles River and the city as she arrived and left from work, and it gave her a much shorter elevator ride to her office. However, it meant she had to fight through all the traffic in the garage on the way in and out each day. When her coworkers were being ignorant twats (a surprisingly common feat for a bunch of people who were all graduate school educated), it took her upwards of twenty minutes just to reach street level. Worst of all, once she left the uppermost level of the garage there was no cell service until she emerged on the street far below. Not even text messages.

Cunts. Jesus, get out of my way. I gotta take care of my girl.

Alexis pulled out onto the street in her Acura and immediately did a brake stand. Traffic was already piled up. It'd take her at least twenty minutes more to get to the Storrow to start heading home.

I'll kill the time talking to Matty. Bitch better answer. Alexis pored through her contacts and dialed Matty with nothing but her thumb. The car edged forward ten feet, and the call went directly to Matty's voicemail.

Well, shit on a shingle, dammit. She must be on the phone. Alexis sat her phone in her lap and fought the urge to call down God's judgment on the idiots in the road in front of her. She was surrounded by tools. A few minutes later she dialed Matty's number again. The voice mail greeted her.

You know, Matty lives in Beacon Hill. That's not that far, and the traffic is fierce. Maybe I'll just sneak a lane or two over and shoot down the city streets to her place. I'll see what she wants for dinner, and we'll get takeout. I'd like to see her, plus if she's not feeling well she could use some company.

Alexis put her blinker on and waited a minute for the truck beside her to let her merge so she could escape down the main city street and avoid the throngs of cars all funneling towards Storrow Drive. She waved at the man driving the truck and made her best effort to look sultry. The aging man in the needlessly large Cadillac truck (clearly compensating for a boring lifestyle, a loveless marriage, and shitty kids) looked at her with a mix of irritation and disgust.

Motherfucker. Alexis powered her window down and leaned out. She put on her crazy bitch face. "Hey asshole! Let me in! I'm on my period, I got good insurance, and I don't care about your damn truck!"

The older man's eyes went wide with shock. A nut job redhead was a powerful force for change. The man stopped his truck, and once the vehicle in front of his had moved, Alexis fit her smaller car into the gap. She waved and smiled like she'd never cursed like a sailor.

Now, to Matty's place.

*****

Matty had a beautiful apartment in a brown brick building that was at least a hundred and fifty years old. Alexis knew Matty had the third floor all on her own and was probably paying out the nose for rent. Matty's parents had some money, but for her to afford a place like this she must have no college debt and a second job. That, or she had negotiated one hell of a starting salary out of graduate school.

Alexis parked on the street in the single open space and ran up the steps to the ornate door. It was amazingly wide, almost twice the width of a normal front door, and had a beautiful beveled glass window. Through it she saw a wide staircase and a suited man sitting at a desk. He was into his fifties and looked bored as he flipped through a Fish & Game magazine. She opened the door with a grunt.

"Hey, buddy. Can you ring Matty Rindahl's for me? I'm Alexis, her old boss and dancing buddy." Matty flashed that killer smile.

This time it worked. The old man with his tuft of white hair ringing a large bald spot sat the magazine down immediately. "Of course, miss." The old man picked up a phone from the desk and dialed Matty's number from memory. He probably dialed these apartment numbers ten times a week as the residents needed cabs, dry cleaning, or delivery food. He let it ring until it went to voicemail.

"No answer?" Alexis asked.

"No, miss. Perhaps she's on the phone? It's going straight to her messages." The old man had a voice that reminded her of a cartoon character. *Come to think of it, he looks like a cartoon character too.*

"Would you mind if I just went to her place and knocked? Her office said she called out today and I want to make sure she's okay." Alexis hit him up with the smile.

The old security guard made a showing of it being no big deal, "Of course! Head right on up these stairs until there aren't any more to go up. Her door is on the left. Only one on the floor."

"Thank you. You're a fine young man," Alexis said with a wink as she scooted by his desk and up the stairs.

I bet he's looking at my butt.

She was right.

*****

Alexis crested the top step of the building's stairs and started down the hardwood hall. She could see the door that belonged to Matty. Apartment 301.

Alexis reached the broad white door and gave it a solid triple whack with her knuckle. She waited patiently, excited to see Matty.

There was no answer. Alexis knocked on the door again, this time adding two extra knocks to show her excitement.

A minute passed, and still no answer.

"Hey, Matty baby, it's Alexis. Can you open up for me?" Alexis hollered into the jam of the door. Her eye caught something small.

What the hell is that warp in the wood? Alexis saw a crack in the wood that marked the edge of a bulge. It was right about at eye level where the door met the jam. Right about where the chain would be on the other side. *Is that bulge there because the door was forced open?* Without thinking Alexis grabbed and turned the knob, suddenly in a mild panic. The large brass knob held firm. It was locked.

She's gotta have a key here somewhere. Matty's like that. Alexis lifted the small oval rug at the base of the door, but there was nothing below it. She got up on the tips of her toes and felt along the top of the door jam, hoping there was a key hidden there, but like the rug, there was nothing. She looked up and down the hallway. There was a small round table at the end of the hall below a large window. On the table was a potted plant.

There. It's there. Alexis left the door with the strange bump on it and trotted down to the table. She lifted the potted plant and sitting below it, like Bilbo's ring at the bottom of the river, was the key to Matty's apartment. Alexis snapped it up off the dusty white doily and went back to the door. The key went into the lock effortlessly, and she turned the knob. The door swung in with an ominous creak.

This is how horror scenes start. Or how horror movies end for dumb characters. Shit.

The door opened up and revealed a kitchen that was updated to look modern despite the antiquated feel of the high ceilinged building. A small kitchen table just inside the door had a bottle of prenatal vitamins on it, not too far from a bottle of vodka. Between the two was an empty glass.

Oh God, what have you done Matty? "Matty?!" Alexis hollered into the apartment. Her voice bounced off the cold walls and came back at her. Her echo sounded lonely. Alexis left the kitchen and walked down the lone hallway. Immediately she passed an empty bathroom. It was dominated by the presence of a massive claw foot tub. Alexis let herself into the bedroom after announcing herself once more, and that room too was empty.

"What the fuck?" Alexis spun and walked back into the kitchen, turning into the adjoined living room with its three huge paned windows. She could see the fire escape out the glass and almost laughed at how bad the view was. *That'll cut down on the rent a bit.* One of the windows to the fire escape was open, and Alexis went over to investigate. *Maybe she's sitting out there thinking about life?* Alexis stopped short of the windowsill. Despite the setting sun, her eyes saw tiny flecks of red on white, and she froze. There was blood on the sill.

Alexis backed up, nearly falling on the couch. She turned towards the door and her entire body stiffened. The back of the thick door was indeed damaged. Where the chain had been was a crack in the wood and on the floor behind the door lay the broken security device. More alarming than that were the blood streaks. Long, jagged finger marks of raw, coagulated blood were on the door as well as a clear pattern of spatter where digits had been severed.

With shaking hands Alexis reached into her tiny purse and began to dial 911. Somehow instead, she called Abe.

Chapter Thirty-Four

Abe

"Hey, Alexis," Abe said casually into his phone.

"Abe? What the,,,? I was trying to dial…"Alexis said in a voice that was obviously cracked with fear and tension.

What the fuck? "Alexis are you okay? You sound scared, is something wrong?"

"Yeah, uh, Abe, I'm at Matty's place and something is wrong. Something is like really very wrong. I was trying to dial 911 but I guess I dialed you by accident."

"911? Is Matty hurt?" Abe got up from the couch and started towards the massive staircase. Tesser's room was up the stairs, and the dragon would want to know.

"I don't know. I just let myself in using her spare key. She didn't go in to work today, and she hadn't answered her phone, and I was stuck in traffic so I came over."

Abe waited for her to continue but she didn't. "Alexis?"

"Sorry. I… Abe, there's blood all over the inside of her door. It's finger streaks. Like someone had some fingers cut off. I can't tell if they were hers or not. And Abe, there's vodka on the table and an empty glass. I think she might've been drinking."

Abe stopped at the top of the stairs. *Tesser won't like*

that at all. Shit. I don't want to be the one who pisses off the dragon. "But no body? Signs of a larger fight?"

"There are specks of blood on the windowsill too. I have no idea what happened, Abe. I think I need to get out of here. I need to call the police. Do you think Tesser had anything to do with this?" Alexis sounded near to panic. Abe could hear her short breaths and felt like he could hear the pounding of her heart through the phone.

"Lord, no. Tesser wants that woman safer than all the gold in Fort Knox. Plus, he's been here the whole time. Leave the apartment. Go downstairs. Does she have building security?"

"Yes. Some old fart."

"Okay. Tell the old fart you found blood, and let him deal with it. You'll need to hang around and sign some kind of witness statement, but I'm going to tell Tesser, and we'll be right over, okay? Just text me her address when I let you go." Abe took a few more steps towards Tesser's closed bedroom door.

"Okay. Abe?"

"Yeah?"

"If something bad happens, I know this is like, weird to say, but I'm like, really into you. I know there's an age difference, but, you know. Abe I've got a real bad feeling about this."

Abe smiled and felt a tickle inside his chest. "I'm really into you too, Alexis. Stay calm. I'm going to get Tesser."

"Okay. I'll text you in a minute."

"Okay, bye." Abe hung up the call and took a deep breath. He rapped his knuckles on Tesser's bedroom door. *I'm not sure what to say here, but I hope to God Tesser isn't one of those kill the messenger types.*

Tesser opened the door. He was in one of Abe's Deadmau5 shirts. It was a smidge tight on him, but it looked good. "Yeah?" the man said with a hint of sadness.

"Tesser, I just got a call from Alexis, she's at Matty's

place," Abe said, steeling himself.

Tesser perked up. "And? What did Matty say? Can I call her?"

"Something happened. Something bad maybe. We don't know."

Tesser's gold eyes narrowed, and a flare of red could be seen deep within. "Something bad? Is Matty hurt, Abe? Did she hurt herself?"

"We don't know. Alexis said there was blood in the apartment, and Matty is nowhere to be seen. She's calling the cops and then sending me Matty's address so we can head over."

Tesser turned and searched for his shoes. He found them quickly and slid them on. "I know where she lives. We slept together at her place. It's not far from here. Will you come with me? It might be dangerous, if something bad has happened."

Dangerous? What could be dangerous? "Yeah, I'll go. I've been working on a couple new spells. I think if you're around I'll be able to cast them."

Tesser's eyes were still flared red, but the glow subsided after he calmed a bit. "Thank you, Abe. Let's go."

The two ran down the stairs, but Abe stopped at the bottom. "Hey, Mr. Doyle!" Abe shouted up into the cavernous stairwell. "Mr. Doyle!"

"What have I told you about shouting?!" Mr. Doyle said from the top of the home. The old man leaned over the railing, looking frailer than ever.

"Sorry, Mr. Doyle. Something bad has happened to Tesser's girlfriend we think. We're headed over to her apartment to see what's going on. Keep your eyes peeled. I'll let Ellen know on the way out."

Mr. Doyle looked speechless. "Very well then. Good luck, boys. Losing a loved one is the hardest thing to recover from. I hope it is not as you fear."

Tesser turned and looked up at Mr. Doyle, his hand

still on the front door knob of the house. "Thank you, Mr. Doyle. While we are gone please be careful."

Mr. Doyle nodded from his perch atop the landing rail.

Abe looked back to Tesser as he turned the knob and pulled the wide door inward. Abe was shocked to see several men stood outside the door on the stone steps. *Who the fuck is that?*

The men all wore what appeared to be black tactical gear and were armed with incredibly heavy-duty weaponry. They looked like a SWAT team. The man in the front, his hand frozen as if to knock on the door wore a simple black suit. Abe could see the grip of a large handgun on his waist under the suit coat. The rest of the men behind him all raised the muzzles of their guns several inches, prepared to lift them higher to fire on the two men inside the house. To fire on him and Tesser.

Tesser dropped the tilt of his head a bit, furrowing his brows. Abe could feel a shimmer coming off him, a vibration as the dragon somehow…flexed an unseen power. The hair on Abe's neck stood up as if electricity was coursing through the room.

"You are Tesser, correct?"

"Who are you?" Tesser asked, sniffing the air innocuously. High above, Abe heard Mr. Doyle disappear from the landing, his feet dragging on the thick carpet.

"I am Mr. Host. I need you to come with me," the suited man replied.

"You are not a lawman, and I come with no one. Answer my question. Who are you?" Tesser said angrily, his hands balling into fists. Abe felt the thrums of stored potential energy again. *If Tesser were to uncork whatever he's building…*

"Sir, there's no need to be rude. If you'll just come with us, we have information that might interest you. It's about a woman we believe you care about," the man named Mr. Host said.

"You know what happened to Matty?" Abe asked behind Tesser.

Mr. Host's creepy eyes never left Tesser's. "We do indeed know the state of Miss Rindahl. I can guarantee you her safety as well as the safety of your cohabitants Mr. Tesser. All you need do is agree to visit no harm on my men."

"Dude, Tesser, can you agree to that? This dude knows what happened to Matty."

Tesser sniffed the air again, this time more obviously. He started to nod his head, as if remembering something or approving of a scent on the air. "Your scent. It's the same as the men behind you."

"We must be wearing the same deodorant. I need your answer, Tesser. The longer we wait the more risk Miss Rindahl is in."

"I remember you. I don't remember where I remember you from, but I remember your scent. Right before I fell asleep." Tesser said quietly, almost angrily.

"Tesser, don't do anything stupid. I don't wanna get shot," Abe said, taking a step away as he felt that intensity grow again. The chandelier above the dining room table nearby began to vibrate slightly.

Without taking his eyes off Mr. Host, Tesser spoke, "Abe, this man is Veil-Born. From another plane of existence. Not human, not animal. He's unnatural. He is other."

"Nonsense," Mr. Host replied.

"He said he'd guarantee our safety. We just can't hurt his men."

Tesser spoke once more, "He *is* his men Abraham. One and the same, made of the same non-flesh. If we agree to his bargain, then he gains leverage. He can then kill us or harm us at his leisure, and we are bound to his daemon's deal."

"Daemons? What? He *is* his men? Could you be any more fucking vague?" Abe asked as he took a step back behind a coat rack as if it would stop automatic gunfire.

"He's right," Mr. Doyle said from the stairs above. Abe turned and looked up. Mr. Doyle had returned and stood a few feet away, holding a pocket watch at arm's length. The steel disc swung erratically from the still arm of the elder mage. Oddly, the watch repeatedly swung towards the doorway where the strange men were, as if they were a magnet. "This is an Asmodean compass. It senses those from beyond the veil. It hasn't ticked in years, but now it feels like it's coming apart at the seams. These men are not men, they are devils, Abraham. Evil made flesh."

"Well, fuck you," Mr. Host said bluntly. He had a look of extreme irritation on his face.

Abe looked back and caught the glimmer of movement outside one of the living room windows. More men were moving about. Things. *We're fucking surrounded.*

Tesser snarled an ultimatum, "Well, Mr. Host, I think I'll strike a new bargain with you. You tell me exactly where Matty is and I send you back beyond the veil in a pool of your own blood."

Mr. Host shook his head, disappointed. "Tesser, the world is different now. They don't care about magic or gremlins or boggarts or dragons like you. It's money and greed. That is our domain. You've lost this world already and you slept through the fight like a slumbering princess. It's been a long time since we put you to sleep, but we haven't forgotten how. You wouldn't want us to ruin this nice house and kill these poor fools would you?" Mr. Host suddenly looked…different. Indistinct and thorny in a way that defied physical explanation. Abe found his hands shaking and his mouth dry.

Tesser's eyes flared brighter than ever, and Abe felt his heart throb so powerfully it felt like it had stopped beating entirely. "Let's see you try to make me sleep again."

The blink of an eye later, Abe was shocked at how

loud the gunfire was. It almost distracted him from the pain as he fell to the floor.

Chapter Thirty-Five

Spoon

Spoon was sick. Very sick. At least that's what he told his Captain at the station a couple of days ago. He needed some time off, and his union rep told him just how to phrase his request to get it without raising too many questions. Spoon needed the time off to get his head straight, to pull it out of his ass, and get away from this Tesser obsession.

It wasn't healthy, it wasn't safe, and it wasn't professional in the least. It was almost insanity.

I'm good now, though. I took a couple days off, I checked in with a department shrink, and I feel better. I still can't explain why I got so fucking obsessed with this European dude, but I'm good now. Better. I'm back to work in the morning, my boss never found out I was up to weird shit, and I collared my perp. So what if he turned himself in, I closed the case. All is well again in Spoonville.

Spoon was driving down the street in the Back Bay in his cruiser, his window down in the chill autumn evening. It was dark, and he was making one last trip down Tesser's street to wash his hands of the whole affair.

Just one last wave goodbye.

Spoon slowed his cruiser several blocks away when

he saw three very peculiar black sport utility vehicles double-parked in the street at the home Tesser lived in. They looked exactly like the SUVs the Secret Service used when the President was visiting.

Oh, fuck me. He's some kind of dignitary. That's why he was setting off all my alarms. That makes so much sense. Probably some Bulgarian prince on vacation in Beantown.

Spoon stopped his unmarked cruiser entirely when he saw the crowd of heavily armed men at the front door of the home. Three large males wearing tactical gear stood on the steps behind a man wearing a black suit. Even in the darkness of the impending night Spoon could see that they were equipped for war. They had M4s, full head to toe armor, and were ready to fire. The man in the suit at the door looked cool as a cucumber.

At the vehicles stood several more men dressed the same, watching the neighborhood for movement. Moving around the front of the house were two more of the men. They were flanking the front door and getting a firing angle on the interior through the massive windows. Several more could be seen forming a perimeter around the SUVs and the house. Without thinking Spoon picked up his phone and dialed his Captain's office. Spoon knew he'd be there.

The caller ID told the Captain who it was. "Yeah? Spoon?"

"Hey, I'm on Beacon Street. I'm sitting here looking at a trio of heavy duty black SUVs double-parked, and there's about ten guys dressed up like a breaching team at a house. They aren't BPD SWAT, and they aren't identified with any kind of unit or bureau markings. Do you know anything going on here? Can you find out fast because something is about to go down."

"Yeah, hold on." Spoon's boss put him on hold. Spoon's sixth sense was flaring hard and he pulled his cruiser over and double-parked it the same as the suspicious trucks. He got out of the driver's seat and went to the trunk. His Kevlar was there as well as his own department issued M4. Spoon sat his phone down and put it on speaker as he started to get his SWAT gear on over his tee shirt and shorts.

As Spoon put his helmet on his Captain came back, "Hey, Spoon?"

Spoon took the phone off speaker and held it to the bottom of the helmet, "Yeah Captain?"

"I just checked and we've got nothing. Either it's an off the record hit that BPD HQ doesn't know of, or something fishy is going on."

"Can you get some black and whites over here right now? We need a uniformed presence here stat. I got bad vibes, Captain. I dunno why."

"You're a cop. We get those kinds of feelings as a profession. Okay. I'll make a few more calls too. Don't approach, Spoon, if you're in civvies. I don't want you to..."

Gunfire erupted at the door, drowning out the Captain.

Spoon's mind immediately flashed back to the valleys of Afghanistan against his will, reminding him of all the war he'd fought there. The high-powered weapons created a rapid fire staccato of echoes that reverberated up and down the city street and set off car alarms in every direction. The muzzle flashes lit up the darkened street and caused Spoon to squint slightly. He ducked behind the end of his car, somehow keeping his phone near his ear.

"Shots fired Captain, gotta go!" Spoon said into his phone before hanging up. He slid a magazine into the well of his weapon and chambered a round. With his thumb he flicked the weapon off safe. Spoon tossed his phone into the trunk of the cruiser and took off at a full sprint towards the melee, his weapon up high, ready to fire. When he got closer, he fished out his badge, held it high, and started to holler out, "Boston Police

Department, cease fire! Cease fire!"

One of the men who had been at the hood of an SUV facing the gun battle at the door turned towards Spoon and raised his weapon in Spoon's direction. "Boston Police! Lower your weapon!" Spoon yelled again. He hoped his badge and the giant BOSTON POLICE on the front of his vest would be sufficient identification to avoid being shot.

The man in the tactical gear fired a three round burst at Spoon, and by some freak stroke of good luck all three bullets whizzed through the air around his body. It was almost like something deflected them away from hitting him. Spoon felt them buzz by, and a fraction of his mind drifted back to his time at war.

Motherfucker. Spoon shouldered his weapon and squeezed the trigger twice, putting both rounds center mass, high. The man crumpled to the ground, and Spoon kept running at his collapsed form. The rest of the men present in the street were still shooting at the house and whoever was inside with Tesser. The cacophony in the street was incredible.

What the fuck is happening?

Spoon assessed the situation at the door as the men in tactical gear opened up a hellacious amount of gunfire on the house. Windows shattered immediately, adding more nightmarish noise to the scene unfolding in the Boston neighborhood. He took a knee and reached down to check the pulse of the man he'd just shot, but when he felt downward, the man's neck wasn't where it was supposed to be. Spoon looked down, and all that remained of the man he'd shot was a blank uniform and gear. Right out from under Spoon's hand, his body had evaporated into the chaos of the night.

Spoon's mind immediately flashed back to the scene in the alley with Tesser and the young man. The garbage flying about, the wind picking up from nowhere. His rational mind had fought for days now to dismiss the supernatural origins of that event, but here and now, looking at a set of empty clothes that should've been on the body of man he'd just shot, he knew the truth of it. He had been right all along, and something was fucked up in the world. Real fucked up.

Spoon looked over at the front door of the home just in time to see an enormous flash of light inside. A tremendous explosion happened, and the men at the doorway were ejected out from the building and down the steps. It was like no explosion Spoon had ever seen before. The men got to their feet again and approached the door, firing inside at targets that weren't firing back. Tesser stepped into the direct line of fire of the door jam and sent a haymaker into the chin of the suited man as he reached the top of the steps. The punch hit with the force of a bomb, and over the gunfire that had to be hitting Tesser's body Spoon heard the neck and jaw of the black suit break with a crunch. His body caught air from the blow and sailed the length of the stone steps, stiff as a board, landing with dead weight on the sidewalk ten paces away. It was something from a movie.

Then the man in the black suit sat up.

I don't know who to fucking shoot anymore.

Chapter Thirty-Six

Tesser

Tesser had never been shot before. The last time he'd gone toe to toe with a human he'd been struck with axes and swords, and as you would expect those weapons failed against Tesser's inhuman body. In the instant between when he saw the Legion police-creatures squeeze the triggers of their guns, and the time the bullets impacted his body, he found himself very unsure of how his body would fare against the lethal modern technology.

As the first hail of bullets pierced his Deadmau5 shirt he had enough time to worry about Matty and Kaula. *If I die here, they die with me, I fear*. When he felt the tiny metal projectiles pancake against his immortal flesh, he realized fully that there was no danger from the insignificant weapons.

Tesser then heard Abe grunt in pain and fall to the floor behind him. *FUCK*. Tesser turned and dove towards where Abe's body had fallen without hesitation. Tesser's draconic brain was working overtime, slowing the passage of time to watch the flight trajectory of the bullets heading towards Abe. Tesser inserted his form between their lethal path and Abe, saving his friend from a hissing rain of metallic death. Tesser felt the bullets snap against his back and thighs, further ruining his clothing.

"Abe!" Tesser barked down at his friend. Abe's skin had already taken on a funereal pallor. He was hit twice in the abdomen and was bleeding profusely from the wounds. Abe was already covered in sweat.

Mr. Doyle was above, out of the angle of fire from the men at the door. He looked down to Abe's limp form. Tesser could sense the boiling sorcery in the old mage, near to exploding.

Finally.

Mr. Doyle spoke and sent forth a burst of arcane fury he hadn't summoned in far too long. "Rejicio!" he snarled, holding his Asmodean watch towards the door and the invaders there. A disc of bright white energy coupled with the sound of a thunderclap left his watch, rolled down the steps, and hit the men standing in the doorway. They were tossed backwards as if a tidal wave had struck them, and they tumbled down the stone steps.

"ABE!" Tesser screamed into the young man's face. Abe's eyes were glazing over and rolling upwards. *He is dying.*

"Go! Deal with them. I have a spell that will sustain him, go! Send them back across the Veil!" Mr. Doyle shuffled as fast as his old legs would take him down the stairs of the home that was being shot apart. Dust flew everywhere as Mr. Doyle's prized possessions were torn apart by the assault.

Tesser looked up at the old man and knew he spoke the truth. Their best solution to saving Abe's life was killing Legion at the door. Tesser stood as the living room windows blew apart in another burst of weapons fire. Tesser glared out the window as more of the Legion bodies shot at him.

There are many of them. Killing them all will be difficult.

Tesser walked to the door, his gold eyes burning red

with anger. As he crossed the threshold the men with the guns below were getting to their feet. They fired at him as soon as they could, discarding the safety of the Legion body in the suit that had spoken earlier. The Legion mouthpiece started to speak again, but Tesser beat him to the punch, quite literally. The dragon brought a fist up from low and put all four knuckles into the jaw of the suit before he could say anything else. He felt the bones, teeth, and neck collapse against his fist as the suit's body soared upwards and away. Tesser was shot a dozen more times before the body fell to the ground at the sidewalk.

"Ellen!" Tesser barked at the tree near the door. The tree suddenly twisted, turning towards the walkway of stone where the other armed man-things stood. They looked up at the tree as a two inch thick branch came down like an over handed Big Papi homerun swing. One of the Legion soldier bodies swung his weapon up to counter the branch but it was too late. The hamadryad's blow crashed down with the force of Mother Nature and shattered his frail body. The evil construct from beyond reality burst into nothingness as the branch smashed against the earth below, leaving nothing but black smoke, empty clothes, and weaponry behind.

The suited man's body sat up, and his eyes billowed out an emptiness so foul that it scalded the soul. Tesser's memory flashed again, bringing him back to a moment in time long ago when he'd faced down this Legion before. But now was not the time for the past.

Tesser roared with all his strength at the soldier-copy, stunning its senses long enough to close the distance. As the thing's weapon came up to fire again, Tesser grabbed its burning barrel with his left hand and yanked the gun free, tossing it away like an unwanted toy. He brought a right hook into the face of his foe, and a cascade of teeth flew out, scattering across the ground. He brought his left hand back and punched it into the throat of the daemon. Its entire body burst into black smoke and nothing, evaporating as if it had never existed. Tesser strode down the stone walkway towards the suit-wearing daemon.

I'm going to rip that thing's fucking head off.

"WHERE IS MATTY?!" Tesser bellowed into the face of the suited man. Windows down the street that had withstood the noise of the gunfire broke from the sound of his voice. Tesser was fury given purpose.

Automatic weapons fire rained at him from what felt like every direction. His shirt was ripped apart and his pants were rags. He could hear a deeper, throatier blast coming every so often and thought it was a shotgun. When those shots hit his body they felt like a prickling sensation and not an attempt at being stabbed. They were less effective at hurting him, but far more efficient at destroying his clothes.

My clothes are as important to me as the bodies Legion has created are to him. Discardable.

Beyond the suited man Tesser saw a familiar face. It was the police officer that questioned him at the pizza shop. He was dressed as the others, but looked out of place, and bewildered.

Sergeant Spooner?

A bullet rocked Tesser's skull, striking him directly in the forehead. He took a step back just as the suited daemon reached him and began to pummel his body with blows. These strikes were far more dangerous than bullets. The daemon could summon power from beyond the Veil, from the realities just outside of belief and sanity. Tesser could feel claws at the end of the suit's hands form and slash at his human flesh. Against reason, the claws were starting to sharpen against his skin, and if he didn't rally his balance quickly, the daemon would actually manage to hurt him. The other gunfire abated as the suit pressed his sudden onslaught.

"Die dragon filth! This is OUR world now! Your time is over!" Legion screamed from all the uniformed mouths present. The chorus of voices rang a note that could whiten hair.

A single gunshot snapped the press of the daemon, halting the tearing at Tesser's flesh. The round came from behind the daemon and struck it in the back of the neck, blowing its head clean off. The body gone, the black suit tumbled to the ground empty, no longer dangerous. Tesser took another step backward and saw the man named Spooner in the distance. He had his own weapon pointed at Tesser. He was the one who had rescued him from Legion. He had fired the shot.

Thank you, Sergeant.

The rest of the daemons opened fire on Spooner, sending a hundred high velocity rounds his way. The Boston Detective dropped to the ground immediately, thanks to reflexes honed in dusty, bloody battle. Spooner looked out of his mind to the dragon, and he wanted to help.

Let's end this.

Tesser started to run at the end SUV where three of the daemon soldiers had taken cover. Half were shooting at Tesser and half in Spooner's direction. Tesser gave them no chance to run, hitting one of them at full speed, bludgeoning the man-form like a battering ram. He landed on his back and skidded away into the street, his weapon lost. One of the other things turned his weapon and fired it point blank into Tesser's face, sending sparks and errant ricochets into the neighborhood. Behind them Tesser could hear the earth breaking apart as the hamadryad uprooted her tree body to lend more assistance.

I hope she's strong enough after her sending. I don't want her to die too.

Tesser spat a bullet into the face of the thing that had shot him and followed it with a jackhammer punch. The skull collapsed like broken pottery under his strength, and the body disintegrated like all the others had. More equipment fell to the ground.

The two false men at the rear of the SUV near Tesser turned from Spooner's direction to deal with the furious dragon. They too pulled triggers that spat out useless bullets at the dragon. Tesser literally tore them limb from limb, bursting their ethereal bodies apart in a spray of smoky evil.

The street became quiet for a moment, but a trio of short bursts rang out from near where Spooner had taken cover. Afraid for the worst, Tesser ran around the rear SUV just as the first in the line floored it and started to drive away down the street. Ellen had reached the road, and with one enormous tree branch arm she stove in the windows on one side of the truck, nearly tipping it over. The truck righted itself and drove on, escaping.

In the road lay Sergeant Spooner. He clutched at his chest and side and his face showed pain. Sirens could be heard wailing in the distance, their noise approaching. Tesser ran to the downed cop.

"Spooner? Are you okay?" Tesser crouched at Spooner's side.

Spoon looked up at Tesser, fear and confusion in his eyes. "Tesser, what the fuck is happening? Who are these people? What the fuck is going on? Why are they exploding?"

"Are you okay, Sergeant? Health first. Information after."

Spoon gritted his teeth in anger. "I'm fine. Flesh wound to my hip, just below my armor."

"Good. You'll survive then. Modern medicine is quite able to handle that. Now, I am a dragon, and those were daemons in human form. One daemon actually. I believe they came to kill me."

Spoon looked at him and clearly had no idea how to respond. From the window of the brownstone home Tesser heard Mr. Doyle holler, "Tesser! Tesser!"

Tesser stood and looked over at the old man. He was leaning out the destroyed front windows of the house, and he showed as many signs of injury as the home. His sweater was torn apart, and he had blood running down his face from a wide gash in his forehead. He was covered in dust and detritus and he was sweating profusely.

"What? Is Abe okay?!" Tesser shouted back.

"They took him! They took him Tesser, and I couldn't stop them! I'm sorry, Tesser. I tried but my magic wasn't strong enough! I'm not the mage I once was…" Mr. Doyle started to sob angrily as he put his face into bloody hands. The man had lost another apprentice to violence.

"Daemons just kidnapped your friend?" Spoon asked quietly, a strong tone of disbelief in his voice.

Tesser looked down, fury in his face, and grabbed Spoon by the bulletproof vest. The dragon yanked the cop to his feet as an adult might right a fallen toddler.

"Can you drive still?" Tesser snarled into the distance as the black SUV escaped far down the street, turning a corner with squealing tires.

"Jesus, man. Hell, yeah. Want to ride with me? Let's go get the fucking daemons!" Spoon said, clearly having no idea what he was asking for.

"Follow me. You drive. I'll fly," Tesser said as he pulled open the driver's side door of the truck for Spooner.

"What?" Spoon asked Tesser as he got into the vehicle painfully.

"Mr. Doyle might not be the mage he once was, but I am most certainly the dragon I have *always* been." Tesser shut the door and turned to Mr. Doyle. He shouted to the crying old man, "I'm going after Abe."

"What do I tell the police?!" Mr. Doyle shouted back, wiping tears from his eyes. He looked out the window and up at the massive form of Ellen the hamadryad. She was an animate tree, standing in the middle of the street, and there were police cruisers approaching them rapidly.

"Tell them the past has come back tonight. Tell them

the truth. No more do I hide," Tesser said loudly as he started to run.

Tesser's feet fell one in front of the other as Spoon floored the truck behind him. He felt the wind in his hair as he picked up more speed down the street, starting to nearly outpace the truck. He lifted his arms high and let his mask fall free. As his hands came down, massive golden wings sprang from his back, and his arms and legs burst out of what remained of his clothing. His tailbone sprouted the massive growth that would balance him in dragon form, and his face and neck changed, metamorphosed.

One massive downward buffet of his wings later, Tesser, in all his draconic majesty and terror took to the night sky of Boston, Massachusetts. *This is as it should be. As it once was. The wind in my face and beneath my wings. Let their world unravel. Let it adjust. Let the magic come back. Let them quake in their buildings now instead of their caves so long ago.*

Let them see the fires of dragonkind again.

Behind Tesser, Spoon watched as the incredible beast's launch flipped over half a dozen cars, and shattered all the windows for fifty yards in both directions on the street. He felt the SUV strain against the wind.

"Ho-ly shit."

The city of Boston then witnessed the return of Tesser the third, the Dragon of Life. Everything on Earth would change forever.

Again.

Chapter Thirty-Seven
Spoon

Watching the man Spoon knew as Tesser run so fast that he couldn't keep up in the truck was one thing. Watching that man transform right before his eyes into a full-on creature of legend and myth was another. Tesser's tiny human body shifted shapes, expanding and growing as fast and easily as Spoon might slide on a work shirt, except Tesser was sliding into the gargantuan form of a dragon. It happened effortlessly.

The dragon's wings extended from one side of the street to the other, leaving just a scant amount of space between his wingtips and the rows of massive homes. From the tip of his nose (just above a mouth filled with dagger teeth the size of butcher knives and machetes) to the end of his massive tail Tesser's body was almost half the length of a football field. When he plunged his wings down and launched his body into the air, the incredible force of downward air pressure flipped over a dozen vehicles like they were made of paper mache' instead of steel, rubber, and plastic. More car alarms bleated in panic as vehicles were tossed about like toys. Watching him take flight gave Spoon a strange joy he'd never experienced before. An exultation. *This is better than hearing your voice on the radio or winning a lottery when you least expected it.*

Tesser's gargantuan form slid into the night sky above the buildings and trees as easy as a fish swam in water, impossibly graceful. The whole scene playing out felt surreal. But it was so very real.

Spoon swapped his eyes between Tesser flying fast above and pulling away, the black SUV that was filled with the strange attackers, and the dying young man that the dragon above was trying to rescue. The Sergeant couldn't help but look quickly to the doorsteps on each side of the street at the people standing, their jaws dropped, hands held high holding their camera phones skyward at the majesty of the beast. They hit the pavement hard and fast when the lead vehicle started to open fire back at the dragon. Rounds sparked and skipped off the ground, and Spoon heard and felt them as a couple of rounds spanked into the grille and bumper of the truck.

After this, the image of Tesser as a naked man in an alley dispensing justice to common thugs would be long forgotten.

I cannot believe this shit is happening. Spoon kept the pedal floored in the brand new truck. In a dash mount he saw a Remington 870 shotgun and quickly flicked the catch that'd free the weapon if he needed it. He put both hands back on the wheel and let his adrenaline drown out the pain of the gunshot wound in his hip. It burned, but nothing was broken, and the pain was already manageable. He just had to keep looking up at the giant fucking dragon to distract himself. *This is beyond words.*

He cornered twice, fast onto streets that weren't always moving in a friendly direction. Vehicles that had just pulled over to let the first wild truck spitting out gunfire speed by were nearly hit head on by Spoon's. He was a tenth of a second away from a head-on collision for miles. The situation was exacerbated by the distraction of the enormous dragon flying a hundred feet above.

"Get the fuck out of the way! Move!" Spoon screamed out the window, his hand waving the traffic over. *My left nut for a flashing blue light right now.* Somehow, as they pulled onto a wider street, Tesser heard Spoon. The incredible dragon angled its wings and swooped low so it was soaring just above the reach of the orange streetlamps. The dragon's tail lashed to and fro, dangerously close to the roofs of the cars below, and to further ruin the nights of thousands of Bostonians, Tesser let slip a proper dragon's roar.

It was earsplitting, glass shattering, and bowel loosening. Spoon had a grin from ear to ear and felt like a modern day medieval warrior, an honest and true champion of all that was righteous and good. And he wasn't far from the truth. He grabbed at his pants pocket to get his phone, and realized it was in the trunk of his unmarked cruiser. *Fuck. I need to call the station to let them know where I'm going and what vehicle I'm in or I'm gonna get lit up bad.* Spoon did a sudden brake stand next to a handful of pedestrians filming the dragon's flight. His brake pads squealed in protest but the SUV stopped quickly.

"Boston Police! I need a phone fast!" Spoon screamed out at the dumbstruck citizens. Thankfully one of them turned and simply handed his phone to Spoon without a second thought. *Fuck, yeah.* Spoon dialed 911 as he punched the accelerator on the Yukon. This time it was the tires that squealed as he laid rubber down. The male 911 operator answered, and Spoon validated his police credentials quickly. Tesser had relaxed his roar, and Spoon could hear.

"What can I help you with, Detective Spooner?" The operator asked.

"I'm in pursuit with an unknown number of heavily armed suspects fleeing in a black Yukon, plates unknown. They've kidnapped a man in his mid-twenties named Abe. Last name unknown. I'm also in a black

Yukon. We just turned onto Tremont, heading towards Park. We are at a high rate of speed, and there's a giant fucking dragon flying above us."

"Is that a kind of helicopter?" the operator asked.

"No, a golden winged dragon. Creature of myth and legend? They live in dungeons? About two hundred feet long I think. Can't miss it," Spoon said quickly, swerving around a pair of college students standing in the middle of the chaotic street.

"A dragon?" the operator asked as if he thought Spoon was drunk or high.

"Yeah, I am dead serious. By now your lines should be lighting up with reports of it. The real deal. Big angry motherfucking dragon, but get this, he's the good guy. The people in the SUV are the bad guys."

"I ah… Jesus shit we just lit up like a Christmas tree in here," the operator exclaimed. "Good God, I think you're right."

"Don't say I didn't tell you so. Get the word out. I'm in pursuit, the lead SUV are the bad guys, and the dragon is a good guy. Don't shoot the dragon. Don't shoot the pursuing SUV, that's me. He isn't the bad guy and I don't think the BPD have a gun that's gonna do shit to him anyway."

"Yeah, okay. I'll uh, let the responding officers know…" the 911 operator was clearly drifting, and in a level of disbelief over what was being said on his call as well as his fellow operator's calls.

"Tell the officers. Now. 'K, thanks, bye!" Spoon said quickly before hanging up. Normally he'd stay on the line, but he knew the operator would be distracted. Plus, he had his hands full already.

Spoon punched the accelerator and watched as Tesser's wings swept back, launching him forward and nearly over the top of the fleeing vehicle. Spoon wanted to see how a dragon did a high-speed traffic stop.

As it turned out, he was uniquely suited for the job.

Tesser's massive front arms ended in claw tipped hands big enough simply grab the roof of the SUV and lift it off the ground. The motor of the truck started to rev out of control with no weight to power, but the noise was quickly drowned out by the chattering of point blank automatic weapons fire from within it. Spoon watched as a hundred holes opened up in the roof of the truck, punching hot bullets upwards towards Tesser's face. Tesser didn't even react as he planted his back legs down, his rear claws ripping apart the pavement to stop his flight. Like a gargantuan cat with a toy, Tesser peeled back the roof of the truck as Spoon slammed on his brakes. The tires gave out another squeal, but it was still quieter than the sound of the Yukon's roof being ripped away.

Roof gone, the occupants of the truck were at Tesser's mercy. The dragon's enormous hand ate a blistering amount of fresh gunfire from the shooters inside, but he ignored it. With the tips of two insanely large black claws, Tesser plucked one of the attackers out as If he were no more than a chocolate from a box and flung him. The man kept silent as he sailed end over end, his gun escaping from his grip. His flight ended powerfully against the dome of the Massachusetts state house. On impact he burst into nothingness, his empty clothing sliding down the well-lit curve of the ornamental roof.

Tesser sat the truck on the ground and pulled the other man out, this time far less gingerly. He windmill slammed the driver into the pavement of Park Street, plunging his talons into the surface so deeply Spoon thought he'd never get them out. Then Tesser spoke. Roared, more aptly.

The dragon had the man pinned flat on his back and leaned over him, looming. With a wide reptilian mouth he rumbled out the question, "WHERE IS MATTY!?" Tesser's breath came out so powerfully roadside trash flew away, and more car alarms went off. A window nearby broke from the strain. Spoon had the truck in park and was running towards the dragon, his hip doing its own version of a scream. He held the borrowed shotgun at his shoulder.

"She's mine now. So is the child in her womb, dragon!" Spoon heard the pinned man say savagely. When the sergeant rounded the massive dragon's hindquarters he saw that the man under Tesser's hand was actually the person who had worn the suit earlier. *Wait. That doesn't make sense. I saw Tesser punch that man's head practically clean off, and then I shot the cocksucker. I watched him die. He's dead on the street a mile or more away, how can he be here now?*

"THE CHILD IS NOT YOURS! WHERE IS SHE?! WHERE IS MY MATTY!?" Again the roar sent trash and debris everywhere. More windows broke. People were starting to stand from where they'd dived for cover, trying to understand what was happening. Some were elated, others crying. No one knew how much this moment was changing the world, but they were all entranced with it. Spoon was circling Tesser more, attempting to get a better look at the dragon's face.

"You've tried me before dragon. You failed then, and you'll fail now. Nothing has changed. Your fragile woman, your unborn child, and your pathetic world will all fall to me. Human greed and ignorance has opened the doors for my kind, and across the Veil we march. Soon, there will be too many of us for you to fight. There are too few of you left now that magic is dying away." The suit faced man taunted Tesser despite the level of danger he was in. Clearly these weren't the words of the sane.

Tesser leaned his massive form over even more, his snout just a few inches from the face of his captive. He lowered his voice to a gravelly rumble that made Spoon's hair stand on end. "Your kind have fought to cross the Veil since time began, and my kind and our allies have pushed you back time and again. You're right, nothing has changed."

"Magic is gone. Kaula is ours and all her soul is slowly being drained away, sent to the other side as fuel for our young," the man whispered. His eyes rolled upwards, and he took on a look of intoxication. It was as if he'd just been shot full of the most powerful heroin ever and it had only then met up with his mind. But all he'd done was taunt the dragon.

Spoon watched as Tesser's golden eyes grew dark red with fury. The sergeant had to take a step back out of fear. There was no stopping it. The dragon smiled suddenly. "You underestimate her will, Legion. As you underestimate mine. I shall send you back. Run. Dig deep and hard daemon. I'm coming for you."

Tesser's claws ripped free of the pavement faster than a strike of lightning. The dragon formed his hand into a fist the size of a boulder and rocketed it down through the body of the man sinking three feet deep into the street, erupting his bodily form into a cloud of black, wispy evil. Tesser ground his fist into the pavement and then withdrew it, savoring the eruption signaling the daemon body's destruction. After he opened his eyes, he looked around at the massive crowd that had gathered. Hundreds were capturing the image of the dragon and filming the event. Tesser turned down to Spoon.

"Abe is in the back. Please take him to the hospital. Quickly," Tesser's voice was low, but it still shook the chest.

Spoon lowered his shotgun and nodded. "I will. There's a few places right near here. What now? What do we do? You're a goddamn dragon."

"I've always been a dragon, Detective. Now? Now the world wakes up. Let me rouse the human race from its dark slumber of comfort and safety. Let them know what walks among them. What flies above. Ignorance will no longer be acceptable. I shall return soon. See to it my friends are taken care of." With that, Tesser launched his gigantic body back into the air, leaving massive claw marks in the road. His wings shoved the air around so violently Spoon was nearly toppled. He kept his balance through the pain in his side and watched as Tesser flew up, higher and higher between the city structures towards the pinnacle of one of the city's tallest buildings. Suddenly, Tesser banked and flew around the top of the building, circling it. He found something he liked and landed onto the top of the building, and his feet and arms locked on. He looked like a gargoyle gone mad, alive and writhing with inordinate power and energy. Tesser looked down at the crowd near the eastern edge of the Commons, and then clearly made eye contact with Spoon, even at that distance.

He's smiling.

Tesser leaned his long neck back and pointed his mouth to the sky. From the most powerful place deep in his dragon lungs he let slip a roar that shook the ground like an earthquake. It went on and on, tearing the sky in half and sending shivers down the backs of the bravest. There were some that couldn't hear it from where they were, but all knew something powerful had stirred. The roar broke through the shared fabric of consciousness and affected everyone within hundreds of miles. Then he unleashed his flame.

A column of fire came forth from deep within the dragon, setting his scales aglow from heat that came somewhere inside. The fire was as bright as the sun, and as it jetted upwards, boiling the clouds apart, the people below gasped at the warmth coming down. To be kissed by that flame would mean instant immolation. The flames reached higher and higher, creating a tower of brilliant energy and radiance that lit the city and state as if the sun had risen again that night.

How far can that be seen?

Tesser stopped his god-like gout of fire. He grinned

into the sky like the pleased Cheshire cat from Wonderland and vaulted off the skyscraper, slow powerful sweeps of his enormous bat like wings taking him higher and higher, piercing through the hole in the clouds his breath had cleared. The wispy remnants of white in the sky still kept light as if they were the coals in a hearth.

And with that, Tesser set forth more into motion than could be imagined.

Chapter Thirty-Eight
Fallout

The world changed immediately and on many levels.

The first response to Tesser's reemergence to the world stage was not by social media or the television networks. Instead Logan Airport and the Federal Aviation Administration were the first to react. Tesser's enormous body showed up as a brand new plane in the sky, and when an air traffic controllers attempted to contact his body, there was, of course, no response. Tesser did not have a radio to respond with, nor would he if he had one. Within minutes the proper emergency protocols were followed and the east coast air defense fighter jets were scrambled to the metropolitan Boston area to gets eyes on the rogue plane. No one wanted a repeat of 9/11.

Tesser disappeared off the radar about the same time they were crossing into Suffolk County, the home of Boston. The jets reported nothing amiss when they flew over the city, and no signs of a plane crash in the direction the unidentified object had flown in. But of course by the time they reached the area, the internet was already spreading the word.

It was less than ten minutes before photographs of Tesser were live on Tumblr, Twitter, Facebook, Pinterest, and all of the local television stations. Ten minutes after that, Youtube started to see a massive uptick in new videos loaded from the metro Boston area, and the spike in hits to those videos would be later described as a 'bandwidth tsunami.'

The initial reactions were as you'd expect and divided sharply. There were the disbelievers. No matter how many videos were made available over the next week (thirty-eight, if you're counting) they simply refused to believe the event was true. Special effects for a new movie. Government conspiracy. Sunspots. Hackers. Democrats. Republicans. You name the excuse and someone in that camp thought it up.

The second group was to embrace the wonder of the return of a dragon to the world. Signs of the massive golden dragon that could breathe flame were extolled and nearly worshipped by some. Seeing his near two hundred foot length ascend into the highest reaches of the Boston skyline inspired songs and poems of incredible beauty and imagination. Several of those songs went on to win awards, but that's a much different story, for a different day.

The third group responded quietly, preparing for the worst. They looked at the incredible destructive power of the dragon and stepped into their bunkers fearfully. They looked at the 24 vehicles Tesser destroyed by simply *flying over them* and the stretches of pavement punctured and shredded by his immense claws with absolute ease, and his mile high pillar of white hot flame and thought the worst. It was a monster movie come true, and many minds in the government wondered what exactly they would do should that dragon return vengefully. Contingency plans were made ready. Another pair of F15C fighters was put on ready alert in Westfield, Massachusetts, and another two F16C fighters made ready in Burlington, Vermont. Should the flying, fire breathing lizard return, the military felt itself ready. Of course, no one could say what the result of a dragon versus high tech aircraft battle would be.

The fourth group started to react immediately, though it took days for their voice to be heard. Tesser's sudden appearance triggered a burst of intense arcane energy into the world. Despite his role being the Dragon of Life and not the Dragon of Magic, his validation of the supernatural brought belief to the subconscious of billions and the active minds of billions more. As Tesser once said, belief defines experience, and when billions of people suddenly begin to think that magic *just might be real*...it becomes more so, and so do the creatures that are inherently magical.

In Buenos Aires a tribe of goblins erupted from their subterranean lair and into the city streets, emboldened and attempting to claim the city for their own. Luckily there were only a few hundred Goblins and their knowledge of modern technology was woeful. When the Argentinean military responded the goblins were dispatched with haste. Many were killed, but just as many escaped back down into their under city hive, led by their hulking goblin king. The city officials continue to search for the lair of the creatures, but as of yet have not found it.

To the north in Europe, far from where humans normally tread came the trolls. Hulking creatures stretching to nearly nine feet in height with shaggy moss-like fur from head to toe, and with large tusks and claws, they sent their shamans to the humans to make peaceful contact. They didn't know why now was the right time to do it, but they took the risk anyway. The Norwegian, Swedish, and Finnish governments took the high road and met the creature's diplomats with open (albeit protected at a distance with extremely powerful weapons) arms, and the first Troll-Human meetings in several thousands of years were held. They were peaceful, unlike many of the previous interactions between the two species. Especially the last encounter that sent the trolls into hiding long ago—but again, that's a much different story, for a different day.

Gardens all across the world where it was still warm started to flourish and bloom. The fairies had come back, their shy nature cast aside so they could bask in the glow of the surge of magic. Very efficient creatures at the spreading of pollen and the nurturing of flowers and all things botanical, the greenery and wonder of the previously mundane terrace flower collections erupted into a riot of life. People began to snap pictures of the tiny flying fae, drunk on the fresh flow of magic in the world and share them on the internet. The now famous photo of a female fairy smiling through a kitchen window at an eight-year-old Moroccan boy became an icon for the time.

The darkness came with the light, as one cannot exist without the other. Glasgow's night fell quickly into the hands of a large vampire nest that had been dormant for a century. Nightclubs, bars, pubs, museums, and many businesses were taken over by the creatures of the night. When the police attempted to investigate they too were taken over to the dark by the vampires, and to this day the Scottish city is not safe when the sun goes down. It isn't particularly safe during the day either. But as you might expect by now, that's a very different story, for a different day.

Then, and only then, the world accepted what was really and truly happening: it was the rebirth of a lost age. Magic had returned.

Poor Mr. Doyle's life was upended in the most stupendous of ways. He was blessed in the sense that his enchanted wine glass began to work once more. His body began to turn back the clock immediately after his first glass of fermented grapes, and he drank many, many glasses. Not for their restorative effects, but more to cope with the attention the world thrust upon him and nearly losing yet another apprentice. Nevertheless, the end result was the gift of a decade taken off his body, and the banishment of his arthritic pain.

He was first visited by the Boston Police, and then the FBI. Soon after, the ATF made their appearance, and after them came a string a mile long of government agencies with three letter acronyms. And they all asked the same questions.

Where did the dragon come from? Is he dangerous to National Security? Why did he destroy so much property? What happened to the men he killed? Why is there a talking tree in your front yard?

And on and on they went with their questions, pressing for more and more information. They attempted to seize all of Mr. Doyle's possessions, citing a string of laws that allowed them to do so; Mr. Doyle, ever the thoughtful and witty character, informed them that too few of the lab geeks would know how to handle such rare things of arcane power, and that the dragon might be very, very angry that the old man's things were taken from him. It was agreed by all that angering the dragon was a bad idea, so they allowed him to keep his artifacts. And Mr. Doyle was happy because he loved having all of his things and having them work again. The joy of bending the U.S. government over wasn't lost on him either.

Abraham Fellows, friend of Tesser and Mr. Doyle, was shot multiple times in the abdomen by Legion. He suffered a perforated lung, a shattered clavicle, multiple broken ribs, and his intestinal tract took it even worse than that. A doctor described his innards as being 'Swiss cheese' more than once. As Tesser had requested, Sergeant Spooner was able to rush Abe straight to Beth Israel which was only a few streets over. In the emergency room there the doctors were able to stop his bleeding and repair the incredible amount of damage done to his body. They surgeons later credited a spell cast by Mr. Doyle in his home for his survival. Their news conference after the fact started an entire industry of arcane medical study.

Sergeant Spooner was put through the ringer right alongside Mr. Doyle, though they took Spoon back to the station first. Had Spoon not taken the few days off that he did, he would've been fired for sure, but his explanation of being out for a drive that night was solid enough to pass the sniff test. It helped that Spoon was the sole Boston Police Department employee who had met Tesser in human form and could claim to have a good relationship with the dragon. Tesser's words to Spoon the night of his emergence helped smooth over any of the Sergeant's failings. He was put on paid leave as per department regulations while an investigation was made into the shootings. Granted, there were no dead bodies to account for, but that didn't make the incident any less interesting to a slew of already interested parties. When they realized that Spoon had been shot in the massive firefight, they rushed him back to Beth Israel to get patched up. Spoon never said anything about being hurt.

Perhaps most interesting of all the incidents during Tesser's two week-long absence from the world was the complete and utter fumbling of the investigation into Matty Rindahl's disappearance. She suffered from the poor timing of having been allegedly kidnapped on the same day as the first sighting of a dragon. Matty's parents were beside themselves, and after the world simmered down enough, they flew straight to the States to head the push into finding their daughter. Alexis, of course, was torn in two directions; she wanted to help find Matty, but she also wanted to be by Abe's side. In the end when Matty's parents arrived, she went to Abe. It was just easier to be there for him, and defending him from the thousands of questions levied in his direction was something she was very passionate about. He was *her* man after all. Plus, when Abe regained consciousness he assured Alexis that all would be well. After all, Matty had a dragon for a boyfriend.

No one told the media about the connection between Matty and Tesser. Perhaps if they had, Matty would've benefitted.

And through all this, slinking through the silence in which they had they carefully shrouded themselves, were the people in charge at Fitzgerald Industries. The paragons of modern science and medicine, slowly ushering magic out of the world and into oblivion, and allowing in the ever growing foothold of one of the most powerful of all the Veil-Born.

Legion.

Of course, when Tesser returned to the public eye two weeks after his world-changing encounter in the city of Boston, they would eventually be dragged out into the world spotlight.

And there would be blood, and there would be death.

Chapter Thirty-Nine

Mr. Doyle

In the aftermath of the daemonic assault, Mr. Doyle's home received immediate, extensive repairs. His thick and wide custom made front door held strong against the daemons that had come knocking. As was right, they were unable to cross the threshold of the ash door, but they did put hundreds of high velocity rounds through it. As he had feared, Mr. Doyle's arcane protections weren't designed for 21st century warfare.

In addition to his very expensive door, his rugs and hard wood floors were either torn up by more automatic weapons fire or were stained by obscene amounts of Abraham's blood. His entire dining room and most of his living room was run through with more destruction from the gunfire. It didn't help that when the wards on his bay windows failed and Legion came in with three of his false bodies, Mr. Doyle was forced to use an Incendium spell. He was able to kill one of the daemons with the arcane fire, but the other two…they left with Abraham before he could muster enough strength for a proper spell.

I should've been stronger. If there had been more magic for me to wield that night he would not have been shot at all. My wards shouldn't have failed. The spells and runes are centuries old, tried and true. But the magic that night was still thin, though it is better now with this sudden influx of arcane power since Tesser's true reveal.

And what a reveal it was. Mr. Doyle was dealing with the fallout from that now as well. The FBI brought in a special home contractor for Mr. Doyle that worked with the government. The Brit's home was rebuilt by the same men who worked on The White House. He was so *very* honored. When they finished he also ensured that there were no special listening devices worked into the repairs. He'd found none, but still refrained from talking to himself aloud.

The state of Mr. Doyle's rejuvenated home was in direct conflict with how devastated he was internally. His failed wards, his doubt of Tesser, and how impotent his magic was when it mattered most. Even though his apprentice Abraham had survived the daemonic assault, it would be some time before Mr. Doyle would be able to forgive himself for his failures. It was strange to be alone again so suddenly.

The pain of the teaching mage. To watch your apprentice learn a craft that will most likely kill them no matter how much knowledge you impart. It is akin to teaching a suicide bomber, albeit with no fanatic religious belief to make it acceptable. All I've taught poor Abraham is how to fail.

Outside the house on the street were uniformed Boston Police officers standing behind a ring of steel barricades. The city had brought in the metal fencing to keep curious folks away. This was, after all, where the dragon was first seen. Almost around the clock the iron bars kept someone out of the neighborhood and allowed him and the hamadryad some peace and quiet. Inside that outer ring of police was, of course, Ellen, the hamadryad. After the battle in the street she helped to swing in their favor, she had returned to her home in the garden. Not before the police saw her move there, of course. She was the subject of near constant scrutiny by a small cadre of scientists and government officials, but when a tree wishes to be left alone…it simply is. As the scientists were learning, Ellen was powerfully good at ignoring their questions. *I suspect she's waiting for Tesser's return before she speaks.*

Besides all the scientists and police, there were no less than twelve heavily armed government agents making constant patrols up and down the street. They reminded Mr. Doyle of the Legion bodies that had come for Tesser. *Fake men wearing fake uniforms, trying to trick the world into dying. At least these men are real. Born on the correct side of the Veil. The side where good at least has a chance to flourish.*

No one had been allowed into his home since that night, and he hadn't been allowed to leave. *That suits me. I've nowhere to go, and they keep bringing me suitable meals. Being protected by the government in this instance feels welcome, even though I know their guns will be useless if Legion returns.*

Mr. Doyle's phone had rung several times, but he kept his calls curt and to an absolute minimum. It was almost certain that the government was tapping his calls, and the last thing he wanted to do was give them time to trace an incoming call back to old friends. He'd never get over it if his incompetence led to a friend dying or being arrested. Many of Mr. Doyle's friends were wanted for various crimes that the modern world wouldn't understand the need for. *Abraham's near death would be enough guilt for a good long while, thank you.*

Mr. Doyle heard a noise from the kitchen. The now much younger man got to his feet and fingered a small pendant around his neck. His fingertip tickled with buzzing energy emanating from the smooth, plain brown stone. A single spoken word would unleash a terrible elemental force from the necklace at whomever or whatever he wished it upon. *At least I hope it will.*

Cautiously the old man left the living room and walked through the entranceway that still smelled of paint and treated wood. He crossed the spot on the floor where Abraham's blood had been spilled. A flash of memory of the deep red streaks from where the daemons had dragged Abraham's body came to him. The floor might be new, but those dark images would last for some time to come.

Mr. Doyle moved slowly but confidently down the short hall, past his pantry, and into the kitchen. He stopped when he saw a giant rat sitting on the counter near his sink. The rat was on its hind legs, sitting up like a tiny person might. For a moment, both froze, looking at one another.

Dear me, a large rodent.

Then the rat nodded its head in a far too human way. The rat had golden eyes.

Oh then. That might be Tesser. Let's attempt some subterfuge. "Well then, I think I'll retire upstairs. It's getting late." Mr. Doyle then backed away a few steps back towards his pantry, and the rat jumped off the counter. Then as it fell as smoothly as a curtain blows in a summer breeze, the rat transformed into a proud house cat. It thumped its feet onto the floor and skittered away, past Mr. Doyle and up the stairs with purpose.

Well, that settles that.

*****

When the aged British sorcerer reached the pinnacle of the stairs and wandered into his office, fighting to catch his breath, he saw that the Tesser-cat was on the desk, curled into a tight ball, and looking as mundane as any cat on Earth.

"You're a crafty one, dragon. Now get off my desk."

The cat stood up immediately and sprang off the fine oak worktable. Before the paws could hit the ground, Tesser's body morphed once more. The effect looked as if a cat had jumped off the desk, but a person had walked away from it.

"Sorry to enter like this, but I felt it was a good idea not to alert the suits outside," Tesser said. He was naked.

"Modesty first son, go get some clothes while I ready some protections," Mr. Doyle said, averting his gaze. Tesser left and scampered downstairs to his room, while Mr. Doyle fetched a handful of small scarab beetles from an aquarium in the back of his massive vault-room of artifacts. He delicately placed one beetle inside three different beautifully painted palm sized boxes. He closed a golden mesh lid over the insects, and within moments each box began to hum an unearthly tone. He arranged the three boxes in a very specific triangular pattern around his desk before sitting down. Tesser joined him as he leaned back comfortably.

"What are the beetles for?" Tesser asked as he sat down in a chair.

"When placed in those resonant boxes they emit a magical field of noise that cancels out most forms of eavesdropping. I think our privacy here is suspect and I see no reason to allow the government any insight into our conversation."

"Smart. It's impressive how much innovation the human race has brought to the magical world. I saw on the news that Abe is doing well. Thank you for helping save his life. Your spell seems to have saved him."

Mr. Doyle shook his head, the tiniest amount of frustration pressing his lips together tightly. "It was only partly my spell. Your friend, the Sergeant...I forget his name, but he was able to spirit our friend to the hospital. They were able to bring him back from the brink. Thankfully."

"I am very happy, Mr. Doyle. Abe is a friend of mine. If he had died, things would've been worse. I don't think I could've controlled myself."

Mr. Doyle paused before speaking again. "You have been gone a long time," Mr. Doyle said.

"The world needed time. I needed to hide, think, plan."

"Hide? Think? Plan? I should hope you have a right bloody good plan by this point. Stirring the pot is one thing. You've gone and upset the entire kettle. Your display at the top of that building the other night has unsettled the entirety of the human race. Other races as well it would seem. It was selfish, Tesser."

"It was necessary. Humans have forgotten what this world is about. They needed a slap in the face."

"People don't like being slapped in the face you arrogant sot!" Mr. Doyle cursed under his breath lowly. "You must understand people are *frightened* Tesser, and frightened people have wreaked a wretched amount of destruction and misery on this world. You stormed through one of the world's largest cities like a monster, not a creature of beauty and wonder and life, filled with wisdom and goodness. You ripped men from cars and flung them about like a spoiled child would cast aside a no longer amusing toy. You destroyed cars, you damaged homes, and to put icing on the cake, good friend, you climbed to the top of a building and breathed flame so high that the clouds burnt away. You sir, are no better than a monster in a Hollywood film. You're bloody Godzilla."

Tesser sought for a response but found none. He hadn't seen that movie, but he knew Mr. Doyle was right.

"You are a being of a different age, dragon. When last you were among our kind you dealt with uneducated, near feral heathens. But now we have science, mathematics, cities, cultures, and economics. Yes, I grant you we've left behind the finest art of magic, but Tesser you cannot simply *scare* humans into behaving as you wish us to. We can split the atom now, and that is a force that you cannot persuade or threaten into doing your bidding."

Tesser's ire grew at that scolding from the old man.

"Then what now? Men are responsible for who have taken away Matty and my unborn child. I searched high and low all across the city looking for her to no avail. Men have reached across the Veil and brought into this world foulness that cannot and shall not be tolerated to exist here. If you continue to tread the path that you walk I will have no other choice than to *cull the herd*. It is my task to manage the life of this world, and if I deem you a liability, then you *shall be removed*."

"Your threat is childish, Tesser, and I say that knowing you probably mean every word of it. I also know you're apt to be the kind of chum that can follow through on that threat."

"I am," Tesser said hotly. The dragon's anger had raised the temperature in the room. Literally.

"But you've failed to realize that you've the talent to change things. A great opportunity still lies within reach for you, and you need to seize it before it slips away." Mr. Doyle started to smile. *Let's see how patient he can be.*

"Talk," Tesser said leaning forward in his chair. The room cooled a bit.

"The media sees a bat winged dragon scaring a city, and immediately you become the villain. Tried and found guilty in the court of public opinion. The boogie monster, the bogey, the bump in the night. But we both know different. Abe knows different. No matter how many television news casts show Ellen standing in my garden peacefully, the world is still frightened by what happened here in this city, and that is your fault. And Tesser, scared humans do very stupid things. I remind you of the atom. But I tell you this, humans who are excited, and see good and kindness…they can change the world. You want to bring magic back? You want to rescue Matty and your sister Kaula? Then tell us the truth to our faces. Show the world who Tesser really is and why he is here once more."

"You want me to speak publicly?"

"In a calm, rational way. In this form, your human form. Of course, you should arrive or leave in a way that people will not be able to look away from. Something majestic and beautiful. Something that people *must* watch and will *never* be able to forget."

"You've got an idea already. Sneaky old bastard," Tesser said wryly.

Mr. Doyle grinned. "Guilty as charged, your honor. As someone under what amounts to American house arrest, I feel as if though I have a certain amount of clout in the political arena. I have access to something they want. I feel like I could arrange an event the likes of which the whole world wouldn't be able to turn away from it."

"When would this happen? I don't want to delay the search for Matty."

Mr. Doyle considered some thoughts. "I think three days. Yes. Give me three days. I think this event would need to be held in a different place. A different city."

"I fly very fast old man. You should see it."

"I'm sure before the end of my days I shall see you spread your wings in more peaceful times. But now, prepare a statement to the world. Think of what you can say to billions of scared, confused people, and all the strange little creatures of the night you've stirred up. You've poked the hornet's nest, now it's time to calm the hive."

"Interesting metaphor."

"I am a very interesting person Tesser."

Chapter Forty
Matty

Matty's consciousness was elusive. She spent most of her time in a deep well of dreams that she couldn't climb out of. Her mind drifted to and fro in swirls of color, memory, and precognition. Some of what she saw she knew would come to pass, but in her haze she could never quite hold on to what she saw. It was exhilarating and frustrating all at once. Matty's spirit was strong, however, and she fought. She fought in her own way.

"She's a tough one," Matty heard a technician say to a colleague. Matty kept still, her eyes closed. "It's always the quiet ones. We've got her on double the normal drip of sleepy juice, and she's still coming to at least once an hour. It's like trying to sedate a fucking elephant. She's something else."

Whoever the man was speaking to responded, "And she's pregnant too. I wish we could hit her up with stronger shit."

"Stronger shit? This stuff that came up from R&D is the same shit we keep Purple tied down with. She's on dragon dope man. I just hope it doesn't fuck with the baby."

"Maybe that's the whole point of this. Maybe she's not

sick like Mr. Fitzgerald says. Maybe this is all some kind of evil conspiracy to mess with the fetus. Maybe we're in the dragon making business now."

There was a moment of silence, and then the two laughed at the absurdity of it all. A few seconds later Matty felt a tingling running up her forearm where the IV was, and soon after she drifted back into an unhappy slumber.

"Why are you here?" a feminine voice asked.

"Me? Why am I here?" Matty asked in response.

"Yes, why are you here? This is not a good place. You should leave if you can." The voice was old, but had a youthfulness to it at the same time, like a child who says something wise when you least expect it.

"I don't know where I am. I was taken here." Matty suddenly realized where *here* was. She sat on a wooden bench in a room, a large room about the size of a high school gymnasium. Her toes were in short but thick gold grass. There was a roof above, impossibly high and speckled with lights that glowed like fluorescent stars. All around her were computers and printers, tubes and wires, tables and desks, all decayed and overrun by vibrant purple flowers. In the corners, just on the periphery of her vision, she could see tall trees reaching toward the ceiling. She couldn't see if they reached it or not.

"Hm. Being taken here is a very bad thing indeed. I was taken here," the voice said sadly from nowhere.

"Who are you?" Matty asked.

"I'm Kaula."

"Kaula? That's a pretty name. What does it mean?"

"Thank you. It means many things to many people Matty. Eventually it will mean something to you."

Matty felt queasy. "How do you know my name?"

"This is a dream Matty. The impossible is possible here."

Matty suddenly felt much better. "Oh yeah. Well, I

thought I was all alone down here. After Mr. Fitzgerald sent his goons to get me I thought I would be killed."

A tall, young woman came around the edge of Matty's vision then. She was long of leg and had platinum hair that picked up the purple from the flowers and trees. She had eyes with a hint of an almond shape to them and looked faintly Asian. She smiled at Matty as she took a seat on the wooden bench next to her.

"You're far too important for them to kill Matty. Besides, you aren't what they really want." Kaula's eyes drifted down to Matty's tummy.

"They want my baby, don't they?" Matty's hands moved to her stomach defensively, protecting the tiny growing child within.

The woman named Kaula nodded and looked back up to Matty. "They want your baby and her father."

"*Her* father? I'm going to have a girl? I wanted a boy. Well, I wanted *another* boy." Matty's mood swung dark. Her emotions welled inside and she felt a tinge of physical pain.

"I know. Poor Aiden never had a chance, and such a pretty name for a young boy. I'm sorry Matty, but these things happen for a reason. Had Aiden been born, your daughter would've never come about. And she is so *very* important."

That made Matty feel a little better. "They want Tesser?"

"They do," Kaula said firmly.

"Why?"

Kaula smiled, and then thought about how best to phrase her answer. "Tesser is very special. One of a *very* small group of *very* important people. It was no accident that you two met. You too are special. And your love, it will change the world Matty. It is such a beautiful thing to watch happen. There is more magic in that than you can imagine. You have been strong Matty, and brave, but you will need to be so much stronger before this is all over."

Matty's vision was clouding. It felt as if a mist were forming in the strange indoor-outdoors she and the woman in her dream were in. The mist came with a matching fog in her mind. "I'm sorry, Kaula. But, I'm special?" Matty blinked her eyes repeatedly, trying to get the haze to go away.

"You are not *just* human. Tesser can sense it I'm sure, though I cannot say if he knows exactly how or what you are. It is not important right now, though. All will come to light soon though, Matty. For now, protect your child as you have been. Fight against the Veil toxins they pump into you. Do not succumb to their manipulations. You must be strong as I am. Keep hope alive, my child. In the end, you are needed to keep all the balance."

Matty lost the dream as Kaula spoke. She drifted backwards as if falling through clouds, and once again the ill comfort of forced sleep was upon her.

One thought echoed in her mind, bouncing off all the others. It came in Kaula's voice. "In the end, you are needed to keep all the balance."

Chapter Forty-One
Sergeant Spooner

Henry Spooner was in Beth Israel hospital on the same floor as Abraham Fellows. The Feds felt it was easier to protect the two of them that way. Spoon wasn't sure what good a bunch of uniforms and suits were going to be if those damn things came for him.

What kind of fucking person explodes into smoke when they die? Tesser said daemons? What the fuck is up with that? First he says daemons are real, then a goddamn tree starts moving like in that Lord of the Rings movie, and then he turns into a fucking fire breathing dragon? Man. What next?

Spoon's hospital room door swung in and a handful of officers came through. They were all detective rank or higher and wore suits that were purchased off the discount rack. All except for one gray haired man. He led the pack like an alpha wolf right up to the side of Spoon's bed. *Oh yeah, the inevitable ass reaming, that's what's next.*

"Sergeant Spooner, I just wanted to stop in personally to say hello. I'm Commissioner Kearney. May I call you Henry?" The well-dressed cop asked.

Yeah, I know who you are. "It's nice to meet you Commissioner. Henry will do just fine." Spoon extended his hand with a small wince. His hip was still smarting, even after the painkillers. Spoon noticed under his suit jacket he wasn't wearing a sidearm. *I think if I were the Commissioner I'd carry my piece, now more than ever.*

"I just wanted to let you know how much the city appreciates your actions the night the dragon happened. Quite the story, eh? What was it like to be right there? At that thing's feet?"

Spoon fought back a small wave of nausea. A side effect of the medication he was on. "That *thing* is a man, sir. At *his* feet. It was scary sir. Real scary. I'm glad I was there, though. Lucky."

The commissioner nodded emphatically, apologetically. All the sycophants around him did the same. "Luck, yeah. Hey, you want to talk about luck? None of the weird shit that's happening in other places is happening here. Have you been watching the news, Henry?" The Commissioner asked, pointing at the remote hanging on the arm rail of the bed.

"No, sir. I'm trying to watch as much sports as I can. I find the news is mostly bad news, and I get enough of that at work. It always seems like I get a call when the Patriots are on."

"Ain't that the truth, Henry? Well, weird stuff; not dragons, but still real, weird stuff all over. Santa Barbara had these flying, singing things lure a whole shitload of folks right off a pier to drown. They looked like feral winged bat people. SWAT had to bring 'em down with sniper fire. They lost a whole tactical team trying to move out on the pier. The singing. Made 'em crazy. And Cincinnati, whoa nelly. They got that abandoned subway system under the city, right? And a couple days ago these giant fucking rats just appeared down there. Huge things, each one the size of a Doberman. They came out of those tunnels and started to bite people. They have eight dead there tonight. They're getting flamethrowers from the Army to go down in there and burn them out. But not here, Henry. Not in Boston. I think the weird shit in the world is afraid of old Beantown. I think they know not to mess with us. Boston strong."

Spoon snickered, shaking his head.

"You don't agree, huh? You think something else is going on here?"

"Commissioner, that dragon, Tesser, is likely one of the most powerful creatures this world has ever seen. Nothing in the fossil record tops it, right? So we got two things going on here as I see it. I figure either all the weird shit in this city or near this city knows a dragon is here and doesn't want to risk getting burnt up, eaten alive, or thrown off the side of the fucking state senate dome like a discarded chicken wing. What scares me Commissioner, is that I don't think that's what's happening. What I believe is that the things, and I do mean the *things* that were going after Tesser are so fucking horrible, nothing wants anything to do with the city of Boston right now. We've got a problem no one wants any part of. I'd bet not one weird incident has happened in a hundred mile radius of here. I think there's a cancer in this city, and it's keeping folks that know about it away."

"Well, you're right about some of that. Some strange things up in Maine and northern New Hampshire but not much else nearby," the Commissioner said.

"I thought as much. Same as back in Afghanistan, sir. When everything goes quiet, the locals go to ground, and all seems safest, you prepare for the worst. You're usually a hundred meters from a friend dying." Spoon looked down at his feet. He imagined them encased in his old Army boots and could almost taste the thin mountain air again.

"You alright, Sergeant Spooner? You look a world away."

"Yeah. For a minute there. Thinking of friends I don't have anymore."

The Commissioner let the room stay quiet for a minute, respecting Spoon's reflection. "Sergeant, when you're healthy there's something I want to talk to you about. An opportunity of sorts."

"Oh, yeah?" *What the hell is this all about?*

"Well, you've got a connection with this dragon, this Tesser. If he were to return to the city, to anywhere, would you be willing to try and talk to him? Be America's envoy to dragonkind? It might mean some travel. I understand if you don't want to go anywhere near that thing again, but there are people above my already high pay grade who think you should strongly consider it."

"Please stop saying 'that thing' sir. He has personality. A sense of humor. Honor. He's a good person. Don't forget he rescued a woman who was about to be raped."

"He caused several million dollars in property damage and managed to scare the shit out of a lot of people too. Call him what you will Sergeant, but the government wants someone to talk to him, and your name keeps coming up as the best option far and away. I'm buying you, *we* are buying you time, but eventually the men in black suits are going to come knocking and by then it'll be out of my control. Just think on it. Until you're out of here I think I can protect you, but kid, you're in demand right now. This was a courtesy visit."

Shit. "I appreciate that, sir. More than you know. I don't know if I'm qualified to be a dragon diplomat or whatever that job might entail. I can tell you, Tesser was a good person to me, and if there's anyone who might be able to talk to him, it might be me. Emphasis on might."

"Fair enough. We're also trying to wrap up the investigation into the shooting. We'd like to spring you from here and get you back on the job. And Sergeant, don't take any goddamn book deals. You're a better cop than a writer."

"Maybe I'll do the morning show circuit. Bang some actresses."

The Commissioner grinned and shook Spoon's hand.

"That's the spirit."

"Oh, and tomorrow make sure you're watching the television at two. Something's happening down in DC. We were told to pay attention, so heads up. I think I'm going to fly down later tonight to attend whatever it is. I know the mayor and the governor are heading down. I figure there'll be enough space for me to stand somewhere and look important. When you're given a chance to rub elbows with the big folks, you might as well push for it."

"Yeah, you bet. Have a good time if you go. Represent the force well. Thanks guys, appreciate the visit. Tell the men to stay frosty. Strange times."

"I will, Sergeant. Hey, what did you call those armored people from that night? Devils?"

"Daemons, sir. Tesser said they were daemons. Creatures from Hell, I think."

"I wonder if you're the first Boston cop to kill a daemon? We're gonna need to draft up some kind of service award for that, I think. The people love heroes, Sergeant. They love 'em, and right now they're scared, and they need a hero. You'll do just fine. Get well soon, kid. My office or an office much larger than mine will be in touch about the job offer."

"Of course, take care guys," Spoon said after another handshake. The Commissioner and his lackeys walked out of the room, all very animated and happy about how the strange visit went. The door shut with a soft medicinal click, and the wounded cop was alone again.

Ah, shit. I wish Bobby was here. He'd actually make me smile.

Chapter Forty-Two
Abraham

I wish this little fucking button worked more often.

Abe was propped up in his hospital room. No longer in the Intensive Care Unit, he was on a recovery floor of the Beth Israel Hospital, and he had the controller for his pain medication in his hand. The smooth rubber depressor in the center of the plastic controller had a button beneath it, and the button only released so much of the pain relieving love so often. He pushed the button rapidly, trying to intimidate the machine into giving him an extra dose early. It was a cruel game.

I feel like there's a chainsaw inside my abdomen. A running chainsaw. Covered in lemons. Seriously. They should double how often I can hit this fucking switch, and that might let me get some goddamn relief. I haven't slept decently since I woke up in the ICU.

Abe heard Alexis just outside the door of his private hospital room. She was talking to the two suits in the hall. "Look you two. You let me in. I was here this morning, and I was here last night. I'm on the list. Look at the damn list." There was a pause. "See, right there. Top of the list thankyouverymuch."

The door opened, and the feisty redhead came through it. She was all smiles.

"Hey, you," Abe said. It hurt to talk.

"Hey. How are you feeling today?" Alexis asked as she approached. Her arms were filled with sweet treats and soda, as well as a handful of books Abe had asked her to retrieve from his apartment. Apparently there was no way she could get into Mr. Doyle's home. It was under heavy guard ever since the attack.

"I was just thinking of lemon coated chainsaws lodged in my large intestine."

"That bad, huh?" She stroked his forehead and gave him a kiss. He was the tiniest bit sweaty from the pain.

Abe nodded sadly, "Yeah, pretty bad. I'm still on a liquids only diet, babe. They won't let me eat that stuff. Thank you for bringing it, though."

"Should I take it home and run it through the blender? Want a milkshake? Tell me what I can get for you."

"Just hang out with me while this thing happens on television. Supposedly the President is announcing something to the world. Has to do with Tesser and all the weird shit he stirred up across the world."

Alexis pulled the uncomfortable hospital chair over to the side of his bed and sat down. "Okay. Put it on, and let the President wow us with his intellect, charm, and power."

Abe grinned. *At least smiling doesn't hurt.* Abe popped on the television and found a station he liked. It seemed like most were carrying the 'event.'

"Jesus. Look at that." Abe swallowed down a wave of pain as he adjusted his bed upright. On the screen was a wide-angle shot of the Lincoln Memorial. Where the steps should've been was a massive tiered stage and grandstand filled with hundreds of suit wearing politicians, dignitaries, religious figures, and government officials. It was a who's who of important people and served as one of the most impressive gatherings in remembered history. Security in the background looked incredibly heavy, as was to be expected. Men wearing head to toe black body armor and carrying military grade weaponry were standing every fifteen to twenty feet.

At the foot of the stage stood tens of thousands of people, all huddled together against the bitter chill in the autumn air. They carried signs that ran the gamut of human emotions on the current state of the world. "God Save Us!" "The End is Nigh!" "Peace and Love!" "Dragon for President, '16" "Impeach! Elect a troll they have tusks!" "I blame the GMOs!" And so many more. Hundreds of signs were held high, some proudly, others sarcastically.

On the stage was the podium of the President, flanked as always by his two panes of teleprompter glass. The camera pushed in on the podium as a chorus of cheers and jeers greeted the President's arrival on the stage. He walked with confidence, waving to the crowd as he walked up to the podium and microphone. Once there, he let the noise linger for a minute before talking.

"Today marks a unique occasion in history. As we know, the world has changed in many ways the past few weeks, marked by the arrival of a creature out of myth and fiction. Many of you are now calling it the Great Boston Dragon." A round of applause came from the crowd.

"Many of you have seen the news since then. You probably have heard of all the bad looking things that are starting to appear in the dark. Monsters, some say. New animals, some say. And we all know that our world has always been filled with wonder and magic, but now that magic is here in a very literal and real sense. Many of you are excited by the opportunities this has afforded our civilization, but many of you are also frightened of this new world, understandably. I am pleased and proud to be here on this American stage as humanity and planet Earth step into a new age."

These don't seem like scared people to me. They seem

excited.

The President waited for the cacophony to die down. "Many of you listening to this, watching this moment of history on the television aren't from America, and you're probably thinking and wondering, 'why America?' I want to tell our allies all across this world that The United States was approached by a very special person recently and they are here to address the public. I'll be honest, at first I was hesitant to be the host for this event. I thought it would be safer to do it somewhere remote, somewhere we could contain it away from population. But I said no to that. To be unafraid of change is to show courage, and to change we need to embrace this new world we live in courageously. Ladies and gentlemen, I present to you America's and the World's newest friend, Tesser." The President stepped back from the podium and gestured to the side of the stage where he had stepped up himself just minutes before. A tall blonde man stepped onto the stage and strode across it to the leader of the free world.

"Oh, holy fuck look at that. It's Tesser. Shaking hands with the President." Abe's heart monitor started to alarm he was so excited. Alexis took his hand into hers and the machine gave up its dismaying cry.

The golden eyed, blonde man wore a sky blue button down shirt and slate gray slacks. He looked professional but not political. With a thin shirt and slacks he was underdressed against the cold wind of the day. His attire looked humble but intentional as he shook the President's hand firmly, thanking him away from the microphone. The President put a strong hand on Tesser's shoulder, showing firm positivity, and holding him still in the moment as a hundred thousand camera flashes lit up. That image would be shared for years.

After saying his two cents to the new friend of the world, The President let go of Tesser, and the man in dragon form walked up the podium. He was smiling, handsome and charming, quickly and easily eclipsing the charisma the President had. He adjusted the microphone upwards.

"Hello, World. As the President said, my name is Tesser. It's a pleasure to be able to address so many of you in this way. I'm not accustomed to all this, so please bear with me as I stumble through this speech."

People were going hysterical cheering, and Abe knew they had no idea why. If Tesser wanted to be elected President of Everything right then, he'd win in a landslide.

"The world has changed for what I know to be for the better. You see, I come from a time where what you see as new and frightening is old and common. I see a world that has lost touch with its sense of wonder, filled with people who do nothing but wake, work, and sleep. There are too few fireside stories told, and too few days spent lost in the warm summer sun. Too few fairy tales, and too many school shootings."

Tesser had to pause. He was drowned out by raucous applause again. When it died down, he continued.

"This may alarm you. It may also scare you, but the world has been sculpted over time by a race of creatures that have stayed out of your memory for too long, and I come here today before you all to apologize for our lack of presence. On behalf of the seven dragons of Earth and all that we hold precious and dear on this big blue world filled with magic and life and laughter, I say I am sorry for the lack of effort we have put into making your world a better place."

The people lost their minds again. Some of the audience had expressions of shock on their faces. Disbelief was scattered in, but most were roaring with approval and admiration for the statements Tesser had made. So many people craved a change. Abe and Alexis watched it all, but after a minute Alexis turned to Abe.

"What is he saying? On behalf of the dragons? He's apologizing for them? Like he's a messenger? Is he part of some ancient conspiracy or something?" Alexis was confused.

Abe sighed softly. "Alexis, he *is* a dragon. He's Tesser, the dragon of life. The same one who rescued me the night of the attack."

Alexis stared at him. "Fuck you."

"Really. He's a dragon, Alexis. The real fucking deal."

Tesser spoke again, and the couple fell silent. "The other night the city of Boston was taken by surprise by an entity that has forced its way across the Veil, invading Earth from a realm beyond reason, beyond hope, and polluted by evil. The Bible has referred to this entity as Legion. Some of you saw the end of the battle against Legion that night. You saw a dragon fight that battle."

Murmurs of fright came from the crowd.

"Legion is a daemon. What we have grown to call a 'Veil-Born.' An alien to this reality that must be sent back before he opens a rift wide enough to let loose a flood of pure, unadulterated evil that cannot be stopped."

Now the crowd was near panic.

"But I assure you Earth, there exists a force that eclipses even that of Legion's. A force for good and kindness greater than the force for evil Legion represents. I am Tesser. I am the tender of your flock, and you are my charge in this life. You are all my children, and like the vengeful father I am, there shall be no rest for Legion, no hole deep enough to hide in, no mountain too high for me to climb in my quest to rid this world of him. Legion is not welcome here, and let this serve as his eviction notice."

The crowd was going insane with energy. The politicians and gathered people of importance in the grandstand were all standing now, emphatically clapping their hands, even though Abe could see they weren't quite sure what the hell Tesser's deal was.

Tesser walked away from the podium and onto a wide area of the stage set off to the side. *How did I not notice that the podium was off center like that before? It's like there's enough space for him to...*

Tesser undid the top button of his shirt, and somehow spoke loud enough for the crowd and the nearby microphones to hear. Even through the television Abe could feel his voice resonating somehow. *It's like he's right here in the room with us.*

"I will take the fight against all that threatens humanity and the creatures of this world we call home together," Tesser said, as his shirt opened up. That image would be on posters and shirts the next day. "I cannot do it alone. I will need you to help me. Many of you must step into the breach to protect one another from the things that have forgotten that they need to fear me. That they need to fear all the dragons. But rest assured my people— " Tesser shrugged his shirt off, and let it drop to the floor of the stage. "I am Tesser, and I am YOUR Dragon."

Tesser crouched low with a smile so joyous and so pure that Abe couldn't help but let slip a squeal of delight. Then, as sudden as a mongoose's strike, he propelled his body into the air and shifted form into what he truly was.

Nearly every television station in the world watched live.

Tesser's massive golden form elongated from his human form, bursting all of his remaining clothing as he transformed into his full dragon body in just seconds. Before he could fall into the crowd, his sail-like wings flapped powerfully once, and he took off up and over the assembly, taking flight down the length of the Reflecting Pool, heading straight towards the gray spire of the Washington Monument. Cameras spun on their mounts to track his tremendous first public flight, catching the awed faces of those present. The water below him formed overlapping ripples as the air cascaded down from his flight. His tail swung back and forth as he ascended up to the peak of the Washington spire where he circled once and then perched impossibly, all four massive clawed hands gripping the stone gingerly, keeping him suddenly still like a gargoyle.

Tesser launched another stream of white-hot flames from deep within his throat across the sky above, lighting up the already bright day. The flames evaporated in the air, and the dragon let loose a triumphant roar, announcing to all he was present, and he was the new guardian and leader of the world.

Tesser propelled his body into the air with his legs and a flap of his wings, and he took higher and higher to the sky.

Abe hadn’t lost his childlike glee from the showing. He looked over to Alexis, and she too had a smile that couldn't be explained. "I told you. He's a dragon. He's *our* dragon."

From outside the room Abe and Alexis suddenly heard a stern voice, "Sir, Sergeant, you need to return to your room." Then the door burst in.

The cop, the same cop that had brought Abe to this very hospital the night of Tesser's first appearance came in. He was leaning hard on an IV stand, using it as one might use a tall walking stick and was clearly straining against a good amount of pain.

He was shot at least once too. What he's doing here?

"You're Abe right? Tesser's friend?"

Tesser's friend? Man. That has such a different meaning right now. "Yeah. You're the cop that saved my life, right? Spooner?"

The cop shuffled over as two uniformed policemen followed him in, exchanging looks of dismay and irritation. Neither wanted to be the one to put hands on the "Dragon Cop."

Spoon made it to a second uncomfortable hospital chair and collapsed, exhausted. He caught his breath and then waved the two policemen away dismissively. They shrugged and left the room.

"Yeah, I'm Spoon. Nice to meet you. You know this gunshot wound didn't hurt until they dug the damn bullet out of me. Now I can barely fucking walk."

"Thank you for saving Abe's life officer. We owe you a huge debt of gratitude," Alexis said, getting up and moving over to him. She kissed his cheek.

"It's not officer. I'm a detective. Detective Spooner. I'd normally say no biggie, but I busted ass to get rid of the officer title, so I feel entitled to it," Spoon said, forcing a grin through his pain.

Alexis made a sympathetic face. "Okay, Detective. You earned that for sure. Thank you."

"Yeah, man, thank you," Abe said.

"You're welcome. So kid. We need to talk."

Abe shrugged. "About what?"

"Well, the world was a fucked up place before the two of us got shot to shit, and with all that happened that night, and with the stunt our mutual friend just pulled for all the world to see, I get the distinct feeling we're gonna need to work together to figure out what all needs to happen before he rips the world in half looking for that Legion thing."

Abe's mind raced. "Sergeant, he's probably not even all that pissed about the daemons. He's got other problems."

"Say what?"

"Unlike my good rap friend Jay-Z, Tesser has 99 problems, and one of them *is* his girlfriend. She's pregnant, and those daemons snatched her up. And if you think we're in trouble with him angry, he was already pissed about one of the other six dragons being missing. If we don't get this figured out there could be wrath and ruin on a scale that makes the worst stories in The Bible look like a coloring book."

I didn't think he could get any paler.

Chapter Forty-Three
Alec Fitzgerald

Alec was sweating. He'd just finished watching the on air reveal of the dragon that had escaped Mr. Host's snatch attempt.

Everything is going to come apart. The world knows now that dragons are out there, they're going to realize that they are intelligent and have souls, and then they're going to start looking for them. And what the fuck do I do about my staff? Everyone here at Amethyst knows now that the fucking dragon we've got knocked out downstairs is alive and kicking and would want to wake up. And let's not forget that there are just seven of these damned things in existence, so it's not like we can hide behind the idea of 'well, it's just one dragon out of many.' One peep out of any of these people and we're exposed. Fitzgerald Industries is shitcanned. What the fuck am I going to do? We're doing so much good work here. Saving lives.

Alec's phone rang. He picked it up. "Alec here."

"We need to discuss a plan. Are you free?"

It was Mr. Host. "Yes. Come up to my office." Alec hung up the phone before Mr. Host could say anything else. The minutes long wait for the otherworldly security man felt eternal to Alec. He couldn't decide which was worse, meeting with an angry Mr. Host or dealing with the fallout of the revelations handed out to the world just minutes before on television. It didn't help that Alec knew deep down inside that the 'Legion' creature Tesser spoke of was most likely something Mr. Host had control over. Alec shuddered at the thought. Mr. Host entered the room and caught Alec's gaze with impassive, soulless eyes. He strode over and sat down in a chair. They were silent for a few too many awkward seconds.

"What do we do? I thought we could keep everything quiet so long as everyone was scared of the other dragon, but now they know he's a good guy. What's our biggest problem right now? Is it Tesser finding us?" Alec blurted.

Mr. Host stared at Alec like a hawk looking down on field mouse. Alec shrank down, suddenly afraid. "In a way, yes. The purple dragon's presence here must be kept absolutely secret. We must ensure that no employees here speak about it. We must pay bonuses immediately. We must ensure that they are aware that this dragon was found brain dead, and that we are keeping it intact as we are for medical reasons. They must be made complicit, Alec. Willing. We must convince them that what we are doing is righteous and good. Do you understand?"

"Yeah. What do you think is a fair bonus to pay? Five grand each?"

"For the lower level employees with minimal knowledge, yes. Twice that for middle level or informed employees, and four times that for those with extensive knowledge."

"That's a lot of money, Mr. Host."

"It is nothing weighed against the potential loss of your entire business empire, Alec. An occasional and temporary financial setback is inevitable when you deal with the stakes that we play with. Celebrate that you have the fiscal power to purchase your way out of this situation." Mr. Host smiled.

God, that's creepy as fuck. "What do we do if people ask tough questions? What if they refuse to stay quiet?"

"You're a smart man, Alec Fitzgerald. You are your father's son. You will say the right things because you're intelligent, and charismatic, and they will love you for the truth you give them. And should they refuse to cooperate with this plan then I will speak to them, and convince them with a more archaic means of diplomacy."

"You're going to threaten them, aren't you?"

"Everyone has something to lose, Mr. Fitzgerald. Exercising leverage over someone simply requires the knowledge of what they do not wish to lose. You'd be surprised how quickly the staunchest opponent of an idea can be swayed when they stand to lose something precious. I would point you towards the example of Matilde resting peacefully below us."

"I don't know if I like that idea," Alec said, thinking of a series of terrible scenarios where his hard working employees were terrified by the strange and evil man sitting in front of him. Assuming he could even be called a man.

"I don't think what you like matters, Alec. There is only what must be done for the greater good. You are doing amazing things to advance humanity here. Sometimes those with a lack of vision must be brought to heel to see the future. Let me handle the less pleasant aspects. You do what you do best."

"I guess that'll work. When do we do this?"

"Now. The Human Resources department informed me this morning that all but four employees came in today. We should assemble them in the cafeteria immediately. They would be expecting some kind of all-hands meeting at this point."

"True. I'll have my secretary page the building. Make sure they all come?"

"I already have the doors to the building staffed with my men."

I don't like the way he said that.

*****

Fifteen minutes later Alec stood in his company's cafeteria surrounded by a large group of his employees. Alec surveyed their faces, trying to get a feel for the assembly.

Most look worried. These meetings are rarely good for morale. Everyone thinks there are going to be cutbacks and their head is on the block. I've got to get that whole idea out of their heads fast. Some look rightly afraid. They know we're involved in this dragon shit, and they expect the worst. I need to make sure those people know they're safe. Some of them look angry. They know something is wrong with what's happening here, and they want answers. I'll need to give those people something to chew on. Some kind of moral ownership of it, and some kind of moral reasoning for how what we do is good. All smiles, and here we go.

"Thank you all for coming to this last-second impromptu gathering, folks. I know this is a disruption to your day, but in light of the events down in DC earlier this afternoon Fitzgerald Industries, and me, mainly, felt it was vital to have a conversation about what happened down there and how it relates to what we're doing here."

Okay, so far, so good.

"For those of you who were unable to see the worldwide broadcast down in Washington, a second dragon, the same dragon that was seen down in Boston breathing fire into the sky, held what amounts to a news conference. He claimed that he was now 'our dragon' and that he was here to help protect humanity."

The group of people had a wide array of responses. Some cheered, some gasped. Most simply murmured. This development was significant for them in a personal way.

"I can completely understand all of you thinking and wondering about how this development affects you personally as employees here at Project Amethyst, as well as how this affects the whole of Fitzgerald industries. Well, I'm here to hopefully address your concerns and fill you in on some details that have been kept secret for some time."

A few people clapped.

"Our dragon, Amethyst, was taken into our protection after an expedition found her in Asia. I can't say exactly where, as that's still secret. I can assure you that when Amethyst was taken here, she was already well on the way to being brain dead and that my father's wishes were for her to be brought to a place similar to the one we have created for her where she could help others live better lives. I am told her last words to the team that stabilized her were something to the effect of, 'Please use me to make the world a better place.' And people of Project Amethyst, for ten years we have done just that. We have given back so much to humanity by harvesting the incredible gifts this dragon has provided to us. We are doing her an honor by providing our services to civilization, and I want to thank you for all that you do." Alec clapped hard and put on his best show of emotion. He thought forcefully of his kitten, the one that died in his arms when he was seven. The memory dredged up old emotions, and tears started to run down his cheeks immediately. Alec could see multiple people well up in response.

Perfect. "Obviously with the knowledge that our dragon is not the only dragon in the world we need to change how we do things around here. We'll be reaching out in the next few hours to get in touch with the Federal Government on how we can best talk with this new Tesser dragon, and how we can move forward in a way that is both respectful to this new community in a way that protects humanity's best interests, as well as the best interests of the company at large. We want to be a responsible corporate partner with the world, especially as it changes so dramatically. Also, as we are heading to the end of fiscal quarter four, we'd like to make another announcement as well. Due to Fitzgerald Industries' incredible success this year, we are sharing a package of retention and loyalty bonuses. As a thank you for your incredible dedication to the work we do here and your discretion in keeping the privacy of the corporation, I'm happy to announce bonuses for every person in this room, starting at no less than five thousand dollars."

The applause was immediate and tremendous. *Money talks, baby. So far, so good. Here's the last big hurdle.* "Now, I know some of you have questions for myself and the organization, and I want you to know many of them will be answered in the next week or two as we sort out what those answers actually are. This is news to us as well. Having said that, do any of you have a pressing question about the bonuses or the events of the past few weeks?"

A hand shot up from the middle of the crowd. Alec pointed at them, and they asked a question. "When will the bonuses show up in our paychecks?"

Alec nodded, agreeing with the sense of the question. *I know him, perfect.* "I can't say for sure, Tony, but the paperwork has already been submitted to payroll, and unless I'm mistaken, it'll take a week or two for them to get everything in order. I'd say you'll all have your money no later than Thanksgiving. Pretty exciting."

Another hand shot up. The girl asked her question before Alec called on her. "What do we do now as far as telling people what we know? I'm having a real hard time not running my mouth at night right now to my roommate."

"Well, I think our Human Resources department would remind you that you signed a very binding contract to keep everything we do here at Fitzgerald Industries very secret. That includes pillow talk with spouses and slipping up with our roommates. Medical Research and Development is a very cutthroat industry to work in Megan, and nothing has changed so far as that is concerned. I'd say now more than ever your respect for the company's need for privacy is needed. I know I'd appreciate it, and I know all the people here in this room want to keep their jobs and making sure that we keep our tongues from wagging will ensure that. Great question Megan, thank you. Anyone else have any questions?"

An older man on the edge of the group raised his hand. Alec recognized him as one of the senior biotechnologists. Alec inclined his head, and the man spoke. He had a faded European accent. "Mr. Fitzgerald, I watched the announcement on one of the televisions in the break room. I'm feeling overwhelmed as I'm sure many of us here are. All of what's happened here in the world has made me rethink everything. Goblins, Trolls, Dragons, warlocks, and witches. It's almost more than the rational mind can fathom. But I am working on dealing with this change. What I am left wondering in the wake of all that we know, is how much of the truth of the world that has been hiding for so long has Fitzgerald Industries has been aware of?"

"I don't follow, Peter." *Shit. I don't like where this is going.*

"I mean to say, what of the world have you known about? It strikes me as very peculiar that for a decade now you've had a formulated medicinal cocktail that has kept a dragon in a sustained coma, brain dead or not. It would've taken months to invent such a substance at best. Most likely a year. It may seem convenient to some, but to the prying mind, your story rings as false."

"I don't appreciate what you're implying Peter. I wouldn't lie to my own people."

The older man took a step forward, emboldened by the tiniest sound of defense in Alec's voice. "I think you *would* lie to us, Alec. I think you're lying right now. Some of our neuroscientists have written reports at length detailing significant cerebral activity in the purple dragon downstairs. She is not brain dead. She is sleeping.

She dreams. We are not keeping a brain dead dragon alive. We are keeping her asleep. When I thought she was a pacified savage beast I had no qualms about this, but now I worry about the morality of it all, and I think we are not the heroes, we are the jailers."

Fuck. Fuck fuck fuck.

"Mr. Ehrlichmann, your accusations are beyond the pale. They border on treason to the company," Mr. Host said. Alec hadn't even seen him arrive in the room.

"Mr. Host, with all due respect, your job is to keep us safe and to keep the dragon and this facility secure. Your opinion on my observations is not needed." The German scientist was animated now.

"Yeah, Host. Piss off. We want to hear what Fitzgerald has to say," another scientist said. *I think he's in neuroscience. Shit. I wish I'd had longer to prepare for this.*

"Gentlemen, ladies. I don't know what to say. We're dealing with a species that defies all logic and reason. They're too big to even be alive according to what we know about biology, yet there is a dragon a hundred feet below us. How are we to know what her mental state is? Perhaps a dragon brain has a completely different network of neurons that would trigger what appear to be dreams. I think we've a lot left to learn about the world, Mr. Ehrlichmann. As for us being jailers, I'd be unable to sleep at night if that were the case. My father founded this company to save lives, not incarcerate them."

The German scientist stared at Alec. After a tense moment, he threw up his hands. "You're lying. I can see it in your face. This goon, this Mr. Host is here to intimidate us. This is no different than the Communists or the Nazis."

"No, Mr. Ehrlichmann," Mr. Host said quietly, "this is very different than the Nazis. I was only able to control them for a few years. You, I've controlled for more than a decade."

"What?" the German man asked confused.

Mr. Host suddenly drew his stainless steel sidearm and calmly blew the scientist's brains out. The gore sprayed across the gathered crowd, hitting more than ten employees in the face.

"Wipe them away," Mr. Host said to no one listening. The ear splitting crash of automatic weapons fire ripped the room apart. Alec covered his face and dropped to a knee in shock as he watched hundreds of highly trained scientists, accountants, and technicians murdered by a hail of bullets. Mr. Host calmly again walked over to him and shielded Alec's body from a stray bullet. None came; all of the weapons fire was pouring in from the edges of the room where Mr. Host had carefully placed his men. Alec watched in horror as each of his people died, dropping to the floor with pierced hearts, shattered bones, and destroyed skulls. One of the bullets flew high and struck one of Mr. Host's men, and instead of dropping to the floor wounded, he erupted in a nebulous black cloud of mist, vaporized. His gear fell to the floor, empty of the person who wore it moments before. The gunfire stopped as suddenly as it had begun.

"What the FUCK have you done?! You're a fucking MURDERER! These were MY people!! HOW COULD YOU?!" Alec reached out and punched Mr. Host in the face hard. The security agent's jaw rocked sideways, but he was otherwise unharmed and entirely indifferent.

"You'd lost them. The German had made a compelling case. At this point, it was wiser to cut your losses and start anew. Look at the bright side. You no longer have to pay out any bonuses."

"BY KILLING EVERYONE?! YOU FUCKING MANIAC! Kidnapping Matty, that I could almost stomach, at least we were protecting a baby, but this is too much!" Alec's mind was broken. He tried to punch Mr. Host again, but the infernal guard stepped aside and caught the fist easily. He squeezed hard and Alec's legs buckled from the pain. Mr. Host's crew of men were closing in on him like sharks at a feeding frenzy. They too wanted a taste of Alec's blood.

Sweet Jesus, he's going to break every bone in my hand.

"Shut up, you little bitch. You and your short lifespan and inability to see the big picture. Your father wanted me to help you. Your father signed a contract, Alec Fitzgerald. One that I must remind you yet again that you ratified when you came of age and took this corporation over. We are bound as one, Alec Fitzgerald. Your successes are inextricably linked to my presence and my assistance, however it may come. You're nothing like your father. He was strong. Bold."

"I don't want this. I don't want the death. These people were INNOCENTS!" Spittle flew.

"No one is innocent," Mr. Host said with confidence, letting go of Alec's hand. It felt like Alec's bones were throbbing in pain.

Alec collapsed on the floor, overcome with emotion. "How can we go on? How can I live with this?"

"Today is insignificant when weighed against the loss of all we've achieved, Alec. Rest assured. In short order all will return to normal."

All Alec could do was rock back and forth on the blood-smeared tile as a dozen of Mr. Host's men passively watched him cry.

Chapter Forty-Four

The Dragons

Surrounded by earth miles deep underground Garamos dug, as was his task in life. Garamos didn't need to breathe down below the surface of the earth. He subsisted on the sheer presence of so much precious soil, stone, water, and mineral. This was what he was meant to do, and he loved it. The packed earth parted for his claws as easily as his seldom-used wings would part a cloud. His goal was simple: sculpt a continent then the world. His goal was ever just out of reach, as was the design of things.

Garamos was titanic in size, even compared to the other dragons. He was twice the length of Kiarohn and a hundred feet longer than his brother, Tesser, the next largest dragon. His immense size made grinding away at the stone and rock near the edges of tectonic plates that much easier. It also meant that when he breathed flame into a volcano, causing an eruption took only moments. Garamos' breath was second only to his red sister's.

Garamos was happy to do this, his job. It was slow, deliberate, and it afforded him the luxury of living in a world that was by his design. Granted, he did have to suffer the machinations of the other dragons, but what they did was fleeting. Tesser's living offspring were flashes of irritation to Garamos despite their widespread influence on the world. If he had it his way, Garamos would eradicate all of humanity, but dealing out death on that scale wasn't his task. He would no sooner boil the oceans his other sister lorded over.

As Garamos tugged away a massive stone, setting free enormous chunks of plate, he felt an itching sensation at the back of his skull. *I must've gotten some wretched insect under a scale again. I will never understand why that of all things bothers me.*

The itching came again, more severe this time. Garamos stopped his digging and reached back to scratch at his tough brown scales. As he used a claw the size of a black bear to dig at the edge of a scale as hard as steel, he suddenly realized the itch was coming from within.

Garamos would've closed his eyes to concentrate, but they were already sealed shut against the dirt. There was no need for eyes to see the presence of light miles below the kiss of the sun. *What is that sensation?*

"It is me, brother," a friendly voice whispered faintly inside Garamos' mind. It was almost drowned out by the pulse of the Earth all around.

I know that voice. "Kaula? I can barely hear your voice. Where have you been? Are you okay?

"You must go to Tesser in America now. With haste. I can say no more."

"Kaula? Sister?"

Garamos was suddenly at a loss for emotion, something he was unfamiliar with. Garamos was, of all the dragons, the prepared one. To have a variable like this thrown in the air was unsettling in the extreme. *She must be where he is. She must be in grave danger. It is time to find my sister. My brother will answer for it if her disappearance is linked to his return.*

Garamos tilted his gargantuan head upwards and

with a great cough, erupted flame from his throat at the ceiling of the tunnel he had been carving. The flame liquefied the earth and stone instantly, and he began to etch away an open column that would lead to the surface. As the molten stone fell all around him, Garamos reached up and began to rip away even more burning earth. The surface couldn't come fast enough.

*****

Kiarohn, the smallest of all the dragons, flew high in the air above the Pacific Ocean. Kiarohn was slender, built more like a winged serpent than the dragons of western myth and legend, and the whole length of that body was covered in fine white and blue scales. Some cultures had memories of Kiarohn, and they named those memories the great Coatl. Blue eyes surveyed all the ocean below. Two pairs of great gossamer wings, three times as wide as Kiarohn was long, flapped powerfully. They should've moved the dragon's body far faster through the air, but no matter the speed of the wing's beat, the dragon moved along lazily. But Kiarohn's wings were meant less to keep a body aloft, and more to move the air about.

Kiarohn was the father and the mother of the wind.

"Kiarohn." Kaula's voice whispered to him high in the nighttime sky. The voice came from the pure ether of the magic she was made of.

Kiarohn's mouth formed a mischievous grin. The dragon expected the sister to return soon. "Hello, sister. It is a pleasure to hear your voice once more."

"Tesser will need you soon. Find him."

"He won't be particularly hard to find now. Is it important?"

"Yes. Leave now. The world must wait."

"So be it," Kiarohn said into the sky. He wheeled about in the air and started to head east, towards

America. This sudden change of plans might result in terrible storms in the southern Pacific, but such was the way of the world. It wouldn't take long for him to find Tesser, and hopefully, he could return to his stirring of the world's winds quickly.

*****

A blonde woman was relaxed naked in the white sand on a sunny beach on the eastern coast of South Africa. She was tall, impossibly tall, well over six feet, yet still beautiful and dainty. Several men gawked at her from the nearby resort bar. She would've been an impressive site even if she hadn't simply appeared out of the rough Atlantic surf, striding languidly. After building up some courage by downing several drinks, one tall man walked over.

"Hey, miss, saying hi, testing the waters is all. A man can't be too cautious now that all the weird things are coming back. You might be a mermaid," he said, joking. He had no idea how accurate his statement actually was.

The blonde leaned her head back, exposing full sun soaked breasts that dripped with delicate drops of seawater. She looked to him with bright eyes that danced between blue and green. The man thought of the ocean, almost as if he had no other comparison to make.

"A wise man tests all waters before jumping in. I won't be here long. You should go enjoy another drink with your friends. I'm not a very friendly lady. I think you'll find these waters unwelcoming." Her voice was husky, and her intonation off. It was almost as if she didn't interact much with men.

"I see, well, before I leave you, may I at least get your name? So as to save some pride?" the man asked, defeated.

"My family calls me Fyelrath. Now go. Thank you."

The man walked away, shrugging at his friends. It

was a valiant effort.

"You should be nicer to the humans," a small crab said to Fyelrath from a few feet away.

Now what is this? A speaking crab? What has Tesser been up to all this time he's been gone? "I keep my own counsel crustacean. And how is it you've learned to speak? All my time in the ocean and you're the first crab with a burning desire for conversation in English?"

"I use what I can to speak now. My sister, it is I, Kaula."

By the tides, it is. Fyelrath sat up, luring out a bunch of open-mouthed stares from the bar junkies behind her. "Kaula, you've returned. How delightful."

"I cannot speak for long. You need to head to Tesser. He will need your help soon. Very soon."

"I will find out where he is," Fyelrath said to the tiny crab. The crustacean stopped for a moment, clicked its claws twice, and then shimmied sideways towards the white foam of the ocean's edge. Kaula's magic was gone. Fyelrath got to her feet and walked abruptly towards the men still staring at the bar. Her nakedness stood out even more robustly.

"I'm looking for a dragon. I know he's been on your news. Where is he?"

The same man who approached her mere minutes ago replied. The liquor he'd downed was hitting him hard now. "A dragon, eh? Tesser, America's flying cunt. Crocodile with wings that one is. He was in Washington on the news a week ago. But I hear he's back in Boston. Starting a new tea party."

Why would he be so disrespectful? "Tesser is a dragon. A noble creature tasked with incredible responsibility. Were it not for him, you'd be nothing. More respect would be advisable."

"He's had nothing to say about my life, mermaid. Back into the ocean with you. Go find your Tesser."

"And so I shall," Fyelrath said with a whimsical smile.

She turned and ran hard and fast toward the surf, and at the last moment she let free, and shifted into the form she loved most. Fyelrath became a blue-green wingless dragon, more like a sea serpent than the flying creatures Tesser and Kiarohn were. Her long body and shorter legs coiled powerfully and launched off of the white African sands and high in the air before she dove into the water, thirty feet offshore. Her long back slithered side to side in the waves as she swam out deep into the ocean, eventually slipping under the surface.

The men at the bar hesitated for a few seconds, and then all downed their drinks, and headed inland. The need to be on the beach had been drained away.

*****

Zeud, the red dragon, sat atop a cliff that overlooked the Aegean. She was wandering today, far from the area of the world that her family had decided was hers. *I hate Asia. I hate the word, I hate all the damn islands, and there's far too much water for my taste. Why couldn't Fyelrath be assigned Asia? I wanted Europe. Far more rocks and cities. I would so love to set fire to one of their ancient forests as well. Perhaps the one that the seven stones are in. I wonder if they would burn under my breath now.*

Through her dinner plate sized nostril Zeud snorted out a javelin of flame into the crystal blue waters of the Mediterranean. Steam erupted upwards. Zeud smiled. It thrills me to be this visible now. Ever since Tesser returned and went public he's given us permission again to be revealed to his progeny. It has saddened me to watch their growth from the shadows without his tutelage. But now…

At the edge of her vision on the sea's horizon she saw the white shape of a cruise ship come into view. There was no way they could see her from that distance, but she could see them clearly. Dragon eyesight was some of the worlds finest. Zeud stretched her wings wide, allowing the cool sea breeze to buffet her wings full and nearly give her loft. It made no sense according to man's science that a dragon could achieve flight. They were too heavy, their wings too small to gain enough lift.

But man's science didn't account for the magic inherent in the dragons, and that made Zeud smile. They think they know everything, but my brother has shown them different.

"That he has," a soft voice whispered on the breeze.

Zeud knew immediately whose voice spoke to her. "I haven't heard from you in a long time sister. You've been away like our brother. Missing for a decade."

"I cannot speak long. Our existence requires you to find Tesser. You must move quickly."

Zeud took off flying immediately, deciding it would be most fun to fly over the cruise ship. "Kaula, my dear, I'm already headed. I miss you."

"I miss you as well. I will see you soon."

Zeud's heart soared as she flapped her wings. She set free a rapid-fire burst of flames from her mouth. They exploded like comets against the sea's surface. She smiled like she hadn't smiled in a long time.

*****

Ambryn was in dragon form below the city of Paris. The ancient catacombs below the city served as a quiet lair for him, and he appreciated the food above. He also felt better when he was able to chase down the teeming masses of rats under the city. Bringing balance to life was his duty, and when he rested under the city it was satisfying to burn away legions of the little rodents.

Ambryn's pitch-black body was reduced in size to move through the tunnels. He was not much larger than a good-sized horse, albeit one with a long tail, neck, and bat like wings. Ambryn slinked along in a tunnel almost a hundred yards below the streets above, hunting a particularly voracious pack of rats.

Come here little ones. There are a few too many of you. We just need to restore the balance for a bit. Don't make me cough up a virulent plague that will wipe you all out, because I will…

"Hunting rats now, Ambryn?" a hollow voice carrying on the wind in the ancient tunnels said to him.

Ambryn chuckled. "Kaula? Gone for a time, and now returned. What say you?" Ambryn abandoned his hunt to listen for the faint voice of his sister.

"I have great need for you. Find Tesser. He will lead you to where I need you."

"As you wish my sister. Might I ask what I'm required for?"

The air suddenly became stale in the tunnel, matching Kaula's thoughts on his answer. "Grave tasks brother."

The dragon of death looked around at the piles of rat feces and exhaled in a frustrated way. Ambryn spat out a small glob of pestilent saliva on the dirty floor. The rats would die, and that made Ambryn happy. What his sister might need of the dragon of death did not make him happy.

Chapter Forty-Five

Tesser

Tesser sat at Mr. Doyle's dining room table. It was just after their dinner, and all gathered were drinking tea or coffee. He wore a tee shirt that had arrived in the mail a few days prior. A gift. It had a logo for the role-playing game Dungeons & Dragons on it. Tesser found it amusing. The government had been forced to bring in a team of special postal workers to sift through all the mail being sent to Mr. Doyle's home.

Presently there were over a thousand letters and packages arriving each day from all around the world. Shirts, gifts, endorsement deals, inquiries to learn magic, scientific studies, and marriage proposals were the most common. A few letters containing potentially dangerous substances had come too, but they'd done no harm.

Around the table sat Mr. Doyle, Abe, and Alexis. The dining room window was open so Ellen outside could hear. She had somehow managed to relocate her 'face' to a lower portion of her tree trunk and was actively watching and listening on their conversation. Presently Alexis was staring at Tesser, still fighting the idea that he was actually the dragon he was. She looked at him, trying to find an errant scale or claw that might reveal

Tesser's true nature. Tesser looked over to her and she blushed.

"Sorry. I'm just still struggling to get accustomed to all of what's happened. It doesn't seem possible. I don't mean to stare," Alexis said.

I know. "It's okay Alexis. If you have questions, go ahead and ask."

Having been given permission, Alexis started to speak, but Mr. Doyle cut her off. "Tesser, I'd say that your performance was brilliant, though there are still a good many people out there who don't understand yet. You'll need to do many more public showings of proper behavior to convince everyone."

Tesser shook his head. "I don't want to make that a priority, Mr. Doyle. We need to find Matty, and we need to find Legion."

Abe chuckled. "Tesser, as you made it out to be, this fucking guy lives in a hundred bodies or more all at once. Like a hive mind. How the fuck are we going to find him and kill him?"

Tesser agreed. "It'll be difficult. But if I can just get the scent of one of his bodies I can track him down. It was foolish of me to kill all of them that night."

"And to be clear, you've gone on record and said that the only way to kill this Legion daemon thing is to destroy ALL of his bodies at the same time. Isn't that like saying the only way to kill an ant colony is to kill each and every fucking ant? Isn't there a Queen Legion we can kill? A brain Legion?" Abe asked.

"There is an executioner's stroke that can be done. But it could be as much of a challenge as attempting to exterminate all of Legion's bodies."

"How would one perform this 'executioner's stroke?' " Mr. Doyle asked.

"No daemon may cross the Veil without being beckoned first from this side for a specific reason," Tesser said. "They must be summoned intentionally and willfully. That desire to have them here serves as an anchor. The more substantial the desire, the more power the daemon can exercise on this side."

Abe wrinkled his nose. "This side?"

"Creation. This plane of existence," Ellen added through the open window softly.

"Our reality. Our dimension. Existence. Whatever you wish to call it. For Legion to able to manifest so many bodies here, and to be so established as to have vehicles, armor, and guns, it means he's strongly fettered to this world now. Bound. Contracted."

"Contracted?" Mr. Doyle asked, already knowing the answer.

"A written contract. Some form of physical document. Often done in blood or feces; most effectively on stone. Tens of thousands of years ago when humans were only barely taking their first steps with me, my kind fought against the daemons periodically. The humans would trade something to the daemons for a service. To control the daemon and to give it more power they would document the task at hand. Many of the ancient cave paintings your scientists are finding are actually daemonic contracts. Help my tribe hunt mammoths. Teach us how to make beer."

"No, shit. So what's the killing blow?" Abe asked. "Destroy the contract?"

"No. Once written the idea of the contract survives its destruction. It *did* exist. Therefore, it still has some validity. It will weaken the daemon certainly, which is something still worth trying for. The true killing stroke is to remove the person with the desire. If we can find and remove the person who holds the other end of Legion's contract, then Legion becomes unfettered and must return across the Veil."

"So, how do we find this person?" Alexis asked.

Tesser stood up and went to the window of the Beacon Street home. He and Ellen exchanged pained glances. They knew the stakes of the state of events at hand. Outside and down the way remained the government cordon. Metal fencing blocked the street, and heavily armed guards kept watch. Half kept their eyes pointed towards the home that Tesser stood in. *They say it is for our protection, but I wonder what the real goal is. Here they hope to keep me contained, observed. They sleep better at night thinking that they have some control over me. They think asking me to stay here means they are safe. The path of every human civilization seems to be the same. They wish to control what they fear.*

Headlights came onto the early evening street. The lights emanated from a large dark colored SUV very similar to the one Legion arrived in. Tesser saw the plate and recognized it as belonging to the government. The men at the fencing spoke to the driver and front seat passenger, and after some credential checks, the gate was moved aside, and the vehicle drove up to Mr. Doyle's home. A second SUV parked behind it, and all eight doors opened. Men with suits got out. Tesser recognized one of them.

That's Sergeant Spooner. He looks good. Hurt still, but good.

Tesser turned and talked to his gathered friends, "Everyone prepare for company. I think we are to be visited shortly by Uncle Sam."

Mr. Doyle got up and looked out the window. "Yes. Those men are with the FBI, I believe. Perhaps the NSA."

"Spooks? Fuck. I have some real crazy shit on my laptop guys. They might be here for me," Abe said half jokingly.

Alexis slapped him on the arm. "Freak."

"Half of it is there because *you* put it there. Who's the freak now?" Abe said bluntly. Alexis turned an even brighter shade of red.

The men made their way to the door of Mr. Doyle's home and knocked. The British sorcerer was waiting for them, and he pulled the door inward on the second knock. *The last time I saw that door open a daemon was on the other side. Ironic that a government agent stands there now?*

"Good day, gentlemen," Mr. Doyle said. "What brings you to the Back Bay of Boston this evening?"

"Mr. Doyle, I'm Director Roger Fisher. I work with a department in the Federal Bureau of Investigation. We were wondering if we could have a few hours of your time?" Director Fisher was average in height and wore a blue suit. His hair was dark brown with flecks of gray and was slicked to the side in a style that seemed more fitting for the 50's. He had wrinkles at the edges of his eyes that gave away some of his age.

"A few hours, Director? Don't you people normally say 'a few moments?' Being upfront more than usual tonight?"

The Director smiled a real and good smile. *I like him. He has sincerity.* "Mr. Doyle, this is a new day. Things have changed. I don't want to waste your time any more than I have to, but we do have some interesting things to go over with you and the folks who are staying with you. Tesser most of all, as you might imagine."

Tesser was in full view of the Director and stood with his arms crossed. Mr. Doyle turned back to the dragon and with a nod of his head, Tesser granted permission for the audience.

"Come in, gentlemen. But be warned. I've prepared wards against treachery. Should you attempt to mislead us in any way, you'll find yourself paying a price for it."

The Director looked at Mr. Doyle like he thought the sorcerer was kidding, but when the Brit didn't flinch or smile, the Fed simply nodded and came in. On his heels was a cane wielding, suit wearing Spooner.

Tesser grinned and walked up to greet the injured cop. "Sergeant. I thank you for all you've done. I am in your debt." Tesser stuck his hand out to shake Spoon's.

The limping cop took Tesser's hand and shook it

firmly. "It's not Sergeant anymore. I left the force. I'm with the Bureau now. Well, sort of. I don't know what we're calling it yet. I'm federal. For how long is up to you they tell me."

"Up to me, eh? That makes me feel like I have them by the short hairs."

Spoon chuckled as more suit wearing feds poured in. "You have the world by the short hairs my friend. I need to go beat up some assholes in an alley too. Apparently it pans out for you."

"I don't know if all of this could be considered 'panning out.' There have been repercussions since I came to beneath this city. People have suffered. People are suffering."

Spoon nodded. "I'm here to help you do something about that."

"I'm listening."

Chapter Forty-Six
Matty

"You will be a mother soon," Kaula said softly, stroking Matty's hair. Matty had her head in Kaula's lap. The two were on a bed of soft green grass in a meadow. It was night, and the air was still warm. It felt like a perfect summer evening.

God that feels good. "How long? I feel like I just found out."

"Many months still. You need to get fat with the baby first. That time will pass fast so long as everything falls into place," the amethyst haired woman said. A warm breeze came through, rustling their hair.

I suppose she's right. "What things need to fall into place?"

"I've summoned my brothers and sisters. They will be arriving soon. After this I'll use what's left of my magic to summon Tesser. I've almost none left. But we were fortunate. Something very useful has managed to fall into our laps. It has spared me enough energy to have this last conversation with you."

"Is Tesser coming to rescue me? I mean, rescue us?"

"In a manner of speaking, yes, to both of your questions. But I need some help from you for all these things to happen, Matilde. I've an important question."

I hope I can manage the answer. "What is it?"

"I'll be sending for Tesser soon, but I've no way to tell him where to go to find us. Is there someone I can tell him to seek out to find where we are? Someone we can trust?"

Well, the only person who might know is Alexis. "I assume we're at the Amethyst building. They drugged me before I got here. If not, then I think sending them to that place would be the best place to start. Tesser might have to face Mr. Host, or Alec, but worse things have happened. I think Tesser can handle himself."

"He most certainly can."

"Well, I guess Alexis is the answer. My old boss. She works for Fitzgerald Industries in the Boston office. She knows the Amethyst Project is north of the city. Maybe she can get them into the Boston office and dig around to find the address?"

"What does Alexis look like?" Kaula asked.

"She's a feisty redhead. Short, pretty. About forty. She was dating Abe, Tesser's friend. That's how I met Tesser, sort of. I miss her."

"I'm sure she misses you as well. My hope is that this Alexis friend can help lead them back to us. She must. We've not much time to spare."

Matty felt a small wave of relief as Kaula continued to stroke her hair. "When will they come?"

Kaula pondered, running her purple fingernails through Matty's dark hair. She looked down at the glossy strands and seemed to approve of them. "Two, two and a half days. It's hard to say exactly with Tesser. He can be so impulsive. Unpredictable. Like the life he creates. I've tried to orchestrate everything around him but it's taken so much effort. This will be my last act of magic for some time, speaking with you here."

"Magic? Is this more dream-speak? Anything is possible while you sleep?"

Kaula smiled, and Matty suddenly felt the weight of her immense age and wisdom. *Good lord, she's old. Really old.*

"No, Matty. I've been here, fighting against the daemons that brought you here as well for very long. They've kept my body still, but my mind has been too strong for them. I have been able to gather some resources from this hole in the ground, and now, with you here, I'll be able to send the final message to Tesser. Then, my dear Matilde, he shall come for us. You shall be set free, and I shall have the release I've yearned for, for so long now."

I miss Tesser. I shouldn't have been so angry with him the other day. "Kaula? The other day when we spoke you said Tesser was a special person. One of a small group? What did you mean by that?"

Kaula smiled again. "Look into my eyes. What color are they?"

Matty tilted her eyes up from Kaula's lap and looked up. The woman's eyes were a radiant and bright purple. Almost too glimmering and deep to be real. "You have amazing purple eyes. They remind me of Tesser's gold eyes."

"As they should. Tesser is my brother, of a sort."

"You don't look anything alike. You seem Asian, and he isn't. I mean, your eyes look similar, sort of."

"Not all families look alike, Matty. Some of your ancestors look nothing like you do now, though they'll recognize you for who you are when they finally meet you. You're going to be very well known soon."

"My ancestors? Who are they?" Matty sat up on her elbows.

"Tesser is a dragon, Matty. One of Earth's seven. An orchestrator of will, and the creator and guide to all living things on this world. Your schools call what he has done evolution, but we dragons call it his will."

A dragon? That makes no sense and yet doesn't sound

strange in the least. "I had sex with a giant dragon?"

"You made love with a dragon who became a man. He has spent so much time away from his natural form. At first to explore your kind, but then, to be with you."

"Does he love me?"

Kaula nodded. "Yes, though he doesn't know how to love the way you want him to yet. He has never given himself to anyone before. He has always done his deed selflessly, wishing nothing but improvement and change for the better on anything he has come into contact with. Though at times, a father must be wrathful."

"Has he killed? Is that what that means?"

Kaula nodded again. Her choice to not speak on the matter chilled Matty. After a minute of silence, Matty pressed again.

"Will I have a baby dragon? Is my child, my girl as you said, will she be a dragon?"

Kaula started to speak, but stopped herself. She tried again, but failed. After thinking on it a third time, she finally said, "Your daughter will share many traits of both you and her father. But there can only ever be seven dragons on Earth. Seven draconic souls are all the world can bear. Any more would upset the precarious balance of things. For your daughter to become one of us, a dragon must die. Dragons are very hard to kill."

"I wouldn't want that," Matty said sadly.

"It is not yours to want."

Chapter Forty-Seven

Mr. Doyle

Director Fisher sat at Tesser's left hand. Everyone in the packed dining room sat silent, waiting for the man to begin the conversation. After crossing his hands on the table, he started with respect in his voice. "Should I call you Mr. Tesser? Mr. Dragon? I'm not sure what the etiquette is for addressing a being of your nature while an intelligent tree watches you through a window. Oddly enough, there's no manual entry for it."

Ellen chuckled, and Tesser grinned. "Simply Tesser is fine. Fancy titles are an invention for the ego. I'm a dragon. Ego is a strange concept for us."

It's hard to be egotistical when you're god-like?

"I can only imagine. Look Tesser. Mr. Doyle, Mr. Fellows, I've come here with a few of my closest associates at the request of some very important people whom you've already met, albeit briefly for security reasons. I'm here to make a proposal; I'd like you to listen and then ask me any questions you might have."

A proposal. How dear. Whenever there's an offer from a government official I feel like they keep one hand extended trying to shake your hand, and the other with fingers crossed at their back. Let's see how this Mr. Fisher attempts to play Tesser. At the very least this will be entertaining.

"Go ahead, Director. I'm all ears," Tesser said as Abe put a carafe of coffee at the center of the table. Alexis sat down creamer and a jar filled with Mr. Doyle's precious sugar cubes.

Delicious, and right on time.

"Alright. First off, I mean you no disrespect. I want you to know I mean that."

"Just talk Director. I'm not going to set you on fire if you piss me off."

Spoon grinned. He sat at Tesser's right hand.

Fisher began again, "You scare the living fuck out of the world Tesser, plain as can be. I'm here to try and keep you contained and make an attempt at making great use of what appears to be one of the world's greatest natural assets."

"I appreciate your honesty. Continue," Tesser said as he poured a cup of coffee.

"The President and the Armed Forces, Intelligence, Homeland Security, and Energy and Natural Resources Committees all want to bring you into the fold. Bluntly put, we'd like to offer you a job."

"A job? I have had a single 'job' in my entire lifespan Mr. Fisher and that was as a bouncer at a pizza shop just recently. I am a dragon. We do not work for humans."

"Hear me out. Please."

Tesser shrugged and indulged the man.

"There are a rather ludicrous amount of strange happenings in this country right now, Tesser, all across the world, and you're the biggest friend we have. Lots of people are scared by what's coming out of the woodwork and going bump in the night, and too many are dying at the hands of what you seemingly have stirred up. I'd like to ask you to help us deal with these things. Fly out to different places, look into it, take some scary things out, and then go about your business."

Tesser sipped his coffee and nodded. "You wish for me to be a killer."

This should be entertaining.

"What I'd like, is for you to help train a special unit. A division of the Federal Government likely allied to Homeland Security or the FBI. I would be the head of that unit. In my wildest dreams you'd lead us to trustworthy people who can train a cadre of investigators and a counter assault team that can deal with the things our world is now apparently filled with. We're under informed and certainly under armed right now. I'm sending agents and watching front line first responders deal with shit they aren't prepared for. Do you know how many cops have died the past three weeks? EMTs? I think you can help. I'm asking for that help."

"You want Tesser to be your super cop?" Abe asked as he sat down in a plus chair against the wall of the dining room.

"I hate to say it like that, but we need some heavy artillery. God is on the side with the best artillery, right? He's the biggest gun in town hands down." Mr. Fisher started making his own cup of coffee.

Tesser spoke up immediately. "I have many questions. Why is Sergeant Spooner here? He's still injured."

"Special Agent Spooner is the first hire for the Division we'd like to create with your assistance. We'd like him to serve as your direct contact with the unit. A liaison officer. He'll be attached to you and will be able to draw on government resources as you need them. His performance the night of your first appearance was exemplary, and with his prior relationship with you, he seemed perfect for the job."

"I dig it. Why you? Why do you get to run the show?" Tesser asked.

"I lied extensively on my intake poly with the Bureau when I joined. I passed the psych eval with flying colors too. Ever since I was a kid, I've been able to interact with ghosts, Tesser. Dead people talk to me. I see them all the time. I've kept a lid on it for decades. Everyone thought I was just a stellar investigator, but all I was doing was listening to victims and finding the evidence they pointed me to. When all this came out I went from being a closeted freak to a rare agency asset. This is a lot like post 9/11 right now. People are afraid, and they're looking for help wherever they can get it, and they aren't asking too many questions about where it came from, or what they have to give up to get it. Simple as that."

Very interesting. This Director Fisher is quite a character.

"I can help you, but I will not work for you. You will not dispatch me to where you wish me to go, and there are a few things you will need to understand for this to work."

"Okay. We're very flexible on the details. I'm glad you're on board in some fashion."

"First, I am a dragon. I predate all of your species. I am older than the dinosaurs. I have flown over every inch of this world. You claim eminent domain as a nation, I claim eminent domain as a *species*. Your nation is a recent construct that is noble in concept, but has absolutely no authority over me or any other dragon. We do *as* we wish, *when* we wish, without regard for your laws. We are not callous or indiscriminate, but we operate on a scale that you cannot fathom. We work in millennia, not Presidential terms. We do not do what is popular right now, we do what is necessary for the rest of time. We will do things that will cause an uproar, and that is simply *how it must be*. Do you understand?"

"I uh, shit. I think so. You know we have really large bombs, right? If you piss off enough bigwigs doing whatever it is dragons might do, they might react poorly. Push the big red button and give me a whole lot of ghosts to talk to."

"Humanity has not invented a weapon that can kill a dragon," Tesser said simply.

Mr. Fisher seemed to disagree. "Have you considered the nuclear bomb? I don't want you to feel threatened

Tesser, but if you do anything drastic, it might get to that point."

"I understand. I won't be doing anything that drastic, Mr. Fisher. And more notably, your nuclear weapons are powerful, yes, but dragons are immortal. You do not have the means to kill one of our kind. We're the original cockroaches. One of my finer creations, I would add."

"You made cockroaches?" Mr. Fisher said. The suits in the room laughed with him nervously.

"Yeah," Tesser said seriously back.

The men stopped laughing. "Well then. Good on you. What else do you need to tell us?" the Director asked.

"I would have you employ my friends. Mr. Doyle is an able spell caster that can teach many people the art of sorcery. He can also assist you in developing a curriculum to teach others. Abe as well. He has an excellent mix of intelligence, technical skill, and magical ability. If they agree to work for this new division, I require that you bring them aboard. They are the true assets you need. I also will require that you hold them harmless for anything they do when they assist me. You can't prosecute me or them if they aid me. Mr. Fisher, humans must protect humans in the end. Perhaps you can strike up a bargain with trolls eventually, or a few friendly giants as well, but that's down the line, after they begin to respect and trust you. Humanity has burned many bridges since I made you, and that was before I was sequestered away."

"Right. Most of that is done. That's easy. I can't fully guarantee immunity that broadly though. What if you guys decide to commit some vast atrocity together? You have to be held accountable."

"An atrocity committed by us would give you the leverage to do something, should we do that. Trust in me, Director. I won't lead you astray."

"Okay. I'll make it happen."

"Thirdly, you must understand that life is managed

on this planet by two entities. Myself, and my brother, Ambryn. As I am to life, he is to death. We keep all things in check. In my absence humanity grew to a size and level that I did not expect and didn't necessarily wish for. I'm sure my brother Ambryn took steps to bring you into check while I was away. I have a strong suspicion the bubonic plague and a few natural disasters were his handiwork, for example. Put bluntly Director, if a few of you die, it's for the greater good of the world."

"That sounds damn callous, Tesser."

Tesser agreed, "It does. But as I said, we do what we wish, when we wish. I cannot and will not stop every human death. Species suffer. Species go extinct. It is the way of the world. Humanity is not at risk of extinction any time soon, but you are also not out of danger either."

"I think I understand. But you are agreeing to help? Maybe when things get really bad?"

"Only when things get really bad, and only when they are happening for unnecessary reasons. I should also state that I will not act against another nation in the name of America. I am not a weapon, or a political tool. I am a force of nature."

"Jesus, you're like a fucking movie script filled with idle threats, Tesser. I thought you were a good guy."

"I *am* the good guy, Director. I think you need to understand that if I am speaking in this way right now, imagine what the things I am concerned about are like. I fear nothing, Director. Nothing. Understand that. So what concerns me, should horrify you. I am not trying to scare you into thinking that I am a villain or that I am unreasonable. I am attempting to make you understand that while humans have been running the show for a very long time, that is not quite the case any longer. I want to work with you, but you need to understand how this will work."

Mr. Fisher was taken aback but kept his cool. "I get it. I'll take what you've said back to the President and the committee chairs. They're going to take it a little rough, but I'll try and speak accurately."

"That'd kick ass. Mr. Fisher, I appreciate you coming and speaking openly. I expected far less, and you've impressed me."

He seemed flattered. "I'm glad then. In the interim, Agent Spooner will be at your disposal. He'll stay behind and go over all of what he can offer you from an Agency perspective. If you need me, go through him. If you need any kind of official assistance, he is your asset to make that happen. His cell phone has a contact list the Chinese would set fire to Hong Kong for." The older man stood, and the other suits stood with him.

It's like they share a single mind. I wonder if this Legion character works as uniformly.

The Director turned to the open window and looked at Ellen. "Ellen, right? A, uh, dryad? Is that right?"

Ellen somehow managed to nod without moving. "A hamadryad. And yes, I am Ellen."

"Ellen, if you and your people are ever looking for a job, we could certainly use you in some kind of surveillance position. I'm not sure what kind of compensation we'd offer a tree, but I've got some leeway. Consider it. A pleasure to meet you."

Ellen nodded again. Tesser shook Fisher's hand and he left with his entourage, leaving only Spooner behind.

"Exciting shit, huh?" Spoon asked the group. Alexis was giving Abe a hug off to the side. It was a moment for celebration.

Tesser looked unsure. "Are they being sincere, Sergeant? Are these trustworthy people?"

"Agent Spooner. Special Agent, I should say. Just call me Spoon. I'm supposed to lay low. Fisher is a weird cat. He's seen some strange shit, and I think he's telling the truth about how long he has been seeing it. I think he knows you're the real deal, and he's stuck between scared politicians and a fucking real deal dragon. I can't imagine a place that'd be more anxiety provoking."

The man makes a valid point.

Chapter Forty-Eight
A Leaf on the Wind

Outside of the Project Amethyst building the fallen leaves of trees blew about in the early autumn cold. Golds, browns, reds—the colors of fall. It was unseasonably cold that late afternoon. Frost would come after the near nightfall.

One green leaf was lost. It had fallen very far from the tree whose branch it had sprung from, having been carried on a wind that came from a natural and pure magic. The very same wind had given the leaf enough magical power to stay green, to say fresh for the chance it needed to return to its branch with a message. So far, the leaf had received no message. Here it blew in circles, somehow drawn to a parking lot like a moth was drawn to flame.

Deep below the pavement with the painted parking spots, and below the sand, stone, and earth was a manmade cavern. It was enveloped by wires, cables, and all manner of technology. Some of that technology was man-made, and some of it was a hybrid from beyond the Veil. Daemon infused technology rife with raw evil from another reality pulsed with a life of its own. The thrum of evil in the basement thumped like half a dark heartbeat.

The other half echoed, beating in a different, much fouler reality across the Veil. The leaf wasn't aware of that, but the magic of it all drew it to that spot.

Inside that man-made cavern so far below the earth was Kaula. Her body was still imprisoned there, though her mind was strong enough to wander. Maybe the leaf sensed that.

Kaula had a net cast on the world. It was an insubstantial net made of thought and hope, held together by the dwindling magic inside her body. The Veil inspired technology pumping into her was rotten and evil, and it kept nearly all her will at bay but she was able to do this much to fight back. One last whisper on the wind to a beloved brother.

Through the stone and earth the purple dragon spoke to the leaf, gave it a message, and the last bit of uncorrupted magic she had left inside. The leaf took those rare gifts and spun up into the air, reinvigorated with purpose. It would need the purpose, it had a vast journey home, especially considering it was just a leaf.

A magically imbued leaf that had fallen from the branch of a hamadryad, but still a leaf nonetheless.

Once high in the air the leaf caught a wind current heading south towards the city. Its tree, the hamadryad, was currently living in the city, so it was fortunate to find a path through the air so quickly.

Hours passed. The wind discovered so fast turned sour and slow, causing the leaf to stall multiple times. It fell all the way to the ground twice and had to wait patiently for another gust to carry it high. But magic has a way of creating its own luck, and the last of Kaula's magic was no different than any of the magic she'd created her whole life. The wind came…and up the leaf went.

Over trees and highways the green leaf flew south. As the leaf was drowned in the cold whiteness of a thick cloud, a great feathery griffon flew by. Large enough for a grown man to sit astride, it had the head and wings of an eagle and the body of a lion. The majestic creature of ancient myth sensed the noble purpose of the leaf and screeched in approval. It swung round wide and flapped its massive wings strongly, sending the leaf fast and surely further south and out of the cloud. The leaf couldn't be grateful, nor did Kaula know of the griffon's gift, but the world now had a better chance at surviving because of it. Such strange fortune.

As the leaf moved out above the increasingly taller and taller gray and brown buildings of Boston, the wind funneled and sped it up. By then the sun was setting, and the last bits of orange glow had died in the sky, leaving behind only the bitter blue cold of the night.

It was drawn along again, pulled in by the silent song of the branch to which it belonged. Still miles away, the leaf soared unseen above. Down below, tens of thousands of pedestrians and vehicles went about their business, unaware of the leaf and what it represented.

The leaf glided over the water of the Charles River and over the lanes of Storrow Drive as car sped by, heading east and west. Over the massive rows of old brick homes it went, eventually cresting high into an invisible column of air that descended down onto the branches of the silver birch from which it had originally come.

The hamadryad's branch received the return of the leaf without effort or thought. The leaf simple reattached as easily as it would have fallen in the autumn, though that connection sparked something much more spectacular.

Ellen, the hamadryad, was near to the side of her friend, Mr. Doyle's, home. She had been listening in on a very important conversation inside the home, and most of the participants had just left in two cars. She had no interest in cars. They couldn't feed her, water her, or bring her the sun, and they couldn't hold up a conversation either. They were useless.

But then the message in the leaf entered her sap and traveled through to her spirit at the core of the tree. Instantly she knew the message. Her sending had returned successfully.

"Tesser," she said, interrupting the conversation. Her voice was low, but urgent.

Somehow the dragon sensed it, and he turned to the window where she was rooted. "Yes, Ellen. You have an idea?"

"My sending. Something just came back," Ellen was swooning with the magical essence from Kaula. Having a pure element of Kaula's essence inside her was intoxicating. She felt more alive than ever. Taller, wider, and greener.

Tesser got to his feet from the dining room table and strode across the room to Ellen. He crouched at the window. His face was full of hope. "What have your leaves told you?"

Ellen was breathless, almost drugged from the touch of Kaula. "Most of the dryads and hamadryads have been asleep for years. It is the way of our people to sleep for long times, even more so since the magic began to fade. I'd hoped more would've been awake for the sending. But a leaf came back to me. And it came with a message from your sister, Tesser. I have words directly from Kaula."

Tesser's hands dug into the wooden sill of the window, cracking the paint and splitting the wood. At his back Abe, Mr. Doyle, Alexis, and Spoon all moved closer to hear what Ellen had to say. She saw the looks on their faces, and wanted immediately to share the news. Tesser pressed, "What did she say?"

Ellen had no tongue, so she couldn't lick her lips nervously. Instead, her roots wiggled and dug deeper, seeking reassurance in the cold earth. "She was captured by humans a decade ago. She's underneath the earth north of here, in a laboratory. I think it's under a parking lot, but I can't be sure. There were many silver birches all around. Dozens and dozens. That's why the leaf landed there. Birds of a feather is the human expression. That's not from her message, that's just what I can glean from what the leaf felt."

"How can we tell what building the leaf came from? What facility? What parking lot? Did she say anything about Matty?" Tesser asked urgently.

Ellen continued, "She spoke of Matty. She is with Kaula."

"Safe?" Alexis asked.

"I don't think so. Kaula was very clear. You must come fast. Now, if possible." Ellen tilted back and looked up at the cloudy sky. It looked like snow.

"How can I find this place where she is? Is Legion there?"

Ellen nodded knowingly, her eyes rolling up in a sudden surge of positive energy. "Yes. She is surrounded by the one with a thousand faces. She knows how to kill him. How to send it back across the Veil, she said. But she needs you now. Matty needs you now."

"How can I find this place?"

"Kaula said the redheaded one might know."

Tesser spun, still crouched, and looked up to the now confused Alexis. "Where is she?" It wasn't a threat, but any question like that from Tesser certainly carried the unspoken weight of dire consequences.

"I...I uh…I have no idea," Alexis stammered, nervous.

Tesser took a deep breath, and slowed his speech. "You have to think. Kaula knew you'd have an idea where Matty was taken. What do you know about Matty that the rest of us don't know? Something you two share that the rest of us don't."

"We're both girls. That's something." Alexis shrugged.

Mr. Doyle put a soft hand on her shoulder. "Alexis, dear. Something that isn't obvious to us. Something that

Kaula would KNOW from where she was. Think locational. Think personal."

"Well, we work together. Maybe she was taken by someone we work with?"

"The man at the door here who said he had Matty called himself Mr. Host. But he lied, he was Legion," Tesser offered.

"Oh holy fuck, Tesser," Alexis said, suddenly short of breath and nervous. She crumpled up a napkin in her hands reflexively.

"What is it? That name. You're familiar with it."

She nodded emphatically. "Yeah. He runs security for Alec. I've only seen him once, but some of the people I know who went to work where Matty went have said he's creepy as hell."

"Where is your work?" Tesser asked.

"Not far from here. But Matty doesn't work at the same facility I do. She works in a new facility somewhere north of here. Oh shit. It's called Project Amethyst."

"Kaula is the purple dragon, right? Amethyst? Somewhere north of here you say? That's gotta be it," Abe said. He went back to the dining room table and flipped open his laptop. Furious typing ensued.

"How can we find the address for this building, Alexis? Can you search it out on a company computer?" Tesser asked.

"No. It's well hidden. The facility was top secret R&D style stuff."

Abe spoke up from the table. "Says here that Fitzgerald Industries leapt up in the industry about ten years ago. Huge advancements in medical technology out of nowhere. Privately owned and supposedly incredibly profitable."

"Convenient," Mr. Doyle returned. Tesser stood and started to pace. His fists clenched repeatedly, anxiously.

"Guess what a Google search of Birch plus Interstate 93 also just turned up? Silver Birch Industrial park.

About an hour north by car right off 93. No word of Fitzgerald Industries there, but it does line up. Worth a look?"

Tesser stopped pacing and looked over at Abe. "That's it. I can feel it." Tesser turned to Spoon. "Tell your government friend I am headed there, and they are to keep everyone away. Far away. I'll be doing things that could be...highly destructive."

Spoon simply nodded and reached inside his suit jacket for his phone with all the contacts in it. He stepped away to make the call.

"The rest of you are welcome to stay or come as you choose. This is not your fight," Tesser said, his golden eyes flaring red.

"Tesser. There is no sitting this out. I will come. I suspect Abe will as well, and we all know the good Special Agent Spooner will be there. Allow us a few moments to gather our things," Mr. Doyle said confidently.

"You could die," Tesser said.

All Mr. Doyle did was smile, and say, "We are all going to die eventually, Tesser. Choosing how we meet that end is a wonderful human trait you may not realize you've given us."

"Fair point, that."

Mr. Doyle turned to the men gathered. "Abe, Mr. Spooner, when you get off the phone there are a few things upstairs that we should bring with us. Old treasures that might be useful."

Chapter Forty-Nine

Spoon

Spoon hit the first speed dial on his phone. It went straight to Director Fisher's phone. The older agent picked up after a single ring. Spoon could hear the sound of the vehicle they were in still. They couldn't be far away.

"Agent Spooner? Does Tesser have a question?"

"Tesser has a purpose, Director. And you can call me Spoon if you don't mind. People have been calling me Spoon since I was a kid. Agent still sounds funny in my head."

"Yeah, I know that feeling. What do you mean by purpose, Spoon? Is he headed somewhere?"

"Yeah. The tree in the yard just got a leaf in the wind that had some kind of message in it. The tree said there was a missing dragon, and it's somewhere north on I-93 and they think it's under the ground near or in an Industrial Park called Silver Birches. Tesser and the crew here are headed north to check it out. Tesser's got red in his eyes, and the last time I saw that everyone got to watch him pretend to be a volcano downtown. He's asking that we clear that area good and wide STAT. Says it could get messy."

"I can't believe what you just said is my reality now.

It's a god-awful joke, but okay. You stick with them. I'll get in touch with local authorities, and we'll evacuate as fast as we can. How long do you think we have?"

"I'd guess we'll be out the door in less than ten minutes. Not sure on the distance to target, but we might get to this Silver Birches place in an hour maybe. I'd guess at less. Tesser is pissed."

"We'll do everything we can. Showtime as they say, Spoon. Show me why I hired you."

"You got it." Spoon hung up the phone and jogged up the stairs in Mr. Doyle's home to where the old man was gathering relics of a bygone era for their trip. *I hope I get a magical Gatling gun…or two magical Gatling guns.*

"Mr. Spooner," Mr. Doyle said. "What is your first name?"

"Henry. But you can call me Spoon. I like that a lot."

Mr. Doyle looked uncomfortable at the thought of calling someone a 'spoon.' "If you don't mind, I'd like to call you Henry."

Whatever. Spoon shrugged. In the office just off the top of the stairs Mr. Doyle had quickly produced a stack of wooden cases. They were old and ornate, held together by leather bindings and brass nails. They appeared more like luggage that belonged on the Titanic than something in a modern home.

"As you men leave here to fight things from the other side, I want you all to carry with you weapons that I know to be effective against…well, against evil."

Tesser, Alexis, Spoon, and Abe all stood quietly, listening.

Mr. Doyle picked up a small case about the size of an old VCR. He undid a small padlock with a tiny key from his pocket and opened it. Inside were a pair of impressively etched silver revolvers and trays of ammunition. *Nice. Enfield Number two's.*

"Abraham, I know firearms aren't your strong suit, but with your Call of Duty experience, I hope you can manage to operate these. They are vintage 1934 Enfield Number Two, Mark One revolvers. I have thirty rounds of specially made ammunition for you to pair with them. I am unsure of the science on how the shells were manufactured, but a close friend of mine in Texas assures me they are capable of visiting great harm on things of a...supernatural persuasion. They have been blessed by numerous clergy of many different faiths and are infused with essences of a wide array of harmful substances to things made of evil."

Abe was speechless.

"Take care. Familiarize yourself with how they load. They are simple to fire."

"Make sure you don't point them at anyone, Abe," Spoon said.

Abe nodded. "I'll do my best, Spoon." Abe took the case and moved to another desk.

"Tesser, I trust you need nothing from me."

All Tesser did was smile.

"Henry. I am assuming that the United States government has seen to it that you are issued state of the art equipment in support of our dragon friend?" Mr. Doyle asked sarcastically.

"I've got some neat toys. More if I ask nicely."

"I thought as much. For you, I give different gifts." The eccentric British man turned to a larger case; longer by far, but light. Mr. Doyle lifted it with ease, despite being his unclear age. He sat it on his desk where the revolvers had been a minute before. The case flipped open revealing a vintage Air Force horsehide leather jacket. It was worn, well worn, and had some abrasions and dark patches where it appeared to have been burned somehow. It was the quintessential pilot's leather jacket. It looked like it had been dunked in testosterone and wiped dry with Hercules' loin cloth. It screamed macho.

Holy shit. That's old school. "Looks like Indiana Jones' jacket."

Mr. Doyle agreed. "The style was made popular by those movies, yes. This particular jacket was worn by a bomber pilot in 1943. He brought the jacket to a shaman outside of the base in Africa where he was stationed before a bombing run into Italy. The shaman cast many spells on this jacket for the American pilot. The pilot and his crew survived that run and many subsequent runs. Before leaving on a trip to bomb Germany, the same pilot brought this same jacket to an Irish mother who was part gypsy. Roma. She cast more spells on the jacket and somehow the spells entwined and fortified, which is rare and unusual. The pilot took his crew over Europe, and even though the bomber was shot down, he survived without a scratch. As you can see, the jacket has been burnt and shot at repeatedly, and it continues to keep its wearer alive. Now the jacket is mine, and tonight I wish you to wear it. May its magic stay strong and keep you alive as it did the pilot."

Fuck. That's lineage. "Thank you, Mr. Doyle. I don't know what to say."

"Tell me you'll cover me when we get there and that you're a crack shot."

"101st Airborne, Mr. Doyle. Qualified Sharpshooter."

"Excellent. Now if you'll allow an old man a few minutes to get his things together." Mr. Doyle shuffled away after picking up several heavier cases. He went to a back office and shut the door, leaving the others alone to play with their new toys.

Alexis turned to Tesser, having been lost in the mix. "I want to go with you guys. I know I'll be no use, but I want to go."

Tesser thought on it for a minute, trying to think of something to say. I got an idea. "Alexis, how good a driver are you?"

"I drive into and out of Boston every day on my commute. No accidents in six years."

That's better than most of the guys on the force. "You

drive my truck. It's armored, and you can stay in the wings if things get messy. You can always take off if it gets really bad."

"Is that a good idea?" Alexis asked Tesser.

"No. But you might as well come. If we fail to kill Legion or send him back across the Veil, it won't matter if we leave you behind here. Nowhere will be safe."

Alexis looked afraid.

Spoon slid the jacket on after taking his off the rack suit jacket off. The horsehide felt cool against his skin, and there was an unmistakable aura of invincibility he felt with it on. Maybe it was a placebo effect, but he liked how it felt. *I wanna go shoot at some shit. Kick a motherfucker in the chest. Kill me some daemons.*

Across the room Abe was fastening a belt with twin hip holsters for the Enfield pistols. He tied the thigh cords and stood up straight. Spoon could see fear in his eyes as the young man looked at his reflection in the dark window. Abe loaded one pistol and put it into a holster.

"Abe."

The young man turned, and Spoon saw the fear directly. He'd seen it a hundred times before in the Army. Pre combat jitters. The face right before a man's first jump.

"We are going into battle against daemons from Hell. We are going to be shot at. They are going to try and stab us, slash us, and eat our souls. We will have to kill tonight. With guns, and knives, and if things get real bad, our bare hands and teeth. It's gonna be a storm, and we're gonna be in it. But you know what?"

Abe was almost shaking now. "What?"

Spoon leaned his head towards Tesser. "That guy is on our side, and he's a motherfucking *dragon*."

Abe stopped shaking and smiled.

"Yeah, I thought so." *Hope that gives him some balls. Guess we'll find out whether or not quick if this is the real deal.*

The back office door opened and Mr. Doyle strode

out. He had transformed from doddering old eccentric into a warrior straight from a history book. Under a leather duster the old man wore leather leggings and a chain shirt adorned with rings that formed a red Templar's cross on his chest. A pocket watch hung on a chain around his neck. At his right hip he wore a leather holster that held an automatic pistol. Dozens of waist pouches held God knew what, and on Mr. Doyle's left hip hung a longsword in a scabbard that looked expensive beyond belief. It was encrusted from top to bottom with ivory, gold, and silver inlays. Carvings of Latin and older languages ran alongside gems and scrollwork. *I wonder what the sword looks like.*

On Mr. Doyle's forehead sat a pair of mad scientist goggles with thick, darkened, round lenses. He looked out of place, out of time, and out of his mind.

"You look completely fucking crazy, old man," Spoon said.

Mr. Doyle beamed. "That's not the first time I've been told that, and rightfully so. Abraham, don't forget your spell materials, and don't leave until I give you a few potions. Let's go kill some bloody daemons."

Tesser cracked his knuckles and led them down the stairs.

We are going to explode some daemons tonight boys.

Chapter Fifty
Tesser

Tesser flew low and fast, the cold autumn evening wind licking at his eyes and scales. Below him was Interstate 93, the north-south artery that ran from the south end of Massachusetts to the north of New Hampshire. It was a heavily traveled route normally, but right now, as the evening aged, there were fewer and fewer vehicles on the road. The dragon passed over numerous police cars and fire trucks on the way, with Spoon's Agency truck staying close behind.

I could fly faster, but I want them to arrive near when I do. I can't protect them if they get there too early or too late.

Mile after mile gave way as he soared above the trees but below the thick white clouds. His heart raced happily, thrilled to be flying again and to finally be on the hunt for something he wanted so desperately to destroy. He had no fear in his heart.

Matty had better be safe. If that thing hurt her, I swear I'll cross the Veil myself and annihilate everything I find on the other side. Legion may not be able to die here, but I'd bet he'd burn for good over there.

Tesser's miraculously powerful nose caught the tiniest hint of something familiar on the air. It was a taste of family. A memory of millennia eons ago. *Kaula?* Tesser inhaled deeply, swirling his head about to find the source of the scent and immediately he knew it was above the clouds. With a flap of his giant wings he cut through the damp white puffs and ascended to the pure night sky above.

It will be a good night tonight. Tesser saw, flying in the sky and moving in from miles around, his dragon brothers and sisters. To the west, Garamos was the first to catch his eye. He was gargantuan, even by Tesser's ample standard. His enormous red and brown scaled body flapped wings the size of a stadium up and down rhythmically, propelling him forward. He looked over at Tesser and snorted a ball of flame from a nostril the size of a sewer lid. It was a greeting and a threat. The two brothers often argued over how things were done.

To the east Tesser saw Kiarohn, the blue dragon of the sky. Beyond the need for a gender, Kiarohn was truly neither male nor female. Kiarohn existed to stir the winds and make Earth more habitable for Tesser's life. Kiarohn's glittering and glimmering wings moved almost hypnotically, and Tesser could feel that the wind in his face he'd felt so long that night had been from Kiarohn the whole time. The thought of that put a smile on his enormous face. Tesser looked up. High above, far, far above, a glimmering red comet slid downward.

Sweet sister Zeud. How is that you were able to focus on this for so long to travel here from wherever you came? The only thing that's ever captivated you is fire, and the only thing burning right now is you. Zeud came down from the heavens like the mythical phoenix that was often confused for her.

We are far from danger, but this will be much easier with them here.

Tesser dropped down below the clouds and made sure Spoon's truck was still moving safely on the interstate. Its flashing blue lights kept the traffic ahead of it out of the way, and Alexis kept the pedal to the floor. She was a good driver, as advertised.

Tesser closed his eyes and reached out with all his senses. Like the flashes of storm clouds appearing in a darkened sky, Tesser could sense the minds and presence of the other dragons. Small sparks were below in the truck as well. *That must be Mr. Doyle, and Abe.* Tesser looked into the darkness, searching for more clues. He tried to attune all his senses into one—smell, hearing, taste, and the magic his sister had seen fit to trust to him. *I don't expect to see Kaula, but I might be able to find the silver birches Ellen's leaf found. I'm glad Ellen let me eat the leaf. Now I have a connection to it.*

Tesser pushed his senses out further than was safe, risking an intrusion by anything aware of his psychic vulnerability. It was dangerous, foolish really, but the dragon was desperate to find the woman who carried his baby. Then, suddenly, a scent came to him. It matched the scent of the leaf Ellen had given to him. It was only a few miles away.

Tesser opened his eye and skimmed the earth just above the truck. He matched its speed, and they rolled down their windows. Spoon looked to him with an expression of childlike glee. Tesser tried to speak at a tone that would be suitable for humans. "It is near," he said a little too loudly. The words came out as a roar and Alexis swerved, frightened by the incredibly loud warning that came from above. Spoon responded with a thumbs up out the window.

Tesser tilted his head back and let his wings lift him higher before he flapped powerfully. Too low, and he'd flip the truck over with the downward air pressure. The stroke propelled him upward and nearly doubled his speed. *Fuck this highway. I'm heading straight in.*

The span of a handful of heartbeats was all the time it took for the dragon of life to leave the road and find the entrance to the industrial park. Like its namesake, the gates and grounds of the complex were saturated with silver birch trees. They were leafless, unlike Ellen, but the bright white and silver bark was unmistakable. Tesser buffeted his wings and landed in the middle of the main road of the park, his front and rear claws digging in to the asphalt to stop his sliding decent.

Seconds later Garamos landed as well, but he took no care in what he destroyed on the way down. His body crashed into a three story office building, utterly flattening it with his weight. The noise was ear splitting as steel girders folded like balsa sticks and concrete blocks simple vaporized under his immense bulk.

I think that fucker is smiling. Tesser walked over towards his larger brother as Zeud, the bright red dragon, landed softly in the street like he had. She was huge like all the dragons, but she was far smaller than her two present brothers, and elegant instead of brutal. She almost seemed to sway and dance like the fire she lorded over.

"Garamos, you've no right to just destroy the human's things like that. Now they'll need to rebuild that, and people will be out of jobs. What if there were people inside there? Needless murder brother," Tesser scolded in the draconic tongue. It was older than time and equally hard to understand.

The giant earth dragon shrugged in a very human way. "Sorry Tesser. I've been too busy doing my job for the last few thousand years to notice this building. Maybe if I had more time to nap and recover my patience I would've landed there in the street. Maybe if you spent less time revealing our presence to the human race and more time trying to find Kaula we wouldn't argue so much."

"You're testing *my* patience," Tesser stated plainly.

Zeud walked over and interjected as Kiarohn circled above. "You two will never get along. What is it that makes you two wish to tear at each other's throats every time you're in each other's presence?"

Tesser spoke first, "He's an insufferable asshole."

Garamos chuckled, and shrugged again. "I've no time to spare on his impulsive ways, Zeud, and you're just as bad. Humans are no more important in my opinion than the moths or the squirrels he's made. The difference from the two of you is that I have use for fire in what I do. I can't think of a single good reason why anything is alive on this planet. Creatures just gum up the works. Life is an irritation."

Zeud laughed herself this time. "Oh Garamos. Spoken like the true hermit you are."

"Enough about the ugly one. Why are you all here? It is no coincidence that four of us meet in the same place at the same time like this," Tesser said.

"True words brother," Kiarohn said. "I was summoned by our missing sister."

"As was I."

"I as well."

Tesser nodded, understanding that Kaula had been planning this for some time. *For her to orchestrate our presence so accurately as to have us arrive nearly simultaneously…she had to have been planning this for a good long while. Oh Kaula. Ever the crafty one.* "What of Ambryn? Or Fyelrath?"

Kiarohn answered, "No sign yet, but Ambryn is subtle. It is likely that he is here already, watching. Waiting. Fyel must be late coming across the ocean, if she is coming at all. Last I knew she was halfway across the Atlantic, swimming with the sharks."

"She is a fast swimmer. We are not far from the coast. If Kaula sent for her, she will come soon."

"What are we here for Tesser? Where is Kaula?" Garamos asked in a grumbling, impatient voice.

"Kaula got word to me that she was imprisoned below ground under a building I believe is near here. There's a human woman here as well that I've mated with. She carries a child."

"You will fuck anything…" Garamos said shaking his head.

"Well, we weren't all born to tear apart the continents and build mountains with the pieces brother. To each their own," Tesser said.

Garamos shrugged once more. *He looks like the mountains he builds.*

"Imprisoned Tesser? How does that happen? We are dragons," Kiarohn posed to the creator of life.

"I believe the same way I was sent asleep. I cannot remember all the details, but I think I was poisoned by something from across the Veil. I think Legion did it to me. Legion is here now, and if I am right, he has kept her pumped full of something vile from the other side."

The dragons were silent. To imagine the pain and suffering Kaula must be enduring if that were the truth was beyond thought.

"I will head into the building and move below in the form of a human. We cannot risk damage to whatever it is that might be keeping her alive or sedated. If we set free something from beyond the Veil there could be disastrous consequences for the whole world."

"We could've been lured here by Legion for that exact purpose you know," Kiarohn said.

"Yes. But let's hope that's not the case. I will go below. Kiarohn, swirl the winds, and keep the skies clear. Helicopters will come soon. Keep them away, but don't kill them. We need to be allied with the humans, and we need them to trust us. Some things are best left unseen, though. We don't want to let Legion have a public stage."

Kiarohn seemed a bit worried. "There will be consequences. Weather will…be erratic in many places."

"I'm aware. The world will survive. Zeud, I ask of you to allow nothing to leave. Human, animal, or otherwise. Legion can take on a million faces, and I want you to immolate them all."

"As you wish," Zeud said, licking her lips with a tongue of flame.

"Garamos, as much as it pains you to take any instruction from me, I ask you to dig down, and dig deep. Make us a moat so nothing can escape, but more importantly, I need you to find this burial hole where our sister is. There can be no underground escape for Legion. He must pay for what he did to Kaula and me."

"I do this for our sister. Your plan is reasonable." Garamos stood up off his nest of broken building and started to walk towards the deeper portions of the industrial park.

Above, Kiarohn flapped gossamer wings and the clouds blew apart as if they had been an illusion all along. The brilliant stars twinkled, and Tesser smiled. *I missed my family. I'd forgotten how much.*

"What of Ambryn and Fyelrath?" Zeud asked, excited to hear what kind of destruction the two missing dragons would be tasked with.

"I don't know. I made all that up just now."

Zeud clapped Tesser on his massive back with an almost equally massive clawed hand. "That's my boy. I'm sure Fyelrath will find something to drown and Ambryn something to kill. Let's hope he doesn't take it too far and annihilate everything. You remember the chimera incident? It took you almost five hundred years to save them from extinction. Did you know they all died out about two thousand years ago? Sad really."

Tesser shook his head. "I've been asleep for a very long time. You'll have to fill me in later. Damn, I really liked the chimera."

Spoon's black SUV rounded the corner doing eighty behind them. The grill was smashed up from crashing through the park's front gate. Alexis stomped on the brakes and put the truck into a power slide, stopping a car's length from the tip of Tesser's tail. Zeud, not knowing who was in the car, spun around and bared her fangs, flames as thick as lava dripping out from the spaces between her teeth and melting the pavement like an acid. Far behind, Garamos grumbled and shrugged again, and kept walking. One car wasn't enough trouble to turn around for.

Spoon got out of the passenger seat of the car with a look of awe. He saw all four dragons and when his mind drew a blank on what to do or what to say, he started clapping. He looked silly.

Tesser switched to English. "Spoon, this is my sister Zeud. She made fire. Zeud, this is Spoon. He works for the government and is my friend. The grumpy fat one is Garamos and flying up there is Kiarohn."

Zeud's flames died out and she put on a congenial, almost silly smile. "Nice to meet you, Spoon. You're the first human I've met that's been named after cutlery." She spoke English as well.

"That's fucking awesome," was all Spoon could manage. She grinned. *I think she likes him. I like it when friends get along.*

Spoon backed up into the truck and got into the passenger seat. He was speechless. Tesser and his sister turned and started to follow Garamos. He seemed to want to lead.

"Did you frigging see that? I love my fucking job," Tesser heard Spoon say inside the truck.

I hope he can still say that tomorrow.

Chapter Fifty-One

Abe

They were in the right place. All the gunfire was a dead giveaway.

Jesus H motherfucking holy crap in a handbag.

Alexis drove the SUV at just under ten miles an hour. She kept the armored truck no more than twenty yards behind the end of Tesser's tail, and that was far too close to an avalanche of incoming gunfire and dragon sized wrath.

Garamos was the same distance ahead of Tesser, and he was in the locus of the onslaught. Fitzgerald Industries' building in the industrial park was set back and away from the other structures. It was only a part of the park in name, based on how far back it was set. The parking lot in the front was as Ellen had described, full of silver birch trees. Now they were shot apart into mulch or cast aside like matchsticks by Garamos. Standing outside the building in a completely exposed firing line were well over a hundred security personnel. They were exact replicas of the men who'd attacked them at Mr. Doyle's house. Daemons in human form.

That gives me the fucking creeps. I was nearly killed by ten of them. There's no way I'm getting out of this alive. I'm already limping and fucked up. Hell, so is Spoon.

Garamos ignored their gunfire. All the high velocity bullets (tracers included) streaming at the behemoth brown and red dragon impacted his scales and did no more damage than dust falling on a clean floor. They served as a nuisance, at best. Garamos smashed a claw the size of a small swimming pool into the asphalt parking lot and ripped a piece of it up. He tossed it at the soldiers like an enormous baseball, causing ten of them or more to explode into their daemonic, bloodless, nothingness. Garamos grinned, and with a roar that shattered every building window for miles around, produced a narrow cone of flame that was hot enough to nearly liquefy the pavement it streamed over, never mind what it hit. Garamos swept his head back and forth along the line of daemon guardians, and as the flame touched their quasi-human bodies they ceased to exist. There was no puff of smoke, no belch of brimstone. They were utterly and completely disintegrated by the dragon fire.

That fire is like a reality eraser. Garamos isn't even the dragon of fire. What the fuck does Zeud's breath do?

The siege was over in thirty seconds, and Alexis stopped the truck. The scene out the windshield was something apocalyptic and something altogether unreal. *This is my life now. I can't believe this is really happening.* Like a mad man, the limping Spooner got out of the truck, loaded up his agency issued firearms, and started walking towards the trio of walking dragons. Above, circling like a butterfly, was Kiarohn, the dragon of air.

"Where the fuck is he going? He's hurt. I'm hurt," Abe said.

Mr. Doyle chuckled, giddy at the events of the night and amused by Abe's comments. "Abraham my son, calm yourself. Please drink this." Mr. Doyle fetched a small glass bottle out of a satchel he'd brought at the last second. "This is a potent, difficult to brew concoction that is similar to the enchantment on the wine glass I use to slow my aging. It will mend some of your wounds, make your body slightly more resilient to injury, and most of all, clear your mind of pain for a few hours without dulling your senses. A taste from the fountain of youth. Drink deep."

Abe took the bottle from Mr. Doyle as the dragons outside conferred about their plan. One of the daemons burst out of the front door of the building with his weapon streaming out a lethal hail of bullets. Tesser snapped a claw out and backhanded him so powerfully he exploded on the spot. *Shit, I bet he could do that to an elephant. A real elephant.*

Abe looked down at the bottle and unscrewed the metal cap. A sniff told him the fluid inside was sweet. *It smells like cream soda.* Abe put the bottle to his lips and when the drink touched his tongue it was sweet, as expected. Warm as well. Abe let the whole bottle go down in a few gulps, and when the warmth hit his belly, he began to itch all over. *This feels like when I broke my arm in fifth grade. I itched like crazy while that bone was knitting up.* Within a few more moments he felt invigorated, repaired considerably. All of his aches and pains had set sail. Alexis watched as her man blossomed back into health in the backseat of the SUV.

"This is some GOOD shit, Mr. Doyle," Abe said as Garamos started to punch holes in the ground large enough to lose a car in. The truck they sat in shook with tremors with every dragon punch. He was digging his moat, one rip of the earth at a time.

"Wait, Abraham. Try this on for size," Mr. Doyle said, handling him a second glass bottle. This one was filled with a blue fluid that looked like Gatorade or Kool-Aid. The fluid shook as the dragon continued to rip the ground apart outside.

"What does this one do?" Abe asked, looking at it.

"It is distilled magical energy. All the spells you've struggled to cast the last year will be fueled by this potion for the next few hours. Perhaps when this Kaula dragon is free, it'll simply be the way you are from then on. I sincerely hope that is the case. Until then, use this as your font of power."

Abe looked down at the blue bottle and laughed. "Are you shitting me? This is a fucking mana potion."

Mr. Doyle smiled. "A mere coincidence. Drink it, and let us join our dragon leader. He's in a bit of a hurry to find his sister and lady friend, and I fear he shall leave us behind."

Abe already had the cap off and the bottle tipped up. Unlike the first drink, this was cool and refreshing. It felt like an oasis in the center of an ocean of desert. Abe could feel a queer tingling running up and down his arms and legs as the drink settled in his stomach. It felt like when Tesser was around during a spell. It felt like…

Magic.

Abe jumped out of the car and drew one of the Enfield pistols. I feel like a fucking comic book hero right now. He looked over and up at Garamos as he tore further and further into the parking lot. The earthen dragon had already excavated a moat large enough for multiple semi-trailers to fit in, and he wasn't even working hard yet. Tesser's winged body was shrinking down to match Spoon's at his feet. They would be heading into the building shortly.

Mr. Doyle got out of the truck as well, and shut the door. The two sorcerers, one the master, the other the apprentice, met at the hood, the four dragons nearby working at making the scene of disaster more controlled.

"I haven't taught you enough yet, Abraham. This is more than I've ever been brave enough to tackle, and I've done many stupid things in my very long time here on Earth. I hope that this becomes one of the first of our shared conquests, my young friend."

Friend? "I'd say I'm not scared, but that'd be a big fucking lie."

"Must you with the profanity? We're having a

moment. I'd appreciate it if you were to take it seriously, and use the English language in a civil fashion, Abraham," Mr. Doyle chastised, a smile on his face.

Abe tilted his head over towards the dragon creating a small scale Grand Canyon in the parking lot. "The last thing on my mind is language, Mr. Doyle. For what it's worth, one way or the other, I'm glad this is happening. I always wanted this. I always wanted to see dragons, cast spells, and save the world. Dying now wouldn't be the worst thing. I've achieved my dream."

Mr. Doyle put his hands on Abe's shoulders and embraced him. "All young wizards want the same, Abraham. Well, all that but the dying. That is why we trust our lives and souls to the magic we love. Now, kiss your woman passionately, tell her you love her, and let's go send some daemons back across the Veil."

Abe nodded and walked around to the other side of the truck. Alexis rolled her window down and leaned out. *She looks afraid.* "We're gonna head in. Try and find Matty. Rescue the dragon. You know. Handsome guy hero stuff. No big deal." Abe blustered, trying to break the tension.

"Yeah. I know. Be careful." Alexis' voice shook.

"We're past being careful. I'll stick to being badass. I think that'll be my best chance." *Shit that sounded GOOD. Movie quote right there if I ever heard one.*

A tear ran out of Alexis' face, and for a second, Garamos' smashing seemed quieter. "I think I love you Abe. I don't want to lose you."

Whoa. "Alexis, I…um. I'm not really mature enough for this. I like dick and fart jokes. I love the idea of being in love with you, and you know, I totally think I love you too, but right now my testosterone is flowing like the Mississippi River, and I need to kick some ass. I got a magic potion inside me that's begging to get out."

Alexis started to laugh and cry at the same time, and Abe leaned in and gave her a strong kiss on the lips. The kiss was hot and wet from the tears. It was strange, but it fit them perfectly.

"I'll see you in a bit?" Alexis asked, her makeup ruined.

"If I'm not back in a couple hours, you come looking for me. I'm more scared of you than those daemons." Alexis grinned, and Abe walked back to Mr. Doyle as Spoon came running back as well.

"Need more guns, Henry?" Mr. Doyle teased.

Spoon shook his head and went to the passenger side of the truck. "No. Tesser's naked again. I just came back to get him some pants and a shirt."

"Oh modesty. Such a perfect time and place for that."

This is gonna be fun. Until one of us dies.

Chapter Fifty-Two

Mr. Doyle

Upon stepping into the building, Mr. Doyle realized this would be a strange encounter. *The outside smelled of gunfire with a faint odor of brimstone underneath. Truly there are daemons here. But here, as we walk along these plastic and metal corridors, searching room to room for Matilde and Kaula...all I can feel is fakeness. This place is artificial in every way. The wood is plastic, the rug is synthetic. The lights are fluorescent, and the air pumped in by machines. Nothing is real about this place. Not it's physical makeup or its purpose. This was a place of evil, for evil.*

Tesser strode at their lead. Spoon was just behind him, limping strongly but moving forward with his carbine up and at the ready. He looked professional and calm in this dangerous environment, especially with the horsehide jacket, and his presence helped to steady both the spellcasters nerves. Abe and Mr. Doyle were at the rear, keeping an eye on their backside, and standing ready to support them if they were assaulted. Mr. Doyle held his longsword at the ready and Abe one of his Enfield pistols.

They were walking down a broken window lined hall that followed the outside wall of the building. They were only thirty paces inside the building. To their right, out the window frames filled with broken glass, they could see Garamos tearing up his enormous ditch around the building. It was already several hundred feet long, and deep enough for the dragon's entire arm to disappear in. To their left in the hall was a smooth taupe colored wall with periodic office doors spaced out along the way. As they met each door, Tesser would boot it open effortlessly with a bare foot, and they would move in, ready to visit incredible violence on anything inside. Since entering, they'd met no resistance.

Tesser launched another kick into another office door and erupted the entire thing off the hinges and frame. The door rocketed inward and smashed into a large desk, flipping over and going through another window on the other side. They'd discovered that this front face of the building was thin and obscured a central garden in the middle. *A piece of fake paradise, surrounded by falsehoods.*

Inside the office stood three of the daemons dressed like soldiers or guards, and all frantically trying to pick up the contents of the room. The tumbling door decapitated one of them, exploding its body immediately.

"Contact!" Spoon yelled as Tesser dove into the room recklessly. As soon as the dragon was out of the doorframe Spoon squeezed his trigger finger and brought down a second daemon. The door had been open less than a second, and two daemons were dead. The dragon and agent were a pair to contend with.

Tesser grabbed the daemon's weapon with his left hand as it tried to bring it up to fire at him. The gun went off on full auto and the clip emptied into the floor and wall as Tesser gripped the mundane looking monster by the throat and smashed it into the drywall of the office, its feet dangling.

"Where is Matilde?!" Tesser screamed, his throat giving him a voice deep and terrible.

"You'll never reach her in time dragon. She's already dying. Just like your sister," the daemon said, his face melting and reforming into the man Mr. Doyle recognized as Mr. Host. *That must be the face the thing has chosen to represent its true voice. Bastard.*

"You have crossed me before Legion, and you know how it ends. I'll rip your blackened souls apart and cast you back. Spare yourself the pain, trouble, and embarrassment. You don't want the other daemons mocking you for being routed again. Tell me where they are and leave now," Tesser snarled.

The Mr. Host clone laughed. "I do know how this ends dragon. The same as the last time we faced one another. You'll be buried under the earth, sleeping for twenty thousand years. Or more likely this time, until this world ends far sooner than that."

Tesser screamed and tore the man-thing's head off. He tried to throw it through the window but it burst into smoke as he swung his arm.

The three men stepped back, suddenly scared of his anger. Tesser hammer punched the corner of the desk and it collapsed to the floor, splintered and broken.

"We keep looking, Tesser. Time is of the essence," Mr. Doyle said urgently.

Tesser stopped his fury with a deep breath. He inhaled through his nose, and out through his mouth. He nodded in agreement. "Yes. I'm just..."

"Yeah, man. We get it," Spoon said.

Tesser sniffed the air again. *Something has caught his interest.* Tesser pushed past the three men and back out into the hallway. He strode quickly to the next office door and grabbed the handle. He yanked the door free straight off the frame and threw it out the wall of broken windows. He leaned into the office to smell and caught a face full of automatic gunfire. Mr. Doyle watched as the bullets impacted his skin, pancaked, and fell to the floor. *Well then. It appears as if though that room is occupied already.*

Tesser was unharmed by the gunfire, and he

disappeared into the office as Spoon and the two wizards ran to catch up. By the time they reached the doorway they could already smell the noxious fumes caused by the exploding daemons. *Three weapons on the ground. Nice work.*

Tesser was practically snorting air into his nose recklessly. Despite the cordite, drywall particles, floating wood bits, and lingering black smoke in the air, he was ravenously inhaling the room. He turned and went around the back of the desk and sniffed the chair, his nose millimeters from the faux leather. "This is Matty's office."

"How can you tell?" Spoon asked.

"Because he smells her Henry. The hound dog behavior seems like a straight away clue," Mr. Doyle said sarcastically.

"Fuck you, old man," Spoon said with a grin.

"That's the spirit," Mr. Doyle said back.

"If I can find her scent, maybe I can track her in the building."

"Stop," Mr. Doyle said. Tesser stopped, confused. "They didn't snatch her from here, right? They took her from her flat. All you're apt to find in this room is the way to the cafeteria and the lady's loo. I happen to have a bit of a piece of wonder that might be able to help us."

"Good. Go for it," Tesser said.

"Are there any hairs or physical elements of her at the desk?" Mr. Doyle asked, slipping past Spoon and Abe. They moved back to the doorway, providing some cover.

Tesser turned and snatched a dark hair from the back of her chair. He gave it a whiff, and handed it to the old wizard.

Mr. Doyle looked at the hair carefully. "This will do." He reached up to his forehead and took off the thick goggles that had been resting above his eyes. He unscrewed a round lens from the right eye, revealing a small space between that and a second lens beneath.

Carefully, he coiled the dark hair up in the tight space and replaced the outer lens. "Oculus circumspicio. Velox bene facis," he whispered, turning the device on.

A gentle flare of warm light ringed both lenses and gave off an electrical tingle. The British mage slid the goggles back over the top of his head and placed them carefully over his eyes. *Ah, there we are.* Inside the vision provided by the mad scientist goggles, Mr. Doyle could clearly see the presence of Matty in the office. Motes of warm yellow-orange lights appeared on the keys she typed the most, as well as the handset of her office phone. Her seat was glowing like the embers at the base of an old fire, and the edges of her desk where she rested her elbows were alit.

"Yes. I can see her presence. Now, allow the magic to grow, and it'll lead us directly to where she is now."

"Good. Make it work faster," Tesser said.

"It would work faster if your sister wasn't imprisoned somewhere below us, her magic fading. I'm sorry Tesser, but it's going as fast as it…"

Gunfire from the hallway interrupted the old man. From the open doorway Spoon and Abe started to return fire, shooting down both directions of the hall.

"There's like, five of them in each direction!" Abe yelled, snapping off a third shot.

"Make them count, young man! Those bullets are rather expensive!" Mr. Doyle said as the faintest of floating lights began to form in the air in front of him. *I'll have the path in a moment. She must be very close.*

Abe took a deep breath as Spoon loudly emptied his magazine to the left. The younger man knelt and leaned over, popping his head out. He squeezed the trigger smoothly and ducked back into the room. "Got one!" He was jubilant. "Keep firing, Spoon! We got this!"

"I already shot all of mine already. You want help on your side?"

"We're not all professionals, Spoon," Abe said,

somewhat deflated. Another ripping tear of gunfire stitched up the wall near the doorframe, causing Abe to dive into the room. Spoon responded by popping out into the hall and letting off several short bursts of fire.

"Two more down. One left. Wait. One's getting up." Spoon snapped another shot off. "He's down."

Abe leaned out the door and fired his last shot, hitting one of the daemons square in the crotch. The enchanted bullet tore into the artificial person and wrenched it free from this reality, sending it back across the Veil in an explosion of blackness. Abe looked positively ecstatic.

"Nice shot, Abe. Reload. More will come soon," Spoon said as he dropped a magazine and reloaded his weapon. He left the doorframe and picked up a few full magazines from the webbing of the dead and gone daemons. *Fortunate that so many assault weapons use the same standardized ammunition magazine.*

"Can you see where she is yet?" Tesser asked desperately.

The orange path was now well lit in the goggle. It streaked out the doorway and down the windowed hall like a long exposure shot of a neon light being moved about. It was mystical, and it led the way to the woman they needed to save. "I have her. Follow me."

"No. Follow me. Tell me where to go," Tesser said.

"That's very intelligent. You are notably more bulletproof than I. Head out, turn left. She's a good distance below us, but we need to find the stairs or the lift first. I'll know it when I see it."

The four men left Matty's office and started down the hallway, ready to find what they came for. Abe smiled enthusiastically at Mr. Doyle.

Careful what you wish for, Abraham. We are *one step closer to hell on earth, my boy. One step closer.*

Chapter Fifty-Three

Alec

"Alec, this will be a very dangerous night. As things stand, I cannot guarantee your safety. I may need more of your assistance," Mr. Host said calmly.

Need my assistance? What the fuck can I do for you? Alec and his security team leader were walking surrounded by a diamond of Mr. Host's men. They were deep underground in the secure complex near the purple dragon's sedated body. The earth rumbled and shook every few seconds. Alec had no idea what was happening, but he envisioned Tesser ripping the earth apart just a few feet above the hardened concrete.

"What do you need from me?" Alec asked.

"Alec, you are sure to die tonight. I can guarantee you of it. I do not have enough power at the moment to defeat the dragons that are at our doorstep."

I don't want to die. Not here, and not like this. "Dragons?" *What the fuck is he talking about? And power? What does he mean? Jesus shit I'm going to die right here in this fucking lab hole in the ground.* Alec's hand was shaking as they passed through another set of vault doors into a different section of the lab complex.

"Dragons, yes. Tesser has summoned more of his kind

to combat us. To destroy your company and everything your family has worked to build. To kill you."

"Kill me? What the fuck did I do?"

"Your company has kept a dragon in a coma for ten years, Alec. You are part and parcel to something they feel is a crime. These are savage beasts, Alec. Intelligent, yes, but still very savage. They care only for their own kind and will destroy whatever they must to preserve their wealth and power. I can fight them, but as I said, I need your help. Time is short."

"What kind of help can I offer? You're something supernatural, I know that much. My father told me some things before he died. You've already far more power than I have. Whatever power really is."

Mr. Host nodded; he seemed almost absent for a moment, like his mind was elsewhere, or he was lost in thought, talking to someone else. The only sound in the room was the steady beeping from Matty's heart monitor and the thunderous booms of something loud hitting the earth above. "Alec, your father summoned me from a very faraway place many years ago. It took him years of study to learn how to properly do it and after he did he struck a bargain with me, and we worked together to build a better world for both our purposes. A give and take. He gave up a piece of his being to bring us across something called the Veil, and I in turn gave up some of my freedom here. Together we were able to subdue the dragon, and you know how much good has come of that single act. When your father was about to die, we drafted a new contract, and you signed it, passing along his portion of responsibility to you, thus allowing for us to remain and continue to work together on our goals. But we are bound by that contract. Your father was a shrewd and wise man, conceding only what he absolutely had to, to obtain my loyalty and…shall we call it my skill set."

Alec's stomach turned over. *I don't think I like where this is going.*

Mr. Host continued, his men oblivious and robotic. They seemed like walking mannequins. "If you were to write a simple addendum to the contract allowing us more power for the fight that we will be entering in just a few minutes, we can survive it. You and I, and most importantly Fitzgerald Industries and all the work we've accomplished, will continue. But I cannot do it without your permission."

"How do I know you won't just kill me and take over if I give you more…power?" I'm not going to die for this fucking weirdo. Not tonight, not ever.

"Alec, in the contract I am forbidden to harm you. Should harm come to you or the contract we share, I would be weakened. If you were to die I would be sent back from where I came, and we would lose everything we've fought so hard to achieve together. It is in my best interest to keep you safe and sound."

The group of men rounded a corner, and with a swipe of a security card, a pneumatic door hissed open, and they entered a hospital room. Alec immediately recognized the immobile woman in the bed. *Holy shit that's, Matty. I did NOT want to see her like this. Have they got her sedated?* "That's Matty, right? Why is she under like that? Isn't she pregnant? Isn't that baby priceless, and we're running the risk of fucking all that up? Unplug her this second!"

Mr. Host shook his head as a scolding parent might at an insolent child. "No, no, Mr. Fitzgerald, we wouldn't want that. If you had read your genetic reports on her, you'd know she has some…unusual markers. Traits that are potentially dangerous. Ask yourself this: what woman could bear the child of a dragon? No woman I want awake. Trust me in this, she is safe, the baby is safe, and when you write another contract to empower me further, we too will be safe."

"I don't know. I am thinking I might just want to…"

"Alec, your father would want this. His whole

empire, *your* whole empire, will crumble to dust tonight if you fail in this very moment. Within the hour, in fact."

"I don't think my father really knew—"

"Shut up, Alec. Think of what your father would want. He would want you to continue your work, saving lives."

"I guess." Alec couldn't take his eyes off of Matty's body. She wore an oxygen mask, and there were multiple IV lines running into her, pumping similar looking bags filled with the solution the dragon was kept asleep with. *What am I doing?* Alec sighed painfully. His hand was forced, and he knew it. "What do I need to do?"

"Write the following: I give Legion a greater footing to channel his power across the Veil this night. I allow his rage to flourish so that I may survive."

"Rage? You need permission to be angry?"

"Yes, and hopefully you never see why with your own eyes."

"Okay. Give me a piece of paper and a pen."

"Blood is better. That failing, use your shit. Write on the wall." Mr. Host pointed to a sterile white wall in the room. The four guards stepped out of the way in unison, leaving a clear path to the writing surface for Alec.

Scared and afraid, Alec walked over to the wall and stood there, unsure of what to do next. After a moment, one of Mr. Host's men drew a large combat knife and handed it to Alec. He took it with trembling hands.

"Write quickly. They are almost in the lower levels."

"All this money spent on security for nothing." Alec looked down at his finger, then back at Matty, then at the knife. His emotions felt detached. *This is the wrong thing to do. What was my father thinking?*

"Alec, quickly, or we risk losing everything."

With a very unsure, shaking hand, Alec cut the tip of his finger. *Shit that hurts.* He then put the bloody tip to the white wall and began to write what Mr. Host asked of him. His finger shook from the pain and uncertainty. *God help me. God help us all.*

"That's very good Alec. Now we have a chance to survive this. Make sure to sign the bottom to make it official."

I'm going to puke. Or worse.

Chapter Fifty-Four

The Dragons

On the surface of the world Tesser's family had things completely under control. Zeud's ability to command fire coupled with her dragon's breath meant laser precision bursts of heat and flame that struck and incinerated daemon bodies as fast as they appeared. For every ten that shot at her or the other dragons, ten were annihilated by a bolt of her incendiary fire. Over all of this, the cold autumn sky spat snow.

Garamos was disinterested by the violence around him. He was head down into his moat work, and the bullets were harmless. His hide was so thick and naturally dense that no practical man operated weapon could hope to penetrate it. The daemons relying on modern technology had no nope of harming him. The massive earth dragon kept his focus and continued to tear the parking lot apart, preventing any kind of subterranean escape. He was almost deep enough to reach something below the earth. A massive false stone structure. He was reminded of a human tomb, but the size was far too large. It was dragon sized. The thought angered him, and he dug faster.

Far above, the four winged Kiarohn circled in the

night sky. Each wing buzzed faster than any other dragons could and stirred the wind in such a way that the human helicopters that approached were tossed about and had to turn away. Kiarohn could see hundreds, perhaps thousands, of human vehicles with flashing lights cordoning off an area for miles in each direction, keeping all the innocents away. The blue and red lights were almost pretty from that high up. But for Kiarohn, the view was always from up high.

The three dragons dealt with the steady stream of Legion's bodies and kept everything manageable. But then a change came.

A small group of the daemons burst through a series of broken windows on the front facing of the windows. Zeud expected them to raise their guns to fire, but they did not. Instead they landed on all fours, hands and feet pumping, running them across the rubble strewn parking lot as if they were hounds. As they moved, their bodies changed.

Joints broke and reformed at irregular angles, becoming longer, more muscular, feral and animalistic. Their heads elongated into some hellish mixture of wolf and insect. Canine jaws with powerful pincers wide enough to slice through a human torso formed, and multiple sets of faceted eyes sprouted alongside the wolfen eyes. Their skin rippled and buckled, forming chitinous armor plating mixed in with black and gray fur. Saliva dripped, etching and burning holes into the pavement, and their claws sparked as they loped aggressively towards the dragons. The daemons had somehow brought more of their infernal presence across the Veil, and it was the stuff of nightmares.

Zeud was temporarily frozen, her dragon jaws agape at the rape of sanity the daemons presented. To have something so evil, so wholly unwelcome here on Earth was a violation of historic proportions. She started to spit out gouts of flame at the Legion hounds, but they were already leaping through the air to land on Garamos' back.

His digging stopped. Now he had to take notice. The incredible dragon lifted his body up, flinging two of the daemons off his body like a dog would shake free a tick, but Garamos roared in pain. The daemon hounds may not have technology, but their Veil born teeth and claws were able enough to rip through his previously impenetrable hide. Zeud and Kiarohn could see fresh red blood running out from holes torn in his skin.

Garamos grabbed one of the daemons and squeezed it until it popped, but this time there was no smoke. Greasy, sticky blood and gore erupted from his hand as the more materialized daemon body died. They were real now, no longer half on this side of the Veil and half on the other. They were present and poisoning the world with their very presence.

A hundred more leapt from the windows of Fitzgerald Industries.

*****

Alexis had parked the agency issued truck far away from the monster movie happening down the street. She was in the industrial park road and watched the three dragons rip apart everything that moved, and some things that didn't. If she stopped thinking about it, the show was easily the most amazing thing she could ever witness. Front row tickets to the wrath of dragons.

Some strange dogs burst out from the building and charged at the biggest of the dragons, the brown one. Those are some big assed animals. They look almost big enough to be bears. The strange dog things leapt through the air with a predatory power Alexis had never seen before. They landed on the back of the monstrously large dragon and started to bite at his scales. *Fat chance that'll do anything.*

But it did. The huge dragon reared up from his massive earth-moving project and shook off two of the dogs. They flew up into the air like water droplets off a shaking dog, going so high Alexis lost sight of them. The dragon roared out, so clearly in shock and pain Alexis gasped in fear. She could see streams of blood running down the dragon's back as wide as her arm. *That thing could bleed enough to flood the world if they kill it. And if they can hurt that thing…*

Two of the daemon creatures that the huge dragon launched skyward landed in the road twenty feet from the truck. Alexis stared at them as they impacted the ground and got back to their four feet. They shook their heads, regaining their senses.

Fuck. Fuck me. Oh shit. Stay still Alexis. They'll go back after the dragons in a second. The big, scary, tough dragons. Oh, my God, what are those things? Too many eyes. And the teeth! SO many.

Alexis' hands gripped the steering wheel so tight her knuckles nearly poked through the skin. She trembled her body was so flooded with adrenaline and fear. She stared out the windshield of the vehicle and waited.

One of the daemon things turned tail and immediately ran back towards the dragons, eager to taste that flavor of blood. The remaining four legged monster staggered a bit and began to turn to join its friend, but then it froze. *Fuck.*

The daemon turned and locked eyes with Alexis inside the truck. Somewhere in the back of her mind where madness lived, she realized the thing had more eyes than limbs. More than she'd seen earlier. It snarled. She screamed.

As it started charging down the road, closing the distance between, Alexis slammed the shifter into reverse and hammered the pedal to the floor. The powerful truck engine roared to life and launched the vehicle backwards at a remarkable rate of speed. She was held in her seat only by the strong seatbelt across her chest. *Fuck, it's as fast as me. I can't outrun this thing.*

The wolf-bug ran with a speed that danced around the line of physical impossibility. She had the accelerator pegged, and the truck was picking up speed, but the thing remained with twenty feet. Soon, it began to cut the distance, and then in a feat of supernatural strength, it launched itself forward and latched onto the hood with paws that resembled human hands with insectoid hook fingers. Sharp shell-like spikes punched into the steel hood, and the creature was firmly attached. She thought of a lamprey. On the side of the driver's seat was a handgun, and she knew how to shoot it. One hand came off the steering wheel, and straight through the windshield she pulled the trigger and emptied the pistol. The gunfire was deafening, and the safety glass ruined, but she felt a sudden gasp of relief knowing she'd just shot the thing ten or more times.

When the gun clicked dry she saw the thing was still there, and still very much alive.

Alexis screamed, and the monster started to punch new holes into the hood as it climbed its way towards her. She dropped the pistol and grabbed the steering wheel with both hands. Alexis slammed on the brakes and spun the wheel sideways. *This is your stop thing, get the fuck off.*

The SUV started to make a shaking, 180 degree turn, but a tire caught on something, and before Alexis could do anything, the world turned upside down. The car and everything inside it spun over and over uncontrollably, tumbling down the road in a self-destructive barrel roll, smashing all the windows and tossing the daemon creature off like a slingshot. Alexis was shaken senseless by the rollovers, and when the vehicle came to rest on its roof, she hung painfully upside down. Above her on the roof of the truck sat a shotgun that had somehow come free.

That seems lucky. I'm going to need that to kill that thing. Alexis reached up with shoulders that were impossibly sore. She picked up the gun and racked the pump with a wince, chambering a shell. *Thanks, Dad.* The safety went off after that, and as the blood ran to her head, she looked out at the street. A thin film of white snow covered the dark pavement, and more fat flakes drifted down, adding more to the coating. Everything was quiet save for the distant sounds of dragon destruction hundreds of yards away. Out of the corner of her eye she saw the four alien feet of the creature moving towards the side of the car. The legs limped, but they moved with purpose. The thing was coming to finish her off.

"Hope you like buckshot, asshole," Alexis grunted. She held the shotgun as firmly as she could and squeezed the trigger. A thunderous blast kicked out and hit the creature in the leg. The foot broke off and the creature collapsed to the pavement. She racked the pump up again as fast as she could and shot again and again. This time, the creature leapt out of the way, and landed on the underside of the flipped truck. She had no shot.

Alexis tried to turn around to face out the driver's side of the truck, but the shotgun was too long, and the thing dropped down on the ground next her. All four legs were back. *Its leg is healed. I'm dead.*

The thing's mouth was beyond rationality. Part wolf, part spider, part leech, and all evil, the monster crouched down and moved closer to the window. Ropey strands of yellow poisonous drool slid out from the creature's mouth as it opened its maw wide to kill Alexis.

Then thunder struck.

Alexis felt something wet hit her in the face as the world shook, and her stomach churned from the awful smell and taste of it. She wiped her eyes and saw a wall of green out the window of the truck where the monster had been only a second before. The wall moved, and Alexis saw the buildings in the park as the car rocked back and forth from some insane ground impact. *What the fuck just happened?*

Without warning the vehicle moved. It lifted upward off the pavement and rotated around until it was righted. She felt like she was on an amusement park ride. Once her motion sickness passed Alexis realized she was looking out of the cracked windows at an incredibly large and bright blue eye. *It has flecks of jade in it. So pretty.*

The eye was the size of dinner table, and it peered into the vehicle at her. A massive clawed hand appeared, grabbed the roof of the truck, and tore it off as easily as Alexis might crack a can of peel-tab cat food. The sound of shrieking metal did her rattled brain no favors, but it did reveal the fact that she was easily thirty feet off the ground and held by a new dragon. The dragon looked at her with curiosity in its eyes as the melee raged on at Fitzgerald Industries just down the way.

"Who are you? You smell of my brother and daemon innards," the giant blue-green dragon asked in a feminine voice. *How I know that's a female dragon's voice is beyond me, but this is definitely a girl dragon.*

"I'm Alexis. I came with Tesser. He's in the building up there trying to rescue his girlfriend and another dragon."

The dragon nodded, as if that were the answer it expected. "I am Fyelrath. You did well in fighting this daemon. This is a very powerful manifestation. It was fortunate that I arrived when I did."

"Damn straight," Alexis said with a smile. A trickle of blood ran down from the top of her head and went in her eye. She wiped it away.

Fyelrath smiled back. "I'm going to set you down. Stay here."

"What are you going to do? The daemon things are changing, mutating. They can hurt the dragons now."

"We've been hurt before. Pain is unavoidable, even for dragons. It is very much unavoidable for those that would harm one of our kind."

"Kick some ass," Alexis said as the dragon sat her down on the pavement. Something structural in the vehicle gave way as the dragon let go, and the truck tilted to the side comically. "Please."

"Oh I will. I swam an awfully long way to not taste the blood of my enemies, Alexis," Fyelrath said before nodding and taking off at trot that shook the earth.

Alexis felt much better about the odds of this fight ending well.

Chapter Fifty-Five
Tesser

The elevator wouldn't work. The doors wouldn't open when the buttons were pushed. The security card reader sat quietly on the wall, daring them to do something about it.

"Shit," Abe said. "How do we get down there?" he asked, his pistol held up at the ready. *His hand is shaking. Not much. He's trying to be brave, but he's scared. He's a good kid.*

"We find the stairs," Spoon said, stating the obvious. He too held his firearm up and at the ready. They hadn't seen a daemon in several minutes. The sudden safety was starting to wear on them. *The adrenaline fades, leaving the fear and anxiety behind. I suppose that's an error in design on my part.*

Mr. Doyle spoke up, adjusting his goggles, "There are no stairs. My ocular apparatus would've detected a secondary route if there was one. Its enchantment is strong enough to source out alternate routes. If we wish to find Matilde, we must find a way to make this lift work."

"I think making the elevator work is beyond us, Mr. Doyle. What I can do, is make the elevator shaft work for us," Tesser said.

"I don't think I follow," Mr. Doyle said, lifting his goggles in an attempt to make Tesser's statement make more sense.

This should amuse them. Tesser turned and jammed his fingers into the tiny gap between the elevator doors. The metal gave way under his superhuman strength, and he worked his way into the gap between the two sheets of steel. It groaned loudly against the power in his hands, but it was a failing sound. Tesser had his hands wedged in between the doors in just moments. He gritted his teeth and pulled the elevator door apart easily, if not painlessly. On the other side was an empty elevator.

"That helped," Abe said out of the corner of his mouth at an elevator that wouldn't work.

"Patience, Abe. Garamos didn't build the Alps in a day."

"Garamos built the Alps?" Spoon asked, looking over his shoulder at Tesser as the dragon walked into the elevator.

"Look around. He built pretty much everything you see when you step outside. That or put the events into motion so they would build themselves," Tesser said as he stomped a foot down into the carpeted floor of the lift. Something metal cracked below.

"Are you for real?" Abe asked.

Tesser stopped and looked up, his foot coming down again, breaking the floor like a jackhammer. "I am for real. Garamos built everything, and every ounce of life you see came in some fashion from my work."

"You made the platypus? I would love to hear your reasoning behind that," Abe said. Spoon snickered and nodded in agreement.

"Gentlemen, let's not provoke our dragon friend as we are about to descend into our enemy's lair," Mr. Doyle said.

Tesser hammered his foot down again, this time

punching it right through the floor. *There we go.* Tesser knelt and used his hands to rip the floor up like it was no more than cardboard. Strips of carpet were tossed aside with wood and metal. Before long, a hole big enough for two men to fit through was made, and Tesser leaned down into it, searching for something below.

"It's a very long way down. A hundred feet at least. More. It smells like daemon shit."

"How do we get down there?" Abe asked. "And what does daemon shit smell like?"

"It smells like evil. Corruption most thorough. And lies. And to get down there I just need to get a little creative. Spoon, you first." Tesser waved Spoon over and the ex-cop came over immediately. "We'll fall fast, but don't worry. Are you okay with falling?"

"I'm a Rakkasan Tesser. Falling from the sky on my enemies is what I did for a living," Spoon said with a smile.

Very good. "We have much in common Spoon. Stand here." Tesser pointed to the floor near the hole. He put his arms around Spoon at the chest as the man pointed his weapon downward, and the two stepped sideways into the hole. They plummeted in the dark for several seconds at full speed, then there was a tearing sound and a whoosh of air, and they suddenly slowed as if a parachute had deployed. Spoon looked over his shoulder as they drifted downward. Tesser had sprouted smaller dragon wings off his human back. His shirt was torn.

"You can just grow wings at will?" Spoon asked as they descended down the shaft. He returned his attention to where they were about to land in case a threat appeared.

"It is tougher to create a hybrid body like this. Taking on the form of something that already exists is easier."

"Why?"

"I don't know. I suppose rules are rules, Spoon; even we dragons have to abide by some." The man and dragon touched down at the bottom of the vertical tunnel. The closed doors of the shaft bottom greeted them at chest height, speaking of a threat too frightening to talk about on the other side. "I'll be right back." Tesser launched into the air, and with a few flaps of his wings he reached the hole in the floor of the elevator above.

It took less than five minutes to get the other two men down.

Tesser's wings shrank and folded, eventually absorbing back into his flesh as if they had never existed. He tore free and dropped the shirt he'd been wearing. Abe and Mr. Doyle were in faint awe at the spectacle of transformative power. Tesser smiled. He addressed his allies.

"I don't know what greets us on the other side of this door guys, but I do know Matty is down here, and I'm pretty sure Kaula is as well. Legion, the daemon who took Matty and my sister, he'll stop at nothing to prevent us from freeing them. His foothold on this plane depends on us failing. Dying."

"Yes, yes, Tesser, on with it. There's no need to rally the insane. We're already here and willing, and I'm not getting any younger," Mr. Doyle said.

Abe turned with a look on his face. "The fuck you say? You got ten years younger just this month using your damn magic wine glass."

Mr. Doyle conceded the point with a guilty shrug and pulled his goggles back down.

I love these people. "If anything happens, I want you all to know I'll never forget you. I'll see to it you're remembered."

"Said like a true immortal, Tesser. Skip the speech, rip this fucking door open, and let's kill these motherfuckers," Spoon said

"As you wish." Tesser skipped the subtlety of trying to wedge his fingers into the space and instead just punched the gap where the doors met. The metal folded and warped out with a screech. He inserted his hands in the hole and ripped them apart, driving them into their recess and revealing a stark white hermetically sealed passage. At the end of the hall was a thick industrial door with no handle. A card reader was on the wall. To each side were glass walls behind which multiple heavily armed security personnel stood. They were daemons, the same as all the others.

They fired.

Tesser shoved the men back as the glass walls shattered and a wall of lead came at them. There was almost no place to hide in the cramped area they stood, but if they went prone there was some space. Spoon hit the deck immediately at the recessed bottom of the elevator shaft, and right as the bullets came crashing through, the other two men dropped as well. As soon as they hit the ground two grenades rolled through the door opening and into the area they'd taken cover in.

"Fire in the hole!" Spoon yelled. He reached out and grabbed one grenade and flicked it over the lip of the elevator. Tesser saw the small explosive weapon and dropped on top of it, smothering the blast with his body. It went off with a wet WHUMP, but his body absorbed it. His already ruined shirt was now long gone, but the men survived. It was the smallest of prices to pay. In the hall, the second grenade went off, and the men heard a near simultaneous series of muffled explosions as some of the daemons were destroyed by the shrapnel.

Abe was to his feet first somehow. "Telum!" he barked, pointing a tiny shard of sharpened wood at a staggered daemon. It was no more than a pencil really. Abe channeled a tremendous amount of magical power into the simple spell, and the wooden dart rocketed out from his hand trailing visible waves of force and hit one of the daemons in the face. It exploded. "Holy fuck, it worked!" Abe said to his friends, grinning ear to ear.

Gunfire made him drop to the floor.

Tesser stood and stepped up from the lowered shaft bottom. His skin puckered where dozens of bullets struck him. If it caused him pain, his friends couldn't tell. He strode into the hallway right over the broken glass in his bare feet, ignoring that as easily as he ignored being shot, and launched over the short wall to the one side of the room that still had guards remaining. Two strikes later, and they too were nothing but a cloudy stain on the wall and ceiling.

I am angry now. Tesser hopped back into the hall from the security booth and started to punch the heavy sealed door. The steel dented and then caved in as he punched it repeatedly. The walls and floor shook from his anger. Blow after blow smashed into the door, destroying it, and with a soul wrenching scream he kicked the door, blasting it apart. It was a scene of supreme hurt and savagery. On the other side of the door was an airlock space with lockers for sealed environmental suits.

"Shit Tesser, what'd that door do to you?" Abe asked.

Tesser turned, and the men saw the rage on his face.

"I think that door called your mom fat," Abe said, pointing at the second door beyond. Tesser made a grin that had a few too many sharp teeth in it, and he turned and went after the second door. That one didn't last half as long as the first. What greeted them on the other side stopped Tesser cold.

The smashed open door revealed a vast chamber as large as a small supermarket, and twice as high. It stank of the smell of cleaning solutions, medicines that tasted badly, and something dark and indescribable, like the scent of a person you hate, or the color of a sound that makes your skin crawl. Surrounded by a hundred of the nondescript daemon guards and a wall of plastic sheeting was the body of a massive purple dragon. It lay on its stomach, pipes filled with wretched bile masquerading as medicine pumping into it at multiple locations, its wings restrained, and its beautiful face covered by a mask that surely wasn't giving it just oxygen. The creature was comatose and pathetic. No dragon should ever be pathetic.

Kaula. "LEGION!" Tesser bellowed. His rage consumed him. Before their eyes the man dragon shifted forms to another hybrid body. His legs extended, as did his arms and torso. His skin shifted from soft mammalian flesh to the hard scales of his true dragon form. His neck lengthened and his face elongated into a half dragon-half humans. His wings, the same as the ones he'd used to drift down the elevator shaft were back. He was nearly ten feet tall and was barely restrained fury given form.

In the middle of the pack a single familiar face walked forward. He wore a suit, and a face that should've been far more afraid. Mr. Doyle, Abe, and Spoon took cover in the airlock room and watched as the two primordial forces met again.

"Tesser, oh, Tesser. Why do we do this dance over and over? Every time we meet it seems it always ends up the same. How many hundreds of thousands of years has this been going on? Aren't you bored? When will you learn to play for the right team? Sign a contract. Become one with my side of the Veil. Imagine what we could achieve! Legion bound to a dragon. Two of the most powerful creatures in all of existence allied together! This is such a rotten, fleshy world anyway. It needs purging, and it's all your fault. Let us help. Have a clear conscience over all your mistakes made with this world. Sign a contract with me. Last chance…"Mr. Host teased. The thumping above had stopped. Garamos' digging had been interrupted.

Through a half-dragon throat, Tesser wordlessly snarled.

"No? Well, don't say I didn't offer it to you. You should know, I've got a new contract," Mr. Host continued. "I think you'll find the terms quite unsuitable for the long term survival of life here on Earth." Mr. Host ripped off his suit and shirt, revealing a pasty white chest underneath. He had no nipples, belly button, or body hair. He looked like a malformed plastic toy, absent of humanity. Like a tidal wave spreading out from his body, the guards dropped their weapons and ripped off their body armor and clothing the same as he. They too were featureless, almost made of clay. Then, like Tesser had, Mr. Host changed.

His body warped, darkened, and twisted on itself, losing all semblance of humanity, becoming an amorphous blob of raw dark reality. Looking at it brought back memories of nightmares long forgotten, of shapes under the bed, and eyes in the closet. Its black presence was madness made real. The rest of the daemon forms shifted into the same ooze, and soon after they began to coalesce into fewer, larger daemonic forms. Each form was different, and they all matched Tesser's new body in size.

One took the shape of a massive white spider, as large as a car. It bristled with twitching hairs that looked more like spikes and had fangs that glistened with acidic venom. All eight of its otherworldly eyes fixed on Tesser as the fangs rubbed together, emitting a strange vibration that made stomachs churn.

Another molded multiple human bodies into the shape of a many legged worm creature. Each leg terminated in a small child's hand, and the head was an infernal amalgam of five human jaws, arranged in a circle and all hinged to chew its prey to death. Ringing the outer jaws were a hundred human eyes, each staring with lidless malice.

Seven other horrid forms stood in the room, but perhaps the worst was what Mr. Host became. He mocked Tesser. He became a white dragon in mirror image. His eyes were as black as the void he came from. The white dragon laughed.

Tesser snarled, and a war that would decide the fate

of Earth began once more.

Chapter Fifty-Six

Spoon

Spoon's mind came to an abrupt halt as the daemon things shifted forms in front of his eyes. He'd managed to keep it moving, processing, planning even after seeing the new dragon restrained and poisoned in the middle of the huge subterranean chamber, but when those…things changed into the forms they took, shucking the rules of reality, his mind couldn't take it anymore.

In the back of his head where he hid away his fears, doubts, and the memories he never wanted to visit again, there was a dark stirring. There were voices.

"You'll never amount to shit, Hank," Spoon's dad told him once from the recesses of his mind. Spoon could hear his voice in his ears as clear as day, almost as if he were in the room with them, telling him again. The judgment was palpable, and Spoon felt small.

I don't have to take this. He fought back. "Fuck off, dad. Worthless drunk. You died years ago. I made my peace with you. I need to get my shit together right now or my friends are gonna die," Spoon said. No one seemed to hear him. Abe and Mr. Doyle were faced forward, staring at the monsters. *Is time even moving right now?*

"Why weren't you laying down more cover fire?" Spoon's fire team leader asked him harshly, pointing a finger at him. Spoon could feel the familiar, crusty, sweaty fatigues rubbing against his skin and could feel the weight of his US Army issued body armor and helmet again. He could taste the dust of Afghanistan on his tongue. His heart raced. He could see two worlds overlapping, intermingling.

"I was. I…What are you talking about, Sarge? I was…" Spoon's mind struggled to realize he was hallucinating. He could hear the hammer beat of a Browning fifty laying down suppressing fire in the background, but he knew there was none. He was in Massachusetts, in the bowels of the basement from Hell. It was actually a worse place than a firefight in Shahi-Kot valley.

"You're gonna catch a court martial you lazy Irish fuck. I told them about you. Worthless piece of Yankee shit. You can't trust no one from the north!" the Sergeant hollered in his ear. It seemed like his Tennessee accent grew stronger as he got angrier at Spoon. The Sergeant was spitting in fury.

With no regard for sense, Spoon stepped back and raised his weapon, pointing it at the NCO in his mind. He slipped his finger down and rubbed it against the trigger, ready to end the Sergeant's tirade. In his mind, he saw the gravel voiced, dirty faced soldier of the 101st look back at him in shock, but a small piece of rationality appeared, and he saw Abe's face instead.

What the fuck am I doing?

"You are about to shoot your friend in the face," a soft feminine voice said over the din of two battles, one real, one false.

"Who are you? Why are you in my head?" Spoon asked two worlds, his finger coming off the trigger.

"I'm the big purple dragon in front of you, Henry, and if you don't listen to my voice, you're going to shoot your friend and then be killed by Legion. There won't be enough of you and your friends left to have a funeral my friend. You must listen, and listen hard."

For some reason, I trust her. "What do I do?"

"Look up. Not with your mind, but with your eyes, the ones you haven't blinked with, the eyes that feel dry. Focus on that dryness. Feel the reality."

Jesus, she's right. Spoon felt the scratchy surface of his eyeballs and blinked. Each time his lids opened the view changed. Afghanistan. Massachusetts. A dirty, gunpowder soaked battlefield on the side of a cold mountain. A subterranean lair filled with nightmares. A half dozen blinks and his eyes locked into the real world. He was looking down at Abe, frozen, cowering, and confused as Spoon pointed his weapon at him. Just to Spoon's left Mr. Doyle was calmly shooting his 1911 out of the doorway at the giant spider monster, oblivious to what was happening just behind him.

"Spoon, what the fuck are you doing?" Abe asked loudly, his voice shaking. *He has another one of those magic sticks in his hand. One word and I'd have been killed.*

"I don't know. Something came over me. A... darkness. Hallucinations. I saw and heard my father and then my Sergeant yelling at me, and I was about to shoot him, but then it was you, and then I heard...Kaula. Kaula, are you still there?"

She was gone.

"Spoon, you're fucking crazy. Shoot the monsters, not your friends. And Kaula's asleep man. She's right fucking there. Get yourself together. Fight against it. Use your will, not just your trigger finger." Abe stood, suddenly brave and wise. He wore it well. He turned and pointed out the door at the spider monster that was stalking towards them, each spiked foot hitting the floor oddly making the same sound like an aluminum bat smacking into a phone pole. "Telum!" he shouted out, and the same wave of force burst from his fingertips. It might've even been more powerful. The wooden missile screamed out over the shoulder of the elder wizard and struck the spider's foremost leg at a joint, bursting it from the main body and hitting the floor like a side of beef. The spider body reeled in pain, but it pressed forward.

"Good on you, Abraham!" Mr. Doyle yelled, a huge grin on his face. He swapped the magazine in his pistol.

Spoon's mind snapped back into action. We're button holed up in this entranceway, and that spider is going to kill us. The soldier's brain worked overtime now, taking in the entire scene. Tesser was locked in a three-pronged battle in the center of the room near Kaula's body.

The worm thing with a hundred baby arms was trying to pin Tesser's half dragon-half giant body down with its massive girth. Teeth snapped shut on the air as it tried to bite the dragon. The thing was ten feet long if it was a foot, and it must've weighed two thousand pounds. Tesser had one long arm outstretched with a claw at its neck, holding it at bay. His right claw was slashing like a flurry of broadswords, ripping the flesh of the dragon clone straight from the bone. The monster cackled madly as its dark blood flew through the air. Tesser paused his slashing and spat out a rope of white-hot flame into the face of a creature that looked like a bear mixed with a toxic orange octopus. The creature erupted into flames and staggered back wildly, trying to extinguish the most powerful fire in all of existence. It was engulfed, though, and on the floor in a moment, dissolving under the intensity of the fire. More lumbering monsters in a myriad of shapes were closing in on him. Nearby, Kaula sat impassive, drugged, and still.

He's holding his own for now, but he's going to need help fast. Spoon looked at the massive arachnid marching at them and a plan formed in his head. They couldn't help the dragon until the spider was dead.

"Blind it! Shoot it in the fucking eyeballs!" Spoon yelled, and all three men lifted their weapons and fired. Spoon's M4 dumped the entire magazine before Doyle and Abe emptied their guns. *Hooray for a high cyclic rate.*

Spoon was on the move, dropping the empty mag and slapping in a new one. He aimed and dumped that magazine straight into what passed for the face of the giant spider. It screeched in pain.

We're hurting it.

Spoon changed mags again, moving fast. The monster was halted, and when it hesitated, Spoon took three steps at it and ripped another long burst at one of the thing's hind legs, severing it completely. The creature staggered, losing its balance for a moment. Spoon twisted and dumped another fifteen rounds into the leg nearest to him, blasting it free from the body. The creature's enormous weight bogged down the five remaining legs, and it swayed, barely staying up.

From the hall Mr. Doyle stepped out and produced a small leather bag from his belt of tricks. He sheathed his pistol as Spoon reloaded and with both hands threw the contents of the bag at the daemon spider. Tiny shards of metal spilled out, and just before they were about to hit the floor impotently, Mr. Doyle spoke a single calm phrase.

"Crescat, et fuge." The shards of metal leapt out, launched from the floor they were headed to and sprayed at the spider. They grew in size until they were the size of gleaming steel machetes spinning with the ferocity of a chainsaw. The whirling blades bit into the white carapace and flesh of the swollen misshaped spider, tearing large pieces free and sending more black blood than could be imagined all about. The floor was thick and slick with it now.

"Fuck, yes!" Spoon screamed as his bolt returned forward, chambering a fresh round. He put a tight grouping into another leg of the spider, and finally it went down. It hit the floor like the body of a massive alien cattle and made a whining, whimpering noise that reminded Spoon of a hundred dying babies screaming in unison.

Abe limped out of the hall into the massive room and shut the cylinder of his Enfield. Without fear he stepped up to the face of the monster, just out of the reach of its spasming fangs. He pointed the gun at the center of the beast and squeezed the trigger until his gun stopped firing. Black jets of foulness shot into the air from where his heavy enchanted bullets struck, and when the gun clicked empty, he wiped the blackness from his face and spat.

"Eat my ass," Abe said.

The monster exploded.

All three men were tossed backwards through the air as if a massive landmine had been stepped on. Spoon landed on a desk, then slid over it and hit the floor on his shoulder. His collarbone strained and nearly cracked under his own weight. A sharp jab of pain hit him at his shoulder joint, but the bones stayed where they belonged. Mostly. *Fuck that hurt.*

Spoon was up quickly and took in the scene, wincing in pain. Mr. Doyle had gotten lucky. He'd been tossed clear back towards the relative safety of the door they'd come through. Nothing had stopped his flight path, so he'd landed on the floor and skidded along, relatively safely. *He'll be back in the fight in a minute. Just need to help Tesser, buy some time, and hold on.*

Abe had hit a desk the same as Spoon, but instead of landing atop it, he'd hit the front of it, back first. He was slumped sitting on the floor, face on his chest, red blood running down his neck from a wound on the back of his head. *Shit. He's done. Might be dead. Goddamn it.*

Tesser was still at perilous war with the creature surrounding him. He'd ripped the face off of the worm. All of the faces. Spoon did a quick count of the daemons still remaining and got to five before Tesser was attacked by a new thing. It was ropy, and other than the fleshy bag of a torso it dragged on the floor behind it, it was made entirely of tentacles covered in fish hook barbs. As Tesser stood toe to toe with the false dragon creature that mimicked him, the octopus daemon launched itself at his back. Too many tendrils to count wrapped around and up over the dragon's torso, the barbs digging into the scales with alarming effectiveness. Tesser roared in pain as his arms were lashed with the ripping tentacles, immobilizing him.

I can't get a shot. I can't get a fucking shot. Shit shit shit.

"Tesser, shift! Go big!" Spoon screamed.

"I can't!" He roared. There was confusion in his voice. Something very wrong was happening to him.

Tesser's arms were ripped wide, spread like he was about to be crucified. The dragon shaped daemon roared in delight, mocking Tesser and spreading his arms as well. "I may not be able to kill you, but you shall suffer dragon! No sleep for you this time! Just pain. Eternal pain!"

Out of the fleshy knot at the center of the tentacle creature another massive appendage appeared. It raised high into the air, and it was tipped with a clear spike. *It looks like a fang.* As Spoon watched, a green fluid pushed towards the tip of the tentacle fang, and it reared back to stab Tesser in his exposed throat.

He's a goner if that hits.

"Does this bring back any memories, dragon? So much like the last time you challenged me. You never learn dragon," the daemonic dragon taunted.

Without thinking Spoon raised his weapon, exhaled softly, and calmly shot the fang off the tentacle. It burst in a halo of wet acidity, and the slimy appendage writhed in agony, flinging more of the green fluid around the room. Wherever it hit, a hissing sound came, followed shortly by smoke and the smell of burning. Tesser tried to recoil from the eruption, but he was held firm. He wound up being sprayed by the acid and many of the scales on his face and chest began to melt away. He roared in pain.

The white daemon looked beyond Tesser and saw

Spoon standing there, holding his weapon. The thing was enraged. "KILL THEM!" the dragon mockery bellowed. Three of the monsters turned their attention from encircling Tesser and started towards Spoon.

I've only got five magazines left. I don't think that'll be enough to kill all these daemons.

From the corner of his eye Spoon saw Mr. Doyle appear. He had drawn his longsword from his hip again. Much like the gem encrusted scabbard that held the weapon, the sword was similarly bedecked in ornamentation. Of course, you could hardly see it through the blue arcs of electricity running up and down the blade currently. The blade was now charged with the power of a lightning bolt. With a joyful whoop, Mr. Doyle brought the blade down in a slash that completely split a daemon monster in half. A sound like the crash of thunder filled the room and bruised Spoon's eardrum. One side of the monster, the one that looked like snakes, fell to the floor wetly, snapping its limb-serpents around while the other side, the one that looked like a piranha, flopped down, instantly dead. There was no explosion, just Mr. Doyle's celebration. He spun the sword around his body like Conan, arcs of electricity creating a dangerous halo around his body.

"Not just yet, daemon. You've yet to hear my voice in the matter, and I love a good conversation. Shall we debate the merits of you going and fucking yourself?" Mr. Doyle said.

Two insane creatures closed in on Mr. Doyle, both the size of refrigerators. One had pincers on each of its four arms large enough to pick up and rend a steel drum. Behind them, Tesser was still screaming in pain and the creature with the tentacles had grown another tail with a stinger.

I hope that sword doesn't run out of ammunition because things do not look good.

Chapter Fifty-Seven

Alec

Alec was crying.

There are few real things that a human being can experience that are truly chilling. Really and truly frightening, not like a movie thrill or the discomfort one experiences when reading a scary book alone late at night. When a parent hears a cry of pain from their child, or when you see something that shouldn't be there, like the image of a dead relative in the mirror, a human might be chilled.

Alec was finding out that the cries of a dragon in pain were chilling. It was a primal response that required no thinking, like a rabbit hiding from the shadow of a hawk, or how an octopus squirts ink when fleeing. Hearing the dragon roar in pain was alien and frightening. On some level he didn't know he had understood that a dragon should *never* be in pain. They should *never, ever* be harmed because they are integral to something larger than he could understand. *If I had ever heard the purple dragon make that noise, I would set her free. How could my father allow her to be taken? He must've heard her cries of anguish. Who was my father really? What good are we really doing keeping her here?*

Alec was sitting in an uncomfortable blue plastic chair in the center of the room. He wiped the tears from his eyes and looked around the small room. Standing at the door flanking the drying bloody contract on the wall were two of Mr. Host's men. They stood hunched over slightly, breathing heavy and making strange expressions every few seconds. They were detached, almost not even in their skin, and they were paying little attention to what was happening in the room. *One of them is drooling.*

Alec looked over at the heavily breathing Matty. She too seemed too restless in her drugged up state. *What do I do? What can I do? I'm a prisoner here.* Alec looked back at the two guards. One of them had rolled his eyes up, leaving nothing but white visible. Alec stood, and after pausing to see if they would react, he walked over to Matty's bedside.

Fuck this empire. I need to do something. I may die tonight, but I am going to set this woman free. Maybe she and her unborn child can escape and have a good life, far from me and this fucked up life I've made for myself. Alec reached out to pull Matty's IV, but the moment his finger touched her flesh, he felt an electrical jolt, and the world went black.

A moment later (or was it ten years?) he opened his eyes and he was in the same room, but things were different. A picture of a Japanese village hung on the wall where a landscape had been before, and Matty wasn't in the bed. Instead it was a completely different woman. This lady was pretty, almost to the point of seeming created and not natural. But Alec knew she was real. She had Asian descent in her eyes and skin tone, and despite her unnatural paleness and the sweat on her brow, she radiated some kind of warmth. It pleased him to stand near her. It was fading though and fading fast.

She opened her eyes slowly and cracked the faintest of tired smiles. She had intense violent colored eyes. "You must be Alec, the son."

Who is this? Why do I know her? "Yes."

"I never got to talk with your father before he died. I understand he was a man of tremendous achievement," the woman said. She coughed.

"Yes. Who are you? You're familiar to me. I know you."

She nodded meekly. "I am Kaula. The dragon you have had kept in a coma for a little over ten years, Alec. I've tried to reach out to you, but Legion has kept us apart."

Good lord, her eyes. And her hair, it's a shade of dark purple too. "You can shape shift. Amazing. Are you in pain? I was assured you were brain dead. I'm so sorry, Kaula."

She nodded again, as if she understood and believed him. Alec was relieved. "How much you've been manipulated saddens me. I am in constant pain, Alec. So little of me is left inside now. I'm rotten to the core. Maggoty. This conversation could be the end of me, but that's alright. I've led a very long life. Will you help me? Will you help the world? Bring magic back? Give life back to the things that have seen their essence fade away?"

Alec nodded emphatically, understanding without question that her course of action would help the world far more than the one his company had pursued for so long at her expense. "Of course. This has gone too far. I never wanted so much pain, suffering, and death. Just tell me what to do."

"It will not be easy."

"I do the impossible all the time, Kaula. I need this insanity to stop."

"It will mean giving up everything, Alec. But it will mean saving the world."

I'm not going to like this. Alec's voice was shaky, but he had the courage to say what needed to be said. "Tell me what to do."

*****

A few minutes later Alec came to in the still room. He looked over to make sure his remaining guards were still far and away, then pulled out Matty's IVs, and lifted her oxygen mask off. A small squirt of blood jetted out from the hole where the needle came from, but it stopped quickly, and she was otherwise unhurt. Alec brushed her dark hair off a sweaty brow and hoped she was okay. He could hear more violence coming from down the hall in the main dragon observatory. He wiped the wet tears from his cheek. *I know what to do now.*

"Alec…" Matty whispered out of a dry mouth. "You prick."

Well, when you're right, you're right. Alec shushed her softly. "Matty, quiet. We're in danger. Another dragon is here. Several actually. They're destroying the facility."

She perked up considerably. "It's Tesser. He's here to save Kaula and me."

"Yes, it would seem that way. You talked to Kaula too?"

"Yeah, in a dream. She spoke with me. Undo my hands Alec, let me go. Please, I'm pregnant."

Alec shook his head. "Not yet, Matty. You need to be kept safe. I'm not scared anymore. I know what to do."

"What? Free me Alec. I can help, I just need to be let go…" Matty struggled against her bonds, but she was exhausted and weak.

Alec fixed her hair again. "It's okay. They'll come for you soon. It'll all be over in a few minutes. I can undo it all. I understand so much of this was a great big mistake, but I can make it right. Kaula told me how." Alec turned and lifted a bag of saline solution from her IV stand. He removed a small syringe from a chest nearby and walked over to the white wall where his blood had helped him write a new deal between him and the daemon his father had summoned to this world. One of the guards, the one with the rolled up eyes suddenly came to and stared at him as he stabbed the needle into the bag. He drew the plunger back and filled it with the clear solution.

"Mr. Fitzgerald, what are you doing?"

Fucking you over. "Righting some wrongs my family has made."

The other guard suddenly snapped to attention and drew his sidearm. When he spoke, he spoke in Mr. Host's voice. "Now let's not make a hasty decision Alec. Years of hard work... We can't just throw it away. We can discuss changes to the terms of the contract when things have settled down. Think of your safety, Alec. Changing the deal now would be catastrophic."

Alec ignored the daemon and squeezed the syringe out, drawing a line of fluid on the white wall above his bloody writing. It started to run down, ruining the words he'd written, sending pink, watery streaks down to the floor. He stabbed the needle back into the bag to refill it.

The guard lifted his gun and pointed it at his face. "Stop, or we'll be forced to shoot you."

"You can't shoot me. It's in the contract. The original contract my father drew up. Shrewd guy, my dad. You can't kill me. You can't even hurt me. All these years I never remembered the fine print of that dusty old piece of evil. I was so scared. Scared of failing my father. Scared of you, but you know what? I'm not scared anymore. I talked to Kaula. She told me what I had to hear. What I wanted to hear all along."

The guard's face rippled, as if a stone had been thrown into the water of his skin. He shook his head and suddenly he was Mr. Host. "How? There were precise instructions. Measures taken. You were to have NO contact with the dragon."

"Oh Mr. Host," Alec said as he sprayed another stream of saline into the words. "You can't stop dragons. You can only hope to contain them, and even that doesn't last, now does it?"

"You'll pay for this treachery, Fitzgerald. Your family will be cursed for the rest of time for this. You'll die slowly. Painfully," Mr. Host spat, his features twisting into a devilish caricature of himself.

"That's not the plan I have. Mr. Host, I renounce this contract. I'm sure my lawyers would agree it was signed under duress," Alec said as he used his very expensive shirt sleeve to wipe away all the blood, destroying the newly minted contract.

From the other room where the battle waged on Alec heard a tremendous cry of pain. Except this time, it wasn't the sound of a dragon in pain.

This time, it was Mr. Host.

Alec set the bag down and bit the cut on his finger, setting free a new stream of blood. He started to write something new on the wall. A new contract that would help set things right.

*****

Alec walked down the concrete hallway into the main room, stopping only to remove a handgun from the holster of a dead and disappeared security guard. His thumb throbbed. He didn't really know how to use the gun, but he only had to shoot one thing in the room to achieve what needed to be done. He knew from watching movies how to check to see if it was loaded, and he made sure the safety was off. No sense risking a small mistake now.

The carnage in the main dragon observatory was incredible, and the destruction matched the chaos and the noise. Three men were fighting against a dwindling number of Mr. Host's now naked security men. How they had lost their clothing was beyond Alec, but they looked afraid and disorganized. *They don't have any junk. Or nipples. Look at that*. The three men (two younger, one older) were all shooting guns into the daemons that were highly effective against them. Each pistol shot seemed to kill instantly, and the man with the automatic weapon was firing so many bullets even the daemonic bodies couldn't withstand the attack. The old man held a sword in his hand that crackled with an electrical charge. A naked guard tried to sneak up on him, and an arc of electricity shot out and destroyed him. A black puff of smoke was all that remained.

Alec watched as a smaller but similar golden version of Kaula literally went around the room, tearing Mr. Host's men limb from limb as easily as Alec as could tear off a sheet of paper towel. *That must be Tesser. I thought he'd be bigger.* Each of the mangled bodies disappeared into a puff of smoke instead of gore, and right as each was destroyed, their faces shifted into that of Mr. Host's. *It's almost like he's trying to catch up to Tesser to fight back. Above* them in the earth a terrible thumping, scraping noise resumed. Something was digging down to get at them again. Something very large.

"STOP!" Alec screamed. Suddenly the gunfire abated, and the daemon guards turned towards him, concerned and apologetic. They raised their hands in a calming gesture, attempting to appear nonthreatening.

"Now Alec, don't do anything rash," Mr. Host said. Another Mr. Host added, "Please leave, it's for your own safety. You don't understand how much I care for you, Alec. Please, listen."

Behind a row of the face shifting bastards Tesser's face changed. He'd seen Alec enter the chamber. "YOU!" he screamed out a half dragon's mouth. From above, a massive crack appeared in the reinforced concrete ceiling and gray dust fell like dirty snow. Something was nearly inside the room.

Alec nodded sadly. "Yeah, me. Me, all along. But I came out here so we could set things right, Tesser."

The half dragon stormed across the room, knocking aside several of Legion's remaining bodies, but he stopped short of dismembering Alec. As the men that came with him dealt with the surviving guards, it crouched slightly, coiled and ready to end his life. "Speak," he said, his voice full of restrained anger.

"I'm sorry for everything. I'm sorry for taking Matty, and I hope to God nothing is wrong with your child. God only knows what the fuck these things were pumping into her. She's safe, right back there. I wrote something on the wall for you too. Make sure you read it. Make sure the lawyers read it. All I wanted to do was help people like my dad did, Tesser. Well, like I thought he did. Here now, I'm starting to realize that my father may not have been the good person I thought he was. All I wanted was to do well. Be a hero. All I wanted to do was follow in his footsteps, make him proud. And you know what? I did. I took every step the same as he did, and in the end it got me the same thing it got him." Alec looked down at the handgun, then back at Tesser. "In bed with a devil, and dead."

Kaula, I'm sorry this took so long.

"Nooooo!!!" Legion screamed through all his remaining mouths in unison.

Alec put the handgun to his chin and pulled the trigger. A forgiving blackness took him away from the world filled with the consequences of his family's mistake.

Chapter Fifty-Eight
Tesser

The handgun went off with a crack, and Alec Fitzgerald met a messy, but honorable end. Legion's multitude of now human forms all spun to face Tesser, their identical faces covered in humiliation and anger.

"I guess this time it ends a little differently, eh?" Tesser said through the incredible pain he was in. The dragon's body was torn up by the daemonic assaults that had been laid against it. His flesh was torn, bloody, and agonizing.

"Like you, I cannot be killed, Tesser. I will return, and next ti—" the bodies of the daemon ceased to exist in the blink of Tesser's dragon eye, leaving a strange popping noise in their wake. *The sound of Earth's air rushing in to fill their void.*

The ceiling continued to crack from Garamos' loud assault above. He'd be through the concrete in just a few seconds. The smell in the room was beyond horrifying. Daemon blood and the rapidly rotting carcasses of the manifested bodies that didn't disappear gave off enough of a stench that the three men in the room had to cover their faces.

Abe is alive. I was worried there for a moment. Abe had

been tossed into a desk by the explosion of the massive spider's corpse. His head had been racked up hard against the wooden top of the desk, and he'd lost consciousness and a lot of blood. Mr. Doyle was tending to the young man as he leaned up against the desk that'd nearly killed him. His eyes swayed to and fro, unable to focus. The aged British warrior was producing another bottle of reddish liquid from a pouch for the boy. *He'll be okay in time.*

Tesser turned to Spoon, who was nursing a hurt shoulder. He was covered in slime, dirt, and a hundred small cuts that wept just enough blood to make him look like he'd been thrown through a pile of plate glass windows then tossed with salt and lemon. He looked bad. "Spoon. Can you go to where Alec said Matty was? Make sure she's okay. Bring her to me. Please."

"On it," Spoon said before limping away towards the hallway Alec had come from. *Strength personified. This is the best of the human spirit.*

Tesser turned to the giant, torn plastic enclosure that held his sister away from him. The room was too small for him to shift into his full form , so he simply began to rip the plastic apart to get at her. The soft clear substance gave way easily under his claws, and before long the scaffolding holding it up came down too. She was exposed now, ready to be freed. *I hope she hasn't suffered too much. Let me set you free, sister.*

The ceiling broke apart, raining down television sized chunks of concrete. Garamos' tree trunk sized fingers poked into the room before tearing back a sheet of concrete, letting in fresh air and the soft rain of white snow. Tesser looked up and saw his brother's face. Garamos seemed relieved.

"Is she safe?" Garamos rumbled from above. Tesser could see Kiarohn circling above and Zeud leaning over the hole.

"I don't know yet. She lives, but she seems…not well,"

Tesser said. The dragon of life leaned over her face and removed the massive oxygen mask as Zeud fell to the floor of the massive chamber in naked human form. She was back to being a long legged, incredibly beautiful redhead. She came to her sister and brother, her face full of worry.

"Jesus shit. You are beautiful," Abe said, holding the back of his head.

"Thank you," Zeud said politely back.

"Son, you already have another redhead," Mr. Doyle said, never taking his eyes off of Tesser and the purple dragon. Abe looked sheepish.

"Zeud, pull that tube out," Tesser said pointing to a large IV tube with the diameter of a human's wrist. It entered Kaula's body at the point most aptly described as the dragon's armpit. Zeud did as she was asked as Tesser removed another tube from her rear leg. Bright red blood feebly spilled out when the evil feeds were taken away.

Another woman appeared, dropping from the hole in the ceiling. She landed on the floor deftly like a cat, rolling and coming up already on the move. She was tall like Zeud but had a paler skin tone and long blonde hair. Her eyes sparkled green, and she too was remarkably beautiful, though there was something uncivilized about her.

Tesser stopped and smiled at the strange woman. Her appearance was the dawn after an endless night. "Fyelrath. I've missed you so. I'm glad to see you," Tesser said, pausing to greet his sister.

"Is she alive?" Fyelrath asked. Her face was wrought with fear for her sister.

"Only in the strictest sense," Tesser said sadly. He stood near her face and shifted down into his human form. He was naked again, like his sisters.

Each of them moved to their sick sister and rested a reassuring hand on her still face. Her sides inflated slowly as she breathed through her nose gently, in hitching inhalations. It was weak, but her breathing was her own finally. She seemed to be returning to some kind of life, though slowly.

"Tesser?"

"Matty?" Tesser stood quickly and turned. Behind him Spoon helped Matty walk. She looked drained and weak. She had an arm around his shoulders and leaned on him heavily. Tesser went to her and took her weight, wrapping his arms around her strongly. He lifted her off the ground in an embrace and inhaled her scent. She smelled of cool running water that had been fouled ever so slightly. She smelled like the drops of evil that were scattered all around Kaula. He didn't care. She was in his arms again. He found her mouth and kissed her passionately, ignoring the grossness of their bodies. *I have missed this woman so. Mother of my child, and…woman I love.*

"You're naked again," Matty said with a smile, her nose against his.

A tear ran down Tesser's face. A tear of joy. "I have a lot of trouble with clothing."

"More of that prolific need to be naked, eh? Sexy times again? Cross off another species?" Matty taunted, squeezing him tightly again. Their argument was long lost. All that was left between the two of them was the joy of being back together.

"No, nothing like that. Been too busy today. Maybe if you're free later?"

Matty started to cry, and the two simply held one another. Everyone else watched, and there were more tears.

"Freedom at last," a weak new voice added.

Kaula. Tesser turned and sat Matty down. The purple dragon's sad eyes were open, though they were flecked with black and grey. She had been invaded by the evil from across the Veil. Her body was tainted and profoundly ill. "Kaula. It is so good to see you. To hear your voice again."

"Oh, my darling brother, it is good to see you again as well. Fyelrath, Zeud, Garamos. Kiarohn, I am not strong enough to lift my head to look up at you, but I feel your wind against my face. It is a welcome sensation." A small gust of wind picked up in response. Kiarohn's kiss.

"What can we do? How can we revive you? Put life back into this body to make you well again?" Zeud asked, rubbing her sister's snout.

"Who else is here? I can smell four humans. I recognize two of you. Henry, is that you I smell?"

Spoon stepped forward, overwhelmed by the moment, "Yes, Kaula I'm here. Thank you for the help earlier. You saved Abe's life, probably all of ours." The other men looked at Spoon, wondering what he was talking about.

"A small token of my appreciation, Henry. Thank you for dealing with my urgings all this time. I've pressured you so much of late, and you've handled it very well. Better than I expected." Kaula was proud, but tired.

"Urgings?" Spoon asked.

"I compelled you to follow my brother. The alley? Your presence at the restaurant that day was partly due to me whispering in your ear, Henry. Were it not for your instincts, I would not have been able to reach out to you in the first place. I'm glad you were able to avoid punishment for my compelling you." Kaula's voice became more exhausted with each word, but she finished her statement.

"It's no problem. I'm glad you did what you did."

Kaula closed her eyes, seemingly nodding. "Who else is there? Two men. You smell of magic. A most welcome thing to breathe in. Who are you?"

Mr. Doyle stepped forward first. "I am known as Mr. Doyle, Kaula. I am but a modest wizard, channeling your magic for the greater good."

Kaula snorted a weak laugh. "Mr. Doyle, your

channeling of magic has not always been for the greater good. I can smell the years on you, and they add up to far more than what your body says. Although you are a good person. I am pleased that you have aided my family this night. Welcome."

Mr. Doyle stepped away, speechless at last.

"I'm Abraham Fellows, Kaula. It's an honor," Abe was still unsteady from his injuries and used a discarded carbine as a cane. *At least he has the sense to keep the barrel down.*

"The honor is mine, Abraham. To be surrounded by men and women of such valor does me a credit that I can never repay. Thank you for your sacrifices, Abraham. You have done a great thing this day."

"I'd do it again in a heartbeat, Kaula," Abe said, puffing up proudly.

"I know, and in time you'll be called upon again. And Matty, you are here too? No longer a dream? Step in front of my eyes so I can see you in this world finally."

Tesser helped Matty move so Kaula could see her. The couple stood near her left eye. "Hello, Kaula. It's nice to finally meet you," Matty said. *She seems almost as weak as my sister.*

The tiniest dragon smile cracked Kaula's lip. "The same to you, Matilde. I'm very proud of you. My brother chose wisely."

"Thank you," Tesser said.

"No Tesser, thank you. It saddens me to say this, but here is where one journey ends, and another can begin, and we all have the two of you to thank for that chance," Kaula said.

"What?" Fyelrath and Zeud said simultaneously.

"Kaula, what are you speaking of?" Tesser asked firmly. *She's scaring me.*

Sadly, but proudly, the dragon of magic spoke. "Tesser, brothers and sisters, I am too far gone to continue. My body is full of the evil Legion pumped into me from across the Veil, and it shall not last. I am hollow now. Near all of my will is spent to stay alive for this moment. I can live only so much longer, and the longer I remain, the worse the world will be for it. All my magic is corrupted and darkened, and should I survive, the world's magic will reflect what they have made of me. I am their success in failure. If I survive, they have won."

"But you cannot die. Dragons are immortal, right?" Abe asked aloud, his voice filled with the same fear and uncertainty the dragons felt.

A new voice, a man's voice spoke, "I suppose there is one way for a dragon to die."

Everyone turned and laid eyes on the speaker. It was another dragon, a small one, half the size of the others and as black as midnight. His wings were folded, and his tail wrapped at his feet. His neck was long and topped with a skull that was wreathed in six curving horns, two upward, two back, two forward, framing the jaw. The dragon's scales gleamed with a sinister slickness, and his eyes were a strange, sad, soul filled black. His very existence seemed mournful.

Tesser snarled and stepped in between the strange new dragon and Kaula. The other two female dragons did the same as Garamos' massive dragon fist slammed into the chamber floor, cracking stone and threatening God-like violence.

Tesser threatened the dragon, "Ambryn, away with you. You were never made for this purpose! It is anathema to even think of it. The balance would be cast to oblivion! All would be lost! There must always be seven! Always! Never six."

"Silly brothers and sisters, Ambryn is here at my request," Kaula said, sounding even more exhausted than before. Ambryn sat back and crossed his arms patiently, a sad expression coming across his face as his eyes drifted to the floor.

What? Tesser spun and faced his sister. "Are you

insane? If you die, all magic will fade. The world will fall into even more chaos. There must be seven. We cannot carry on without you."

"Kaula, this is madness," Zeud, the dragon of fire pleaded.

Kaula sighed. "I've arranged for everything." Kaula turned a massive purple eye to Matty. The eye drifted down to Matty's stomach. "Matilde. Your daughter."

Matty understood. She nodded.

What? "Kaula? Matty? What is going on here?"

"Tesser, you chose wisely. So very wisely. I had to nudge you a bit once. Had to urge you to take the risk. You couldn't simply make a baby dragon with heedless lust. You needed love too. And you did it. You loved her. You still love her, and you always will. And that love, your love…is enough. To birth a child capable of being the seventh dragon in my stead, I needed the dragon of life. I needed you, and I needed Matilde, a woman strong enough to bear the burden of a dragon in her womb. With your union and my passing, your unborn daughter will become the seventh dragon unborn. Rejoice. As one life leaves this world, another is poised to join it."

"Noo…" Tesser said, dropping to his knees sobbing. He put his hands on Kaula's face gently, pleading. "No, you can't. You mustn't. We've had forever together, the seven of us. You mustn't give up. It's too soon. We'll find a way."

Fyelrath stood shaking her head, her arms crossed over her breasts, salty tears running from red, sad eyes.

Zeud backed away, incredible pain on her face. She shook her head and mumbled unintelligible words of sadness. She backed into a bank of computing equipment and began to cry as more snow fell softly on them all. Above, the winds churned powerfully, stirred by Kiarohn's grief.

A single wet tear fell to the floor from Garamos' eye above. It splashed as if a bowl of water had been tipped over. His lips curled in anger. "Ambryn, if you do her bidding, so help me I will destroy you."

The much smaller dragon was crying as well. To watch death cry was more emotional than any present could handle without joining in. "I suffer this duty for my sister, Garamos. I've wept since she beckoned for me and I realized what she needed. I've wept for this whole battle, fighting my own daemons. Hate me not brothers and sisters. I do this for her, for us, and for the balance."

Garamos roared into the night sky above. He punched the earth above repeatedly, trying to vent his anger. All he managed to do was shake free several tumbling chunks of stone and iron. He was shattered with grief.

"Matty," Kaula said softly.

"Yes, Kaula?"

"You will be the first mother of a dragon. I cannot imagine the hardships you will endure. But your blood is strong, more than just human, as is your will. And my brother, as foolish and impulsive as he can be, he loves you and will be by your side through it all. As will my whole family. Your whole family."

Matty started to cry. She nodded rapidly as Tesser put his arm around her.

"I love you all. I always have, and forever shall I. Now Ambryn, as I wish, set my soul free so it may be born again."

The black dragon gritted his teeth and fought his instincts to do exactly NOT that. In the end, his sister's wishes won, and he approached her throat, sobbing, wracked with spasms of grief. He stood at her side and raised a single obsidian claw. It hesitated high in the air, shaking, unable to do what Kaula wanted.

"Give my magic back to them, Ambryn. Give me peace. Set me free," Kaula said before shutting her eyes for the last time.

The dragons watched as Ambryn nodded, crying

uncontrollably. He struck down at her throat, and for the first time in all of ever, a dragon died.

And then the dragons wept.

Epilogue

I am a nervous person right now.

I am Tesser, and I am a nervous dragon.

And yet here I sit, rich, powerful, and successful, and I am far more nervous than I have ever been.

Very nervous.

It is late June. It has been almost nine months since the events below Fitzgerald Industries. Since the death of my sister, Kaula, the dragon of magic. I still cry for her now and then, more often than I should, but I suppose I always will. You can't live with someone in your life that long and expect their absence to not affect you from time to time. Yet in her death, so much good was to be found.

She was buried in what is now Germany, near the circle of stones that predate dragonkind and all other life on Earth. Garamos carried her across the ocean with the rest of us in tow, and by hand we dug her grave in the dark forest. She lies there now, under the guard of many proud sorcerers, trolls, werewolves, and more.

She rests in peace.

With his own blood on the wall of the room Matty was imprisoned in Alec Fitzgerald wrote a new Will and Testament. It was simple, and in the wake of the revelations at his company the courts said it was to be allowed to stand firm. He handed over control of his medical business empire and all of his assets to me. I am now wealthy, though I don't need the money.

I gave Alan, the man at the Starbucks who gave me a small coffee and lessons on English, a million dollars. Hell of a tip for a cup of coffee.

I have since dissolved much of the company after the investigation learned that much of the scientific advancements made were only because Kaula was abused so. It didn't help the company's chances when the taint of daemonic influence was found time and time again. I made sure that each employee who lost their job was compensated handsomely, and I took the time to track down the families of all the employees who were slaughtered by Legion. They too will want for nothing for the rest of their lives. I hope they use their economic freedom to better the world. Fitzgerald Industries is now a hollow shell of what it used to be, and that is still a company to be reckoned with.

Alexis is now in charge. I have faith they will do the right thing from now on.

After being dressed down for allowing so much destruction, Henry Spooner was lauded with commendations. The night of our great confrontation he was able to direct the appropriate official assets in the short amount of time to the site of greatest need and engaged a daemonic enemy fearlessly. Without his work that evening, undoubtedly hundreds if not hundreds of millions of lives would have been lost, and the country and world saw to it he was recognized.

He now serves as a senior agent at a newly formed multi-government agency headed by Director Fisher. In the wake of the assault on their reality by Legion, most of the governments of the world agreed that national boundaries would only serve as hindering barriers in the protection of Earth from outside or paranormal threats. I laugh at the idea of the word and concept 'paranormal.' They still think what they have known all along is 'normal.' Eventually, they'll realize all the things that have been weakened or in hiding have been here longer than they have. They are just as normal.

Silly humans.

This agency Spoon works at bears the moniker of The International Agency for Paranormal Response. They often refer to themselves as TIAP-R, or simply, 'The Agency.' The CIA doesn't like that at all, understandably so. The media likes to call them Tapper. Agents are often referred to as 'Tappers.' I like that. That's what I call them. Tapper has set up several locations across the world. Their headquarters in the United States is in Manchester, New Hampshire. The location had something to do with the airport being convenient and not what lies beneath the city. Such is the way of the government.

This past Spring Mr. Doyle was able to set up the initial phases of a teaching college for Tapper. The Agency wanted him to relocate nearer to Manchester, but he was unwilling to move. He's set up his home in Boston, and after a little flexing, he persuaded them to relocate their college to Weymouth, near Wampatuck State Park. It's pretty there, and when they're done building the school, it will be beautiful as well. Mr. Doyle is seeing to it that the school is built with magical sensibility rather than modern styling and economic design. Things are different now, and he knows it.

Abraham has learned a lot from his mentor. So much so that he has entered into the FBI's academy so he can join Tapper. So far, Abe has performed admirably, though it is very difficult for him. He is a shoe-in for admittance once he graduates from Quantico. He and Alexis are engaged. I should've mentioned that already. I am apparently forgetful when I am nervous.

Spoon continues to serve as my liaison to Tapper, and though they haven't called on me for assistance yet, they maintain a steady flow of information to me. I am able to advise them as needed, and one day, I am sure, they will get in over their heads and call in a panic.

Until that day…

The rest of the world aches in growing pains. Kaula's death released an invisible rippling explosion of magic across the world. Pure, primal energy flowed out from her and helped to reconstitute what the world had lost in her absence. Things are still not where they need to be, but the practitioners of magic across the world have rejoiced with their invigorated powers. All the creatures born of magic are back, for better or for worse. Mankind has created an uneasy truce with these creatures of magic, and I hope sincerely that the truce holds. Man has lived in fear of nuclear winter for many years, but what could happen in a war between humans and a race made of the ephemeral magic that binds all of reality together…

Well, that would be bad.

I am sitting in a hospital in Boston. The same one that Spoon and Abe were brought to the night Legion made his assault on me. The night I revealed myself to the world.

I am in a waiting room. There are dozens of Tapper security men all about. They are nervous as I am, but they hide it. Today is a day for excitement, not fear. Matty's parents are here from Norway. They still fear me – I can smell it on them – though, they also love me. I have taken care of their flesh and blood and very soon will give them a granddaughter. They hold each other's hands excitedly. Near me is my sister, Fyelrath. She sits in human form, waiting as nervously as I am. Across the room is Ambryn, the slayer of Kaula, dragon of death. He has been racked with guilt ever since, despite having received our forgiveness. He has his fingers interlaced in his lap, and he, too, is nervous. So many dragons, all so nervous. Outside in the street below is Garamos. He is managing the crowds that have come here today and for the same reason I am here. Above us all flies Kiarohn, stirring the winds as always.

Zeud is in the delivery room with Alexis and Matty. That's why we're all here today. Matty is giving birth. She is in labor, and any moment now our daughter will come into the world, the seventh dragon of Earth, the second dragon of magic, and the first dragon born and not made.

Her birth will usher in a new age of wonder and magic, bringing back all that was lost.

And that's why I'm nervous. I am about to be the first father to a dragon.

The double door leading to the birthing room opened. A young nurse, clearly more nervous than everyone else in the room, walked out and saw Tesser. She approached him. "Mr. Tesser?"

"It's just Tesser."

"Everything went well. They'd like you to come back now." The nurse motioned for Tesser to follow her.

"May I bring my brother and sister? Matty's mother and father?" Tesser looked at Ambryn and Fyelrath, both of whom had slid forward in their seats, excited.

"I don't know how I would stop you," she said laughing.

Tesser grinned, and the three dragons and Matty's parents followed the young nurse. It took less than a minute to reach the birthing room. It was colorful and clean, with plenty of comfortable furniture and a spare bed off to the side. They'd intended to come here a day early and stay the night, but their daughter had a different idea. She was several days early. Magic worked on its own schedule. It arrived precisely when it meant to.

Zeud stood on the opposite side of the bed, all smiles. Her bright red hair made for an interesting bookend with Alexis who stood on the other side of the bed. Both women turned and looked at Tesser as the dragons entered. Alexis went to Tesser and wrapped her arms around him proudly.

"She's beautiful, Tesser. So beautiful," Alexis said. She had eyes filled with tears of happiness. Tesser did too. Lindsay, Matilde's mother, went straight to her daughter and embraced her happily.

"Kaula was right, Tesser. This child is special. Dragon-born, look at her," Zeud said in awe, looking down at the baby.

Daniel, Matty's father, stood proud. "It would take a woman with troll's blood in her veins to bear the first dragon, wouldn't it?"

"Troll's blood? What?" Tesser asked him, laughing.

"You didn't know? I thought it was the ramblings of my insane grandfather for years, but now I know he was telling the truth. He once said that our family had been part troll. They're strong you see. And Matilde has that strength in her."

Of course. The smell of running water and cold nights. That scent I was attracted to. She's more than just human. Tesser's realization made him love her more.

Tesser approached the bed and finally laid eyes on the mother of his child. Lindsay and her husband backed away slowly so Tesser could get close. Matty looked spent, but in a far different way than when she'd been poisoned at Fitzgerald Industries. She was exhausted from the exertion required to bring life into the world, and through her fading pain she glowed. Her sweat and her smile made her more beautiful than ever.

She held their baby.

Tesser and Matilde's daughter was born with a near full head of violet colored hair. It was a soft purple, the shade of a summer New Hampshire lilac. Tesser loved that color. It reminded him of his sister.

The baby girl had a round, cherubic face that already faintly resembled Matty. She was calm, already sleeping dreamily, happy to be in the arms of her mother. She had one tiny hand wrapped tight around Matty's index finger, clutching on to her mom, wanting to be a part of her despite not being aware of the world just yet.

"She's here," Matty said, looking up at Tesser.

She's everything. Never have I had a child I've loved so much without ever having laid eyes on her. "She's so beautiful, Matty. She looks like you."

Matty agreed with a nod and a smile. "Yeah. Little like you too. Do you want to hold her?"

Whoa. Now there's an anxiety spike. "Yeah. I do." Tesser reached down and the mother and father exchanged the baby. She was heavier than Tesser thought she'd be, but he lifted her carefully, as if she would break, beaming with pride.

Ambryn and Fyelrath leaned over his shoulder and looked at the baby. Both dragons were overcome with emotion. The tears flowed, though this time not in grief, but in exultant celebration. True, selfless, joy. *I am the father of a dragon. The greatest of all life.*

"What will you name her?" Ambryn asked, sniffling.

Matty answered him. "Tesser once knew a Valkyrie named Astrid. Her name means to be fair, beautiful, and of God. Her name will be Astrid Kaula Rindahl. The eighth dragon born."

"That's an incredible name you two," Alexis said softly.

Astrid opened her eyes and looked up at her father for the first time. Her eyes were the same soft purple as the shock of hair on her head, but tiny vibrant flecks of green were there too. The tiny baby smiled and her feet fluttered. She cooed.

She knows I'm her father. Or maybe...my sister's soul recognizes me.

Tesser walked over to the window holding his baby and looked out on the city of Boston. Down in the streets below, he could see Garamos looking up at him eagerly. The two caught each other's eye, and Garamos looked at the baby as Tesser presented her. *He is happy. And finally, after all this time, I think he might approve of a life I created.*

Tesser smiled.

Garamos reared up on his two hind legs and began to clap thunderously. The crowd gathered at his feet, lining the city streets almost as far as the eye could see went wild, for his celebration signaled the birth of Tesser and Matty's child, ushering in a new age for the world. Their applause and celebration could be heard through the window, many stories above. Tesser watched as several helicopters came into view, attempting to get a good view of their window to capture the first images of the new dragon child. Tesser held his baby girl aloft in front of the window and let them drink in the majesty of Astrid.

"That's right. Take her in. Get used to her world, she's going to be a big thing for a long time."

"Aren't you the proud papa?" Matty said from the bed.

Tesser turned, disappointing several billion television viewers around the world. "Have you seen this child? She's perfect. She's the best thing I've ever done. Aside from meeting you."

Matty looked at the man she loved, the dragon she loved, and rested her head back on the pillow. Zeud took her hand and squeezed it.

Tesser turned back to the window and held his daughter to his chest. He whispered, speaking to the world, but only loud enough for his daughter to hear. "You're going to want to pay attention, Earth. This is my daughter, Astrid. I love her, and you will too. Now that she's here, everything will start getting back to normal. Back to the way things should be. But different too. And I'm okay with that. But it's time to get back to work, Tesser. This world has missed you fiercely, without even knowing you were gone. But it'll be easy."

Tesser kissed his daughter's forehead.

"I am yours in the way a Princess owns a King."

Tesser kissed her forehead again and looked out at the sea of people celebrating the birth of his child with him.

"There is a new dragon among us."

About The Author

CHRIS PHILBROOK is the creator and author of *Tesser: A Dragon Among Us*, as well as the popular webfiction series *Adrian's Undead Diary* and *Elmoryn: Wrath of the Orphans*.

Chris calls the wonderful state of New Hampshire his home. He is an avid reader, writer, role player, miniatures game player, video game player, and part time athlete, as well as a member of the Horror Writers Association. If you weren't impressed enough, he also works full time while writing for Reemergence as well as the worlds of Adrian's Undead Diary and Elmoryn.

Find More Online

Check out Chris Philbrook's official website **thechrisphilbrook.com** to contact the author and keep tabs on his many exciting projects, or follow Chris on Facebook at **www.facebook.com/ChrisPhilbrookAuthor** for special announcements.

Visit **adragonamongus.com** to access additional content and learn more about Tesser and the world of the Reemergence Novels.

Don't miss Chris Philbrook's smash hit: *Adrian's Undead Diary*. Follow the exploits of Adrian Ring in this epic eight-book series as he searches for meaning, survival, and hope in a world ravaged by the dead. Visit **adriansundeaddiary.com** to learn more about Adrian's world. Available in print, Kindle, and online.

Read more by author Chris Philbrook in *The Kinless Trilogy*. Explore Elmoryn, a world of dark fantasy where death is not the end. The story begins in *Book One: The Wrath of the Orphans*, available in print, Kindle, and online. Visit **elmoryn.com** to learn more about Elmoryn, view concept art, and much more.

Can't Wait for More?

Look for Chris Philbrook's **FREE** short fiction eBook, *At Least He's Not on Fire*.

Find it on Amazon, Goodreads, or Smashwords today!

Amazon: http://www.amazon.com/dp/B00JSGEKIK

Goodreads: https://www.goodreads.com/book/show/21948978-at-least-he-s-not-on-fire

Smashwords: https://www.smashwords.com/books/view/430970

Made in the USA
Middletown, DE
10 June 2021

41701260R00262